THE

HIGHLAND WATCH TOWER;

OR,

THE SONS OF GLENALVON.

A ROMANCE.

BY THE AUTHOR OF " KATHLEEN ; OR, THE SECRET MARRIAGE ;" "THE HEBREW
MAIDEN ; OR, THE LOST DIAMOND ;" " FATHERLESS FANNY ;" &c. &c.

" Not always vice does uncorrected go,
Nor virtue unrewarded pass below ;
Oft sacred justice lights her awful head,
And dooms the tyrant and the usurper dead.''
BOYCE.

LONDON:

PUBLISHED BY E. LLOYD, AT THE OFFICE OF " THE
PENNY SUNDAY TIMES," 231, SHOREDITCH.

1842.

PREFACE.

It was imagined that a romance, calculated to give the reader some insight into the manners and customs of our forefathers, might be generally interesting to the reading public, and the result of the present attempt has proved that the idea was not an erroneous one. The period chosen for this purpose is one of the most interesting in both English and Scottish history; and, though much of our narrative is of course fictitious, there were opportunities for blending instruction with amusement, and it will be found that we have adhered closely enough to history to afford a tolerable insight into the causes which led to the invasion of Scotland, and, at the same time, to show the noble feeling of independence that inspired our northern neighbours to repel the inroads of a haughty and presumptuous foe.

The character of the Chief of Badenoch, though haughty, cruel, and vindictive, has not, we believe, been overdrawn. Such men, unfortunately, existed in the dark age to which our narrative belongs, and it can scarcely create surprise that it should have been so when we consider the anarchy and confusion that existed ere society had been formed as we now happily see it. The barons, in fact, were restless and ambitious, and, knowing their power, they seldom failed to exert it, whether it might happen to be against the sovereign or their equals.

The struggle between the two kingdoms has been described with as much accuracy as the nature of the subject would permit; and, if the writer cannot take to himself the merit of being a faithful historian, he may at least hope that the perusal of the following pages will induce some of his readers to consult those authorities from whence he has derived his own information.

The Princess Isabel a captive in the presence of Edward, King of England.

The fearful vision of Angus Glenalvon.

THE HIGHLAND WATCH TOWER;

OR,

THE SONS OF GLENALVON.

CHAPTER I.

"Murder most foul, as in the best it is,"
But this most foul, strange, and unnatural."
[SHAKSPERE.

"DEATH to my foes," muttered the stern chief of Badenoch, as he noiselessly led his ruffian followers through the silent chambers of Glenalvon Castle. "The midnight hour suits well the direful errand that has brought us hither, and as you value your own lives, let none escape the death to which I have doomed them. The name of Glenalvon shall become extinct, and then shall I at length have achieved that vengeance for which my soul has so long thirsted. Strike to your victim's heart, I say, and let no puling mercy save one of those whom I have adjudged to perish in this night's slaughter."

Thus spoke the vengeful chief to his awe-subdued followers, as he led them through the castle, to which they had gained admittance by the treachery of a faithless domestic. In each chamber they found the inmates buried in sleep, and all perished by the hands of the ruthless assassins who had thus stolen upon their unconscious slumbers. But the blood that already flowed quenched not the fury of the implacable chief, who, mindful only of the accomplishment of his fell purpose, still continued to lead his ruffian throng towards the chamber where slept the Earl and Countess of Glenalvon, unconscious of the dreadful tragedy that was acting around them. At length, he approached the only door that now interposed itself between him and his intended victims, when, glancing fiercely round upon his followers, he said :—

"Remember the commands I have given you; the inmates of this next chamber little think of the destiny that so speedily awaits them. And now, proud Helen of Glenalvon," he muttered to himself, "thou shalt feel the vengeance of him whose love thou wert mad enough to slight for another. I will bring down thy scornful spirit even to the very dust, and compel thee to be mine, or send thy soul to join that of thy husband. This is, indeed, a triumph, and well requites the agony of my tortured soul. Aye, Helen, thou shalt become mine, or perish by the hand of my meanest slave."

"My lord !—my lord !—arouse you !" exclaimed Roland, the faithful steward of Earl Glenalvon, who at this moment rushed in to give warning of the danger which threatened his beloved master. "Awake, in the name of Heaven, or your life will fall a sacrifice to blood-thirsty ruffians !"

"Peace, brawling idiot !" muttered the chief, seizing the old man by the throat; "peace, I say, or even thy white hairs shall not save thee from my vengeance."

"I care not for your threats," said Roland; "slay me if you will, but my latest words shall be uttered in giving warning of your presence to my honoured lord."

"Nay then, this to thy heart !" exclaimed the chief, plunging a dagger into the bosom of the old man, who, reeling from the effect of the blow, staggered a few paces, and fell dying into the arms of one of the men.

"You have slain me," he said, "and I regret not, since my life has been lost in an attempt to preserve my master. I die, and let my last prayer prevail upon you to spare those who are guiltless of any crime towards you."

"Liar !" answered the chief, fiercely, "they have been the bane and curse that have beset my path of happiness. I loved the Lady Helen, and she rejected me with scorn to bestow her hand upon the worm I am now about to crush. For thee, old man, I sought not thy life, but thou hast provoked me to an act which has sent thee to the grave ere thy time."

Roland had no power to reply to this, for his life's blood was fast ebbing, and with one last effort to reach the chamber-door, he sank to the ground, and yielded up his spirit.

"Heed not this carrion," exclaimed the chief, spurning with his foot the bleeding corse of his aged victim. "He will give us no more trouble, so now, hasten with me to the chamber of my foes, and stand prepared to do my bidding, even at the slightest signal."

With these words he entered the room, and perceiving by the light of a lamp that the countess and her husband were still sleeping, he motioned to his followers to stand aside, and stepping towards the couch, stood gazing upon the forms of those against whom he had formed so terrible a plot. Yet, even their happy state of unconsciousness, and the beauty of the countess, awoke no feelings of pity in his breast, for the demon of revenge was still lurking there, and it was not without some difficulty that he could restrain himself from bursting forth into a loud laugh of demoniac triumph. But he soon shook off the reverie of exultation in which he had indulged, and raising the poniard which was still reeking with the old man's blood, plunged it with fearful force into the bosom of Earl Glenalvon.

At that moment a wild shriek of agony burst from the lips of the countess, who had been awakened by the act that had robbed her of a beloved husband, and throwing herself upon the bleeding form of Glenalvon, she besought the assassin to complete his vengeance by sending her spirit to join that of his other victim. The earl, however, still retained some sparks of life, and faintly imploring his countess to allay her agony, he directed a look of hatred towards the murderer, and in hollow accents, exclaimed :—

"For ever be accursed the villain who has thus, like a base coward, stolen upon my slumbers to do a deed which will bring upon him the blasting lightnings of Heaven. Take with you the imprecations of a dying man, and may they cling to you even to your own dying hour. With my last words I curse you ;—may the horrors of an evil conscience be your everlasting scourge, embittering each moment of your life, and inflicting upon your soul the torments of hell !"

Awe-struck at these words, the chief of Badenoch stood as if rooted to the spot ; it seemed to him that the curse had already fallen with withering effect upon his soul, and for an instant he regretted the passion that had urged him to the execution of so fiendish a project. But this feeling was quickly subdued, and resuming his haughty air of defiance, he gazed upon the dying man with an expression of triumph that gave his countenance an appearance that was almost supernatural.

At this juncture the countess slowly recovered from the swoon which the recent horrors had produced, and throwing her arms about the bleeding form of her husband, she gave way to her agony of grief in those tears which alone could afford relief. Still, however, the chief was unmoved by the misery and desolation he had caused, and hastily advancing a pace or two, he attempted to remove her by force from the beloved object to which she so fondly clung.

"Why," he exclaimed, "dost thou still indulge in grief for an act which no tears or aid of thine can prevent ? Thy husband is dying, Helen, and I, who have been rejected with scorn, now offer thee a home and protection. Cease, then, these tears, and, instead of wailing for the dead, bestow thy smiles upon one whom thy scorn has almost driven to madness."

"Villain, forbear !" cried the countess, slowly raising herself, and directing towards him a look of mingled horror and contempt. "Leave me, murderer as thou art, and never again present thyself before her who can never again regard thee but as a foul and accursed monster !"

"How !—art thou still obdurate ?"

"Canst thou," she asked, "look upon this bleeding form,—the victim of thy cruel hate, and yet believe that I can ever forget the deed which has robbed me of a beloved husband ?"

"Thou hast thyself to blame for it all," he replied sternly ; "thy coldness and disdain prompted me to an act of vengeance, and now thou feelest the bitter pains of thine own blind obstinacy. Yes, Helen, from the day thy hand was given to Earl Glenalvon, I have meditated this deed, and now thou art a witness of the act to which slighted love has impelled me."

"And that act," she exclaimed, "has rendered thee for ever hateful in my sight."

"Dost thou brave my power then ?"

"Thy power is nought," she replied, with scorn, "since Heaven will aid the innocent against the oppressor."

"Nay," cried the chief, fiercely, "if thou wilt not yield to persuasion, thou shalt to force. This very hour shall make thee the bride of the man thou dost treat with scorn, and never again shalt thou have an opportunity of thwarting the will of one who has the power of compelling thee to accept his own terms."

"Villain!" she exclaimed, "thy boasts are uttered in vain, for, great as thy vaunted power may be, thou shalt never subdue her who thus sets thee at defiance. Thou art armed, and perhaps may slay me, but even though thy dagger was upraised to kill me, yet would I still refuse to purchase life upon such terms as thou hast had the baseness to propose."

"And yet," he said, "thou hast no tie, seeing that the earl, thy husband, now lies at the point of death."

"To which condition," exclaimed Helen, "thou hast thyself brought him. Thou art his murderer, yet canst thou basely propose a union with her whom thou hast robbed of the dearest treasure of her heart!"

"Beware how you speak thus, Lady Helen," he cried, "for words such as those thou hast just uttered, may haply drive me to desperation, and then bitterly wilt thou regret the madness that has urged thee to this course."

"I heed not thy threats, monster!" answered the countess; "for, say as thou wilt, I have yet the means of escape left that will preserve me from becoming the bride of him whom I can regard only with loathing and detestation."

"Nay, there are none here to aid thee," returned the other, with an air of triumph. "Thy castle contains not one friend in this, thy hour of need, for all have perished by the hands of my followers ere we reached this chamber."

At this moment the last groan of Earl Glenalvon was heard, and the countess again throwing herself upon the dead body of her husband, was for a time unconscious of the perilous situation in which she was placed. Still, however, the heart of the chief remained callous, and he gazed upon the afflicting scene with apathy and unconcern. At length, a dark scowl passed over his countenance, and stepping forward a pace or two, he seemed about to sacrifice the countess to his fury, when a vivid flash of lightning shot across the chamber of death, and immediately afterwards there followed a peal of thunder that shook the castle from the battlements to its very lowest foundation. Horror-struck at this apparent interposition of Heaven, he started back, and hastily concealing the poniard in his vest, he stood with folded arms looking upon the lovely wreck before him. Yet, her distress softened not his stubborn heart, for his haughty spirit could brook no contradiction, and though appalled for a moment, he was still resolved to accomplish the purpose that had brought him to the castle. At last, suddenly reviving as a dreadful thought passed across her brain, she started up, and with a look of mingled agony and horror, inquired if her children had shared the hapless fate of their unfortunate father.

"They both live," answered the chieftain, sullenly; "but it depends upon yourself whether they behold the next rising sun."

"Ah!" she cried, frantically; "for mercy's sake bring them to me, that I may know they live. Slay me if thou wilt, but spare, oh, spare my children!"

"They are captives in the hands of my men, yonder," answered the chief, pointing to the further end of the chamber: "at present, you see, I have spared their lives, and it now only remains for you to say whether they shall escape the doom to which they will otherwise be adjudged."

"Monster!" she cried, "would you slay my innocent children, who have never harmed you?"

"It remains for yourself to say what shall be their fate," answered the chief of Badenoch. "Promise to be mine, and I pledge my word they shall be safe."

"Promise to be thine!—never!" she exclaimed, shuddering, as she saw her helpless offspring struggling to release themselves from the villains who held them.

"Am I to understand that as your final answer?" he inquired sternly.

"I can give no other," she replied.

"Then they die!" he exclaimed, hoarsely; and turning towards his men, he continued: "You remember your orders,—plunge your weapons into the hearts of those children the moment I give the signal."

"Mercy!—mercy!" cried the distracted countess; "spare them, I implore you, and a mother's blessings shall attend you."

"We ask for no blessing, lady," said the chief, scornfully; "you have dared to reject the offer of my hand, and it now only remains for me to accomplish the full measure of vengeance that I have vowed. The lives of your children hang upon your word, and yet you would consign them to a dreadful fate, rather than wed one who loves you."

"Dare you speak of love," she cried, "to her you have widowed by your lawless violence?—Have I not seen my husband butchered by your own hands, and think you I can ever become the wife of such a monster of iniquity?"

"Your words of scorn, lady, do but add to the fire of my wrath," exclaimed the chief. "I have given you sufficient warning of my intention, and you have only another instant to speak those words which will either save the lives of your children, or consign them to a dreadful fate."

"Is there no alternative?" she wildly cried, "no other way by which I may save them from destruction?"

"There is not," exclaimed the chief of Badenoch.

"Then my own fate is decided!" answered the countess, in accents of despair.

The chieftain eyed her with a look of doubt, for he knew not how to understand her last words, though he felt inclined to construe it into an augury that she was about to yield to his demands. He, however, could not fail to observe that her countenance had assumed an expression of desperation, and that her wild and haggard looks denoted some fearful thoughts which were passing through her almost maddened brain. At last, addressing herself to the inanimate form of her murdered husband, she exclaimed in frantic accents:—

"Why, why dost thou look so sternly upon me?—Dost thou reproach me for not having followed thee ere now, rather than yield assent to the monster that has robbed thee of thy life? But thou shalt not wait long for me, Glenalvon, for my soul is weary of the world, and I will seek peace and rest beside thee in thy grave. Yes, dearest husband, I have brought thee to this, and deeply will I atone for the fault that has made the fierce chief of Badenoch thy foe."

"Wilt thou save thy children?" demanded the chief, impatient of further delay.

"I will."

"Ah!—then thou wilt be mine!" he exclaimed triumphantly. "Thou wilt be my bride, and thy children shall find a protector in the man thou regardest as thine enemy."

"I have not yet said that it shall be so," she replied, with more composure than she had hitherto manifested. "My answer is yet to be given, and, hating thee as I do, it is scarcely to be expected that I can ever consent to become thy wife, ere the body of my slain husband has grown cold."

"Your consent may be extorted," answered the chief; "it may be given reluctantly, perhaps, but I care not even for that, if I do but triumph after the defeat I sustained when thou didst become the willing bride of Earl Glenalvon."

"Wilt thou," she asked, "grant me a little time, that I may consider thy proposition?"

"Not an instant, Helen."

"Nay, I ask but for a day," she replied, "and at the end of that time I promise to give an answer."

"Will it be in the affirmative?"

"That I cannot say, at present," answered the countess. "I must reflect well ere I consent to this union, and the time I have asked for is so short that surely you will not refuse me?"

"I see how it is," replied the chief of Badenoch; "thou hast some scheme in view,—some hope that events may arise to prevent our union. But I will not be trifled with, Helen, and the present moment must decide the course I am about to pursue."

"Then let this be my answer!" exclaimed the countess, in accents of desperation, and snatching the dagger from the body of her unfortunate husband, she plunged it deep in her own body, ere the chief could rush forward to arrest the fatal blow. As she did this a gleam of triumph passed over her countenance, and glancing scornfully at the monster who had driven her to this alternative, she faintly said :—

"Thus, remorseless villain, have I escaped the loathsome fate to which thou wouldst have doomed me. Soon shall I join those whom thy cruel hatred has sent, ere their time, to another world; and thus has my own hand defeated the deep designs that urged thee to the murder of all our household. I am now free, accursed assassin, and thou art left to curse the chance that has snatched me from a doom that was more terrible to me than death!"

The countess had by this time grown weak from loss of blood, yet, with a last effort, she pressed to her bosom her children; who, terrified at the scene they had witnessed, broke away from their guards, and flew to her side. No one, indeed, attempted to prevent this last sad interview, and even the chief of Badenoch himself, harsh and cruel as was his nature, forebore, at present, from giving any orders for their re-capture. He would have advanced to support the dying countess, but she motioned him not to approach; and so earnestly was this expressed, that he shrank back, apparently unnerved by the unexpected and tragical occurrence that had taken place. Silently he watched the scene that was going forward, but soon the usual sternness of his nature became apparent, and joining his ruffian followers, he stood a little apart to whisper the directions he had to give for their next proceedings. The countess, however, gave no further heed to him, and observing the distress of her children, she made every effort in her power to soothe and console them.

"Do not, my dear children," she said, "weep at the approaching death of one to whom life possessed no charms after the fearful events of this night. I have escaped a doom from which my soul revolted with horror, and could I but be assured of your safety I would quit the world without a single regret."

"You have been over hasty, Lady Helen," exclaimed the chief, advancing a few paces nearer; "I did but propose marriage, and you have laid violent hands upon yourself."

"It was done," she replied faintly, "to escape from a villain whom my soul abhorred. Death will now soon release me from the miseries you would have planted in my bosom, and upon Heaven do I rely for mercy and forgiveness, for a deed which was prompted by your own base deeds. Upon you will a heavy retribution fall, and in this, my last hour, do I call upon you to desist from persecuting the two unfortunate orphans whom your own foul crimes have rendered friendless.''

" I need no council from thee," exclaimed the chief sullenly; " the deed, which was my own, I must answer for, and as for your children, Helen, they are still in my power, and shall die to fill up the measure of my vengeance."

" "Oh, in mercy, harm them not, I implore you," exclaimed the countess, vehemently. " Beware, and seek not that injury, for my spirit shall guard them from thy acts, and avert the crimes thou would commit towards the innocent! Let thy vengeance now be satisfied, for even in death will I hover over them, and save my helpless offspring from the machinations of the wicked! And now, my children, farewell—Heaven will not forsake thee, and thy prayers will never be unheeded by——"

Here her voice faltered, and shuddering convulsively as she pressed the children to her bosom, she sank back and expired by the body of the murdered Earl of Glenalvon.

CHAPTER II.

" Seest thou yon mouldering ruins?
How darkly frowning in their sad decay,
Yet still magnificent.''　　　• THE FEUD.

THE horrible incident narrated in the foregoing chapter occurred early in the fourteenth century, when Scotland was unhappily the scene of the wildest anarchy and confusion. The death of the late sovereign without children, gave rise to those princes who conceived they stood nearest to the vacant throne, and the disputes that subsequently occurred between Baliol and Bruce—both having nearly equal claims to the kingly dignity—lit the flames of civil war throughout the country for many a long and wearisome year, and gave occasion for that foreign interference, which for a time lost the nation its independence, and made it a mere territory to Edward the First, King of England.

It was then that such acts as we have related, could be committed with impunity, for even the shedder of blood could escape punishment, and the powerful chieftains dwelling in the mountain fastnesses could breathe defiance to any power that might be brought against them. They were, indeed, greater than their monarchs, for there was nothing to control them, and secure in their own strength, they exercised a species of tyranny around the neighbourhood of their castles, that was far more galling than any other submission their victims might have been compelled to make. In many instances they usurped the sovereign functions, ordering those who had offended them into their presence, and in most cases dispensing death to all who had rendered themselves in any way obnoxious.

Nor was it of any use to complain of the injustice to which the humbler orders were subjected, for an appeal to the sovereign was in vain; he himself being too weak to afford that redress which his will might probably have induced him to give. Occasionally he would intercede in behalf of any applicant, but even this was attended with some hazard to himself, as the haughty barons were seldom disposed to listen to him, and sometimes they would threaten him with rebellion if he again remonstrated against a continuance of their self-assumed powers.

This brief explanation has been rendered necessary in order to show that the deed of violence and bloodshed we have described was no fiction. The chief of Badenoch had his own private revenge to gratify, and being resolved to annex the territories of Earl Glenalvon to his own, he had entered the castle as we have seen, and slaughtered the sleeping inhabitants without fearing that any evil consequences could overtake him.

The hapless Countess Glenalvon perished as we have seen, but the rage of the chief of Badenoch was too great for description. He had expected to make her his in spite of the hatred he knew she bore towards him, and even at the moment when he felt most secure of his prize, she fell by her own hand rather than become the wife of the monster who had slain her beloved husband. Helen had, indeed, long been the object of his love; he had named the subject to her, yet she listened to his words with coldness, and in a few months afterwards, gave her hand to another. Still, however, the fire in his heart was unquenched; he had been disappointed, but was not yet subdued, and in secret he resolved to avenge himself at the first opportunity that offered, and how fatally he fulfilled his oath is already known to the reader.

Glenalvon she had loved from the first time they had ever met, for his soul was pure and generous, and the whisper of calumny had never uttered a word against his honour. This was another source for the hatred of the chief of Badenoch, for he was no friend to virtue or those who professed to honour it, and when he beheld his rival in possession of the prize he had himself contended for, he gave way to the bitterness of soul that terminated so disastrously. Years, however, passed without the accomplishment of his murderous designs, but when the moment arrived that he could safely carry it into execution, he summoned the fiercest of his band, and having instructed them in the project he had at hand, he led them forth, and by means of a bribe to one of Glenalvon's faithless domestics, found admittance at midnight into the castle.

That the children had not shared the fate of their hapless parents, was owing merely to a caprice on the part of the chief, who, being satiated with blood for that night, resolved to spare them for a time in order that he might glut his vengeance at some future period. He, however, ordered them into the custody of his principal confidant, who was desired on no account to let them escape, but to be ready to produce them whenever the period for their execution arrived.

When all except the children had been slain, the followers were permitted to plunder the castle of all they might think worth carrying off as a reward for the share they had in that night's fearful tragedy. This done, they set fire to the castle in order to conceal the dreadful deed they had performed, and thus shield themselves from the suspicion that would otherwise fall upon themselves and their chieftain. Thus, every sign of the transaction was obliterated by the flames which consumed all that came within their reach.

It is true suspicion fell upon the perpetrators of the crime, yet no evidence remained to prove its truth, or lead to any discovery which might bring punishment upon the guilty. The whole neighbourhood was thrown into consternation on the following morning when the dawn broke, and showed the devastation which reigned where once had stood the noble castle of Glenalvon. Many rushed through the mouldering ruins in the vain hope of saving the inmates from destruction, but no living creature was to be found, and the general supposition was that all had perished in the flames that had reduced the noble castle to an unsightly ruin.

It was a sad spectacle for those who had been used to gaze upon the spacious edifice when it was in the zenith of its magnificence; they now beheld a shapeless mass, where once joy and hospitality had reigned; and

again they sighed in the bitterness of their hearts as they thought of the dreadful fate that had befallen those who had perished in the all-devouring flames.

But the origin of the dreadful calamity was enveloped in an impenetrable obscurity; it might have been the result of an accident, or—and the latter supposition was but too probable—the destruction might have been caused by some secret foe, who had taken this method of avenging himself for some fancied wrongs endured at some previous time. At present, however, there was no clue by which the mystery might be cleared up, and applying all their energies to the task of subduing the flames which still raged in some parts of the building, the neighbouring peasantry at length succeeded in conquering the devouring element.

This done, they were enabled to institute a more careful search through the desolated edifice, and as they traversed different portions of it, they saw enough to convince them that most, if not all the inhabitants, had perished in the flames that had destroyed the ancient halls of the Glenalvons. In all directions the ghastly forms of bodies half consumed met their view, and though it was impossible to distinguish amongst them those of the noble owner and his beloved countess; the fact of their not having sought refuge at any of the neighbouring cottages but was too convincing a proof that they had perished in the flames, and the only question that remained, was, as to the perpetrator of the deed, and the motive that had induced him to commit an act so cowardly and inhuman. It was certain, however, that many persons must have been engaged in it, and whilst a universal horror was excited by the base transaction, a general determination pervaded the amazed spectators to avenge the crime whenever it should please Heaven to point out the guilty parties.

"This has been a sad day for the noble lord of Glenalvon," said an aged

No, 2

peasant, who stood leaning upon the blackened walls before him. "All, alas ! have perished, and desolation frowns upon us even from the place where we were wont to witness happiness and peace. Yet the evil doer shall not escape the punishment due to his crime, for the hour shall come when he, and all who aided him, shall perish even as have his victims."

"You say, truly, Donald," exclaimed another, who stood near while these words were uttered. "The day of retribution will come, and I, who am a younger man than yourself, will never cease to hunt after the villain that has done this deed. Let him beware, I saw, for all who have witnessed this sorrowful sight are pledged to devote themselves to the task of bringing the foul authors of this ruin to the doom they merit."

"Can any among you guess who has done it ?" asked the old man.

"At present all is involved in mystery," replied the other, "but the monsters cannot long escape the searching enquiries we shall make after them."

"Is it known whether the noble Glenalvon has perished?" enquired the elder.

"There is but too much reason to believe he has," replied the second speaker, "for no one has heard anything of him, though the messengers that we despatched in every direction to search after him, have returned some time since. Nor is that the worst part of this sad tragedy, for it is not to be doubted that the countess and her two children have shared the melancholy fate of their unfortunate relative."

"How !" exclaimed the old man, "have they not even spared the women and children ?"

"It is feared all have perished," replied the other; "I would have searched among the ruins to recognise the bodies that are not utterly consumed, but the falling walls convinced me of the danger, and I was compelled to desist."

"And it would have been a vain and fruitless task," returned the aged man with a sigh. "There let them sleep amidst the ruin that has fallen upon their house, and though no marble ornament may be raised over their remains, yet will they live in our remembrance, and prompt the young men among us to aid in bringing justice upon those who have done this deed."

"There is little need, father," answered the other : "for aught, save our own feelings, to spur us on to accomplish the design you speak of. For my own part, I am ready to make any sacrifice to obtain ample vengeance, and glad should I be were it my lot to hurl destruction upon the head of the monster who has thus sacrificed many to his fiendish vengeance. From henceforth I will devote myself to the task, and with Heaven's aid it shall be accomplished, even though years may pass away ere the time arrives for it."

"Hear me, youth," exclaimed the elder; "if treachery has had ought to do with this fearful deed, there is a power above that will in its own good time discover the guilty, and bring them to a just punishment. Let the wicked tremble and repent, for there is no escape for them, though for a brief period they may triumph in their fancied security. Let us not, then, forget our duty, but rather endeavour to preserve that which it is in our power to save, than by indulgence of idle grief, allow ourselves to abet the destruction which it may yet be in our power to avert."

"And what can we now avert ?" asked the other, pointing towards the smoking ruins; "is not yonder castle levelled with the dust, its beauty and strength faded, and those who but a few hours since dwelt within its walls, numbered among the dead ?"

"We know not all are dead," answered the old man ;—"the earl and his family may have had a forewarning of what was about to occur, and in that case it is likely they have sought shelter in some distant place. Should it be so, it remains with us to prove our love and devotion by saving that which may have escaped the ravages of the flames from future destruction."

The suggestion of the last speaker was promptly acceded to, and in the course of a few hours all that had not been consumed, was conveyed from the ruins and carried to a place of security, in case either the earl or any of his family should have escaped the destruction what had fallen upon Glenalvon Castle.

From that time, the remains of the edifice went to decay, and years passed by without any discovery taking place that might in the slightest degree lead to the revelation of this fearful mystery. Stories of a wild and fearful character were, however, circulated respecting sights that had been seen, and sounds that had been heard around the mouldering ruins. Terror-struck by these reports, most of the inhabitants removed to distant places, and never again returned to visit a scene which was impressed with so many horrible recollections. The neighbourhood, indeed, became depopulated, except by a few hardy peasants, who dwelt amidst the lonely waste, and obtained a scanty subsistence from the produce of the earth.

Yet, even these, sitting of winter evenings by their fires, would ofttimes relate tales of terror such as had been handed down to them by their forefathers ; and as the howling winds swept mournfully round their rude hovels, they would tell of the dismal fate of the castle, and gave a sigh for those who had perished on that terrible night of blood and rapine.

Yet, even the boldest among them would not pass the ruins after the darkness of night had set in, for the rumours of the ignorant had peopled its interior with spirits of another world, and there were not wanting persons who were ready to affirm that they had perceived sights there which they scarcely had the courage to relate. The belief that it was haunted, indeed, became general, and the once peaceful mansion of the Earls of Glenalvon was looked upon with suspicious terror, and timidly shunned by the few rustics who were compelled by circumstances to live in the neighbourhood.

CHAPTER III.

" Such constancy as hers I ne'er did hear of,
For, spite of dangers or the threats of foes,
She still was faithful to her generous task."
THE CONSCRIPT.

UPON the night when the murder of their parents took place, the orphans of Glenalvon were hurried away by the ruthless villains, and conveyed to the lonely tower of the chief of Badenoch, where they were to be confined till further orders were given respecting the fate to which they were to be doomed by their blood-thirsty foe. Fergus, the ruffian to whose care they had been given, had been inspired with a momentary feeling of pity in their behalf, and desirous of saving the orphans from the fate that he knew awaited them, he had formed a project for concealing them in a place of safety, when suddenly the chief presented himself before him, and in a sullen tone, commanded him to strangle them both, or dread the terrible punishment that would certainly fall upon himself.

Obedient to the commands of an imperious monster whose will he **dared** not thwart, the retainer hastened away to complete the deed of blood. **But** he was too late, for his wife, to whose care he had committed them during his temporary absence, had removed them beyond his reach, nor could all his threats of vengeance or promises of future reward, induce her to confess what had become of the two unfortunate orphans. Nay, so resolute was she in the cause of injured innocence, that, in spite of his denunciations of vengeance, she hurried from him, and abruptly entered the presence of the haughty chief of Badenoch, who, in his own chamber, was contemplating with savage joy, the triumph he would achieve when the two children, the only barriers that remained between him and the possessions of the Earl of Glenalvon—should be laid in the dark and desolate grave.

"My lord," exclaimed Magdalen, as she entered the room, "it has come to my ears that you have a design against the lives of the two children that you have made orphans. They are to be murdered to complete your vengeance, and it therefore becomes my duty,—woman as I am,—to stand forward as their protector."

"Art thou mad to brave my wrath with words like these?" demanded the other, furiously.

"I am not mad," she replied; "but I would warn you against the foul crime you meditate. The children of Glenalvon shall not perish!—Nay, look not on me thus menacingly, for I am as resolute as yourself; and though I perish for the boldness with which I address you, yet shall they be spared the fate that has befallen their hapless parents."

"Thou shall repent this rashness!" exclaimed the chief, gnashing his teeth wrathfully.

"Nay, I shall never repent becoming the protector of those who cannot aid themselves," answered Magdalen, unmoved by his anger. "Death I fear not, nor shall torture make me confess the place where I have concealed your hapless victims. I may perhaps perish by your hands ere another instant has passed away,—yet what will my death avail you, since it will not again throw the orphans in your power?"

"Magdalen!" exclaimed the chief, with startling vehemence, "thy words are bold and fearless, yet is it in my power to punish the insolence thou hast dared to utter. But I will be calm," he continued, after a momentary pause, "and yielding to the pity you have awakened in my heart, will spare these children in whose cause you have taken so great an interest."

"Oh, my lord," cried the grateful Magdalen, "you know not with how much joy those words have inspired me."

"I have said they shall live," he replied, "but it shall not be as the sons of Glenalvon! Be prudent then and keep them from my sight, for shouldst either they or thyself again cross my path, that moment will be thy last. Be silent, too, for should I ever hear that thou hast prated of who or what they are, thou diest!—Leave me woman!—Begone to some lone and safe retreat, where the foot of man never penetrates; and remember, Magdalen, that the sword of vengeance hangs suspended over thy head, for should once I hear that thou hast been unfaithful to thy trust, I will pursue thee to death, even though I should have to follow to the very farthest confines of the earth."

"My lord," cried Magdalen, "grateful for even this mercy, I promise to keep your secret inviolate."

"Swear it then!" he exclaimed, "and should'st thou break thy oath, may thy soul sink to eternal perdition!"

"I do swear it!" cried Magdalen, clasping her hands, and falling at the feet of the chief.

"Then begone from me!" he muttered, hoarsely;—"begone, I say, and never let me see thee again."

Tremblingly she arose from her knees, and quitted the presence of the imperious chief, whose angry looks and gestures betrayed the fierce conflict in which his soul was engaged. As she left the chamber, she hurried to the place where the children were concealed, and as night had closed in, she led the orphans forth, and quitted the castle. Edwin, the youngest, she carried in her arms, whilst Angus, the elder born, walked closely by her side, clinging to her garments, and wondering at the haste with which she pursued her way.

The steep cliff upon which stood the castle they had just left, was situated in the sea, and was separated from the island on which stood the fortress of Glenalvon, which had so lately been given to the devouring flames, by a narrow creek, generally very difficult to pass, on account of the strong current of waters which flowed there with fearful impetuosity, and formed a whirlpool, dangerous even to vessels of large size.

Scrambling with extreme difficulty down the steep declivity that led to the sea, Magdalen placed the children in a recess in the rock, whilst she made her way towards a small boat, which usually lay there for the use of those who dwelt upon that sterile tract. Fortunately at that period the waters were not much agitated, and loosing the ropes that secured the fragile bark to the shore, she returned for her youthful companions, and putting them on board, placed herself at the stern, where grasping the rudder, the vessel sprang from its moorings, whilst little Angus, holding aloft the torch, with which they were provided, assisted her in guiding the boat, so as to avoid the danger there was so much reason to apprehend. A short time served to reach the place of their intended destination, where they landed without encountering any difficulties.

But the way before them was still long and difficult, yet Magdalen shrunk not from the task she had imposed upon herself, and long ere the day was expected to break, she had nearly reached the place to which her footsteps were directed, and where she hoped to find a secure shelter for herself and the children she had rescued from death. The younger boy still slept in her arms, but his brother Angus was wearied with the exertions he had gone through, and it was with no little difficulty that he kept up with his generous protectress.

At length they reached the base of a lofty rock, at the summit of which stood a watch tower, erected there for the purpose of guarding that part of the country against the sudden incursion of a neighbouring foe. Here Magdalen paused for a brief period, and Angus, who had scarcely spoken till now, exclaimed in timid accents :—

" Whither are we going? for I thought we were on our way to the castle of Glenalvon, and yet this place did I never see before. Alas! alas! they have slain my father, and my poor mother perished at the same time, for they would have dragged her away from home, and then she stabbed herself to escape from the fearful men that had entered our house."

" Poor child!" sighed Magdalen, as she gazed upon the sobbing boy, "thou art indeed an orphan, with no home,—no friend in the wide world, save myself. Yet fear not, my boy, for I will be a parent to you both, and shield you from the blood-thirsty tyrant that would have hurried you to an early death!"

" Will you indeed be our friend?" asked the child.

" Aye, as I hope for mercy hereafter," answered Magdalen, " do tell me, darling boy, will you be content to live with me and love me as a mother?"

" Indeed, indeed I will love you," cried the artless boy. "You will be kind to us, I know, for you have already braved dangers for us, and saved me and little Edwin from those bad-looking men that would have slain us as they did our poor father, who was stabbed by them in his sleep."

"Angus!" exclaimed their protectress, earnestly, "I entreat of you speak no more upon that subject, as you would preserve yourself and your brother from a dreadful fate. We are surrounded by dangers and difficulties, our lives are in momentary peril, and should we be traced hither, nothing could save us from the cruel vengeance of those from whom we have escaped. I have risked much, my dear child, to save you both from death, and, therefore, I charge you do not involve us in fresh perils by speaking further upon this subject."

"I will not," cried the child, earnestly, "indeed, indeed I will not."

"Henceforth then," she continued, "regard me as a mother, and in return, I will love you both as my own children. A little patience will serve to unravel this fearful mystery, and when you and Edwin reach the years of manhood, you shall perhaps know all, without reserve. Then, if the villain lives that has done you this wrong, you may revenge yourself upon the cruel author of the deeds that have just been perpetrated."

"Aye," cried the boy, warmly, "and I will revenge them too, or die in the attempt!"

"But you must remain silent on this subject till the time I have named," answered Magdalen, "for should you ever let it be known that you are aware of what has taken place, or that you belong to the noble house of Glenalvon, the wrath of your enemy will be aroused, and you and your brother will perish by a cruel death."

"I will obey your counsel," answered Angus. "For a time, at least, I will keep this secret to myself, but it shall only be that I may the more certainly punish those that have rendered me an orphan."

"Do not, on consideration," she added, "let the least hint escape that you are aware of anything that has passed, for your persecutor has spies in every direction, and it might be the means of leading to a discovery of our hiding place, and then whither should we fly for shelter and protection? Already I have had much difficulty to encounter in my efforts to save you, but should you again be discovered, no prayers, no entreaties will serve to snatch you from the vengeance of your stern foe. And forget not, my dear boy, that the lives of your brother and myself depend upon your prudence, and that all would perish did one thoughtless word upon this subject escape your lips."

"I will not forget your instructions," replied the boy, "but when I grow old enough, and have strength equal to my years, I will find out my enemy, and revenge my father's death."

The generous woman raised her eyes towards the Watch Tower, and perceived a light through the loop holes, near the basement. As she gazed, it ascended slowly, disappearing every now and then, till she could at length see its strong glare upon the summit. Two figures then became visible, both of whom wore armour, and by the torch which one of them bore in his hand, she could perceive them occasionally glancing over the battlements, as if looking either for an enemy or for some one else that they were expecting to meet them in that mountain solitude.

To her alarm she perceived that one of them was her husband, and then, in subdued tones, requesting the youthful Angus to maintain a profound silence, she led the way towards the tower, when crouching with the children beneath some low shrubs, she awaited in trembling anxiety till she could once more venture from her place of concealment.

"Alas!" she thought within herself, "should they happen to see us to what a dreadful fate shall we be consigned. Our blood alone will satisfy the fierce wrath of these dreadful assassins, and yonder brawling stream will for ever conceal the crime that has been committed."

She paused, for at that moment sounds were heard approaching from the direction of the Watch Tower, and it was but too evident that the persons, whoever they might be, were advancing towards the place where she had found a temporary hiding place. Magdalen crept closer into the dark covert, and in a few moments she could perceive by the torch that the foremost man carried, the dark visage of Fergus, immediately behind whom came Stephen, the keeper of the tower, whose blood-thirsty disposition she well knew, rendered him a fitting instrument in the hands of the vindictive chief of Badenoch. Nearer and nearer they approached, till at length she could hear a portion of the conversation in which they were both earnestly engaged.

"I tell you all has been accomplished," said Fergus;—"the Earl of Glenalvon, and all belonging to him, have fallen beneath the poniards of our chief and his brave comrades."

"What!" exclaimed the other, with astonishment, "have none been suffered to escape?"

"I tell you all have perished," answered Fergus.

"Blood-thirsty miscreants!" exclaimed Stephen, who, bad as he was, felt some degreee of pity for those who had thus miserably perished.

"What mean those words?" demanded Fergus, wrathfully. "Do you regret that our noble chief has thus destroyed those who stood in the way of his ambition?"

"No, sir," returned the other, alarmed at the consequences of his hasty expressions; "it was but a momentary feeling of pity for the unfortunates. But it was our chieftain's will, and I no longer regret its execution."

"Why, that's well said," exclaimed Fergus, with a grim smile; "for why should we, who are mere dependants on our lord, express displeasure at the fall of his enemies? But I said wrong when I spoke of all having perished in our attack on the Castle of Glenalvon, for the two children were conveyed to our chief's fortress, where it was intended their execution should take place."

"And have they escaped?" asked Stephen.

"They have," answered Fergus, "and that too, with my wife Magdalen. But doubtless they will come hither for shelter, and should that be the case, it must be your task to aid in delivering them once more into our power."

"It is hardly likely they will come here," said the other.

"It is almost certain they will," returned Fergus, "for they will be weary of traversing the wild and desolate tract they have to pass through, and should they claim shelter, you must grant the favour with as little of your usual surliness as possible."

"Depend upon it I shall obey your injunctions," replied Stephen.

"And remember," continued his companion, "that your own life will be hazarded should you afford them the means of again escaping from our clutches. You must detain them in close custody till our chieftain has been informed of their being safe within his power, and then, I'll warrant you, he takes speedy means to release himself from these brats who stand between him and the object he has most dearly at heart."

"Must they indeed die?" exclaimed Stephen.

"They must," answered the other; "the wealth which would be their's, is destined to fill the coffers of our chief, and never can that be done with safety till the children are disposed of. Remember, Stephen, though once the vassal of Glenalvon's chief, you are now the slave of the chief of Badenoch, to whom yonder Watch Tower now belongs. Should the sons of

Glenalvon escape the search that will be made for them, they may hereafter seek retribution for their parents' death, and then bring destruction
upon us all."

After this Magdalen could hear no more, for they passed on, and their
words became indistinct. She, however, discovered to her horror, that
the Watch Tower was now in the possession of the children's greatest
enemy, and thus was their only hope of concealment at an end. This was
a terrible blow to one who was already wearied with the exertions she had
made to escape, but the greatness of her danger inspired her with fresh
courage, and yielding to the impulse of the moment, she resolved to seek
an asylum in the tower, and, if need be, make a confident in Stephen, who
was her brother, though the sternness of his nature had made them almost
as strangers to each other. No sooner had she resolved upon this, than
taking the still sleeping child in her arms, she conjured little Angus to follow her fearlessly, and with some difficulty they began to ascend the steep
rock upon which the Watch Tower was situated.

In former times Magdalen had lived there, for her father had been
warder when it was in the possession of the Earl of Glenalvon, and knowing every part of the place, she made her way towards the entrance gate,
which she found had been left open against the return of Stephen. Here,
however, she again paused, for she could not help trembling at the danger
to which the children would be exposed should the fears of her brother
prompt him to confess to the chief of Badenoch that the young and innocent victims of his wrath had sought refuge within the domains he had
usurped. But this was no time for hesitation, since there was little doubt
that Stephen would shortly return, and proceeding onwards she was about
to ascend the steps that led to the chambers above, when she bethought
herself of a subterranean vault, which was never visited, on account of the
rumours which were spread of its being haunted by evil spirits.

Proceeding through an arched recess, therefore, she descended a flight of
stone steps, that led to the dreary abode beneath the tower, and having at
length attained the place which had been the object of her search, she
spread her cloak upon the ground, and laying the children upon it, cautioned Angus against speaking too loudly, promised to return to them immediately, and then hastened away to meet Stephen, of whose return she
was in momentary expectation.

At length, as she stood waiting for him at the portal, he made his appearance, and no sooner did he catch sight of his sister's form, than a deadly
paleness overspread his countenance, for he knew her fate would be sealed,
should her presence there be communicated to Fergus, and though his
heart had of late grown callous to all generous feelings, yet was his soul
subdued when the thought flashed across his mind that he might be commanded to become her executioner. For a moment or two all power of
utterance forsook him, but Magdalen, fancying she could perceive some
trace of kindness in the look with which he regarded her, caught him by
the arm, and in earnest accents exclaimed :—

"Brother,—dear brother, save me, I implore you ; I am in danger, and
you only have the means of preserving me from those who seek my life."

" Why art thou here, Magdalen ?" he asked sullenly. "Thou knowest
I dare not shelter those who have offended my lord, and should'st thou
remain in this tower, my own life, as well as thine, will answer for it."

"Alas!" she bitterly cried ; "is there none to help me ?"

"Aye," he answered, "thy husband!"

"Name him not !" exclaimed Magdalen, wildly ; "his crimes have for
ever separated us, and never will I again accept favour or protection from

the man whose soul is stained with blood! Oh, my brother, pity me, I conjure you, and do not reject the prayers with which I supplicate for shelter and protection."

"It is in vain you plead to me, Magdalen," he replied; "for thou art denounced by my chief, and if the news I have heard is correct, thou art accompanied hither by the two sons of Glenalvon. Nay, it is in vain to deny it, and thou must either deliver them up to me, or with this bugle will I call Fergus of whom thou standest in so much dread. Surrender them, I say, and I will bestow upon thee the protection thou hast required of me. Thy life will be safe, for Fergus seeks only those children whose existence is so dangerous to the chief of Badenoch. All thou hast to do, therefore, is to yield them up willingly, and the reward we shall gain from our master, will amply repay us for the service we have performed for him."

Indignant as she felt, Magdalen dared not betray the anger which these words had occasioned, and though scorning a falsehood, had it been to serve any purpose of her own, she resolved to invent some story by which to deceive her brother till a more favourable opportunity occurred for removing the orphans to a place of safety. It was some little time, however, before she could think of anything that would serve her purpose, and Stephen had again demanded where the children were, when driven to desperation, she replied :—

"Alas! my brother, the children you speak of are no more. I fled with them, it is true, in the vain hope of saving their lives, but as I passed the bridge that crosses yonder torrent, my foot slipped, and they were precipitated into the roaring waters beneath! I would have plunged after the helpless objects of my care, but the darkness of night hid them from my sight, and by their dying shrieks I knew that they had been carried far, far beyond my reach."

"Magdalen!" exclaimed her brother, fiercely; "thou hast spoken
No. 3

falsely. This tale is merely invented to deceive me into a belief that the sons of Glenalvon are dead."

" Why dost thou doubt me, Stephen?" she asked. " Have I not spoken it, and didst thou ever detect me uttering a falsehood to shield myself? I tell thee the boys have perished, though well thou knowest I would have saved them had it been possible, even at the hazard of my own life. They are gone, Stephen, and now the only favour I have to ask is, that I may retire to the solitude of this tower, and pass the remainder of my days in the place where first I drew my breath."

" I will not deny thee the shelter thou hast asked," he exclaimed, " because at present I have no proof that the tale just related is false ; enter the tower, therefore, but remember, should'st thou have deceived me, even I— thy brother—will not put forth a hand to save thee from the fury of those who have sworn destruction to the whole race of Glenalvon."

As he concluded, he sullenly placed in Magdalen's hand's the torch which he held, and having desired her to go to the chamber she had been used to occupy when her father, Ronald, was warder to the tower, he turned away and hurried after Fergus, to inform him of what had taken place.

As for Magdalen she quickly hurried through the passage leading to the cavern, where she found the hapless children buried in a profound slumber which their late fatigue had rendered so necessary. To disturb them in their innocent sleep seemed cruel, but their danger urged her to immediate exertion in their behalf, and rousing Angus, she explained to him the necessity for a prompt removal from that place, and then raising the other child in her arms, she retraced her steps followed by the trembling boy whose terrors almost rendered him suspicious of her intentions.

Passing through a door which led from the courtyard to the hall, they ascended a spiral staircase which communicated with the upper portion of the tower, and entering a chamber which had been occupied by Magdalen in former times, she laid down her burden, and touching a spring in one of the panels, revealed an interior apartment, of small size, but sufficiently capacious for the purpose she had in view.

Little Angus expressed some surprise as his attention was attracted towards this place, and would have enquired what she was going to do, but Magdalen motioned him to be silent, and whispering to him, in his ear, to be silent as he valued his life, entreated him to trust her faithful zeal in his behalf, and promised him safety from his enemies if he would rely in confidence upon the watchfulness with which she would guard him from the perils with which his life was threatened.

They then passed through the opening, and Magdalen led the way up another and very narrow flight of stairs, which led to a small chamber situated at the summit of the tower, and so overgrown with ivy, that the existence of such a place was unknown to Stephen, and had only been discovered by his sister by a mere accident, when some years before she had been wandering alone through the tower. Such as it was, however, the chamber afforded an excellent hiding place for the orphans, and she felt assured, that, with care, they might remain in security till they arrived at that age when they would have it in their power to hurl retribution upon the guilty author of their wrongs.

But it was not easy to allay the terror of Angus, to whom the gloomy chamber had communicated a feeling of dread that he could not conceal. In vain Magdalen assured him that he was safe from harm, for he dreaded the loneliness of the place, and uncertain as he was as to the fate that was intended for him, he pleaded hard to be taken to some other part of the tower, declaring that he would rather die by the hands of the ruffians who had charge of the tower, than remain a prisoner in such a gloomy place as that. To comfort him, Magdalen remained in the room till day break, when a loud knocking at the door startled her, and promising to return again as soon as she could get an opportunity, she hurried down, and securing the secret panel, descended to the lower portion of the tower, and gave admittance to her brother and Fergus, both of whom commenced a strict search through all the chambers, but without finding the hapless objects for 'whom they were seeking.

"The brats are no where about, it seems," exclaimed Stephen, after they had completed their fruitless search; "and so I suppose she has told the truth for once. You have done well, Magdalen," he continued, addressing himself to his sister; "by your means the children have been safely disposed of, and depend upon it our noble chieftain will take care to reward you liberally for the service you have done."

"Aye, aye," said Fergus; "you have proved your wisdom in disposing of the youngsters, and I feel half inclined to forgive the folly that made you brave the wrath of the chief of Badenoch, when you suffered your tongue to run so fast. They will sleep soundly enough in the river, I'll warrant, and since it saves the shedding of more blood, I'm not sorry that they met the fate Stephen has been telling me about. So now, Magdalen, if you think proper to return with me to the castle, we may live happily and contented enough, and the past shall be forgotten as if it had never happened."

"The past never can be forgotten by me," replied Magdalen, firmly; "nor will I ever consent to return to the castle with one whom my soul has learnt to abhor. The crimes you have committed will ever be fresh to my memory, and years cannot obliterate the foul deeds in which you have been a willing participator. Leave me, then; enjoy the rewards which will be heaped upon you for your misdeeds, and obtain, if thou canst, in a life of riot and revelry, a forgetfulness of that which, if remembered, must kindle a consuming fire in thy heart."

"Psha! why reproach me for what has been done?" he asked; "it's useless to look back upon the past, and if thou wilt return with me, thou shalt never have cause to repent having overlooked my errors."

"I will never trust to thee again," she replied; "for thou hast already heard the deep detestation in which I hold thee. Urge me, therefore, no more upon a subject in which I am unmoveable. Here, in this dreary solitude, will I pass the remainder of my days, and the only favour I ask, is that thou wilt never again present thyself before me. Leave me, then, I entreat, and may Heaven pardon thee the grievous sins thou hast committed against those who never injured thee, and the blood thou hast spilt at the command of a cruel and vindictive tyrant. Thou hast heard me, Fergus, and as thou would'st avoid my curse, avoid the solitude to which thy crimes and infamous career have driven me."

The rage of Fergus could scarcely be suppressed as he listened to the words of his wife, and drawing his dagger, he would have struck her dead at his feet, had not Stephen interposed and allayed the fury that had risen to so ungovernable a height. His rage, however, soon subsided, for he had long wished to part from Magdalen, whose disposition so ill accorded with his own, and uttering a few contemptuous sneers at the resolution she had formed, he declared that she should never see him again unless he was at any time sent to the tower on the affairs of his master. This done, he turned upon his heel, and accompanied by Stephen, hastened back with the welcome news of which he was the bearer.

When the chief of Badenoch was informed of the supposed death of the sons of Glenalvon, he gave way to a free indulgence of the gratification afforded by the intelligence. Upon Fergus and Stephen he bestowed a large reward for bringing him the information, and immediately advanced them to situations in his service, much higher than they had previously held; and even to Magdalen did he extend his bounty, for, believing that she had been the means of ridding him of the children, he sent her a purse of gold, and appointed her to the guardianship of the tower whenever the duties of her brother might happen to demand his presence elsewhere.

Within a day or two after this Stephen was ordered to repair to the castle and it was some time ere he had leisure to return. This was an opportunity most anxiously desired by Magdalen; who, having free and constant access to the children, was now able to reconcile them to the strange place, and to assure them of their safety in future. The room too, was made to assume a more comfortable and cheerful aspect, so that little Angus and his brother became convinced that she was indeed the friend she professed to be, and in the course of time the tower seemed to be less gloomy than it was at first, and they patiently submitted themselves to the confinement that was thus rendered endurable.

They had now frequent opportunities of taking both air and exercise from the summit of the tower, and attended, as they always were, they learnt the name of each island that was visible from that lofty eminence, and could repeat the many legends connected with them, which were marvellous enough to rivet the attention of her youthful auditors. She, however, would on no account suffer them to descend lower than her own chamber in case of her brother's arrival, for there the secret panel would speedily afford them the means of escape to their own hiding place, and thus they might remain secure till Stephen again took his departure. Indeed, she began to love them with all a parent's fondness, and on no consideration would she have exposed them to the danger she so much dreaded.

Thus frequently left alone with them for long intervals, it became her pleasing task to train their minds in that virtue which she so well knew how to teach, and thus secluded from the world which offered her no temptations to return to it, years passed away unmarked by any circumstance to create alarm, either for herself or the youthful charge to whose care she had devoted herself. It appeared, in fact, that both her brother and Fergus had ceased to remember that she still lived, for they rarely visited the tower, and even when they did so, they stayed but a short time, and then left again without troubling themselves to see her.

Crowning the summit of an adjacent island was seen a venerable monastery, frowning over the waters, and adding solemnity to a scene which was peculiarly rich and grand. It was an object which Angus and his brother loved to gaze upon from their own lofty turret chamber, and often did they sigh for an opportunity to visit a place which had afforded them so much pleasure to gaze upon. The confinement indeed which they endured became irksome to them, and knowing of no reason why they should be thus confined in a lonely and desolate tower, they sighed for the moment when they should go forth, free and unshackled, into that world which their imagination had painted in such glowing colours.

CHAPTER IV.

" The blackest rock upon the loneliest heath
   Feels, in its barrenness, some touch of spring !
   And in the April dew or beam of May,
   Its moss and lichen freshen and revive ;
   And thus the heart, most seared to human pleasure,
   Melts at the tear, joys in the smile of woman."
                                             BEAUMONT.

AIDED by Father Andrew, a monk belonging to the monastery we have alluded to, Magdalen was enabled to afford the children a far better education than might have been expected, for the holy man was frequently at the tower, and great was the pleasure he took in forming the minds of two children who were so willing to place themselves under his care and attention. His efforts succeeded even beyond his most sanguine expectations, and in a short time he was gratified at seeing that they had advanced in their education far beyond that point which is usually reached by children of their age.

To Father Andrew the good Magdalen had confided the secret which so much concerned the future destiny of her youthful charge, and from him she received advice upon all matters connected with the hapless orphans she had generously taken under her care. Through his counsel, however, she still abstained from giving the boys a hint of who they were, or the sad event which had deprived them of the care and affection of their murdered parents. Angus, the elder one, had a faint recollection of the dreadful night when murder and desolation had visited the castle; but he remembered nothing that could in any way assist him in the recovery of his rights, nor did Magdalen wish him to do so till he could act with certainty against a foe whose heart would still prompt him to deeds of vengeance, should he imagine that any of the Glenalvon family had survived the night on which he had set fire to their castle and slaughtered the inhabitants in their beds.

The mind of Father Andrew was excellent, and his birth and education far above what might have been expected from one buried in the small obscure monastery to which he belonged. He had dwelt among the great and the powerful, and unforeseen misfortunes had induced him to quit a world of which he had grown weary. A long period had elapsed since he entered this sacred retreat, yet never had he regretted a change that brought peace to his wounded heart; for he was contented with his lot, and resignation he conceived to be the first duty of a Christian.

His form was still noble, and retained the majestic carriage which had distinguished him in his younger years, displaying at once his illustrious descent and the vigour of manhood for which he had been distinguished. Still, however, his mien and deportment were meek as became the life he had now chosen, and possessing all the attributes of a good man, he was reverenced, not only within the cloister, but by those whom duty or inclination induced him to visit.

Father Andrew visited his youthful pupils twice and sometimes three times a week, and as he had been a warrior in the early part of his career, he was enabled to instruct Angus and his brother in those military tactics which it was probable would, at a future period, be of the highest importance to them. Indeed, so apt a scholar in those martial exercises was the elder boy, that he soon excelled his instructor in the management of the bow, the broadsword, and the spear. In these lessons Angus seemed to take the greatest delight, for though he never mentioned the subject of his parents' cruel destiny, yet in his own mind the thought was constantly present, and as he grew towards manhood, he looked forward with burning impatience when he might avenge a crime that had rendered himself and his brother the victims of a base and sanguinary tyrant.   Both the monk and Magdalen guessed the thoughts that occupied his mind, and earnestly did they endeavour to impress upon him the duty of submission and forgiveness of wrongs, but the boy still continued to indulge in his visions of the future, and though at present he knew himself only as an orphan, he felt well convinced that his parents had belonged to the highest rank in society.   Sometimes he would venture to enquire of his friends the story of his wrongs, but they always avoided his questions, and assured him that his slight recollections of the past were founded in error.

At length, however, being repeatedly pressed upon the subject, Magdalen confessed that his birth was noble, and that he had been deprived of his just inheritance by the same hand that had robbed his parents of life. This only served to make Angus more anxious and persevering in his enquiries, but his foster mother would reveal no more, assuring him that the time would arrive when justice would no longer be withheld from him, and declaring that any further revelation of the secret would but expose him to danger, she implored him to rest satisfied with what he already knew till the hour approached when he might boldly stand forward and assert his claims to the estates and dignity of his father.   But the impatience of the youth was no longer to be restrained, and taking the hand of Magdalen, he exclaimed,—

"Tell me, I implore you, dear mother, to whom do I owe the foul wrongs that have been heaped upon my family; refuse not my earnest pleadings, but reveal to me the name of the blood-stained villain, that I may know him for my enemy, and take those steps which may avenge the murders he has committed?   I have had dreams of fearful import, and beheld the bleeding forms of my parents bending over my couch, as if to stir my soul against the remorseless monster that sent them to an untimely grave.   They call upon me for revenge, and solemnly have I sworn to obey the injunctions with which I have been charged.   This alone seemed to satisfy their perturbed spirits, and never will I rest till the pledge so awfully given has been performed.   Tell me then, dear mother, the author of these cruel wrongs, and I will hunt him through the world, but he shall pay the penalty of the fearful crimes he has committed."

"Alas! dear Angus!" she cried, "most dreadful was the moment when the halls of Glenalvon sunk amidst the flames of the destroyer!   Child of a noble house, may Heaven preserve thee and thy brother from the fate of thy parents, and protect them from——"

"From whom?" demanded the youth, eagerly.

"Dear boy, I dare not tell thee to whom thou owest this injustice," answered Magdalen.   "I have been compelled to swear eternal secrecy, yet, though I cannot tell thee more, I will exert myself incessantly for the safety of yourself and your brother, and will aid as far as lays in my power to restore you to those rights of which you have been deprived.   At some future time Father Andrew may, perhaps, reveal that which I dare not speak of, and till then you must rest satisfied with the slight knowledge you already possess.   Be patient, Angus, and you will yet find that there are friends who will exert themselves in the cause of injured innocence, and who will lose no opportunity that may offer to replace you in those rights of which you have been deprived, and for which your ancestors have nobly fought in defence of their country."

Magdalen now saw with grief that she would not be able much longer to suppress the earnest yearnings of the youth for the vengeance which he meditated against the enemy of his family. He had on former occasions spoken of his anxiety to join a patriotic band which had been secretly formed for the deliverance of Scotland from its present thraldrom, and each day served the more to convince her that it would not be long ere he burst through the restraint in which he had thus far been held, and placed himself amidst the foremost ranks of those who had risen to relieve their country from the ignominy into which she had fallen.

Burning to learn all that his generous protectress had been most careful to conceal from him, Angus hastened to the armoury, and with impatient strides paced up and down the gloomy chamber in which he passed the greater part of his time. Still was his mind occupied in the one favourite subject that occupied his every thought, and as he glanced round upon the arms that hung against the walls, he took shame upon himself that he was thus passing his days in idleness, when the calls of his country should have prompted him long ere that to take part in the struggle which had already commenced for the restoration of her liberties and rights.

Angus was now in the eighteenth year of his age, and his brother, Edwin, about four years younger. He was tall, robust, and of dignified aspect, and a bold spirit of enterprise animated him to exertions far beyond the generality of youth at his time of life. His manners, too, when not excited by the remembrance of his father's wrongs, were mild and engaging, whilst his countenance generally wore an aspect so benign, that there were few persons who could have looked upon him without feeling an attachment that could not easily be eradicated. Even Magdalen felt the power of that noble air, which at once exhibited a manly bearing and a greatness of soul that gave even to his youth the settled steadiness of mind which usually belongs to persons of more matured age.

We must now return for a short time to the chief of Badenoch, who, actuated by the love of gold, had often, but in vain, descended to the subterranean vaults of the Castle of Glenalvon, for the purpose of enriching himself with the treasures they were reported to contain. But his efforts were useless, for if gold had ever been there, it was either removed by other hands, or had perished in the flames which had destroyed the ancient mansion of his victim. At length, terrified by his own superstitious fears, he abandoned a task that seemed to be hopeless, and believing the place to be haunted by the spirits of those who had been its former tenants, he forebore any further visits to the scene of his iniquity, and even went out of his way to avoid the solemn ruins, which never failed to remind him of a night of horror that he in vain sought to forget.

At one time he had frequently endeavoured to trace his way through those portions of the venerable pile in which the destructive ravages of the fire had been least felt. But his spirit quailed as fancy represented to him the gaunt form of the Earl of Glenalvon, who seemed to smile at the terrors he could not conceal, and to exult in the tortures which remorse inflicted upon the vindictive perpetrator of his ruin. It was, indeed, generally reported that the shades of the Earl and Countess of Glenalvon roamed through the melancholy ruins of the place where once they dwelt in peaceful happiness, and though reckless of all else, the guilty chief of Badenoch could never venture to approach the lonely scene where forms so terrible might meet his view and blast his sight with visions that were too fearful even for contemplation. He, however, carefully avoided any outward display of his terrors when his friends and retainers were present, and affecting a carelessness that he felt not, he sought by every means in his power to convince those about him that his soul was as free from care and anxiety as ever it had been. Yet in the silence and loveliness of midnight, what tortures wrung the heart of Glenalvon's murderer! Wild shapes and awful sounds at those times seemed to surround him on every side, and even in his dreams came fearful warnings to his ears, that bade him beware of the not far distant day when retribution would alight upon him for the cruelty and injustice he had been guilty of towards the victims of his implacable rage.

CHAPTER V.

"Here,
If ancestry can be in aught believed,
Descending spirits have conversed with man,
And told the secrets of the world unknown."
                                        DOUGLAS.

UPON one occasion during their long residence in the Watch Tower, Magdalen had shown Angus the gloomy subterranean retreat where she had sheltered him and his brother on the night of their first arrival there. An old legend, discovered by the youth amongst other lumber in the armoury, had often occupied his deepest attention, for it narrated several wild stories connected with the vault, and in one that more particularly impressed itself upon his memory, he learnt that, though of great extent and reaching beyond the distant mountains, it had an opening at its furthest extremity, which had in former times been of great service when the inhabitants of the Watch Tower were besieged by an enemy.

Our youthful hero had on several occasions ventured to enter within its gloomy recesses, though constantly warned by Magdalen to avoid them. Often had he sighed for permission and opportunity to range through the dreary retreat, and explore the mysteries of which he had read in the legend that had first attracted his attention to the spot. From the first, Magdalen had been most anxious to check this desire to roam from the safe retreat afforded by the tower; and for a time she succeeded in diverting his design by relating tales of wonder and terror, which excited his terrors and withdrew him from an object which she had many reasons to feel alarmed at.

High-spirited as Angus was, she dreaded that should he ever pass beyond the boundaries of his hiding place, the tempting desire of liberty, and his love of martial exploits, might serve to withdraw him from her protection. She, therefore, dreaded lest he and his brother should, in one rash moment, undo whole years of that anxious care which had hitherto preserved them from the vigilance of the foe they had so much reason to dread.

The thought of being separated from them was one that filled her with apprehension and alarm, for though often urged on this point, both by the youth himself and Father Andrew, she would reply there was too much danger in it for her ever to consent to their leaving the place till they were well able to protect themselves against the perils to which they would be exposed.

"Your countenance, my dear young lord," she said, "is too much like that of your noble father's to render your departure from this place safe. You will be seen, and, doubtless, some one will betray you to the chief of——"

Here she checked herself, but added presently afterwards,—

"Remain contented as you are for another year, and I will myself be your guide from this place. By that time you will be better able to guard yourself from the evil machinations of your foes, and if the noble brother of

your unfortunate mother is still living—which, alas! I fear he is not—he
will take instant measures, not only to bring down punishment upon the
guilty author of your wrongs, but also to restore to you that inheritance
which has been taken away by fraud and violence."

"Know you not whether our uncle lives?" asked Angus.

"It is to be feared he does not," she replied; "for had he outlived the
destruction of Glenalvon, its injured heirs would, long ere this time have
found in him a powerful avenger of the crimes that have laid them prostrate."

"And yet," observed Angus, "it is possible he may survive. Is it not
likely the same means which could so secretly accomplish the ruin of our
house, has also deceived the world with a forged tale of our death? Let
me, then, go forth," he continued, earnestly, "that I may seek him who
will be our friend in the hour of need. You have told me ere now that he
was reported to be generous and good; if so, when he beholds the children
of his hapless sister, will he not welcome us and make our cause his own?
Besides, he will be grateful to you for the care you have bestowed upon us,
and you will then leave this dreary abode to dwell once more in the world
you have abandoned for our sake."

"Alas!" cried Magdalen, "these sanguine hopes bespeak the kindness
of your heart. Think not, however, that I mean to throw a damp upon
your wishes, or wrong with unjust suspicions the character of your only
living relative. He may be just, my dear Angus, and you have become as
strangers to him, and after this lapse of years we know not that he would
greet with a welcome the offspring of his murdered sister. Besides, I have
other powerful reasons for delaying your departure, and when they no
longer exist, you shall not find me unmindful of your interest, or forgetful
of the promise I have given. Be patient, then, till the period I have named
has expired, and, believe me, I will then no longer oppose a wish which I
see you have so ardently at heart."

No. 4

Yielding to the suggestion of his kind friend, Angus promised to obey her wish, but in secret he indulged more than ever the thoughts which had urged him to desire that liberty for which he so ardently yearned. It was not, however, from any selfish motive that he sought to attain this object, but there were deeds to accomplish which he considered as paramount duties; and bearing in mind, as he constantly did, the remembrance of his parents' murder, he resolved never to rest till he had found out and punished the author of the cruel outrage. This alone could satisfy the burning of his youthful spirit, and when once retribution was accomplished, he cared not how soon he left a world which hitherto had afforded him nothing but trouble and anxiety.

The impressions of terror which Magdalen had from the first inspired, respecting the interior of the subterranean vault, no longer maintained their influence over him, but yielded to those convictions that broke in upon him as he advanced towards manhood.

At last accident presented to him a temptation which he was unable to resist. Magdalen, contrary to her usual custom, had left unfastened the door of the court-yard, which opened upon the descent which led down to the cavern, whose obscure intricacies he was so anxious to tread. For a moment he stood irresolute how to act; but at last, grasping the hand of his brother, he began to descend the winding steps that conducted to the dark abyss beneath. The young one, however, could not conceal the alarm which this sudden resolution had given rise to, and pausing as he tried to penetrate the gloom before him, he enquired anxiously of his brother whether he meant to risk a danger that might terminate in his own destruction.

"I will risk all," replied Angus, firmly, "rather than endure the suspense that tortures me till the mysteries of this cavern are revealed. You, however, need not accompany me, Edwin, and, indeed, I know not whether it would not be better for you to remain behind to comfort our dear Magdalen. Tell her that I go thus suddenly and in secret to avoid the pain of parting from her, and that I absent myself but for a time, to seek abroad that honourable renown which here I never can hope to aspire to. This cavern, if legends speak truly, may lead to scenes we have hitherto been excluded from."

"Nay," cried Edwin, "I cannot—will not part from you thus; where you go there will I follow, even though the path should lead to death!"

"Hear me, brother," exclaimed Angus, "at present I would have you remain with her who has proved to us so kind, so vigilant a protector. Here you may live in peace and safety, for should I not discover that our uncle lives, no place can so securely shield you from those perils of which we have so often heard. Remain here then, Edwin, in that safety which you would in vain seek for elsewhere, and, should Heaven spare me, I will again return to share with my brother whatever fortune it may be my lot to bear. Tell Magdalen that though I have disobeyed her in this instance, my departure was urged by the knowledge that in no other way could I obtain that justice which I have sworn to accomplish. If I survive I will do so with honour to myself, or never behold her more!"

"Hold, Angus!" cried the young Glenalvon, as his brother was about to leave him. "Wilt thou refuse to take me with thee, or thinkest thou I could linger here without the friend I have so dearly loved? If thou art resolved to go on this adventure, I will accompany thee; one fate, whether it be for good or for evil, shall alike be ours, and we will not now be separated. I am young, but my heart is firm, nor shall difficulty or danger subdue my spirit. Together we will go to the camp of our king, and even in the field of battle we will not be separated!"

" Dear brother," exclaimed Angus, pressing him to his bosom; " your generous wish shall be granted. Come with me, Edwin, the moment of action so long desired is at length arrived, and our future deeds shall proclaim us to belong to no coward race."

It was almost night when this determination was formed, and the gloom before them might have inspired any other hearts with terror. Angus, however, put aside all fear, and bidding his brother to keep close behind him, he set forward, aided by the light of a small lamp which had been left burning by Father Andrew during a recent visit that he had paid to the tower. As they proceeded through the fear-inspiring place, the echoes of their footsteps reverberated around them, rendering even more horrible a spot that had long been the scene of superstitious dread. At length the adventurous youths could observe that the arches and pillars became of less gigantic proportions, till the way branching beneath a low chasm, completely shut out the faint gleam of daylight that had hitherto been visible from the entrance. Edwin looked fearfully around him and marked with terror the difficulties they had to encounter, and the probability that in that darksome place they would lose their way and perish by an inglorious death.

At length as they proceeded further, openings occasionally burst upon them, exhibiting to their view stupendous images that were at once terrifically grand and darkly sublime. Rocks piled upon rocks, having their bases deeply buried in the earth, rose frowning and threatening destruction to those who ventured to pass near them. Above ran a broken and irregular vaulted roof, through which there were, here and there, fissures that served to admit the daylight, and which rendered more conspicuous the gloom and horrors of this dismal cavern. The brothers, however, still continued to pursue their way; but the rugged path they trod, often obliged them to cling to the basements of the rocks, to prevent them from falling down the precipitous descents that were continually presenting themselves in their way.

Having passed those winding avenues, they at last found themselves within the wide space of a circular cavern or amphitheatre, that yet received some feeble rays of light, which glancing through the fissures, duskily revealed the gloomy objects of the surrounding scene. Wild, dank weeds hung through the hollows of the roof, dripping their unwholesome dews into the stagnant water that covered the flooring; exhaling a noxious vapour through the damp, chill air that communicated to the wanderers a comfortless sensation of shivering numbness, like the coldest blast of the keen winter's storm.

All around them the rocky walls arose in wild fantastic shapes that might have stricken terror into the hearts of older persons than themselves, and with the aid of fancy, the most grim and fearful object could have well been imagined as ready to start upon those who ventured to penetrate the darksome caverns so seldom trodden by the foot of man. Angus, being the elder of the two, gazed with a feeling of wonder, mingled with admiration on the scene that was thus presented to his view, but Edwin shrunk from the appalling sight, and would have retreated in dismay, had not his brother seized him by the arm, and by force compelled him to pursue the devious path which led them onward through through the fearful labyrinth. It was in truth a fearful task that lay before them, but the elder of the two youths was of a dauntless spirit, and be the result what it might, he was determined never to retrace his steps whilst a chance remained of exploring the caverns in which they were now urging their uncertain way.

From the legends he had read his imagination peopled the place with warriors who had long since quitted this world, and occasionally, as their footsteps echoed through the vaulted recesses, he paused to look around him in the expectation of beholding some grim form either to welcome them to the place, or punish the temerity that had tempted them to visit scenes that were devoted only to the wandering shades of the departed.

At length, anxious to afford rest to the more fragile form of his brother, Angus sought a ledge among the rocks where they might for a brief space rest themselves after the exertions, both mental and bodily, that they had gone through.   Here they seated themselves for a time, and as the elder youth perceived the drooping spirits of his brother, he sought by every means in his power to chase away the dismal thoughts that a scene like this was well calculated to engender.   Calculating from the time since they had left the tower, and the pace at which they had been traversing the interminable cavern, it appeared pretty certain that they must have proceeded at least three miles, and yet no termination of their dismal journey could at present be seen.   To add to their dismay too, they could perceive through the chasms above, that daylight was beginning to close in, and even the proud spirit of Angus began to fail when he thus beheld the prospect of passing a night in the place which his busy imagination had peopled with so many horrors.   He saw, in fact, that their hopes of escape were at an end, and that they must pass the remainder of the night far from all assistance, however great might be their need for human aid.

To add to his perplexities, he perceived that his lamp was upon the eve of expiring, and its flickering, half extinguished flame served but to render more hideous the few objects that were still visible.   At this moment he began to regret the over hazardous spirit that had prompted him to seek this adventure, and the more particularly did he feel vexed with himself as it was entirely through his example that Edwin had been tempted to encounter dangers which his own more timid nature would have avoided. Terrible, therefore, was the prospects before them, for they must either pass the long, weary hours of night and darkness, in that horrible place, or attempt to return to the entrance of the cavern, which was almost impossible, in consequence of the mazy windings through which they had come.

Fortunately, Angus had provided himself with a small portion of provisions, which he now produced to recruit the almost exhausted frames of himself and his brother.   This was, in truth, a most welcome repast, for it served to enable them to encounter the difficulties that lay before them, and at the same time the elder brother took the opportunity to encourage the other with hopes which he himself did not expect to realize.   However, the result was fully equal to his anticipations, and Edwin either felt, or professed to be more sanguine of a successful termination of their adventure than he had hitherto appeared to be.   Finding this, Angus assumed an appearance of gaiety, and proposed that they should continue their onward progress.

"There is no doubt," he said, "but we shall by and by find one outlet from this place, and therefore we should rally ourselves for the task we have to accomplish.   Our lamp, as you see, will not serve us much longer, and when its last feeble rays expire, we shall find our labours more difficult than they are even at present.   So rouse you, brother, and let us not droop in despair, because we have a few hard trials to surmount, and remember, when we become men, as we shall in the course of a year or two, we shall have much greater dangers to encounter than merely finding our way through a dark cavern, which, after all, will serve us to laugh at when we have arrived at a termination of our subterraneous ramble."

Edwin, though nearly exhausted with the efforts he had made, complied with this suggestion, and rising from their rocky seat, they re-commenced their almost hopeless task of pursuing their progress through the dreary abode of darkness and horror. Faint as the light was, they were just able to discover the entrance to another gloomy chamber, which, like all the rest that they had passed through, was wet with the water that dropped through from the rock above them. As they proceeded the way became more difficult than ever, and the fading beams of their lamp now reminded them that they would soon be left to wonder onwards in darkness and uncertainty. At last, however, they arrived at another opening, and passing through it, found themselves in a more spacious chamber than any they had yet been in, and inspired with a slight feeling of hope, the youths redoubled their speed under an idea that they were approaching a termination of their wearisome labours.

The further end of this place was soon attained, and they then discovered another small opening, which was nearly choked up with the stones and rubbish that had fallen from the roof above. To remove these was a task of much difficulty, but when the labour was accomplished, and they were enabled to continue their way, how great was their joy and gratitude at finding themselves once more in the free open air of Heaven! Involuntarily they both fell upon their knees, and offered up to Heaven their grateful thanks for the strength which had thus served to extricate them from difficulties which at one time had appeared to be almost insurmountable. Liberty was now before them, and as they gazed upon the star-lit firmament, they felt how great was the reward that had at length fallen to their lot.

" Welcome, thrice welcome," cried Angus, " is this glorious scene that has thus burst upon our sight. Farewell, my gloomy tower, for no more shall your cheerless walls enclose a spirit that burns for liberty and glory. Till now, never have I known the blessings of which I have hitherto been deprived, and from this moment will I dedicate my days to the attainment of that vengeance for which the blood of my murdered parents has so long cried in vain !"

The youth spoke aloud, and his soul was wrapped in the happiness with which the moment of his deliverance had inspired him. He felt that his actions were now under his own control, and gazing upon the glorious scene presented to his view, a new feeling of rapture possessed his soul, that whispered to him the deeds of glorious renown, that his own arm might yet achieve.

The feelings of his brother were somewhat different, yet not less grateful was he for their deliverance from the scene of their late wearying journey. Seating himself upon the green turf beneath a wide spreading tree, his first thoughts were directed towards the scene in which he and Angus had passed the greater portion of their lives. In vain he looked for those familiar objects that long use had rendered so dear to him. The Watch Tower was not within his view, and all around wore a look of novelty that served to remind him the more forcibly of the dangers into which their unadvised escape from the retreat would most likely plunge them. Of a less ardent temperament than his brother, his soul yielded to dismay when he thus found himself far away from the scene which long habit and attachment had rendered dear to him.

From these reflections, however, the youths were aroused by the black, portentous clouds which suddenly overspread the heavens, and rising from their grassy seats, they once more pursued their way, in the hope of finding some place wherein to shelter themselves from the gathering storm. Proceeding, therefore, towards the summit of some rising ground before them, they beheld by the flashing lightning, the dark outlines of a mansion as it rose above the wood that almost bounded their view.

Somewhat surprised by this, they increased their speed, an l soon found themselves in the forest, whose devious paths presented as many difficulties in their way as they had to encounter in the cavern. They, however, persevered, and at length finding a beaten track, continued their way, and after a long wearisome walk, at last came to an opening in the forest, from whence they beheld at no great distance the castle which it had been their anxious desire to reach. Upon their nearer approach, the castle seemed to be rather a noble, uninhabitable ruin, than a place where hospitality was to be expected, yet even desolate as it was, they thought it might afford them a shelter from the storm, and they, therefore, hesitated not to advance towards it, in the hope that they might at least pass the night there, and thus with renewed strength continue their journey, when daylight would again serve to guide them on their way.

Fatigued as they were, it was with much difficulty that the youths reached the moat which encircled the walls, and upon arriving there, they found that the bridge was down, which gave them immediate access to the cheerless building before them. After much toil they arrived at the darkly frowning tower which seemed to form the principal entrance to the building. The massive portal stood open, and displayed to their view a scene of mouldering desolation and cheerless solitude. Still, however, the edifice retained some bold, majestic features of former magnificence, though its general outline displayed only masses of ruin and decay. Falling towers and turrets, blackened and laid waste by the hand of time, and the more recent attacks of a hostile force, were the sad symptoms of its forlorn and deserted condition.

With the most tender care Angus supported his almost fainting brother through the scene of desolation; the latter was too much exhausted to observe the melancholy ruin which on every side presented itself, but Angus shuddered as he passed along, and fancied he beheld indistinct shapes flitting before him. Proceeding onwards, he soon afterwards found himself in an inner quadrangle, more spacious and ruinous than the first, and still exhibiting no signs of being inhabited. It was surrounded, like the other, with lofty dismantled walls whose summits were crowned with ivy, and other shrubs, which afforded a secure retreat to innumerable birds, which, startled by the intrusion of strangers, flew screaming from their abode, to seek a shelter in some other part of the ruins.

As he now grew more accustomed to the scene, Angus advanced boldly towards a vestibule which he indistinctly perceived at some little distance before him. The portal stood open, and scarcely had they passed through it, when they were once more left in all the terrors of darkness. Presently, however, the flashing lightnings burst forth from the clouds, and thus aided them in continuing their way; but the deeply peeling thunder added solemnity to the scene, increased as it was by the long reverberations of the mountain echoes, till they died away, and were lost in the distance.

By the lightning's gleam, Angus discovered that they had now reached the interior of a spacious hall, through whose lofty casements the angry fires of Heaven gleamed with terrific brightness, and displayed the grim ruin with which they were surrounded. It now became evident that it would be useless to proceed, as there could be no doubt the place was uninhabited, and no aid, save shelter, could be expected in their present forlorn situation.

By this time the tempest had reached a fearful height, and thus forbade their quitting the shelter, which, slight and comfortless as it was, seemed preferable to encountering the fierce and raging storm without. Angus now grew restless and alarmed, for his brother became more and more feeble, and for the first time he experienced a pang of sorrow for the alarm his flight must have occasioned Magdalen, who now, perhaps, was vainly seeking them, or weeping over the terrors to which such a night would give rise in her solitary confinement. As these reflections occurred to Angus, he resolved when the day returned, to retrace his steps, if possible, to the Watch Tower, and by the presence of himself and his brother, allay that terror which he knew she would feel at the discovery of their flight.

"I will make amends for the ingratitude I have been guilty of towards our good Magdalen," he exclaimed, aloud; "and restore my hapless brother to the care of her whose kindness has preserved us through so many perils. He shall again be placed beneath her fostering care, and since the wrongs of our parents are yet to be avenged, I will myself undertake the task, and single-handed seek the villain whose crimes have rendered me thus wretched."

The ardour of his spirit had certainly led him into an error, which he was now ready to retrieve. On the other hand, Magdalen had perhaps been equally short sighted in secluding him so much as she had from the world he had been so anxious to enter. But his self-condemnation relieved him as he made this resolution, and present dangers compelled the noble youth to exert all his faculties for the preservation of his brother and himself. The tempest was still raging furiously, and as the wind shook the lofty ruin, he trembled, lest each gust should bring down the crumbling ruins, and whelm them in destruction.

Supporting his brother in his arms, Angus continued to watch the violence of the tempest, of which, under other circumstances, he would have felt no dread. At length Edwin somewhat revived from the insensibility in which he had been lying, and gazing earnestly upon the anxious countenance of his brother, he said:—

"Fear not for me, dear Angus; the morning will now soon arrive, and we shall then be enabled to leave this frightful place. Till then, I will endeavour to support my drooping spirits, for I know you are near me, and that thought alone, is sufficient to inspire my heart with the courage which our present circumstances so much require. With the dawn of day, we shall quit this inhospitable spot and may perhaps find some peasant's hut where rest and refreshment will soon restore me to that health which will enable me to endure any further toil we may have to encounter."

Edwin attempted to rise as he uttered these words, but all power seemed to have deserted him, and reeling a few paces, he would have fallen to the ground had not his brother sprung forward, and again supported him in his arms. It then became but too evident that nature was completely exhausted, and Angus in frantic accents accused himself of having brought all this on by suffering him to be the companion of his flight from the Watch Tower.

"I have slain him!" he exclaimed bitterly; "he will die ere assistance can reach us, and I alone am the cause of my poor brother's death!"

At that instant a distant sound was heard, and springing upon his feet, Angus listened with eager impatience, in the hope that aid was not so far off as his terror had led him to imagine. Presently, he heard a door closed with some violence as the piercing shriek of a distant human voice struck upon his ears, and again listening with breathless anxiety, he once more heard the same cries uttering accents of the deepest distress.

"Alas! alas! they have slain him!" exclaimed the voice. "Villains! they triumph in my woes, and yet Heaven strikes them not with its only fires! Whither, ah, whither shall I go for shelter and protection?"

Startled by these agonizing words, Angus eagerly looked around him to ascertain from what part of the castle these sounds had come. The voice he had heard was wild but distinct, for he could clearly distinguish all that had been uttered, and it now only remained to ascertain whether the expressions had proceeded from an earthly being, or from one belonging to another world. If from a fellow creature, they implied the most horrible meaning, and in that case, it was evident the place was not so utterly deserted as he had imagined. Perhaps it was the resort of robbers, for Angus had both heard and read of men whose deeds were even more savage than those of wild beasts, and their places of resort were usually such as the place to which the spirit of adventure had thus led him. The cries he had heard were certainly those of distress; and, prompted by humanity, he felt inclined instantly to follow the sounds which had so much startled him; but then, if the place was really the resort of robbers, thus leaving his brother unprotected, would expose him to the fierce rage of those who would not fail to punish him for thus intruding upon their privacy.

By this time, Edwin had sunk into a sleep produced by the fatigue he had undergone, and Angus, excited by a desire to unravel the mystery, resolved to penetrate the affair and satisfy himself upon a point that had aroused his curiosity. It was certain the sounds he had heard were those of intense suffering and distress, and though he felt faint and weary from the exertions he had gone through, he reasoned for a moment or two, and reflected that as almost any state was better than the horrible anxiety of his present situation, it would be prudent to follow this adventure to a conclusion. It was true he must leave his brother for awhile, but he might perhaps procure assistance, and that thought, more than any other, urged him to make the attempt which was to solve his doubts.

Resolving, therefore, to make the trial, he hastily wrapped Edwin in a cloak, and removing him to a more secure place, groped his way along the hall, towards a staircase at the further extremity, which had been revealed to his sight by the strong glare of lightning during the severest part of the storm. Scarcely, however, had he reached the place towards which his footsteps were directed when he heard a slight sound, and looking upwards, he beheld a faint moving flame floating high above his reach, and passing slowly along. The next instant he discovered the tall, graceful form of a youthful female, attired in long flowing robes, and her hair floating wildly in the bteeze; the countenance was as pale as the whitest marble; and her general appearance denoted the most terrible and exciting terror. But the figure was soon lost amidst the gloom that involved the whole place, and Angus was shortly afterwards enabled to discover that the place was a corridor, with which the staircase communicated.

In an instant the figure had disappeared, and with it the light by which alone he could hope to penetrate the darkness with which he was surrounded. He called aloud, and demanded help, but a cry of distress was the only answer returned to the appeal, which reverberating through the hollow space, sank in mournful whispers that appalled the ear, as if the dead had been awakened to speak from their dreary sepulchres.

But the youth had too much spirit to suffer the effects of superstitious terrors to turn him from the fixed purpose of his soul, and now guided by the frequent flashes of lightning, he was enabled to pass without much difficulty along a vaulted chamber. At the termination of this he found another staircase, and began fearfully to ascend the tottering frame which, as as he passed onwards, shook beneath his weight, and seemed to threaten instant destruction to the daring adventurer.

Undeterred, he continued his way, but with more light and cautious steps, lest he should perish ere the task he had engaged in should be fully accomplished. At last, on reaching the arch, through which the figure had so suddenly vanished, he dashed boldly through its dark and dismal windings, for not a ray of light illumined the place, and though the

tempest still roared, not a gleam of lightning penetrated the deep gloom in which he was involved.

CHAPTER VI.

"Marked you the fixed and solemn look he wears
As of virtue to the grief and woe
That men are sometimes heir to?"

ROLAND THE DISSOLUTE.

LEAVING all to the guidance of chance, and feeling confident that the figure he was in pursuit of had gone in that direction, Angus continued his uncertain course, with a determination of penetrating the mystery, whatever difficulty or trouble it might happen to cost him. Groping along the wall, he discovered, with as much rapidity as he could with safety accomplish, and after some little time had been occupied in this manner, without any beneficial result, he again called loudly for help, in the vain hope that the fair vision he had seen would once more present itself to his view. But the roaring of the tempest drowned his cries, and as he still slowly continued to advance, his situation became more and more hopeless.

Still, however, he determined not to be foiled in the adventure he had thus entered upon, and calling fresh courage to him, he urged his way onwards, till he found himself once more turning down another corridor, where a distant streak of faint light burst suddenly upon him, and again aroused him to renewed exertions. With this guide he was able to increase his speed, and excited by the spirit of enterprise, he hurried along a low

No. 5

vaulted passage, whose dark mouldering roof was scarcely visible through the obscurity, which hung like a pall around him.

But resolute in his purpose, Angus hastened towards the spot from whence the light issued, and as he approached nearer, he could plainly distinguish the faint sounds of a human voice, as if in terror. For a moment he paused to deliberate as to what course he ought to pursue, but quickly casting aside all fears for his personal safety, he resolutely advanced, and bursting through the half closed door of the room from whence the light proceeded, and in a voice of supplication, demanded assistance in behalf of his brother.

A young and extremely beautiful female, and apparently the same that he had followed, rose terrified from her seat as he entered, and uttering a scream of terror as she sank almost fainting upon the floor, cried in piteous accents :—

" Spare him !—oh, spare him !—My poor father is betrayed through the incautious madness that has urged me this night to quit my chamber !"

Angus was so much struck with astonishment by these words, that he was unable to give utterance to a word, but venturing to advance nearer to the female, she rose, and was in the act of retreating from the room, when an old man rushed suddenly upon them, exclaiming to the youthful intruder :—

" Away, thou fiend of hell !—away to the darkness that should be thy hiding place ! Oh, if thou wilt tempt the fierce wrath of the incensed Walter Campbell, take from his hand the death his foes have so justly merited."

The youth to whom these words were addressed, was unarmed, and ere he could step aside to avoid the danger, the sword of his adversary entered his body, and after staggering a few paces, the unfortunate Angus fell to the ground. The gloom of the chamber rendered both the scene and the transaction doubly horrible, and whatever might be the cause of the violence that had been committed, it is certain that no sooner did he see the deed he had done, than the most violent remorse succeeded the fury with which he had rushed upon his defenceless antagonist. His wild eye glared with terror towards the door through which Angus had entered, as if he expected to see a host of foes rushing in for his destruction, and his sword was again upraised to protect him against those whom his distracted imagination had pictured as coming to avenge the fall of their companion. Then advancing with cautious steps towards the door, he cast beyond it a scrutinizing glance to satisfy himself whether his fears were but too well founded. But no living form met his sight, nor did even the least sound break upon his ear to confirm the suspicions that had urged him to a state of mind bordering on madness. At that moment a groan of anguish that was uttered by the wounded youth recalled his wandering steps, and gazing upon the prostrate Angus, he started back with amazement, and exclaimed in a tone of horror :—

" Merciful Heaven ! *who* is it that my frenzy has led me to slay ?—It is not he who ——"

Horror seized upon him as he made the discovery of his fatal error, and mutterings of terrible import escaped him as he gazed upon the youth before him.

" What have I done ?" he muttered.—" Who is it that my over-excited fears have destroyed?—Not the villain that has destroyed my peace,—the accursed foe of mine and my daughters happiness, but a stranger,—young, innocent, and, perhaps, an outcast like myself !"

" Help !—or I bleed to death !" cried Angus faintly.

The other started back as these words fell upon his ear, and a deadly paleness overspread his countenance, as he heard the piteous accents in which these few words were uttered.

At this period the female, who had fainted when the attack was made, revived from the shock she had sustained, and approaching her father with faltering steps, clasped him with wild transport in her arms, and exclaimed :—

"Thank Heaven, he lives!—my father has escaped the ruffians steel, and I am not doomed to weep the loss of one who is all the world to me."

The old man returned her warm congratulations with joy equal to her own, and for a few moments their thoughts were occupied in self-congratulation on the escape they had had from anticipated danger. At last, however, another groan from Angus, recalled the father to his recollection, and leading the maiden a few steps forward, he pointed to the almost lifeless form of the unhappy victim of his intemperance. She shuddered, and though influenced by the same dread that actuated her father, yet did her heart kindle with pity as she gazed upon the insensate form before her.

"My dear father," she exclaimed tenderly, "we are, I trust, safe from the danger we so much dreaded. I know your generous feeling towards those who need our aid, and, therefore, do I entreat you to assist me in relieving this poor youth."

Speaking thus, she approached the object of her pity, and as her eyes rested for a moment on his noble, expressive countenance, she shrunk back confused, and in half suppressed accents exclaimed :—

"Alas! can such features treacherous conceal a soul blackened by guilt? —can villany or cruelty inhabit a form so noble as this before me?"

"Isabel, my dearest child, he needs our aid," exclaimed her father, as he raised the youth, whose eyes had just unclosed, and were fixed imploringly on the lovely girl, whose beauty seemed to have entranced him. "Save him, Heaven!" he continued, "save him, I implore thee, from the rashness that prompted me to seek his life. Oh, Isabel! this is no enemy, as in my madness I was led to believe! Speak, youth, and, if thou hast strength to do so, say why thou didst just now pursue my child, and thus rouse my suspicions that thine intents were hostile."

"I am too feeble to explain all," exclaimed Angus.—"I believe I am dying, and if you would atone this act of violence, afford consolation to one that you have injured, hasten to the hall below, and save my—my—brother!"

Here Angus fainted, and as his eyes were fixed on Isabel, he bent on her to the last a look that well explained his intense anxiety in behalf of poor Edwin. Her tears declared her sympathy, for, unconscious of what she was doing, she had clasped the hand of Angus in her own, and knelt down beside him to support him in her arms.

"Forgive," she exclaimed, "this unintentional act which has prompted my father to aim his sword against thy life. Didst thou but know the dreadful dangers that environ us, the unfortunate events of the hapless hour would, perhaps, excuse the rashness of a deed we so heavily deplore. Believe me, the act was not premeditated, and let the aid we will now afford to thee in thy heavy sufferings, convince that thou wert mistaken by my father for another."

Angus made an effort to rouse himself as her gentle voice fell upon his ear, but for the present, utterance was denied him, that every effort to assure the beauteous girl of his entire forgiveness. At length, recovering himself, he said :—

"Forgive, maiden, the alarm my unexpected appearance in this place has occasioned, and believe me no idle curiosity or evil intention conducted me to this lone retreat. Unknown, forlorn, lost in the mazes of the forest, a stranger to the manners of the world, yet rendered desperate when seeking for shelter from the storm, I hurried forward as chance directed my footsteps to seek that aid which was needed more for my suffering brother than for myself. Thus compelled, I broke into the sanctity of your retirement, and if I have erred, let the atonement of my fault be the probable death which will ensue from the wound I have received. And you, sir," he continued, addressing himself to Walter Campbell, "if human kindness dwells in your nature, hasten, I implore you, to the relief of my almost expiring brother. Save him, and thus rescue from death one who is far dearer to me than my own life."

Faint with the exertion occasioned by this speech, Angus could utter no more, but sank back upon the seat upon which the old man had placed him, while the gentle Isabel, aroused from the stupor of surprise and pity that had seized upon her soul, started up, and throwing her arms round the neck of her father, pleaded the causes of the two youthful sufferers. But Walter Campbell's angry glance struck terror to her heart; for the most horrible imaginations seemed to have risen to his mind, and clasping his hands in an agony of horror, he exclaimed :—

"Horrible vision, avaunt!—blast me not with thy sight, and recall not the dreadful visions that laurate my soul with all the anguish of the past. Oh, Emeline, Emeline!—lost—lost for ever!"

"Father!—dear father!" cried the terrified girl, "for mercy sake, for the sake of her you loved, arouse yourself from the fearful disorder that has seized upon your brain. Think not of ever for the afflictions that have driven you to the verge of despair, but look forward to the future with that hope which can alone assuage the grief that thus presses upon you. Remember, too, our hands are steeped in the blood of the innocent, but we are ourselves guiltless of intending to commit the deed."

These words aroused her father from the lethargy into which he had fallen, who, starting up, was precipitously hurrying across the chamber, when a loud knocking was heard at the door, and at the same moment Isabel distinguished a familiar voice demanding admittance from without.

"It is Rupert," she said, and quickly unfastening the door, a tall gaunt figure, bending beneath a load which he carried in his arms, entered the room. He eyed Angus with looks of mingled cusiosity and suspicion, but he was awed into silence, and bowed with respectful submission to Walter Campbell. He then removed the cloak which covered the burden, and discovered to their astonished view, the form of a fair youth, which he placed upon a seat near Angus, who, starting up with joyful surprise, immediately clasped in his arms the still inanimate Edwin. This effort was, however, too much for his exhausted frame, and again he relapsed into his former state of insensibility. At the command of his superior, Rupert now administered such cordials as were requisite, and which, in a short time, served to restore both the brothers to an indistinct knowledge of their present situation.

Upon examination, it was found that the wound inflicted upon Angus was more slight than had been anticipated, and that his exhaustion had been produced more from loss of blood, than from the serious nature of the injury he had received. Campbell then, in low whispers with his attendant, consulted him as to the means they possessed for accommodating their unexpected visitors, whose claims on his hospitality were enforced by the unfortunate event that had occurred through his own impetuous haste.

The ruined castle, desolate and cheerless as it was, had afforded shelter to the father and daughter; but it now became a question where to bestow the youthful strangers. Three wretched chambers besides the one they were now in, were the only apartments that had been used by them, and as there was no time to make the necessary arrangements, Rupert offered his couch for the night to accommodate the strangers.

It then appeared that Edwin had been discovered by Rupert while the latter was absent for the purpose of procuring provisions. Rupert well knew the necessity that existed for the secresy with which his master dwelt in the ruined castle, but the helpless condition of the hapless youth kindled in his breast a feeling of pity, and risking the displeasure of his superior, he raised him in his arms and brought him to the chamber in the manner that has been already described. Rupert had been a soldier, and being tolerably well versed in the remedies most proper under those circumstances, he performed some healing operations to the wound of Angus, which shortly had the effect of assuaging much of the pain he had endured.

Relieved from his anxiety by the assurance that the injury he had inflicted upon the youth was not mortal, Walter Campbell became more calm and composed than he had hitherto been. Raising himself, therefore, he approached Angus, and taking him by the hand, said—

"Alas, boy! you behold before you an unhappy father, driven by calamity and sad reverse of fortune, from the loved scenes of his birth, to seek shelter and protection amidst the crumbling ruins. Here I have lived to endure the tortures of a goaded heart, and suspicious of all the world, I raised my hand against thee, believing at the moment that thou wert sent hither to betray me into the hands of my enemies."

"And are you now satisfied that my intentions was not unfriendly to you?" asked Angus.

"I am," replied the old man; "and you, I am sure, will forgive an act of violence that I so bitterly deplore. Let my future actions convince you of my good will, and accept all the atonement my almost fatal rashness demands."

"I forgive all," cried Angus; "for your present kindness assures me that my life was not sought with premeditation."

"Thou hast said well," exclaimed Walter Campbell; "and now, boy, let me caution you against forming a prejudice through any strange conduct that you may observe. I am as men have made me—hot, impetuous, rash, but my heart is not dead to pity, and I would fain bestow on you and your brother that care and hospitality which you both seem to need so much. Here, for the present at least, you shall find a home, and may it shield you from those troubles and misfortunes which have driven me to seek concealment from my fellow-creatures."

"Your offer, sir, demands my warmest gratitude," exclaimed Angus; "and believe me, no act of either mine or my brother shall ever give you cause to regret the circumstances which have this night thrown us in your way."

"I can believe you, my young friend," he replied; "and here you shall find safety so long as I myself escape the active search of my enemies. Rely, therefore, upon your safety, for here you may rest secure from the assassins steel."

Grateful for the generous offer that had been made, Angus returned his most fervent thanks, and assured his protectors that the kindness he had thus voluntarily bestowed, should never meet a base return. Then turning towards the beauteous Isabel, he poured forth his gratitude in eloquent terms for the charitable aid she had administered to the strangers that had, unbidden, entered his secret abode.

When Edwin recovered from the stupor in which he had lain so long, he gazed round him with wonder, and the thoughts of the last night's adventure passed in rapid succession through his brain. Yet he spoke not, for gratitude choked his utterance, and it was only by expressive looks that he could convey to those around him the thankfulness with which he accepted the assistance which had thus been bestowed upon himself and his brother.

Rupert now advanced at the signal of his superior, and Angus, supported by the attendant and his brother, rose to quit the chamber. Ere he departed, however, Walter Campbell once more bade him rest in confident security; and then leading his daughter from the apartment, they departed through a sliding panel which he had opened, while Rupert led the way through an opposite door.

CHAPTER VII.

" Can no rest find me, no private place secure me,
    But still my miseries, like blood-hounds, haunt me?
    Unfortunate young man, which way now guides thee,
    Guides thee from death?"   WOMEN PLEASED.

A VAULTED corridor of considerable length was terminated by a low portal at the further extremity, whose rusty fastening seemed to offer but slight protection in case any foe should attempt to force the door. Rupert leading them to the other end of the chamber, pointed to an antique bed that stood against the wall, and which was half stripped of its tattered hangings, the remains of which showed that they had once been of a rich and costly texture. The walls too were stripped of the tapestry that had formerly adorned them, and displayed a gloomy comfortless aspect that struck with chilling coldness in the hearts of the two youths.

In silence Rupert lighted a lamp that stood upon a table, and as Angus declined any further assistance, he silently took his departure, closing the chamber-door after him by way of precaution. For some little time the inmates of this dreary chamber sat watching the wretched object which here met their view; a portion only of the place was lighted by the lamp which had been left with them, and the vivid lightning, as it still shot athwart the casement, gleamed brightly on the few objects in the room, and for a moment lit up the gloom in which they were involved.

"This is indeed a miserable abode," Edwin said at length; "and serves only, by the contrast it affords, to make me regret that we ever left the Watch Tower and the comforts it possessed. On such a fearful night as this, how often have we sat beside the good Magdalen, listening to the fierce howling of the storm without, and as the cheerful blaze rose brightly before us, how happy have we felt, as you, dear Angus, read aloud the ancient legends of heroes that were long departed. Poor Magdalen! how deeply does she now grieve for our departure, and what anxious fears does she feel for the safety of those who have left her fostering care without even one parting word."

Awakened to the conviction of his too hasty conduct in departing from the Watch Tower, Angus folded his brother in his arms, and said tenderly,

"Your reproach, Edwin, is justly merited and shall be atoned. To-morrow we will return to the kind guardian of our youth, under whose protection I will again place you, and freely confess the motives that led to our sudden departure from her care. She will then no longer oppose my wishes, nor keep concealed from us the narrative of those wrongs which I feel but too well assured were heaped upon our parents. With her approval I shall once more return to accomplish the vow I have made, and, rendered more injurious in the cause of justice, and of honour, shall be the better enabled to prosecute the scheme of vengeance I have formed."

Angus paused, and his thoughts recurred to the events which had that night occurred. The fair form of Isabelle floated like a lovely vision on his imagination, and then his mind turned towards her father, whose martial air seemed to impress him with the true and faithful image of one of those heroes of whom he had delighted to read. From these reflections he was raised by Edwin, who exclaimed with all the gladsomeness of a youthful mind,—

" Yes, dear brother, we will indeed return to our tower where we have passed many happy, happy days. And you, Angus, methinks, would not be so anxious to leave us again if that fair young damsel was to accompany us, and sure are we that Magdalen would joyfully receive her, for she is beautiful, and, no doubt, as good as she is fair; and mark you, Angus, how her sorrow for your wound drew tears of pitty from her eyes? Ah! Magdalen would love her if it was only because she was so tender and kind to Angus; and then, with such a companion, how happily should we pass our days; you would no longer wish to quit the Watch Tower, and we should no more be separated from each other."

By this time they were in bed, and as Angus made no answer to those last words, they were soon fast locked in that slumber which the recent fatigue had rendered doubly welcome. The dawn of morning had not yet broke through their casement, when Angus was awakened by a hollow moan, and half starting from his couch, he listened anxiously to satisfy himself whether the sound was real or imaginary. Nothing more was, however, heard to excite a further apprehension of coming evil, and the wound in his side was so stiff and painful, that he was unable to get out of bed to search round the room for his own satisfaction. The lamp, which had been left burning, still dimly gleamed in the fireplace, and afforded just light enough to render the chamber even more dismal than it really was, and to present imaginary phantoms that seemed to be gliding round the bed.

Half terrified Angus felt about him, and found that his brother, in calm, deep repose, slept by his side undisturbed by the sound with which he had himself been awakened, and yet, in spite of his efforts to believe the contrary, he could not help thinking that a deep hollow moan had certainly reached his ear.

" Perhaps," he thought, " Walter Campbell, so evidently unhappy, sleeps in the adjoining chamber, and it was from him that the melancholy sound proceeded, which, echoing through the solemn stillness of night, seemed to possess an awe which at any other time would not have created this alarm."

Convinced that such was the case, Angus lay for some time longer, anxiously watching the return of day, and as he at length bent his gaze towards the almost expiring lamp, he fancied he could distinguish the grim forms of beings pacing slowly through the chamber. No sound, however, fell upon his ear, and tired of watching, he again sunk into repose. But his slumber was of short duration, for either awake he heard, or in his sleep most certainly did so, a voice awfully hollow and supernatural, sound through the chamber, as in anguished accents it thrice uttered :—

"Glenalvon! Glenalvon! Glenalvon! awake, awake! revenge the murdered,—punish the guilty!"

Angus did awake, and as his eyes unclosed, he beheld the fierce and furious glance of a human head, covered with a steel helmet, and dimly seen through an opening of the curtain. On the grim visage a lamp shone as it was held in an outstretched arm, which was so held as entirely to obscure every other portion of the figure, though its dark glaring features were, at the same time, rendered horribly visible to the awe inspired youth. As Angus raised his eyes towards the object of his alarm, the expression of the countenance changed, the whole visage becoming suddenly swelled and blackened with disturbed passion and horror ; the eyes flashed with un-governable fury, and the whole scene was well calculated to strike terror into the firmest heart. The lamp then fell from the hand that sustained it, and was instantly extinguished, at the same moment another groan was heard and the figure vanished.

The wound of Angus bled again, and he was unable to rise, but as he drew aside the curtain, he could faintly trace the movement of some dark object gliding through the further part of the chamber, and the next moment was heard a slight noise like that which would be occasioned by the cautious closing of a door. At that juncture the lamp in the fire-place faintly gleamed up and instantly expired, leaving the chamber enveloped in the deepest gloom ; then a deep sigh was heard at no great distance off, and unable to support himself any longer, Angus sunk back upon his pillow, faint and powerless.

When he at length awoke, he found his brother affectionately occupied in endeavouring to restore him to animation. At first he knew not where he was, and the wild haggard gaze with which he looked around, served still more to alarm his brother. The effect of the last night's horrors had dwelt upon the mind of the youth, with so much force, that his dreams had been full of the most frightful images. Agnes heaved a deep sigh as he returned the warm pressure of his brother's hand, and in answer to his earnest inquiries, he said—

"I have beheld them, Edwin! they came to my couch in the solemn hour of darkness, and then vanished from my view ere I could question them upon the object of their visitation."

"Of whom do you speak, Angus?" demanded the other, alarmed at the mildness with which these words were uttered.

"It was no vision of fancy," continued Angus, regardless of the question that had been put to him; "they were the spirits of those whose memory we oft times consecrate with our tears, and they came to reveal the dark secrets which lie buried with them in the grave. Their forms floated before me, and in dismal tones they cried, 'Revenge the murdered! punish the guilty!'"

"What mean you, my dear Angus?" cried the youth, tenderly embracing him. "Who was it that called upon you to revenge the murder of our parents?"

"The spirit of our father," replied Angus in a tone of deep solemnity. "Yes, my brother, he has appeared before me and demands that justice I have so long resolved to seek!"

The dream of the youth had been fearful and harrowing, and the fever which now raged in his blood, left confused ideas in his brain, that might almost be said to border on insanity. In his sleep he had again heard those fearful words which clung to his memory, and fancy had thus summoned to his view the shadowy forms of his murdered parents. Indeed those images were so deeply engraven upon his memory, that it was not till some few minutes after his recovery, that he was exactly sensible of his real situation.

The kind attention of Edwin, however, at length served to recall his scattered senses, but the fever that consumed him, left him so weak and exhausted, that he was for the present unable to rise from his bed. It was therefore, with no little satisfaction that Edwin saw the door of their chamber open, and the melancholy form of Walter Campbell enter.

He approached the youths, and in a voice of affectionate greeting, inquired of them if they had rested well, and whether the wound of the elder brother was better. Angus fixed his eyes steadily upon the old man, but

answered not his questions, whilst Edwin hastened to explain the terrors that had alarmed Angus during the night.

Walter Campbell heard him with astonishment that he sought not to conceal, and muttering a few words that were inaudible to the youths, quitted the room to procure assistance. Angus watched his retiring form, and as he disappeared from the chamber, he exclaimed—

"No, no—it cannot be; I wrong him with the suspicion, for treachery and guile dwelt not in that form. Its erect and noble front proclaims no cause of hidden terror, for his eye beams forth a calm serenity that guilt cannot assume in the presence of those it has injured. His was not the grim and hideous visage whose midnight visit disturbed my slumbers; its features were those of villany and distorted deadly passions. But thine, Campbell, bespeak thee in possession of a mind and spirit free from those crimes of which I suspected thee!"

Edwin heard not the whole of this incoherent speech, for his attention had been attracted by the glittering appearance of something that brightly gleamed upon the floor. Stooping to ascertain what it was, he grasped the object of his wonder, but instantly started back, with a shudder and an exclamation of alarm, as he exclaimed,—

"Whose dagger is this, Angus, that I have just found? Surely—surely no villain has entered the room during our slumbers to murder us!"

As he spoke this, he handed the weapon to his brother, who, as he received it, started, and grasped at it with an ardour that betrayed the indignation which at that moment filled his bosom."

"Some fearful villany has been at work!" he exclaimed, as his eye gazed wildly upon the dagger he held. "Assassins have been in our chamber, and our lives have been sought by those we have most trusted."

"Let us hasten from home, my brother," exclaimed the terrified Edwin.

No. 6

" We will go back to the Watch Tower, and there remain in security till the time arrives when we may execute the vengeance we have sworn to accomplish. There, at least, we shall be safe from danger, and——"

" Hush!" interrupted Angus, "some one come this way;" and as he spoke, Walter Campbell once more entered the chamber.

Regardless of his weak condition and the pain of his wound, Angus sprang from the couch, and seizing the arm of the old man, as he displayed the poniard, bade him claim it, and then unhesitatingly accused him of having entered the chamber at midnight, for purposes such as the instrument of death seemed to declare.

" The weapon is thine!" he exclaimed. "Thou wert the midnight ruffian who, stealing into my room in the darkness of night, wouldst have slain those who rested beneath thy roof in fancied security. Behold and gaze upon this foul evidence of thy guilt, for it is thine, and thou canst not deny it."

The startled host stood gazed with fixed horror upon the speaker, and as his recollection seemed to return, he regarded the poniard with a look that betrayed the terrible agony of a soul that was ill at rest. At length, snatching the weapon from the hand of the youth, he, in the deepest tones of mental agony, exclaimed,—

" Mysterious forboder of evil, whence comest thou, and why do I now behold thee? Horrible remembrancer of ill! art thou sent to prepare me for my fate, and warn me that my hour is almost come, or wouldst thou tell me that my enemies have discovered this retreat, and that instant flight can alone save me from their fierce vengeance?"

A pallid, death-like hue had settled upon his countenance as he spoke these words, and uttering a groan of anguish as he concluded them, he rushed wildly from the room, leaving Angus and his brother confounded with amazement at the violence he had exhibited.

The remainder of this day passed in gloomy suspense, for the wound of the youth was still painful, and, much as he desired to do so, he was at present unable to leave the place where he believed himself to be in so much danger. Walter Campbell, whatever his intentions towards them might be, returned not, nor did his daughter Isabel present herself before them. Once only, Rupert entered their chamber with such refreshments as they required; but the sullen tones in which he addressed them had a harshness and severity that somewhat alarmed them. From this man Angus sought to obtain some information respecting the inhabitants of the castle, but either his fidelity was not to be shaken, or the natural sternness of his mind was too unyielding to gratify the earnest entreaties of his master's guests; for Angus could only learn that the castle was wholly uninhabited, except by Walter Campbell and his daughter, and that he was the only domestic in the place.

In his own turn Rupert became inquisitive, and demanded explanations from the youths which they knew not how to give.

" Have you come from afar off?" he inquired; "or do you dwell in the neighbourhood of this falling ruin?"

" We were travelling through the forest," answered Angus, with caution, " when the tempest that raged so fearfully drove us to seek a shelter in the first place that offered. The castle seems sad and gloomy," he added, and, to speak the truth, I shall not be sorry to leave it."

" Aye," replied Rupert, "it is both gloomy and dangerous, and has, no doubt, witnessed many a dark and fearful scene in its times. For my own part, I wonder you sought shelter here, and if you take my advice, you will leave it with as much speed as you possibly can."

"If it is so dangerous," said Angus, "why does your master remain in it?"

"That," replied the man, "is a question I have no right to answer. He may have some cause that is best hidden in his own breast. Besides, you are not inclined to explain much of your own concerns, and, therefore, have no right to expect that we shall reveal secrets that are best kept to ourselves."

"When the proper time arrives we will explain all to the satisfaction of those that we may consider to be our friends," exclaimed Angus. "At present there are many things connected with circumstances that have happened in our family of which we remain ignorant. But the time will arrive when all must be explained, and if vengeance is to be executed, our foes shall find that there are those living who will die rather than suffer the iniquitous to live unpunished."

"And this," said Rupert, "is all the explanation you will deign to give my master?"

"When I am assured," answered Angus, "that he deserves our confidence, I shall no longer hesitate to inform him of all I know respecting the circumstances connected with our family. We arrived at this deserted castle by mere accident, and whatever may appear strange about it, we have no desire to pry into secrets that we have nothing to do with, and shall expect the same courtesy from those of whom we have been compelled to solicit for shelter. From us your master has nothing to fear; but how far we are equallly safe from any designs he may entertain against us remains to be proved, though the events of last night almost assure me that we had better have encountered the dangers of the forest than seek the protection we thought to have found beneath this roof."

"Your words are full of mystery," said Rupert, eying him with a glance of suspicion. "Did anything occur after I left you in this room last night?"

Angus paused for a moment, and then related as nearly as he could all that had happened during the night, and concluded by speaking of the dagger which had afterwards been found upon the floor by his brother, and of the helmeted head which he had seen gazing upon him through the curtains of the bed.

"Psha!" exclaimed Rupert; "all you have been telling me was the effect of disordered dreams. You were alarmed, perhaps, at finding yourself in this lonely, desolate castle, and in your slumbers beheld some of those horrors that you had imagined whilst awake. The airy forms, it seems, appeared only during the night, and vanished ere the first beams of daylight."

"Be it a shadow or a substance, methinks I can see it now as plainly as I did during the night."

As he spoke, he directed his gaze towards Rupert, who, affecting not to understand him, turned his head quickly round to glance in every direction behind him, and exclaimed,—

"These are but idle fears, young man, and are unworthy of one who it seems intends to live by the profession of arms. I see nothing but ourselves in the room, and once more I say you have been deceived; and whatever you saw during the night, was merely from the effect of fear and suspicion."

"It is possible it may have been so," answered Angus. "My wound pained me, and the fever that seized upon my frame, may have made my brain wander. Even now I feel unwell, and if you leave me for a time I may, perhaps, obtain that repose of which I stand so much in need."

Rupert needed no second bidding, and again bidding the brothers repose all confidence and trust in the good will of Walter Campbell, he slowly quitted the chamber.

CHAPTER VIII.

" The hearth in hall was black and dead,
      No board was dight in bower within,
    Nor merry bowl, nor welcome bed;
      ' Here's sorry cheer,' quoth the heir of Linne."
                                        OLD BALLAD.

FOR some time after the departure of the man, Angus continued buried in deep abstraction, which his brother carefully avoided to interrupt, and busied himself in all those tender offices which he hoped might con-duce to the case of his beloved Angus. In spite of this, however, the thoughts of the latter became restless and unhappy, and often, throughout that day, did he glance through the heavy gloom of his cheerless chamber, whose dismal aspect awoke his curiosity and suspicion. For the first time he now regretted the weakness that prevented his immediate departure, for there was an air of mystery about the place, as well as the inhabitants, that he in vain endeavoured to account for. He fancied that each moment of delay only served to increase the danger, and anxious for the safety of his brother, he bitterly reproached himself for having led him from the fostering care of Magdalen.

It was, however, impossible to quit the ruined castle in his present exhausted state, and in spite of the alarm he felt on Edwin's account, there was a secret and irresistible charm that made him unwilling to depart from it at present. Often did he cast wistful glances towards the door, and as often hope it would give admittance to the lovely object whose beauty had taken so strange a hold upon his heart. Isabel, however, appeared not, and his thoughts over and over again returned to the last expressions uttered by his mysterious host. Yet they betrayed no confession of guilt. The poniard, it was certain, he had instantly recognised; yet, still there might be other causes for his agitation on beholding it, though the maddened words he had given utterance to might give rise to suspicions that it had been the instrument of some crime which he had himself committed."

Angus then once more reviewed the occurrences of the past night, the appearances that had presented themselves before him, and the possible cause that might have led to so fearful a visitation. He could not forget, however, the attentions he had received; and if his accommodations were not greater, the circumstances was only to be attributed to the want of means on the part of his host, whose happy address, though obscured in mystery, betrayed him to belong to no common order of men.

But whoever or whatever might be the form,—whether earthly or shadowy, that had appeared by the side of his bed on the preceding night, Angus was compelled to admit that it bore no resemblance to the countenance of his host, and therefore he now began to hope that from him he had nothing to apprehend. Still he was convinced that he had seen the horrible object of his terrors, and the fearful aspect was so deeply impressed upon his memory that it was impossible that he could have been either deceived or mistaken. But he felt certain that the face bore no resemblance to Walter Campbell, and he therefore dismissed from his mind the alarming suspicions he had so lately entertained. Yet, though he believed his host to be innocent of having entered his chamber with the intention of murdering him and his brother—yet was there a possibility that Rupert was not equally guiltless; for the dark, scowling features of this man had given rise to suspicions against him in the mind of the youth, and he determined to watch him with a careful eye, and thus avert any mischief he might meditate against him.

The dreams of Angus had certainly been wild and fearful, and he now felt almost inclined to believe that the shades of the dead parents, which he imagined to have appeared before him, were the effects of a disturbed fancy; but that he was awake and saw the armed head glancing upon him through the curtains, he even now felt but too well convinced. The sight of an extinguished lamp, laying on the floor, attracted his notice and revived every doubt that he had sought to banish. The hollow groan that had first awakened him, and the sight of the lamp, together with the succeeding noise like the closing of a door, were all perfectly remembered. Each circumstance rushed forcibly upon his mind in confirmation of his suspicions, and he could no longer doubt that this chamber was the haunt of some mysterious beings, who probably were secreted amid the mouldering ruins for purposes that had hitherto eluded the discovery of Walter Campbell.

To pursue the subject any further at present he knew would be useless, and uncertain as he was, he resolved to be watchful and guarded during the period of his stay there, which, unfortunately, would be longer than he desired, in consequence of his strength being insufficient to allow of his immediate return to the Watch Tower.

The day now begun to decline, but to the astonishment of Angus, no one since the morning had approached the chamber. He then remembered Campbell's last words on departing, and that he had said nothing but instant flight could save him.

"Perhaps he is gone," thought Angus, "and we are left here to perish by ourselves. Isabel too, perhaps, accompanies him, and never more shall I behold her lovely image!"

An involuntary sigh escaped him as he reflected upon these words, and in an instant his brother Edwin was by his side.

"You are ill, dear Angus," he said, "and fain would I prevail upon you to lie down and take that rest of which you are so much in need. The loss of blood has made you weak, and rest alone can restore you to that health which I so earnestly pray for."

"I am indeed weak, Edwin," replied the other, "but that is nothing to the thoughts that agitate me. The mystery I sought to discover is more involved in darkness than ever, and even now when I should be exerting myself, I am unable to move from a place where I fear we are both in danger."

"It is indeed a gloomy ruin," answered the younger Glenalvon; "but there seems to be no one in it but Walter Campbell and his daughter, and one domestic, and surely we cannot have anything to fear from them."

"Certainly not from either Campbell or the gentle Isabel," replied Angus, "but Rupert seems to be of a more fierce disposition, and I have my suspicion whether he may not be connected with some of the Highland banditti unknown to his master."

"And what makes you think so?" asked Edwin.

"There are many reasons why I distrust him," replied his brother, "but chiefly, perhaps, because I cannot help feeling convinced that it was he I see gazing upon me during the midnight hour through the curtains of my bed. The countenance was exactly like his, and supposing my suspicions to be correct, what but an evil purpose could have brought him into our presence at such a time of night?"

"Perhaps you are mistaken," exclaimed the youth. "Your dreams were doubtless disturbed by the fever occasioned by your wound, and as Rupert was the last person we saw on retiring to bed, it is likely his image may have remained in your mind, and thus left an impression so much against him."

"I have endeavoured to argue so myself," replied Angus, "but it has been in vain, for I am well assured that I slept not when the form appeared before me, and should it indeed have been Rupert we may be assured his purpose was one that we have reason to dread."

"In that case," said the other, "why not tell Walter Campbell of your suspicions, and ask his protection against the designs of his menial. Our host would surely endeavour to shield us against treachery, and if Rupert was to know that his designs were suspected, he would be cautious ere he ventured to injure those whom his master honours with his esteem."

"How know we that Walter Campbell is in the castle?" demanded his brother. "Do you remember his last words, that instant flight could alone save him, and as he has not visited us once since then, I almost think his terrors have impelled him to seek safety in some other place."

"Do you think he has abandoned us to our fate?" asked the boy.

"I am afraid so," answered Angus.

"Let us then instantly return to the Watch Tower.

"Alas! you forget the wound that has disabled me from making any exertion," returned Angus. "I am weak, brother, and any attempt to leave this place at present would be made in vain."

"I had, indeed, forgotten it at the moment when I spoke," answered his brother. "There is, however, no need to despair, even if things should come to the worst, for I am now strong again after last night's exhaustion, and will go forth to see if some cottage is not to be found in the neighbourhood from whence I can obtain the assistance you so much require."

"At present there will be no need for it," answered Angus," because we are not yet certain that Walter Campbell and his daughter have left the place. There may be some reason for their not having made their appearance all day, and I will at least wait till to-morrow morning ere I suffer you to go out, and perhaps remember perils that may occasion our eternal separation."

"Then you really believe there is danger in this place?"

"I am afraid so," answered Angus, "and, therefore, I would not have you leave this place alone. To-morrow, I may be better and stronger, and if so, we will depart together, and return once more to our safe retreat in the Watch Tower."

"Ah! we shall then again behold our dear Magdalen."

"I trust we shall," replied Angus, "and bitterly do I now regret the imprudent step I prevailed upon you to take when we quitted a place where we had found a safe asylum from the storms of the world."

"Nay, do not reproach yourself," answered Edwin, "for I, at least, was as much to blame as you were yourself. "Remember, you would have ventured forth alone, and it was my own wish to accompany you."

"And what led us forth, my dear brother?" demanded the elder Glenalvon. "Was it not that we might seek the means to avenge the wrongs inflicted upon our house? Such was our purpose, and though the object may have been defeated for a time, never will I rest satisfied till I have poured the full tide of vengeance upon the guilty wretches that slew our parents."

"But how," asked Edwin, "shall we ever find means to discover the evil doors?"

"That, I believe, will not be so difficult a task as you seem to imagine," replied his brother. "Our good Magdalen, I am almost certain, will be able to tell us when the fitting time arrives, for I overheard her say to Father Andrew, that she dreaded our learning the truth, as she knew our impetuous tempers would incite us to instant revenge. Since then, I have frequently urged her upon the point, and though she denies not a full knowledge of the whole dreadful secret, yet she fears to reveal it lest aught should happen to us."

"Perhaps," observed the other, "she is bound never to tell us by an oath."

"I have myself thought so," replied Angus, "and for that reason have forborne to urge her with further questions."

"Cannot we ask of Walter Campbell?" enquired Edwin; "he may remember the circumstance, and thus afford us all the information we require."

"I should have done so last night," replied Angus, "but Magdalen has always entreated that we would not let any one know our name till we had received her permission."

"And why did she do so?"

"That," said Angus, "is more than I can explain. "It is likely, however, that our lives would be endangered were it known where we are to be found, and I suppose she wishes the secret to be kept till we are able to defend ourselves from the treachery of our unknown foes. No doubt it is a prudent caution on the part of our kind protectress, and I am determined to follow her counsel till we have received her permission to make enquiries."

"At least," observed Edwin, "unless there should be any necessity for so doing."

"Why, in that case," answered his brother, "I should not hesitate. I am, however, convinced, that it would be useless to do anything of the kind at present; and, therefore, much as I should like to ask Walter Campbell whether he has any recollection of our parents' inhuman murder, I will restrain my curiosity till the time comes when I can take up arms against the villains that have so fully wronged us."

"And is it your intention," said Edwin, "to return from this place to the Watch Tower?"

"At present it is," replied his brother, "for my wound will be sometime ere it thoroughly heals, and I am, besides, most anxious to place you at once under the care of our foster mother. I was wrong in suffering you to leave her, and the only way to repair my error is to return with all speed. In a few years you will have grown stronger, Edwin, and when that period arrives, you shall join with me in the efforts to discover and punish those that have injured us. But we will speak no more upon this subject, for I grow uneasy at the long absence of those belonging to this ruined castle, and would fain learn whether they deserted the place or not."

"Shall I go and see?" asked Edwin. "I should know my way from here to the room where we were all assembled last night, and should soon return to let you know the success of my mission."

"I will go with you," said Angus, and rising with difficulty from his seat, he took the arm of his brother, and slowly paced towards the door. This exertion served to restore him a little, and as he quitted the room and breathed a purer air, the oppression that had began to steal upon him gradually wore off.

Edwin, with some difficulty, opened the door, and led his brother through a gloomy vaulted passage that was faintly lighted by a distant window, overshadowed with ivy. Thus reaching the farthest extremity, they experienced no opposition to their progress, and silently passing through another door, found themselves in what appeared to be the sitting-room usually occupied by Walter Campbell and his daughter; but at present the latter only was to be found within it.

The beauteous form of Isabel, habited in a dark grey robe, divested of all ornament, sat upon the oaken seat that ran round the oriel window. Her eyes were directed towards the evening prospect that lay spread before her; but her thoughts seemed to be buried in the most profound forgetfulness of all external objects. Yet in her eyes beamed forth radiant lustre, softened to the most entrancing expression of loveliness that can be imagined.

Wrapped in admiration at the beauteous vision before him, Angus could only murmur some indistinct expressions, whose tenor was scarcely inteli-gible, though they had served to withdraw the deeply engaged Isabel from her mental abstraction.

She raised her eyes, now somewhat dimmed with tears, and their speak-ing language encountered those of the no less expressive Angus. A faint glow of evident satisfaction suffused her countenance as she perceived who her visitors were, and rising in some haste, she enquired whether his wound was better, and as she assisted Edwin to draw a chair on which Angus, after some entreaty, seated himself, she apologised for the neglect he had experienced, though it was evident she was not at liberty to assign a reason for what Angus might with some justice attribute to indifference as to his fate. After a pause, however, she said :—

" My father is at present absent, but I am in momentary expectation of his return. His visits to your chamber this morning has—though I know not why—caused him much usual uneasiness and perturbation. This perhaps may be the only time we shall be permitted to meet each other, and let me, therefore, entreat you to form no evil suspicions that my father's conduct, last night, may probably have given rise to. Your soul, I trust, is too generous to refuse forgiveness to an unintentional injury that was inflicted upon you, and which could only have been committed in a moment of ap-prehended danger. Alas! when the mind is diseased, our actions are placed beyond the power of control, and though the duties of humanity should have urged our eager assistance in your behalf, believe me, it was from no want of feeling that my father has not more frequently visited you to day."

Isabel paused, but her looks confirmed the testimony of her lips, and there was in her department an air of suffering that seemed alike to dis-dain the weakness of unavailing complaint, and to forbid the intrusion of pity, at once silencing every question that Angus might have asked.

" You appear," he said at length, " to be the victims of injustice and oppression. Think not an idle curiosity prompts the deep interest I feel in your welfare, for though we should part never to meet again, still the impression of these few eventful hours can never be erased from the mind of him who now addresses you. We, ourselves, are the children of mis-fortune, and have alike been the sufferers from an unknown enemy, and have preserved from death only by the charity of a benevolent friend, whose first lessons taught us how to feel for and to share in those sorrows we behold in others."

He paused, whilst Isabel's entire attention became rivetted to the gentle expressive tones of the youth by whom she had been addressed, and who, after a few moments pause thus continued :—

" The sons of a murdered sire, despoiled of their inheritance and illus-trious name, wandering like outcasts, seeking a place of rest and shelter, not daring openly to avow their claims, yet indignant at the wrongs their hidden oppressors have heaped upon their race, no longer yield in idle sub-

mission to their fate. Impatient to avenge their injuries, declare their birth, and discover, if possible, the secrets they have long wished to know, they have quitted their retreat, and were driven by chance, and the tempest of last night, to seek shelter from the storm within the seeming deserted ruin which presented itself before them."

Whilst Isabel, still more confused, glanced her eye on the wounded youth, but she felt too much agitated to speak, and Angus resumed :—

. " Grateful to Heaven and to you, for the restoration of my brother ; the trifling injury I received from your father's hands is freely forgiven. My heart acquits him of any evil intention towards me, and I trust he will not hesitate to accept the gratitude which I feel for the benefit he has conferred upon us. Gratitude, indeed, is the only return I can at present make, but if my arm, or my whole life devoted to your service can serve my protectors, disdain not to accept them, nor hesitate to command any return that I can make for the benefits so kindly bestowed." ·

The varying countenance of Isabel during the uttering of these words, was frequently flushed with the deepest crimson as he proceeded. Her soul seemed labouring for utterrance, and Angus, with surprise and grief, observed the agitation he had given rise to. He felt shocked, as if consciously guilty of some harsh expression, and would have apologized for it, but Isabel, subduing her emotions, exclaimed, ardently :—

" Oh ! how painful to the ingenious mind of falsehood and deceit. Compelled by a fatal necessity to remain unknown, what expression can I utter to dissipate the suspicions, which an unhappy destiny justifies, but equally forbids to be explained. Do not, I entreat, judge or question what cannot be revealed," she added, " nor tempt me to break a silence which a melancholy destiny, and the commands of my father imposes upon me."

" You have been the victim of tyranny like ourselves," exclaimed Angus.

"Misfortunes," she replied, "may for a time oppress, but cannot make criminal those who are superior to its trials, and conscious of their own innocence. Three days, alas! have nearly passed away since the evils of this hour were unknown to me, but the will of Heaven must be submitted to, and I will endeavour to bear my trials with that fortitude which can alone support me under my severe afflictions."

Wrapt in profound attention, Angus could have continued mutely listening for hours to the music of her voice, and even for some moments after she had ceased speaking he awaited in expectation of her proceeding. Perceiving, however, that she remained silent, and that her spirits were evidently oppressed with some hideous sorrow, he spoke to her in a voice of kindness, and by changing the subject of their conversation, soon succeeded in restoring her to cheerfulness. Her grief, indeed, seem to be suspended, as she sat listening to the words of Angus and his brother, and the evening passed rapidly away. Rupert had twice entered the apartment to prepare the supper, which, however, remained untasted, for Walter Campbell returned not. Isabel's spirits again sunk under the disappointment, for she trembled for the safety of her father, and the melancholy smile struggling with her ill-concealed fears, proved but too plainly the agitation she in vain sought to conceal. At length her impatience could no longer be restrained, and when Rupert again appeared before them, she exclaimed:—

"Did not my father say he would return to us ere the night had set in?"

"He did, lady," answered the attendant.

"Yet 'tis now almost midnight," she continued, "and we are left in doubt and apprehension respecting his safety."

"He will return presently, I dare say," replied Rupert. "He seemed to be agitated when he went out, and has, perhaps, wandered farther from the castle than he intended."

"May he not have returned, and sought the privacy of another chamber?" asked Isabel.

"Why, to confess the truth, I rather think he has," answered Rupert, glancing towards the brothers as if to signify that their presence was an intrusion. "He is, in fact, at this moment in the vaulted chamber awaiting the time when he can speak to you alone."

Angus was anxious to see and apologise to his host for the hasty expressions he had made use of, but he understood the meaning of Rupert's looks and words, and instantly rising from his seat, he said:—

"You will be pleased to convey to your master the thanks of his guests, and say, we will, till to-morrow, trespass on his hospitality, when, if permitted, we will, in person, express our gratitude, and then take our departure.

Rupert gazed steadily upon the youth for an instant or two, and then bowing to his mistress, hurried from the room. Angus immediately bade adieu to Isabel, and taking up a lamp from the table, was departing, when her voice arrested his retreating footsteps.

"Must you then leave us so soon?" she said, in trembling accents; "and at a time, too, when the exertion may delay your recovery, and perhaps open afresh the wound you have been so unfortunate as to receive."

"Could I dare venture to hope," replied Angus, taking her hand, "that Lady Isabel would sometimes vouchsafe to remember me, I should depart with renewed health and revived courage."

"To doubt that I can do otherwise," she answered, "or to suppose me capable of losing the remembrance of those I have found worthy of my esteem is to suspect me of inconstancy and ingratitude."

"You will, then, deign to honour with your friendship an unknown stranger?" cried Angus, joyfully. He would have said more, had not a look of anxiety and surprise from Isabel suppressed the ardour of the moment, and forbade him to delay her longer.

"Adieu, my friends," she cried, as they once more prepared to depart; "hereafter, should we meet in any other spot than this, the seeming mystery of our fortunes may perhaps be explained. Providence, upon whom I rely, will yet, I trust, restore to my father that lost peace which treachery has deprived him of; and should that much-hoped-for moment ever arrive, it shall witness the sincerity of my esteem, and the sorrow I have experienced for the wrong my weak fears have been the means of inflicting upon you. Till then, once more, farewell, for we must no longer trespass on the commands of my parent, to whom both duty and affection prompt an immediate obedience."

As she uttered these last words she retreated from the room, and Angus and his brother once more returned to their own apartment.

CHAPTER IX.

"I am thy father's spirit;
Doomed for a certain term to walk the night,
And for the day confined to fast in fires,
Till the foul crimes, done in my days of nature,
Are burnt and purged away."

HAMLET.

ANGUS had lingered till the last moment, unwilling to quit the charm whose fascinations possessed his every thought, and awoke sensations of exquisite delight, to which the sameness of his past days had been a stranger. To his couch he carried their impressions, where busy fancy pourtrayed a thousand pleasing images of innocent and cheerful happiness.

The night was serenely calm, not a sound floated on the air, or disturbed the death-like stillness of the dreary chamber; but suddenly a moan of anguish was heard, and as the loud and dismal cry aroused the startled youth from his slumbers, he again heard it thrice repeated, as a hollow voice pronounced with solemn accent:—

"Glenalvon!"

"Guardians above!" exclaimed Angus, "whence came that dismal cry?" and dashing aside the drapery of his bed, he cast forth an astonished and inquiring look.

Horror and dismay instantly seized him, for close by the side of his couch stood a tall, gaunt figure, whose death-like visage was bent upon him, but its features were those of a total stranger. His form seemed enfolded in a winding wrapper, or robe, that nearly concealed his whole person, except his pale countenance, and one arm, which was unconfined, and which, as Angus slowly raised himself on the side of his couch, he waved with measured movement, that seemed to invite the youth's attention.

"In Heaven's name, whence came you?" demanded Angus, in faltering accents.

The figure neither spoke nor moved; its eyes were fixed and motionless, but raising its arm, it pointed towards the door of the chamber.

"Speak!" exclaimed Angus; "wherefore this late and midnight visit?—What wouldst thou?"

The unknown again slightly waved his arm and pointed towards the door. The heart of Angus throbbed violently, but presently, recovering himself, he sprang from the bed, and the figure retreated a few paces from him, as he was about to advance. At that instant a hollow groan reverberated through the chamber, and a voice, whose tones were superhuman, exclaimed:—

" Torture not my spirit, son of Glenalvon, for such thou art !—The hour of my stay is short, and will depart ere the purpose of my visit is accomplished. Fear no evil, but follow whither I shall lead you."

For an instant Angus was deprived of all self-command ; yet, impelled by some powerful impulse, he tremblingly exclaimed :—

" I obey thee !—lead on,   I will follow !"

As these words were uttered, the features of the mysterious being underwent an instant change ; their distorted wildness disappeared, and Angus no more beheld those terrific glances which had awed him into compliance. Trembling, and not daring to question the motives of his mysterious visitor, Angus seized the lamp and followed the figure, who, with noiseless footsteps, advanced towards the door, and pursued the windings of the avenue with a swiftness that compelled the youth to hasten his speed. In silence they passed through dark and dismal passages, and often did the unknown pause to await for Angus, and sigh bitterly as he seemed to view him, and as often did the latter feel an irrepressible terror creep through his veins, as he observed the fixed gaze with which he was regarded.

The way had now become intricate and dangerous, and the alarm and impatience of Angus increased as he saw the forlornness of his situation. The unknown had led him over an immense track of mazy labyrinths, and he was now far away from even the most remote chance of assistance, should the stranger's intentions prove hostile to him. And now his heart reproached him for having yielded to the commands of a being who spoke not, but whose designs began to assume the most frightful and dismaying appearances. Edwin, too, he now reflected, might awaken, and be alarmed at his absence. A sudden thought of horror darted through his brain and chilled his heart ;—his absence might be eternal,—he might never again be allowed to see his brother ! The fearful unknown had thus, perhaps, betrayed his unwary footsteps from the habitable side of the ruin, for the most insidious purposes, —perhaps that of murder !

At this very moment he might be in the hands of his early secret enemy, and thus beguiled from all human aid or chance of rescue, be at length slain ; whilst his brother, thus treacherously robbed of his only protector, would fall an easy victim to their destroyer's relentless fury.

He had no sword, nor any other weapon with which to defend himself in case of treachery. Cold drops of perspiration bedewed his forehead ; his limbs trembled beneath their own weight, and every gloomy circumstance tended to confirm his wildest apprehensions.

Angus was often obliged to hold the lamp towards the floor to enable him to discover a safe footing ; and more than once he started from the ghastly objects that he fancied were presented to his view. He was almost certain that he had twice beheld the outstretched forms of three or four dead bodies, but his light was too dim to enable him to satisfy himself ; and perhaps the wild disorder of his mind might have embodied these horrible creations. Alarmed, he determined on instant flight, let the hazard be ever so fearful ; but the mysterious stranger seemed to know his thoughts, and with outstretched arm arrested his intention, and forbade his departure. Again Angus found himself powerless, and compelled to follow the footsteps of his unknown guide.

At length he was conducted down a high descent of mouldering steps, which, when traversed, led to a long, damp, narrow passage, at the extremity of which was a door, which opening, Angus followed the gliding form of his conductor into a small vaulted chamber. The unknown then approached the steep brink of another flight of steps, and beckoning to Angus, motioned for him to descend. But the youth, unable any longer to repress his feelings as he cast an affrighted glance down the dark abyss, refused to proceed.

"I will advance no further," he said, firmly. "Confess freely for what unrevealed motive I have been betrayed to a place so solitary, that I even suspect your design is to put me to death."

"Death!" echoed a sepulchral voice, and every limb of the youth trembled as his ear caught the terrible response. Again he raised his sight towards the grim form before him; its lips were motionless, and though Angus had distinctly heard the reply, the unknown seemed not to have made it. A groan, however, escaped its lips as in an awe-inspiring voice it exclaimed,—

"The spirit of the dead now calls upon the offspring of Glenalvon for vengeance!"

The long flowing robe of the mysterious form fell slowly off, and displayed the dim outline of the figure of a man clothed in the cerements of the dead, whilst in its left breast was beheld a rusted poniard, almost buried to the hilt. Wild pangs and agonies of torment, like those of an expiring person struggling in the last gasp of death, now evidently writhed the pallid visage of the awful form. Its right hand was applied to the dagger, and then it essayed, but in vain, to draw it from its bosom, whilst at every effort fresh streams of blood seemed to trickle from the wound. A flaming brand of lambent light was held in the other hand, the brightness of which revealed completely the former obscured horrors of the scene. The grief of Angus was extreme, for he now felt assured that he beheld the shade of his murdered sire.

Low, dismal groans of suffering torment echoed through the vaulted chamber, and harrowed up the soul of the fear-inspired youth.

"Seest thou these wounds?" exclaimed the spectre. "Look on this pale countenance, and say, shall Glenalvon bleed for ever unavenged?"

"Merciful Heaven!" cried Angus, "it is my father's awful voice that speaks! For ever let me kneel till I have paid the solemn duties of a son. Most injured form, hear me, and deign to instruct me in the performance of thy dread mandates! Say, what must I do—how mitigate thy wrongs and appease thy unquiet wanderings?"

"Swear to revenge my murder!" exclaimed the spectre, in a tone of fearful solemnity.

"I swear by every tie, both human and divine," answered Angus—"by Heaven's eternal justice—by the the lightnings of its dread vengeance—and lastly, by thyself, to perform whatever thou mayest command."

Angus, when convinced by the sudden disappearance of the outward garment of the mysterious figure that he no longer had any danger to apprehend, ceased to regard it with horror. His soul had been oppressed with dismay at the agonising sufferings he had beheld, and he was rushing forward to snatch the deadly weapon from the bosom of the spectre, but the latter mournfully waved its hand, and silently forbade the nearer approach of the youth, and then, after an interval, said,—

"From the depth of death's unfathomable region thy father's spirit is again permitted to revisit the scenes of his former earthly joys and final sufferings. I call upon thee for revenge—wilt thou obey me?"

"I will."

"Thou wilt revenge mine and thy mother's murder!" again exclaimed the spectre. "The hour of retribution is at hand—be its deed prosperous! Helen's spirit sends a blessing on her sons, and bids them haste to appease her wandering spirit! Beneath yon vaults lie concealed the living testimonies and the buried treasures of Glenalvon. I dare reveal no more, but seek them ere the deadly foe to thy existence discovers their hidden recess!"

"Heavenly powers!" ejaculated the amazed and afflicted Angus. "I am, then, beneath the ruined towers of my ancestors; and here—oh, here, my injured parents breathed their last—in this castle they were murdered!"

"Here, even here," answered the spectre, with a groan; "and bitter, also, do our unappeased spirits wander throughout the midnight hour. But our wrongs shall cease, for thou wilt not for ever let our fall remain unatoned! Be it thine to avenge thy parents' sufferings on earth, and to dismiss their spirits to realms of everlasting happiness and peace!"

The spectre moved towards the brink of the gloomy precipice, and then, casting on Angus a last impressive melancholy glance, it murmured,—

"Farewell!—fail not to redress my wrongs!"

"Stay—yet a moment deign to pause ere you depart!" cried Angus, imploringly. "Oh! shade of my father, by every tender conjuration—by all that once was dear to thee on earth, and blissful in the world unknown, I solemnly entreat thee to stay and unfold the accused destroyer of thy life—the base monster that so long has triumphed in his secret crimes!"

"It must not be," replied the hollow voice of the spectre; "forbear, my son, to lift the veil that at present conceals the name of thine enemy. I must begone, for the morning air warns me to depart, and that my hour is past. Thou shouldst have followed me," added the spectre, pointing down the dark abyss; "but seek amidst those winding vaults the knowledge I am not permitted to reveal, and there shall thou find a living evidence. Slight not my words, for they are the solemn admonitions of thy destiny. Depart this fatal spot ere thy threatened destruction leaves not in being an arm to avenge the wrongs of the murdered! Remember well these cautions, for thine and thy brother's future welfare rests on them. Shouldst thou neglect my warnings, thou and my Edwin are lost for ever. Once more, farewell, and fail not to avenge me!"

The spectre began to fade. It raised its shrunk, gaunt form and arms in solemn appeal towards Heaven; then slowly drooping them over the prostrate Angus, its hollow, deadly eye seemed to speak a blessing on his head. It then again shrunk backward a few paces, and the youth in awe-struck silence continued to watch its gradual disappearance, till in an instant it vanished away, and not a vestige of it was to be seen.

All was now silence, and a lethargic stupor stole over the faculties of Angus Glenalvon. Neither the fearful horrors of the place, nor the dangers it evidently concealed, could withstand the irresistible desire to sleep that had seized upon him; his head rested upon his arm, and he lay for hours in a death-like stagnation of every sense and feeling.

A vision now presented itself before him, and he fancied himself still sleeping in the dreary chamber from which the spectre had withdrawn him. The most melodious strains of music suddenly filled the apartment, and entranced his soul with delight. He raised his eyes, and beheld at the foot of his bed a warrior, tall and majestic, gleaming in burnished armour, whose polished helmet sustained a waving plumage of feathers. A lady, beautiful beyond all earthly comparison, stood by the side of the warrior, clothed in robes of radiant whiteness, spotted all over with silver stars, whose sparkling lustre outshone the diamond brilliance, and crowned with a diadem of sapphire and emeralds. Between them stood another female, not so tall, but more exquisitely lovely and enchanting to the eye. There was not, however, the majesty of figure displayed in the latter, which so strongly characterized the form and aspect of the superior lady; but symmetry and grace, joined with an air of innocence and modesty, gave her an appearance even more thrillingly interesting. Her countenance, though full of more than mortal beauty, was pale, yet serene, though her eyes at times beamed forth mingled emotions of tenderness, joy, and alternate sorrow.

The younger female once lifted up her soft, expressive eyes, and bent them on Angus with a melting force that thrilled his very soul. She kneeled between the warrior and the lady, who each laying a hand upon her head, and stretching forth their other arm over the bed on which the brothers reposed, in the act of solemn benizon, the superior female thus exclaimed,—

"Bless ye, oh, my children! Helen's prayer in death ascended to the gates of mercy; unseen she shall still watch over and protect her offspring. The blood of the murdered, like holy incense, shall weigh heavy on the souls of their murderers; the deeds of the wicked shall be their secret tormentors, and conscience the avenger of their guilt. Thrice blessed live my children; be their lives secured from harm, and their days to come prosperous and happy! So prays continually their murdered mother."

"Blessed be ye, oh, children of Glenalvon!" exclaimed the warrior figure. "Awake, Angus—awake to the love of arms and the glories of a hero's fame. Redress the murdered, and hurl from his ill-gotten seat of power and greatness my blood-stained foe. Snatch from the usurper thy sire's arms of war; let them no longer hang ingloriously in the secret halls of his deadly destroyer. Be prosperous, if valorous—be happy, if courageous. Rush fearless to thy just revenge—appease the injured, and the restless spirit of thy sire shall then, and not till then, find that peace which the grave cannot give!"

The younger female then, in soft, melodious tones, exclaimed earnestly,—

"Depart, oh, Angus, from this threatening spot—the secret haunt of danger. The lurking foe of thy safety stalks through the halls of thy ruined house, impatient for his prey. He strides with fiendish joy, furious as the whirling blasts that bow the proud branches of the mountain forests, and strong in the evil design as when the tempest darkens and the furious storm rages. His unsheathed dagger thirsts for the blood of Glenalvon's sons, and the destruction of the last heroes of thy race. Hasten, Angus—hasten from the threatening dangers of Glenalvon, and from those of thy threatening foe!"

Suddenly a misty vapour obscured the sight of Angus; the music died away, and the mysterious forms were completely shrouded from his observation by the obscurity that had enveloped the objects of his vision, and for a time a heavy stupor seemed to paralyse him. At length, however, a piercing shriek of anguish again seemed to awaken him, and as he opened his eyes he beheld the daggers of armed men pointed towards his breast. But an unknown power, while it withheld their arms, seemed to have inspired him on the sudden with superhuman strength, for he wrestled with his foes, and, after a long conflict, subdued them. But ere he could congratulate himself upon his success, his eye fell on the bed, and he beheld his brother stretched upon it, strangled and lifeless. The blood now flowed from his wounds that he seemed to have had in his recent conflict, a deadly sickness fell upon his soul, and in all the agonies of horror he awoke from his fearful vision.

CHAPTER X.

"Who art thou
Whose wandering steps have traced me to this place?
Art thou of mortal form, or some poor sprite
That's doomed to wander on our earth?"   SEBASTION.

ANGUS hastily started from the cold, damp floor on which he had so long rested; his limbs trembled and sunk beneath him with excessive pain, and his blood seemed stagnant and chilled in his veins. Awhile he remained a statue of wonder and uncertainty, not knowing where he was, or recollecting by what strange and incomprehensible means he had been led thus astray from the chamber to which he and his brother had retired to repose.

A faint and almost indistinct streak of dawn light obscurely glimmered through an aperture, and with eagerness and curiosity he approached it; it seemed to penetrate from a deep cavity beneath the place where he was standing, for it proceeded up the brink of a winding stone staircase, and though Angus now began slowly to recover from the stunning effect of his terrible thoughts, yet his memory of the past was too darkly confused to conduct him with certainty through the present extraordinary difficulties of his situation.

He was, however, well and fatally convinced that something horrible had occurred, but his impatience to regain his chamber suffered him not to pause on the gloomy foregoing events, and he therefore began mechanically to descend the broken causeway, for every vestige of any other outlet, as well as the empty void itself, was indistinguishable, and the lamp he had brought with him had expired during the period of his temporary forgetfulness.

Slowly he continued to wind down an immense depth of steps, now and then obscurely visible by a gleam of daylight, that broke occasionally through chinks in the walls, or rocky clefts of what was, doubtless, a subterranean pass; and for a length of time he continued to traverse through innumerable winding recesses, sometimes obscured in total darkness, or, at best, but dimly shown by the remote chasms in the rocky vault, through which the faint dawn struggled for admittance.

At last he began to ascend a staircase, up which he had not advanced many steps when he saw the reflection of a lamp glancing above him. Inspired with hope by this circumstance, he redoubled his speed to reach the summit, and presently he perceived a young female, who, in form and figure, bore a strong resemblance to Isabel. Rejoiced at a meeting so unexpected, he called upon her to stay, but she was startled at the sound of his voice, and instantly extinguishing the lamp she bore in her hand, she disappeared from his view. It was in vain he sought to follow her footsteps, for she had, doubtless, retreated from him in terror, and once more he found himself in the uncertainty from which he knew not how to relieve himself. He, therefore, descended once more to the subterranean vaults beneath, and pursued his way through them, till it was evident that they became much narrower, and even the faint light that had before served as a guide to his wandering footsteps began to die away.

The patience of Angus was now nearly exhausted, and fears of the most horrible nature took possession of his heart, for he now dreaded lest, wandering amidst these unknown and secret caverns of the earth, he should become at length the victim of a lingering and painful death; since, uncertain where he was, or of the means to free himself from his terrific situation, he might thus traverse, without a hope of rescue, these forlorn regions, and sink down at last exhausted and strengthless, a prey to that fate which he had been so anxious to avoid.

To call for help was in vain, since no human aid could be expected to inhabit a place so savage and desolate; to proceed might perhaps conduct him still further to his miserable doom; and to turn back would be equally dangerous, for, should he not choose the path he had already trodden, he might be equally a wanderer from every chance of relief or rescue.

While he thus paused to determine on his fate, amazement rivetted his senses for an instant, as a distant flash of light, proceeding from a lamp faintly gleaming afar off, pierced the murky horrors of the dark profound; and with wild, hasty steps, he pursued its direction, as, forgetful of all caution, he loudly called for assistance. As he advanced still nearer towards the brightening gleam, he was surprised to find the pass terminate in a low grated open-

ing, which stood ajar upon its ponderous hinges, and gave him free admission to the interior of a circular cavern, which he entered with precipitation.

His voice echoed deeply through the spacious void, as he eagerly exclaimed :—

"If aught of human shape, and possessed of gentleness and pity, inhabits this gloomy place, come forth, and for the love of charity afford to the lost, bewildered Glenalvon the succour and relief he so greatly needs !"

"Glenalvon !" repeated a deep-toned sonorous voice. "Holy angels defend me ! Who is it speaks ? What form stalks this way in likeness of the dead, whose voice, breaking the solemn silence, echoes back sounds but too familiar to my memory ?"

At that moment a tall, venerable figure, whose silver locks and furrowed countenance betrayed the long lapse of many a passing year, issued forth from behind a projecting recess, from whence the rays of the light had darted on the wandering Angus their friendly guiding beams. He advanced with cautious steps towards the young man, upon beholding whom he started back, trembling and terror-struck.

"What wouldst thou, awful being?" he exclaimed, in accents of mingled horror and amazement. "Oft has thy shade, as now thou standest before me, disturbed my nightly slumbers. Reveal thy wish, and while the feeble lamp of life yet dimly burns within this withered trunk, faithful to thy commandant, my last drop of blood shall flow to obey thee. Speak, shade of the murdered Glenalvon, oh, speak !"

Wonder and amazement took possession of the soul of Angus, and it was some few seconds ere he could find words to answer to the words he had heard.

"I am Glenalvon," he at length said ;—"say, good old man, knowest thou my murdered sire?"

"Powers of mercy ! who and what art thou?" exclaimed the aged stranger,
No. 8

with strong emotion. "Say, art thou belonging to this earth, or has thy wandering shade burst from the poor, unhallowed grave which the labour of these hands afforded to thy mangled corse? Thou canst not be mortal, or, if indeed alive, thou art Glenalvon's son,—or else his wandering spirit. Speak, oh, speak, and relieve me of the terrible thoughts thy presence has conjured up."

"In me," answered Angus, "thou beholdest the living avenger of the dead Glenalvon. Whoe'er thou art, whose words proclaim thee well versed in the fearful mystery of my murdered sire's fate, if friendly to his memory, reveal, I charge thee, the hidden secret of his end! Teach me to know the name of his accursed destroyer; let the wronged Sons of Glenalvon and his Helen live to hurl theirs and their parents' deadly foe from his blood-stained seat of usurped greatness,—obey their father's awful mandates—appease their mother's piteous injuries, and live with honour unsullied, or die renowned and famed. Say, if thou canst, the fate of Glenalvon, for in me thou beholdest his rightful heir and avenger,—Angus, his eldest born."

"He lives!—he lives!" exclaimed the old man, joyously. "Glenalvon's illustrious son, I bend before thee this aged knee in reverence and duty. But most I bow in thankfulness, just Heaven, for this day's merciful manifestation of thy power. Merciful Providence, thy ways are indeed inscrutable, and with heartfelt gratitude do I pour forth my thanks for the preservation thou hast afforded to him I believed dead!"

The venerable stranger had, as he knelt, embraced the knees of Angus, who, taking him by the hand, gently assisted him to rise from the humble position he had assumed.

"Thou must not kneel to me, old man," he said, "for at present I am poor and unknown. My life has been miraculously spared, and never will I rest till I have executed the vengeance my father's wrongs demand."

"Tell me, thou living presentment of my once gallant lord," cried the bewildered stranger, "how thou hast so long contrived to escape the murderous steel of the assassin? Where hast thou been concealed during the long, wearisome years that have intervened since my eyes beheld thee, as I then feared, for the last time? Oh! deign to reveal the eventful story of thy preservation from death? Tell to thy father's faithful vassal the story of thy younger years, and the amazing adventures that have at length conducted thee to these deep hidden caverns, whose unfrequented recesses and dreary chambers no steps unhallowed have ever—save thrice—pressed their deserted paths. Oh, hasten to unfold the wonderful narration of thy wrongs and sufferings."

"First tell me," interrupted the youth, "wherefore you so earnestly urge me to proceed with my narration; for know, stranger, the spirit of my sire, at midnight, most fearfully led me into the vicinity of these vaults, and half revealed the secrets of its wrongs; whilst, ere it vanished, it pointed towards this direction, and bade me to seek here a living testimony of my wrongs. Say, who art thou, for danger's lurking wiles it also bade me fear. If thou wilt satisfy me in this respect, and it is still thy wish to know my history, I will no longer keep thee in suspense."

"Dost thou doubt me?" asked the old man.

"At present I know not whether thou art a friend or a foe," replied Angus; "and perhaps mine and my brother's safety may depend upon the caution which I use ere I reply to thy questions."

"Thy brother, sayest thou!" cried the old man, in tones that showed the deep emotion he felt. "Does he also live, and has Heaven indeed preserved the innocent Edwin from the perils with which he was threatened?"

"My brother lives," answered Angus; "and I have sworn ever to be his protector, even though my own life should fall a sacrifice to the love I bear him."

"Dear my lord, doubt not my truth, I implore you," said the old man.

"Ronald's love for the race of his once loved and honoured chief was never, till now, questioned." Then sighing deeply, he added, in a voice trembling with emotion,—"Alas! fidelity to their ruined cause long since has banished him from the world, and from those ties of kindred blood that yet may exist to bind him to an existence which ere long must terminate in the grave."

"Ronald!" exclaimed the youth with joyful surprise; "art thou, indeed, that good and faithful friend, of whom my foster-mother so oft, with tears, has spoken, mourning the cruel and untimely grave of a much loved and deeply regretted father?"

"I am Ronald," answered the old man; "and thou mayest have heard of me as being one that was supposed to have perished on that fatal night when thy parents perished, and their castle was given to the flames."

"This is, indeed, a joyful discovery," exclaimed Angus; "for our good Magdalen will find in thee a parent to bless and reward her virtuous deeds!"

"Merciful Heaven!" exclaimed the astonished old man, after a lengthened pause of uncertainty, whether what he saw and heard was real; "what new wonders does thine invisible agency unfold to me! Magdalen was, indeed, the name of my beloved daughter, and can it be possible that she has been the happy means of saving thee and thy brother from the dreadful fate to which thou wert doomed."

"She was," answered Angus, "and to her do we owe that maternal care which has reared us through the dangers in which we were involved. To her we owe our lives, and never can we forget the heavy debt of gratitude her generous conduct so well merits."

"Alas!" cried the old man, "was she not wedded to the vassal of thy house's foe? How then could the care of my daughter snatch the children of Glenalvon from the savage fury of her husband's chief?"

Angus threw himself into the arms of the old man, and having embraced him, he exclaimed—

"I know thee, old man, and am aware also of thy truth and love for the ancient race of Glenalvon. A thousand and a thousand times has Magdalen blessed thy name, and praised the unconquerable virtue of her much loved father; hear then at full the marvellous tale of our preservation, and bless, with Angus and his brother Edwin, their generous benefactress and guardian."

Angus then related, with as much brevity as he could, all that he knew or remembered of the past, from the first period of his entrance with Magdalen and his brother into the Highland Watch Tower to the present moment, and the awful and amazing means by which he had been thus conducted to the only living testimony in whom dwelt the power to make known what he was himself a stranger to, concerning the dark narrative of his parent's wrongs, together with his own unrevealed misfortunes.

As he concluded, Ronald again sunk on his knees in fervent gratitude to Heaven, but his feelings, for a brief space afterwards, deprived him of the power of utterance; at length, however, raising himself, he said, as he wiped away the tear of pity and regret that had been called forth by the sorrowful remembrance of past times :—

"Yes, thou art, indeed, the true illustrious offspring of my beloved lord. Accept, son of Glenalvon, the reverence and allegiance of thy faithful vassal. I will obey the awful command of thy hapless sire, and if Heaven's watchful justice deigns assistance to our meditated revenge, his spirit shall shortly be appeased by the destruction of his accursed foes."

"Thou wilt aid me, then, in a design that has so long occupied my soul?" said Angus.

"I will, my dear young lord," answered Ronald. "And now let us depart from here with what speed we can, for, aged and feeble though I am, the current of my blood has got a warm stream flowing, and my body shall drain its vessels to the last drop to pay my duty to my chieftain's sacred memory, and right the orphan's injured cause."

"And canst thou aid me in bringing retribution upon the foe that has robbed me of my just rights?" demanded the youth in a tone of eagerness.

"I can."

"And thou wilt direct me so that I may know to whom I owe the destruction that has compelled myself and my brother to conceal ourselves from his furious hate?"

"Thou mayest rely upon me as a faithful adherent to the fallen house of Glenalvon," answered the old man. "I had despaired of ever meeting with one of the noble family that I had so long and faithfully served, but since I have at length met with thee, I will devote the short remainder of my days to aid thee in the cause thou hast taken in hand. Let thine enemies tremble, therefore, for though they have hitherto triumphed in the wrongs they have perpetrated, yet the hour of vengeance is at hand, and they shall fall even in the midst of the fancied security they at present enjoy. But come, my lord, delay may cost us much, and your own safety requires that we should instantly take our departure from a place where your life is placed in so much danger."

"Whither wouldst thou lead me, old man?" inquired Angus, with an anxiety that he could not conceal.

"To the Watch Tower," answered Ronald, "once the safeguard of Glenalvon, let us with speed direct our steps, for in that fortress thou and thy brother Edwin will be secure from peril till the time arrives when we may boldly enter on our enterprise. There, once more, I shall clasp a virtuous daughter in my aged arms, and a father's benediction will repay her for the gentle deeds of mercy her generous heart has prompted her to perform."

"Thou art right, my good old friend," exclaimed the youth. "Magdalen deserves our warmest gratitude, and we must not delay a meeting which I feel assured will afford her so much rapture."

"And her testimony," resumed the old man, "will prove an indisputable voucher of your lawful rights, and I shall have lived long enough, should Heaven, in its mercy, permit me to behold the children of my much loved lord restored to their inheritance, and their names graced with the illustrious honours to which their birth entitles them."

Ronald then, in language whose softened expression in vain laboured to soften the horrors of his dark narrative, related the sad fate of his unfortunate lord and lady, together with a knowledge of the cause that had so many years enveloped in mystery the offspring of Glenalvon. And though he sought by every means in his power to assuage the terrors of his tragic tale, as much as truth would permit, yet often during the recital the blood forsook the cheeks of Angus,—broken exclamations of horror, grief, and swelling indignation, burst from his quivering lips; for every feeling in the breast of Angus was outraged, and at length, unable to hear the end of Ronald's narrative, he exclaimed, vehemently,—

"Inhuman fiend!—Hell could alone be inspirer of such monstrous enormities, and be that hell their avenger and their earthly scourge! Can it be possible that there lives on earth a savage so sanguinary and so relentless? Spirit of revenge, on thee I call!—Plant within my soul thine own terrible strength of retribution; nerve my sinews with thy more than human force, that with a blow I may annihilate the accursed villain that has done this deed of blood, and hurl to the bottomless pit of everlasting torment his black and crime-polluted soul! Chief of Badenoch, prepare thyself for that which is to follow, for the son of Glenalvon survives thy deadly malice, and yet lives, the stern avenger of his murdered sire! May the inward vulture of an upbraiding conscience prey on thy vitals, and fear's horrid agonies impress thy mind with all the horrors of a speedy vengeance on thy foul misdeeds, whose anticipating tortures, haunting thine accursed spirit, may become the goading punisher of thy guilt, and turn thy richest joys to curses! Savage and unnatural were thy deeds, and their punishment shall be like them—relentless! May thy perturbed midnight dreams reveal the knowledge of thy discovered crimes, and foretel the dreadful and certain doom that ere long is about to overwhelm thee!"

As he spoke, Angus hurried forward, impelled by the agonizing workings of his distracted mind, and the impatient desire for vengeance that filled his soul.

Ronald followed, but ere he had quitted the long dreary passage that led from the cavern, he paused suddenly, and kneeling beside a raised clod of earth, he seemed to be for some seconds deeply engaged in prayer.

The eye of Angus, as he half turned round, caught a sight of his bended attitude, and remembering that age claims privileges that youth needs not, he hastened to support the old man; for, as the excess of his mingled rage and grief began to subside into a deep, settled resolution of vengeance, he recollected that he had hurried away from Ronald ere his narrative of woe was ended.

The old man, as Angus approached him, was occupied in sad and mournful reflections.

"Come and kneel with me," he cried, with solemn earnestness, "and on this spot pay the last sad duty to those who rest beneath. To Heaven leave the justice of retribution, and fear not that the hour will soon or late arrive when all these wrongs shall be avenged, and when the triumph of guilt shall be crushed and humbled. Remember, my dear young master, that adversity is the lot of mortals, and he is most noble who can bear its evils with patient humility and unrepining submission. Do not, then, my son, displease Heaven with unavailing complaints, but await the allotted period of its decrees, and when it deigns to substitute thee its instrument of justice, it will be time for thee to rouse thyself for the vengeance thou dost seek."

As he finished speaking, Ronald pointed sorrowfully to the two hillocks of earth, raised beneath a hanging projection of rock, on the lower basement of which was distinguished, as the red glare of his lamp shone on its uncouth tablet, the following roughly hewn inscription:—

"Beneath this tomb rest the mortal remains of the murdered Earl of Glenalvon and his countess. May their immortal parts partake of the bliss of angels, and their spirits be translated to an eternity of peace. Their sufferings are past. To Heaven alone belongs the justice of their retribution, and the punish of their wrongs."

Angus fell prostrate and subdued before the sacred repository of the dead. His filial sorrow gushed forth in tears that it was impossible to restrain, and for a few moments he indulged in them without attemping to check their flow. Ronald did not attempt to interrupt the sacred emotions that had been thus called forth, but continued for a little while longer to gaze upon the sad scene before him. At length, however, with gentle words, he attempted to assuage the burst of grief which Angus had given way to, and withdrew him from a spot that must still remind him of his sorrows.

They now turned the broad jutting of the basement, and entering another rocky pass, the tombs of the once noble Earl of Glenalvon and the unfortunate Helen were no longer distinguishable. At the extremity was a small cavity, whose frightful chasm could only be faintly traced when the lamp threw on the blackened excavation a sombre and heavy shade.

"In this spot," said the faithful Ronald, "lies concealed under yon square of earth, an iron chest, removed hither by the labours of many a wearisome hour. In it are buried the immense treasures and riches of thine illustrious progenitors. The sanctuary of the castle, situated beneath the lower chambers of the western tower, where our chief generally slept, was for awhile secreted from the ruffian sacrilege of the spoiler, during which period I found means, when recovered from my wounds, to collect, at different times, all that was valuable to your house's honour and its future greatness. To this unfrequented place I securely consigned them, and now with joy deliver into the hands of its rightful inheritor, the guardian of his wealth."

Drawing from his leathern girdle a large key, and presenting it to Angus, he continued :—

"Take it, my lord, and when again the lofty towers of Glenalvon shall rise, majestic as the sun when it casts aside its shroud of blackened clouds, and proudly rear their ponderous battlements over the head of their noble heir, then shall this spot be remembered and revisited with gladness; for the labours of fidelity will not have toiled in vain, and the aged Ronald, now sinking fast to his silent tomb, will be sometimes regretted, and his memory held in that esteem which he so anxiously desires."

Angus pressed the hand of the old man fervently, and the tear of veneration and regard glistened in his eye. He would have disdained the acceptance of the key, but Ronald pleaded the uncertainty of his own life, and earnestly implored him to retain it in his own possession till the period arrived when he would be restored to the rights which had been so long withheld from him.

He then led Angus to a fragment of the ruin, and seating themselves upon it, he began to relate the horrors of the night on which the Earl of Glenalvon and his countess were murdered, and then proceeded to narrate his own subsequent adventures as follows :—

CHAPTER XI.

"Attend to me, young lord,
And thou shall learn the miseries and woe
That fell upon thy house in former days,
When thou wert but a child."

THE BORDER CHIEF.

"The dagger of the Chief of Badenoch had pierced my side, and I lay for hours in a death-like stupor. My chamber was the anteroom to the tower where my lord reposed, and which my duty, at the hazard of danger to myself, commanded me to guard ; but my cries, enfeebled by terror, were too weak to reach my lord, and ere I could rush to his presence and warn him of the coming danger, the blow of death, as I then thought, struck me to the ground, powerless and speechless. But the last words that died on my fleeting scenes were those of your mother, as she addressed a solemn prayer to Heaven for protection to her hapless children.

"Providence vouchsafed to foil the assassin's purpose, who wounded me, but did not effect his design, and at mid-day, faint, parched with thirst, and feverish, I awoke to a sense of the miseries that had befallen the house of Glenalvon. I was not so totally bereft of strength but I was able to bind up my wounds ; but that was all, for in attempting to move towards the inner room, I found I had not strength sufficient, but fell helpless on the floor, and nearly as reckless of life as I well knew I was of hope or assistance.

"As I lay powerless on the ground, the flames, which had destroyed several of the south-western chambers, flashed their horrid glare around me, and brightly gleamed through the windows. Exhausted, I sank back in a torpor that had again seized me, and I awoke not for some time, when I discovered the dreadful ruin that had been accomplished. Nature now demanded nourishment, and fortunately my chamber contained the means of satisfying my wants. With care I again dressed my wounds, and in a short time began to feel somewhat stronger, and was enabled to pace slowly my forlorn and desolate abode.

" The day, however, declined in heavy sorrow of heart, for my spirit shrunk back appalled from a view of the horrors it anticipated, and I had not courage to pass into the chamber of murder. No soul approached that in which I was now a prisoner, not an echo of human sound broke on its death-like stillness, yet, anxious to know if the castle was inhabited, I ventured to approach the outward entrance of my room. And now a scene was presented to my view inferior only to that which I remembered to have witnessed ere the wound had been inflicted upon me. The fire had penetrated the corridor, beyond the whole suite of the western angle, of which mine and my lord's were the last chambers, whilst the four exterior apartments, that opened through one another, were nearly gutted, and their empty spaces, black with the smoke that streamed through their roofless walls, assured me but too well of the ruin and desolation that had been left behind them by the ruffians.

" I afterwards discovered that the flames had been extinguished by the neighbouring cottagers ere they had reached the three last chambers of the western tower, and to which act I owed my preservation from death. But the grand staircase was destroyed, as was the gallery and anterooms that led to it, and to this circumstance I attributed the desertion of the remaining apartments, since there was no other known access but by the grand entrance, except by a secret pass which led to these vaults, but which was unknown to all the domestics of the castle except myself. It was, therefore, evident the castle had been wantonly destroyed to cover the dark deeds of the Chief of Badenoch from the discovery he had so much reason to dread.

" Nor could I doubt that the neighbouring peasantry had given implicit belief to their fears, which I found they had entertained, for as they were totally prevented from approaching the chamber of the earl, they easily gave credit to any reports that might be raised, and there was but too much reason to fear that all, even the children of Glenalvon, had perished amidst the flames, which had destroyed the greater part of the castle.

" It was not till the third day that I could summon sufficient courage to enter the dreadful scene of murder and outrage. Yet why should I dwell on the horrid sight my eyes beheld,—why wound your soul with the repetition of a scene that you but too well know ? All around was dark, silent, and desolate, and death, with all its fearful terrors, reigned within the fatal spot ! With infinite labour I penetrated the secret passage to this vault, but gaining a second corridor which led to the upper parts of the north angle of the castle, I once more found my way to a place that remained uninjured by the fire. It had, however, been plundered by the ruffians, except of a few scanty remnants which had been overlooked in their haste, or thought not worth the trouble of removing.

" With some of these however, I returned to my solitary chamber, and in the course of repeated visits, removed almost everything that I should be likely to want, for I had resolved not to quit the ruin till I had paid to the memory of my beloved master the last sorrowful tribute that faithful service can perform. Once more regaining my chamber, I retired to rest, resolving on the following day to accomplish the solemn duty I had imposed upon myself.

" The night was passed in fearful dreams, whose images of terror still dwell in my remembrance ; strange groans and cries of torture, bearing no earthly similitude, filled the air, and shrieks of piercing woe rung through the dismal chamber. The spirits of the murdered thrice called for ' vengeance !' and Glenalvon's noble form seemed to stand frowningly before me ; then, leading me to the spot where the riches of his house were concealed, he bade me guard it for his wronged unhappy sons, who still lived to reclaim their lawful birthright. Your mother next appeared before me, pale and careworn, and leading in her hands her helpless children. She spoke, and bade me snatch them from their murderer's grasp, and guard them from their deadly unrelenting enemy.

"Starting from these terrific visions, I fell upon my knees, calling on Heaven to witness my solemn vow, that I would still preserve my own existence to save, if they were yet alive, the innocent offspring of my chief from Badenoch's relentless poniard, and guard their fortunes from his anxious search. Strange indistinct forms seemed to flit before me as I knelt, and groans, awful and solemn, echoed dismally on the deep repose of the midnight hour. Sleepless I watched till the welcomed dawn chased away the horrors of the night, and then arose to execute my alotted task.

"Taking from a closet a plain suit of iron armour, and closing the vizor of the helmet, I passed down the secret vaults, and reaching the hidden grating of the caverns that opened outward towards the hills, found myself at mid-day once more at liberty, and at some distance from the dismantled towers of Glenalvon. The only pass that lay before me wound through a mountainous causeway, which lay still higher up towards the wooded summits. Slowly I bent my way in the direction of the demesnes of my late lord, but, alas! the spirit of enterprise was smothered in the breasts of his vassals, amongst whom reigned anarchy, confusion, and dread, mingled with a fierceness that I had never before beheld in them. The agents of Badenoch had compelled them to submit to the yoke, and the few who had dared to resist his power had either been banished entirely from the domain, or were obliged to submit to force.

"It was not till the return of darkness that I ventured back again to the melancholy castle, where, through the night, I employed myself in performing the sacred offices of the dead. To have revealed myself I knew would be of no avail. Glenalvon's vassals were powerless to avenge their murdered chief, for the spoiler had completely plundered the castle armoury of every defensive weapon, and though removed far from the scene of conflagration, had totally destroyed the interior. To have attempted, therefore, to stir up our clans to vengeance, was but to sacrifice them to their enemies.

"The brave warriors of our chief were but few when opposed to the numbers of the Chief of Badenoch, for, unfortunately, our lord's greatest forces remained at his castle of Clanalbin, from whence the earl had come to Glenalvon for the purpose of settling some feudal differences here, not dreaming that in Badenoch he should have to encounter a foe so treacherous and deadly. And let me here inform you, my dear young lord, that your title to the distant towers of Clanalbin is equal with your noble sire's; but, alas! the dreadful miseries that have so long scourged our unhappy land have robbed you of this inheritance; for the English monarch, soon after your father's death, seized it, and it is now a strong garrisoned fortress.

"But let me hasten to conclude my mournful narrative. The spies of the detested Chief of Badenoch were dispersed in every direction, and it was with much difficulty that I eluded their vigilance. Under such circumstances I forbore to disclose myself to our people, resolving to remain in my present obscurity till a more favourable opportunity should arrive.

"On the following day I bore the honoured remains of the ill-fated Glenalvon and his Helen to a secret tomb which I had prepared for their last resting-place. My voice was raised in prayer and solemn meditation over their lowly grave, as I yielded to their sad end a tear of faithful memory, and closed over them the earth that was for ever to hide them from my view.

"Unhappy, in myself, and reckless of my fate, I have sat for hours in bitter lamentation over the memory of the past; mourning the untimely destruction of all that had been dear to my affections, and unable to tear myself from the

sight of objects that reminded me of my miseries. Months rolled away, and yet my lingering steps refused to depart the ruined, but still loved haunt of happier days. Oft has my rest been broken by frightful dreams, and I have waked and found them realized. In my slumbers, the spirit of my fallen master was ever present, inciting me to seek his wronged children and avenge his fearful death.

"Noises, too, as if produced by human footsteps, frequently echoed through the empty chambers at night, at which period I found I was not the only living inmate of the castle, for on a night when I had wandered till a later hour than was my custom through the secret passes towards the north tower, voices harsh and angry were plainly to be heard. Listening, I soon distinguished that of the villain Fergus—he to whom, in my unsuspicious confidence, I had given my sister Magdalen, and his horrid words soon revealed to me his guilty designs, as the torch he bore flashed on his own and the pallid countenance of his base superior, together with that of Stephen (the son of my wife's first husband), and a few fierce desperadoes that accompanied their hardened leader, to search for any plunder that might have escaped them on their former visits.

"'Whither wilt thou lead me?' exclaimed the Chief of Badenoch, in trembling accents, that betrayed his guilty fears.

"'This vaulted descent, my lord,' replied Fergus, 'will, doubtless, conduct us to the subterraneous pass below, from whence, as ancient tradition reports, there is a private passage which opens on the chambers of the inner western tower. They cannot all be consumed, and it is probable that there we may find the objects which have so long eluded our search. It is amidst these secret recesses that we can alone hope to gain entrance to the repository of the riches once owned by the dead Earl of Glenalvon.'

"They had not yet descended to the vaulted vestibule, behind one of

No. 9

whose deep shaded arcades I had concealed myself. The recollection of my dream now fearfully recalled my thoughts to the still remaining duties I had left unfulfilled, and I resolved to prove myself faithful to the sacred trust that had beeen committed to my charge. I grieved to find my secret retreat so near discovery, because it could no longer afford me the shelter I required; hastily retreating, however, I once more gained its seclusion, and entered the chamber where I well knew was secreted the treasure, and which I was determined still to guard; for my mind dwelt on the hope that even yet the offspring of my chief might have escaped the destruction that had swept away their parents, and live to claim hereafter their birth-right.

"These hopes were not ill-founded, for I remembered to have heard the cries of children on the fatal night, and their mangled forms remained not in the chamber with those of their murdered parents to confirm the certainty of their death. A secret impulse seemed to keep my mind constant to the hope it had formed, and I yet resolved, on this vague image of fancy, to guard the rights of their orphan children. Concealing myself behind the couch, I awaited the approach of the ruffian intruders.

"Fergus was the first to enter through the secret door, and his savage features legibly expressed a mind blood-thirsty and remorseless; his gait was undismayed—no pang of conscience shook his hardened heart, and he grinned horribly as he cast on the bed a dark glance of hardened scrutiny.

"I had thrown myself under the counterpane, and had raised the bed-clothes so as to deceive the villains into a belief that it still concealed the bodies of those who had been basely murdered.

"'All here, my lord, remains as when we last visited the spot,' whispered Fergus, who, in spite of his ferocious nature, felt an involuntary sensation that had the power to awe his hoarse-toned voice into the cautious whispering of conscious guilt. Again casting his eyes around, he continued, 'The place is secure enough from being discovered; no one has entered here since last our footsteps trod these floors, and doubtless we shall here find the object that we have hitherto searched for in vain.'

"'Wait below in the hall,' said the Chief of Badenoch to his attendants, as he passed through the private entrance. His countenance was ghastly and cadaverous, and the hesitation of his steps displayed the inward terrors of his unquiet spirit. He started back as his eye fell upon the couch where he had witnessed the death struggles of his hapless victims.

"'This is a blood-stained chamber!' he exclaimed, in low discordant tones. 'Helen, thou wert once the admiration of heroes! What art thou now?—food for—— Hark!' he exclaimed, in a voice of loud and startling terror,—'the dismal echoes of the grave resound! Shade of the murdered! dost thou answer to my call?'

"'How now!—what means my lord by these wild alarms?' demanded Fergus, who had been attracted to the spot by the cries of his chieftain.

"'Hark!—hark!' cried Badenoch, in a tone of startling terror. 'What was that noise?—heard you not a groan as if echoing from the grave?'

"Fergus paused, listened with apparent attention, and then, smiling sarcastically, replied,—

"'No, my lord; all around is still, and nothing is waking save the weak suggestions of mistaken terror. I prithee, my lord, rouse you from this weakness, for these starts of conscience might shame even an infant.'

"'I heard the cry of death!' cried the Chief of Badenoch, in low solemn tones, and totally regardless of the words that had just been uttered by his attendants. 'It groaned forth a knell of terror, and my chilled soul shrinks dismayed from the deeds of guilt that the sight of this chamber has brought freshly to my mind. See, see, the bed of foul murder nods and tumbles

beneath its burden, and the coverlid unfolds all its ghastly and awful secrets. Away! let us quit this scene of horrors, for to me it brings recollections that inflict upon my soul all the agonies of hell!'

"' 'Tis but the distempered heat of your own imagination, my lord,'
answered Fergus, ' that conjures up these wild, misshapen images of alarm.
Let me but raise the counterpane, and the unreal phantasies of your
thoughts will speedily vanish.'

"I trembled for my life," Ronald proceeded to say, "and the certain
destruction my temerity would bring on me, should I be discovered, for the
hardened, blood-thirsty Fergus approached still nearer to the bed, and with
a grin of malicious triumph cast towards his affrighted superior, seized the
corner of the counterpane, and was about to tear it from the couch, when
the Chief of Badenoch's voice of stifled guilt and vindictive rage exclaimed,
as he hurried towards the secret entry,—

" ' Forbear! Not for the empire of the world would I behold the blasting objects that lie concealed beneath that blood-stained pall. Follow me
instantly, and, for this night at least, we will forego the object that brought
us here.'

" He strode from the chamber as he spoke, and Fergus unwillingly followed him; but ere he quitted the place he cast around him a demoniac
scowl, as in low breathed tones, intended not for mortal hearing, he exclaimed,—

" ' Fool! I thank thee, and will return hither in secret, for thy coward
spirit merits not fortune's gifts, who favours only the bold. These hoards
shall then enrich the dauntless soul that dreads no fancied terrors, and
dares do all that may compel her stores to yield a golden harvest. Ye dead
inhabitants of this gloomy scene, awhile per force I quit ye; but when next
my footsteps tread this place they shall conduct me to my rich reward.
Till then, be ye the guardians of the treasure that shall soon be mine.'

" For some time," resumed Ronald, " I continued to watch the receding
footsteps of the intruders; but when the dawn of day returned, hastened
to disappoint effectually the threatened intentions which had been expressed
by Fergus. My efforts were successful, and in this secure recess I safely
placed the records and vast treasure of Earl Glenalvon beyond the plunderer's reach or discovery.

" Again they returned, but the chief of Badenoch's guilty terrers awed
him from his premiditated deeds of violence; and thrice he entered the
chamber of death, but each time fled from it, and seemed to be rendered
powerless by the secret stings of that upbraiding conscience which Heaven
implants in the minds of the wicked to be their earthly scourge and
punishment. Even the hardened Fergus felt alarm, and whilst his avarice
tempted him to search for hidden treasure, his failing courage no more suffered him to approach the bed, though he left no other part of the furniture
unexamined.

" Enraged at the disappointment, I caught his words as he quitted the
chamber and descended to his superior to relate his disappointed hopes.
At a distance I pursued their receding forms; they entered these vaults,
and commenced an equally unavailing scrutiny; but disappointed still, and
appalled by guilty horrors, they hastened from these threatening ruins,
completely baffled in their hopes of expected riches.

" My mind, after these harrassing events had subsided, sunk into a listless despondency. All that duty impelled, and grateful love willingly performed, had been done to satisfy the spirits whose gliding forms seemed
ever present to my view, and constant to the traces of my memory. My
single arm and feeble voice could not, alas! redress their wrongs; but my
mind seemed most tranquil and satisfied with itself when employed in the

daily task of visiting and mourning over the tombs of my lord and mistress, and lamenting, as if conscious the dead could hear my fruitless complaints, the disasters of their ruined house, and the solitary sadness of my own joyless existence.

"A year had slowly elapsed; much of the castle was yet standing, and many of its once rich trappings had escaped the plunder of the murderous invaders of our peace. I could not quit for ever scenes and objects long grown dear to my feelings, for the spirits of my lord and his lady seemed to forbid my departure, and demand the reverence I daily performed at their unhonoured grave. Now, however, necessity demanded a temporary absence, and beneath the disguise of a pilgrim's habit I often sallied forth, and, unknown to all I met, was thus able to procure for myself the means of subsistence, as well as learn the events that were passing in the world I had no wish to mingle with again.

"My daughter, Magdalen, had long since disappeared from Glenalvon; her absence was ever a mystery, and her husband, once the vassal of my lord, had treacherously sold his faith to the chief of Badenoch. Dreading to find her principles degraded to the level of her husband's baseness, I suffered years to elapse without inquiry, and thus fatally deprived myself of the tender regards of an affectionate daughter.

"This ruined castle I ever considered as my dearest home, though often for weeks and months together I have wandered to distant shrines in weary pilgrimage to pray for the repose of the spirits of the murdered, and beseech Heaven's guardianship over the injured heirs of Glenalvon, if they had been so fortunate as to escape the daggers of their merciless foes.

"At length, when five years had passed away, I once more determined to visit the scenes I still loved to think upon, and, favoured by my disguise, I approached the battlements of Badenoch's tower to learn, if possible, something of the fate of my long-lost child. With much difficulty I reached the gates, and made known my request, but the warder refused to admit me within the walls, and when I mentioned the purport of my visit, and asked for Magdalen, the ruffian bade me seek her in the grave, 'where,' he scoffingly added, 'she had long since been borne.'

"My child, then, was no more, and mourning over her fate, I turned my weary steps towards the spot which I knew contained those who, when in existence, I had loved with a devoted attachment, and where I meant to rest till life sunk into the last slumber, where alone I could look for peace. Forgotten, or rather no longer believed to be in existence, I from that moment devoted myself to meditation, and awaited calmly, but wishfully, the moment which would release me from my cares.

"Every trace of Ronald had long since been annihilated, or if a vestige of what I had once been yet remained, it was entirely concealed beneath the religious habit I had assumed. Under this disguise I found no opposition to my design, but was permitted, unmolested, to take up my abode in a deep cavern, which I had formed into a hermitage near the secret outlet of the subterranean pass which opened from the castle amidst the almost inaccessible steeps that everywhere surrounded it."

Ronald here brought his narrative to a conclusion, and Angus, who had hitherto been wrapt in the profoundest attention, threw his arms round the neck of the old man, and exclaimed with grateful warmth,—

"Oh, my excellent friend, how shall my tongue express the feelings that your words have inspired. To your faithful fidelity and love my murdered parents owe a grave, and their offspring are indebted for their lives."

Ronald would again have knelt, but the youth prevented his intention, exclaiming :—

"Never again shall thy aged form bend the knee to him who, but for thee and thine, had not now lived to bless thy gentle deeds of mercy. Henceforward thou shalt be as the guardian and preserver of Glenalvon's offspring, and equal with my own shall be the fortunes of thy peaceful days."

Angus then led the good old man from the cavern where they had been seated; but as his eye once more glanced towards the spot which contained his parents' tomb, his bosom heaved with convulsive throbs, and stepping once more towards the hallowed spot, he exclaimed,—

"Farewell, dear injured relics! awhile I leave you in your loneliness; but when next I revisit this darksome abode, these tears of burning indignation and revenge shall have shed on your foe all their fiercest rancour. Then, if I survive, I will return in solemn triumph and give thy poor remains an honourable sepulchre. Till then, spirits of Glenalvon and Helen, repose in peace!"

He then turned away, and accompanied by Ronald, quitted that part of the cavern.

CHAPTER XII.

"Virtue, the strength and beauty of the soul,
Is the best gift of Heaven; the only good
Man justly boasts of and can call his own." ARMSTRONG.

ACQUAINTED with every step he took, Ronald led the way through the windings of the subterranean passages, and soon afterwards they reached the vaulted chamber that opened on the foundations of this part of the fabric. Angus shuddered as the lamp half revealed the mystic objects of this dreary spot. But Ronald observed not his emotions, and still he continued to converse upon the subject that was uppermost in his thoughts.

"Of late," he said, "strange, unusual sounds have disturbed the stillness of this place, and I have even at times heard fearful shrieks and moans vibrate through the ruins. Fearful of discovery, I have confined myself to the caverns we have but just quitted, which open by a flight of steps upon the hermitage. Three nights since, I ventured through these passes — for I was anxious to discover who were the intruders—and abruptly turning a dark passage, I beheld the dark figure of a man, cased in armour, gliding cautiously before me through the ruined portal of yonder avenue.

"My eyesight was but dim, and at first I thought I must have been deceived; but resolving to be convinced, I followed quickly, and found it, indeed, no phantom, for though many years are past since I beheld any of the race of Badenoch, yet, if my memory has not failed me, this man most certainly belonged to them. Alas! my lord, this spot teems with treachery, and Glenalvon's towers will not, I fear, afford shelter or safety to their rightful owner."

Angus started, for he remembered the armed head that had, on the preceding night, appeared beside his bed.

"My father's spirit, Ronald," he said, "bade me shun this place. We will conduct Edwin again to the protection of our dear Magdalen, and our deeds shall, better than our words, declare the vengeance which it is our purpose to execute."

At length they reached the door of his own chamber, and with a bosom relieved of its worst fears, he beheld Edwin safe, though much alarmed at the absence of his brother. When told of the eventful discovery he had made, he fondly clasped the venerable Ronald in his arms, and exclaimed joyfully,—

"Ah, what a happy surprise will it be for our dear Magdalen. She will now pardon the rashness that prompted our departure, in the joy of its being the means of restoring to her a long-lost and lamented father."

Angus now remembered those who he had found inhabiting the castle, and related the extraordinary occurrence of his first arrival and reception. Ronald started up dismayed,—

"You are, then, discovered!" he exclaimed with alarm. "Those features, the exact counterpart of your murdered father, have betrayed you to the recognition of your foes, and, perhaps, it was the chief of Badenoch himself that aimed his sword at thy life! Oh, son of my dear master, pause not an instant, but let us fly hence ere a second blow, more deadly and effective, renders his vengeance complete."

Angus was, however, incredulous, nor could his unsuspecting nature harbour an injurious thought against the parent of the beauteous Isabel. The energy of his words declared the interest he took in their welfare, and he laboured to convince Ronald they were not enemies, but, like himself, fugitives from some powerful enemy. Anxious to dissipate every doubt the old man entertained, he now proposed that they should proceed to the outer chamber. Ronald acceded, and, taking the arm of Edwin, led the way towards the spot.

They then entered the apartment, which was now quite empty of the inhabitants they expected to find there. Upon the table still remained the repast which had been placed there on the over-night; the hearth was cold and cheerless, and all around bore a waste and desolate aspect. Ronald sighed over the melancholy change he witnessed, but forbore at present to give vent to the grief that oppressed him.

"This panel," he said, approaching the place he alluded to, "opens on a range of old chambers that were seldom used, even when the castle was in the height of its splendour. The grand entrance commences from the opposite of the northern wing, and is, I believe, still accessible by crossing the banquet hall below; but through this private pass we can with greater ease gain the whole suite beyond."

"Hold!" cried Angus, taking the old man by the hand; "the chambers you speak of are unknown to me, but are still, perhaps, inhabited; if so, they shall still remain sacred to the shelter and repose of the unfortunate. If Heaven should ever restore me to these possessions of my ancestors, the sanctuary of my roof shall never be withheld from the weary traveller, whose wrongs may drive him to seek beneath my walls that charitable aid it may be in my power to bestow. No—no, good Ronald, we will not, to gratify an ill-timed suspicion, intrude upon that privacy which the unhappy may require."

"Such were the generous sentiments of thy noble sire," cried Ronald, delighted at the words he had just heard; "and oh, may Heaven in its mercy shield thee from a fate such as that by which he fell!"

"We will descend," exclaimed Angus, "to the hall below, for my heart longs to trace the scenes of my infant memory, and recal once more, if yet their images survive the long lapse of departed time, the objects most familiar to me."

The young man gazed through the open casement; the sun had tipped the mountains with his morning splendours; their blue summits were dressed in smiles, whilst their lower portions, half veiled behind a soft mist that clothed their rugged outlines, were nearly concealed from observation. Not a cloud dimmed the sky, and the whole scene was well calculated to raise emotions of wonder and delight. For a time, the dismal horrors of the preceding night were almost forgotten, and as he quitted the chamber, he bent on the panel an anxious glance, for he had hoped once more to see the beauteous Isabel appear from the entrance it concealed.

The long passages from the northern chamber were again trodden by Angus, and as they moved onwards, Ronald accounted for their low and peculiar construction. These passes, it appeared, belonged formerly to the fortifications of the outer vallum, and were perforated, or rather excavated within the thickness of the walls, to give egress to the soldiery from the interior to the ramparts of the castle in times of sudden seige; and it was, therefore, evident that the rooms that they had now quitted were the last of the northern suite.

They now found themselves in the lofty extended area of the grand entrance hall, within which scarcely a ray of light was admitted, for the windows were built high under the eaves of the embattled roof, round which was carried a balustrade, that could only be approached from the middle by a flight of winding stairs; so that while the upper part of this immense hall shone brightly, all the lower vaulted aisles were half buried in a misty obscurity, that gave to each object below a deep and sombre shade.

The roof towards the western end was terribly injured, and yet retained the ruinous marks of the fire which had nearly destroyed the whole of the chambers beyond; large cavities were open to the sky, and the damps which were thus admitted had gradually decayed the costly fretwork of the rafters. Angus paused as he rested himself upon a high raised chair, placed beneath the colossal arch of some gigantic pillars which supported the roof. Fancy was aroused, and memory led back his thoughts to the distant period when last his eyes beheld this the ancient hall of his ancestors. He still had some faint and contused recollections, and in spite of the desolation and ruin that every where encountered his view, the obscure dawnings of objects once familiar with his younger habits and ideas flashed like the rapid changes of an uncertain dream upon his bewildered mind. His heart was softened with the recollections that chased each other through his mind, and a tear of fond regret bedewed his eyes as he affectionately pointed out to his brother Edwin each awakening circumstance, which, thus recalled, grew into certainty, and the youthful Angus knew, and was convinced that he had indeed passed the period of his childhood beneath this very roof.

"In this spot," he continued, "I have often gambolled in happier and more blissful days. Yes, Ronald, thou wert that fond, indulgent companion, whose watchful care e'er attended my wayward sport, and guarded me from the dangers that my heedlessness would have involved me in. I now remember well each circumstance: above yon flight of marble steps once rested my father's high chair of state, and by his side my good mother used to sit, smiling on her buoyant Angus, and perhaps anticipating those days of joy and gladness, that, alas! have never been realized!"

"Ah, Angus!" sighed his brother, "how pleasing, how enviable must be the sensations these revived recollections bring along with them. To me, however, they are a stranger, for my utmost memory cannot stretch beyond the transactions that are connected with our residence in the Watch Tower."

His eyes gushed forth a shower of tears as he uttered these words, and upon recovering himself, he added:—

"Such happiness it is not mine to remember the parental kiss of affection that you have known; but my heart shares in your feelings, my dear brother, and I long to trace, from your recitals, those deeds of glory that once rendered the castle of Glenalvon so celebrated,"

The brothers, when torn by violence from this ancestral home by the minions of the chief of Badenoch, were, the eldest nearly eight, and Edwin not quite three years of age.

" But," continued Angus, " those happy hours are gone for ever.   A ruthless murderer broke down the fair promise of our father's greatness, and blasted the hope of his long continued happiness, sweeping, like the fury of the whirlwind, the very record of his name from the face of being, impiously fearless of that dreadful day when he will be called upon to account for his actions committed in this life.   No more shall the feasts of my father's halls resound with the triumph of the victories ; no more shall our mother's radiant eye beam on the faithful clans of her lord the smile of rich reward for their achievements in the cause of their country's freedom and honour.   Silent, desolate, and deserted are the towers of the race of heroes ;—the spear of Glenalvon is blunted and grown rusty, and his armour, perhaps, now protects the body of his deadly foe from that vengeance which his crimes so justly merit.   But say, good Ronald, did the plunderers seize upon the arms of my ill-fated parent ?   Shall not his son inherit the shield of his warlike progenitors, and wield the sword that has been so often drawn in behalf of his oppressed and suffering country ?"

"Thou shalt inherit the shield of thy noble father," answered Ronald, as his eyes glowed for a moment with the inspired fire of younger days of warlike exultation, " and to thy loins shall these hands, brave youth, gird the sword which was once thy father's."

" Thou hast preserved them, then ?"

" They lie concealed," resumed the old man, " within the inner chamber of the western tower ; no unhallowed touch has yet profound their unsullied brightness, and their illustrious inheritor will not stain with a slur of baseness or fear the valour of him who last wore them in defence of his country's rights."

" May thy words be prophetic, good old man," exclaimed Angus, with impetuous ardour.   " I will wear them nobly ; and when my limbs shall be embraced within the steel ribs of my murdered father's armour, they shall no more be unclasped till his wrongs and those of my hapless mother have been terribly avenged,—till I return a victor to these towers, or yield up my birthright in a death of renown and well earned glory !"

As Angus uttered this he rose from his seat, and they continued to traverse the lofty pillared aisles, anxiously observing on each fresh object that called for their attention and remark.   The western angle lay a heap of shapeless ruins on the pavement, and, as Ronald had said, the grand staircase was totally demolished, for not a vestige remained to declare that it had once been passable, whilst, through an open doorway, was presented a view of the blackened interior of the chambers beyond, now totally roofless, and divested even of the smallest remnant of their floors, and their open lower spaces displayed the melancholy ravages that had been occasioned by the fire on the night when the chief of Badenoch had made his horrible and fatal attack upon the castle of his unsuspecting victim.

Dwelling with the privilege of age on each little circumstance of the past and present moments, Ronald pointed out the still remaining emblems of Glenalvon's former greatness.   At length, he led the brothers from the hall along a winding passage that led to the folding-doors of a massive portal, when, taking from his vest a bunch of keys, he with much difficulty succeeded in opening the entrance.   After ascending a flight of broad stairs, and crossing a gallery, they found themselves in an ancient ante-chamber,

which opened on the whole suite of the eastern side. They then passed through them all, and found them crumbling and decaying beneath the all-destroying hand of time. These were terminated by another long, dreary gallery, which branched off at either end under heavy colonnades towards the western and opposite angles. Edwin was here attracted by several large full length portraits, which Ronald stopped before, for they were all of them former possessors of the castle. Angus, however, musing upon his own sad thoughts, had traversed, unobserved, the full length of the corridor.

Rivetted to the spot, Edwin continued to gaze upon the portraits of his parents which Ronald had pointed out.

"Ah!" he exclaimed, eyeing the martial figure of his father; "how like to Angus! Oh, could I but behold my brother in armour, I should think that figure animated, and expect to behold Angus stepping from its panel!"

"It is indeed the almost breathing image of your brother," answered the old man, "nor is its likeness to my Lord Angus less than are your features to the once happy Helen. Let us, however, depart, for the sight of these sad memorials are afflicting to my memory."

Edwin had turned round to make a remark to his brother, but Angus had quitted the gallery, and the distant echoing of a closing door revealed the track by which he had disappeared, so that they had no difficulty in choosing the direction they should next take.

The pensive meditations of Angus had so entirely abstracted his attention, that he had quitted the gallery unconscious that he had left his companions behind. He had passed through a vestibule, and was following its darksome windings, when sounds of human voices startled him, for they seemed like the tones of command addressed to one who answered them with prayers and entreaties.

No 10

Astonished, but not dismayed, he undauntedly advanced towards a low door, which he passed through, and found himself in a gloomy, spacious chamber. Opposite to the portal by which he had entered he beheld another, which stood ajar, and gave him a slight view of the object beyond; the sounds he had heard were now more audible, and evidently proceeded from the farthest chamber, in which he plainly distinguished the drapery of a female's dress, and looking still closer, he recognized the lovely form of Isabel, before whom stood the almost gigantic form of a man, cased in heavy armour, and his helmet drawn closely over his visage. Angus was about to rush forward, when he heard the man exclaim :—

"All hope of aid is now in vain; you know my purposes, Isabel, and, for your own security, must comply with them. Mackenzie's proud lord is powerless to oppose my wishes, or resent the fancied injuries of his beau- teous daughter; for his treasons to the English monarch have banished him from Scotland, and another now holds the princely revenues of his forfeited lands. Not only his liberty, but his very life is at my mercy, and a word from me can in a moment utterly destroy him. Beware, then, lady, how you insult my offered terms by a refusal, lest you arouse my soul to revenge and deadly hate. Either consent to quit this spot with me ere your father returns, or this night shall behold him the victim of your ob- duracy."

When Angus was convinced that it was Isabel who stood before him, he was eagerly rushing to her presence, but surprise rivetted him to the spot as he listened to the words which had just been uttered. Again he would have advanced, but the voice of Isabel once more arrested his purpose.

"Traitor!" she indignantly exclaimed, "knowest thou no reverence for my birth and sex? Hast thou dared presume to imagine that the Princess Isabel, and the daughter of thy sovereign's sister, will bend from her high- born station, and stoop to the offered indignity of one like thee? Begone from my presence! hence!—nor dare to hope, though now beset by mis- fortunes, that my soul will ever acknowledge a traitor's power. Remember, too, that my father has yet means to punish thee for thy baseness."

"Proud girl!" retorted the other; "long ere thy father reaches these deserted ruins, the crisis will be accomplished, and Isabel far beyond his search. Aye, tremble, for thou art in my power, past hope of rescue, or the means to save thee from my determined purpose. The intruders have already quitted these towers,—no succour can now reach thee, and for the reward of my bold achievement, the English monarch, whom I now serve, will take care of my safety, since the usurping Bruce no more shall grasp the sceptre of Scotland, or tyrannize over its resolved opposers. My arts have proved successful,—alone, deserted, and bereft of every human aid, I will now make thee mine in spite of every obstacle."

The villain grasped the princess in his hold, and her desparing shriek resounded through the dreary chambers of the castle. At that moment Angus, who by that time had been joined by Edwin and Ronald, rushed into the apartment. The ruffian suddenly drew over his face the vizor of his helmet as his eye caught an instant glance of his unexpected antagonist : and ere the blow which Angus aimed could reach him, he quitted his almost fainting victim, and in an instant disappeared. Angus would have followed him, but Ronald's timely interference saved him from dangers of, perhaps, a fatal consequence.

The Lady Isabel had fallen to the floor, when Angus, convinced by the old man's words, desisted, and beholding the situation of the hapless girl, he hastened to support her. At that moment a sound was heard at the opposite door, and the majestic figure of her father hastily entered. Isabel soon after revived under the care of her father, who, however, not without astonishment and a frown of displeasure, had beheld the extraordinary scene. The princess, for such, indeed, her own words had bespoke her, hastened to explain its meaning, and to acknowledge the timely aid of her youthful preserver ; whilst Ronald, with eager inquiring glances bent on the features of her father, exclaimed :—

" If thou art, as this lady's words proclaim thee, her sire, and Lord of Mackenzie's princely territory, Helen Glenalvon's offspring shall, in their uncle, find a noble and illustrious avenger."

" Helen !—my sister !" exclaimed the old man with sudden emotion. " Alas ! these ruined towers bear witness of her melancholy fate, and that of her unfortunate children."

" Unfortunate indeed, my lord, but not for ever lost," cried Ronald ; " for in these thou dost behold Glenalvon's heirs—thy murdered sister's sons !"

Ronald now led the astonished Angus and Edwin to the equally amazed uncle.

" Heaven," he exclaimed, " has deigned to snatch them from the daggers of the assassins, and in Mackenzie's care they may yet find a friend and protector."

" Yes," cried the other, as the youths kneeled before him, " my sister's features are indeed stamped here. Isabel, my child, in thy preserver embrace the son of my much lamented Helen. But, say," he added, addressing himself to Angus, " how wert thou saved from the ruin which involved in death their injured parents, and why so long hast thou lived in obscurity as to be strangers to thy birthright ? From you," turning to Ronald, " I expect an answer, for you, it seems, have hitherto been their guardian. Speak ; if these be the sons of Glenalvon, why have you not sought till now an avenger ?"

" If it please you, my lord," answered Ronald, " to retire to the outer chamber, I will unfold the wondrous tale of their deliverance from death !"

Walter Campbell, or Mackenzie, as we may now call him, attended by the princess, and followed by the brothers and their faithful companion, proceeded to the chamber that had been named. Ronald then commenced his narrative, and ceased not till he had closely substantiated every proof of the birth and claims of the much injured orphans, and banished from the mind of Lord Mackenzie every doubt he might have entertained. As the old man concluded, their noble relative pressed them to his bosom, saying :—

" Alas ! my sons, wayward is the evil tide of that fortune which forbids us to revive the long concealed ties between us, and we have now only met to part almost as soon as chance has thrown us together. Beset by dangers, and flying ourselves from the cruel search of tyranny and injustice, I am powerless to avenge thy wrongs, and tremble every moment at the further woes that may attend us even here. The late outrage offered to my child has alarmed my worst fears, but each moment I expect assistance to lead her from hence. Time, however, presses, and I cannot now explain the seeming mystery of my actions ; hereafter, you shall learn all, and when assured of my Isabel's safety, my mind will have recovered itself ; I shall then be enabled to pursue the only means that can effectually unmask the deep concealed treachery of your foe. But hark ! I hear the signal for our departure."

At that moment the blast of a bugle sounded beneath the outward walls of the castle, and after a brief pause, Lord Mackenzie continued :—

" We must now begone, but we part not, I trust, for ever. Early on to-morrow's dawn, expect me, for I will return as soon as I have placed the princess beneath the strong tower of Dunbrae, where, guarded by its venerable earl, (mine and thy mother's uncle,) she will, I doubt not, be safe for a time from the lawless violence of the times, and from the intrusion of private baseness. Await, then, my arrival here, and together we will seek for Scotland's noble heir. the kingly Bruce. His generous soul, I know, will feel the wrongs of Glenalvon's heirs, and royally redress the injuries they have endured."

It was already dark when Isabel, led between her father and Angus, quitted the chamber, and in silent agitation descended to the hall below.

"Conceal the light," whispered Mackenzie, "or we may be discovered. And now, brave youth, awhile farewell; await my return, and be assured to find in me a friend not unmindful of the justice of your claims, and ever watchful for the moment when they shall be established in the ruin of your foes. Farewell,—at early dawn expect me."

Isabel's hand trembled in that of Angus, as he supported her through the hall and over the grass-grown pavement of the courts beyond.

"Adieu! dearest cousin," he whispered, falteringly; and, could I hope you will sometimes deign to remember me, the parting pang would find a solace in the sweet charm of such a blessing!"

"Believe me," she replied, with emotion, "the remembrance of our meeting will not be easily effaced from my mind; and when my prayers ascend to Heaven for the protection and safety of my dear father, they will also express my gratitude for him whose timely succour has this day saved me from the violence of a cruel foe."

Mackenzie now led his daughter towards some persons whose dark out-lines only were perceptible, for night had veiled each object, whose deepening shades disclosed not the silent tear of a princess, as, with a softly-uttered sigh, she bade farewell to Angus, who lingered at the lower port-cullis till long after the swift-flying steeds had borne their riders far away, and the earth no longer reverberated the echoes of their hoofs.

With a pensive step Angus slowly returned; and, closing, as well as their dilapidated state would permit, the great heavy gates of the hall, he drew across them a strong chain-bolt, and, sighing forth the name of Isabel, retraced his way towards the upper northern chamber.

CHAPTER XIII.

"There cannot be a pinch in death more sharp
Than this;—should we be taking leave as long
A term as yet we have to live,
The loathness to depart would grow."—SHAKSPERE.

THE last few hours had proved so varying and interesting, that another night had already far advanced, unmarked in its progress by either of the brothers or their companion, who still continued to converse on the occurrences and wonderful discoveries, till at length Edwin, feeling weary, declared the lateness of the waning night. To quit the castle at so late an hour was impossible, even if a nearer interest had not demanded their sojourn; and as nothing alarming, since the preceding events had disturbed them, Ronald's fears of danger died away, and he assented to the delayed departure.

They had been conversing on the wonderful means which had, at a moment so unexpected, and in a place so remote, revealed to them the only living relative that survived the ruin of their parents; and while Angus paused to listen to the imperfect account the old man was able to give, the latter was, equally with his young lord, a stranger to the misfortunes which had thus driven the brother-in-law of Scotland's king, and his daughter, to a place so desolate. Ronald often paused in the midst of his narration, and more than once thought he beheld the shape of a human countenance appear in the distant shaded angle of the chamber; but when again he cast back his anxious glances, he saw nothing, and was compelled to own that these suggestions were but the images of his own imagination, which was too ready to take alarm upon the slightest occasion; for his heart was bound up in the safety of the sons of Glenalvon, and he now shrunk from the evils that might befal them, and thus magnified dangers that never might occur.

Angus had, unknown to his brother, declared that as he must spend one more night in the ruined castle, he was determined to visit the chamber in which his parents had met their terrible fate. At length Edwin rose, and retired to the sleeping-room; and, when it was imagined that he was fast locked in slumber, the old man led Angus to the secret passages that conducted to the private entrance of the western tower.

At length Ronald paused at a door that led to another flight of stairs which yet remained to be ascended. He fixed his eye mournfully on Angus, as in an agitated tone he said,—

"The scene above is desolate and terrific, for it will forcibly recal to your memory the woes it has witnessed. To me it is familiar; but of late my soul sickens when I enter it, for the guilty deed seems renewed, and I feel all the horrors of the past fresh as when they were first perpetrated. Let me entreat you, therefore, my dear lord, to forego the melancholy task till daybreak, or suffer me alone to enter, and bring from thence those accoutrements you are so anxious to possess."

"And wherefore, good old man, should I impose upon thee a task which must indeed be afflicting to encounter?" demanded Agnes. "Or why dread from me the want of that firmness which the enterprise demands?"

"No," he added undauntedly. "I will act as becomes the sons of Glenalvon, nor shame, with the weakness of fear, the noble race from whence I proudly date my being. That my father's shade, if yet it hovers round me, may well regard my deeds, is my dearest hope, and I will therefore pass on; but do you, Ronald, await my return here, fearless of danger to myself."

Angus had ascended the opposite stair; and Ronald, disdaining the weakness of his first fears, followed. The former reached the top of a narrow flight, and his further progress was arrested by a blackened wainscot. He struck upon its panel, whose noise reechoed internally a hollow sound. Ronald's accustomed touch soon removed the obstacle, and they were quickly within the gloomy interior of the dreadful chamber.

Awhile, in speechless horror, Angus gazed around; a sacred awe seemed to hang on each solemn object, and the feelings of both were silently impressed with its involuntary impulse. Ronald spoke not, for his suppressed grief choked all utterance; whilst the active fancy of Angus pourtrayed to his mental vision the dark and horrific transactions of this fatal spot, in all their harrowing forms, heightened and rendered more keen by those which his imagination conjured up.

Ronald endeavoured, by every means in his power, to soothe his agonized spirit; and Angus, struggling with the violence of his sorrow, and the strongly aroused indignation of his feelings, assumed an outward appearance of returning composure.

"These," he said, "are the last tears of weakness which sorrow for the injured dead shall wring from me. Chief of Badenoch, grim demon of darkness! tremble at the justice of my burning rage, and the shortness of thine own base triumphs! No ineffectual curse is it which my soul now breathes on thy foul misdeeds. Here, in the spot of thy savage butchery, I swear to live but to avenge thy crime, and dedicate my future being to this, my solemn oath. And you, ye injured spirits, if yet ye wander invisibly in air, receive the firm, unalterable assurance of your son's obedience to your awful mandates."

"It is enough, my lord," exclaimed Ronald, as he raised him from the prostrate position into which he had cast himself. "It is enough," he added—"To Heaven leave the rest ; and now let us obtain the objects of our search, and retire from these dismal scenes at once, for the morning will dawn ere we have accomplished our errand."

The old man now led Angus towards an opposite door, which opened on a small oratory, beyond which was a similar sized apartment, where still remained the armour and warlike accoutrements of the once heroic Lord of Glenalvon.

The reverential attention of Ronald was here apparent, for his zealous care had still preserved the polished mail free from rust or dimness ; and as the light flashed on its glittering bosses, they returned a sparkling beam of brightness that dazzled the eyes of Angus. He approached the lofty pedestal on which the armour rested ; every part remained entire,—the spear raised its sharp and glittering point, and supported the casque, whose armorial crest sustained a waving plume of sable feathers. Each portion was carefully preserved, each screw affixed and free from the effects of long disuse, unspotted by a single stain, save those which declared the prowess of him who had last worn it. The shield leant against the basement of the pedestal, and shone conspicuously. The eye of Angus brightened as he raised it to his hand.

"Prophetic duty !" mournfully ejaculated Ronald ; "thy work is at length achieved ; once more these aged hands shall help to clasp on the arm of my beloved lord, and in his exact image I shall fancy Glenalvon still survives and breathes ! Yes, the secret hope which for years has possessed my mind, is realized. Oh ! may no adverse chance destroy my dearest wishes, and when again this armour shall be laid aside, let me but have lived to behold my chieftain's sons restored to their rights, and all my prayers will then be gratified. Ah ! well do I remember the night when these arms were last worn ; the brave Glenalvon had returned victorious from the raging battle's heat, and Badenoch's hosts had felt the vigour of his deeds of war. The proud invader, under the sanction of the usurping Edward, had received the merited chastisement of his hostile attack on this castle, which had never yielded, had not treachery betrayed its gallant defenders, at the silent, unguarded hour of midnight."

The tears of sorrowing memory flowed down the aged face of the venerable Ronald, as he thus talked over past scenes, while he slowly encased the limbs of Angus in the iron mail. The heart of the latter bled at the recollections which were thus called up, yet he suppressed his feelings, for his thoughts were now centred in the one object that occupied his mind.

At length he was completely encased in armour, and when Ronald placed on his head the plumed helmet, he stepped back a few paces, and fondly exclaimed,—

"Ah ! thou art indeed Glenalvon's image ; such was his manly look, his martial air, and tall majestic height ! Let my eyes once more gaze thus delighted on thee, for as I behold thee now, so once was thy sire ; and to me the past twelve years seem but as a day."

Angus grasped the ponderous spear of his father, and giving to Ronald the helm, led the way from the chamber with sensations of a nature too tumultuous to be described. Passing into the interior apartment, he cast on each surrounding object a woful glance, and with his faithful follower quitted the room, impressed with a sadness which forbade the relief of consolation.

Again they descended the stairs, and after a considerable lapse of time, found themselves, without any new occurrence, in the northern chamber. At the entreaty of Ronald, the youthful warrior then consented to take a brief repose, and as the old man threw himself upon a couch in this apartment, Angus took the lamp and proceeded to his brother's room; but as he incautiously unclosed the door, a strong current of wind instanly extinguished the light, and left him involved in total darkness.

The spirits of Angus were depressed, and his senses weighed down with melancholy, for the occurrence of the last two or three hours hung heavily upon his mind, and he felt a depression that it was not easy to conquer. To return was useless, for the fire had been some time out, and Ronald he knew had no light; it was therefore impossible to revive his lamp.

As thus he groped towards the bed, a low noise faintly sounded through the chamber; startled at this, he drew his sword and stood defensively, awaiting a danger of he knew not what nature; the noise, whatever it proceeded from, grew fainter, and soon afterwards totally died away. He spoke to Edwin, but received no answer, and fearful of disturbing his slumber, he approached the bed with caution, resolved to refresh himself with sleep, since it was now impossible for him, without a light, to visit any other part of the castle. Unwilling to disturb his brother, he threw himself quietly on the side of the bed, and soon fell into a heavy slumber.

But again his sleeping fancy wildly ranged in the fearful mysteries that had before disturbed him, and in imagination the spirits of his parents passed slowly and mournfully by. Their countenances were wan, and as they raised on him their eyes, glances of anger, sorrow, and reproach were flashed upon him. The heart of Angus failed him, but hastily pursuing their forms, and kneeling before them, demanded why they were thus displeased with him.

Glenalvon then stretched forth his bloodless arm towards the suit of mail that seemed still suspended on the pedestal; it instantly fell to the floor with a heavy crash, and vanished from the sight!

"It is the omen of thy destiny," exclaimed Glenalvon, in hollow tones of anger. "Thou hast disregarded my solemn warnings, and misery awaits thee! Mourn, Helen, over the fall of thy sons; Edwin is lost, and Angus shall bleed. Mourn, son of Helen, for thou hast slighted the warning voice of death, and fate malignantly smiles and triumphs in her victory!"

The spirits slowly vanished into air, and Angus started from his sleep, but still terrific recollections floated on his thoughts, whilst their connections with the appalling objects he had beheld the previous night somewhat alarmed him, and he started from the couch, resolved that not another hour should elapse ere he quitted these scenes of threatening danger and mystery.

Impatient to be gone, he drew aside the curtain, and to his horror and dismay, discovered that Edwin was not there! He then remembered the words of the spectre as they audibly sounded in his dream—"Edwin is lost!"

"Edwin! Edwin! speak to me!" he loudly cried as he searched round the apartment; but his brother neither replied nor appeared, and all the most terrific forebodings of Angus seemed to be fearfully realized. "Perhaps he is in the next chamber," thought he, and soon his footsteps reached the interior, but only the still sleeping Ronald was there, and again every dreadful fear became painfully confirmed.

Starting in affright from his deep and calm repose, Ronald awoke, and learnt with horror the dreadful circumstance.

"My worst fears are then confirmed," he exclaimed. "Badenoch's emissaries have discovered that Glenalvon's sons still live, and even now, perhaps, they surround this castle. Ah, fly, fly, unhappy youth, ere yet thou art sacrificed to thy foe's relentless fury!"

"Never," groaned forth the tortured Angus; "I will not quit this spot till my brother's fate is revealed."

"Be calm, and despair not," cried Ronald; "Edwin may yet,—nay, I doubt not,—still lives; for in his death alone Badenoch's fears are unallayed. If, then, you would preserve the life of your brother, be careful of your own. Be patient, and await the lapse of time, which alone can unravel the clue of his mysterious absence."

To satisfy Angus, the old may led him through every part of the castle, but the day was passed in a useless search. It then became certain that Edwin had been taken away during the absence of his brother, and not a doubt remained by whose agency. Ronald well knew the fierce bands of the Chief of Badenoch resorted thither, and to their agency the deed could only be ascribed.

Hopeless, and nearly distracted with the fruitless search, Angus sunk down, and the voice of Roland for a time ineffectually essayed to convince him of the absolute necessity for immediately quitting the castle. Angus was deaf to his entreaties, for the most gloomy feelings of despair pervaded his mind, and he could at that moment have welcomed death. At length the old man suggested that they should return to the Watch Tower, where the counsels of Magdalen might direct their future proceedings, and yielding to the hope thus faintly excited, he rose and followed Ronald through the subterranean pass that led to the tower. At last the whole extent of the cavern was traversed, and they emerged once more to the light of day, and Angus, with a melancholy smile, again recognised the early scene of his past happiness.

Evening was setting in when they began to ascend the steep ascent that led towards the upper portal of the Watch Tower, which stood open, and Ronald's heart glowed with all a father's fondness as he thought how soon he should clasp his daughter in his arms.

They passed the lower court and entered the open vestibule, but its interior was silent and vacant, and now nearly obscured in darkness. Each object to Angus wore a saddened, melancholy aspect, reminding him that Edwin was not the companion of his return thither, but was, perhaps, already sacrificed to the precipitation of their flight from a secure home. The sighing of the breeze mourned sadly through the place as if in lamentation, and hurrying onwards, Angus called aloud on Magdalen, but no answer was returned to him.

Some few moments of suspense elapsed, but the echo of his cries died away, and all again was still.

"Let us ascend to the upper chamber," said the impatient Ronald; "she may be there, which accounts for her not having heard us."

They passed upwards; the first and second tier of chambers were all empty; but a track of blood stained the stairs, and awoke other fears in the breast of Angus, who alone had observed its appearance. Hastily he ascended to the upper story, and entered the well-known chamber of Magdalen. It was, however, like the rest, silent and void, and his soul sickened with his fears, as, bursting open the battlement recess, he found that also vacant.

"She is gone!" he cried, descending the stairs, and casting his eyes round the apartment, he beheld with horror a large track of congealed blood upon the floor.

"It is all over, and fate can afflict us no more," exclaimed Ronald, in an agony of grief; "my daughter has fallen a victim to the savage ferocity of her husband, and this is her blood."

Angus rushed from his chamber, still doubtful of what he saw; but the track of blood that marked each step as he descended, spoke a language too horrible to doubt the cause, and sufficiently attested the foul deed which had recently been committed. Edwin was gone—for ever gone, and Magdalen was doubtless murdered. Her fidelity to their ruined cause had at length involved her in the fate of the race she had so loved and served;—she was too certainly no longer an inhabitant of the Watch Tower.

"Or of this world," groaned forth the deeply anguished youth, as he vainly searched through each well-known recess, which were all vacant; and conjecture yielded almost to certainty of her melancholy fate—that she had been murdered in the upper chamber, from whence her mangled form was borne, and hurled from the ramparts into the deep abyss of waters that roared beneath its basement.

Wild with grief and despair, Angus again rushed up to the chamber where he had left Ronald. Alas! the good old man lay upon the floor speechless, and apparently without life.

"He is dead! Ronald also is taken from me!" cried the frantic youth. "Merciful Heaven! why am I still spared? Edwin and Magdalen are murdered; but, vengeance, thou art yet mine, and, come what may, I will have blood for blood!"

Awhile he hung in anguish unutterable over the venerable Ronald, till night and complete darkness gloomed heavily around, and each object could no longer be distinguished. Despair was at his heart, but his thoughts were still busily occupied in forming plans by which he should discover the murderers and bring them beneath his vengeance.

No. 11.

CHAPTER XIV.

"Alas! poor country,
Almost afraid to know itself! It cannot be
Called our mother, but our grave, where naught—
But who knows nothing,—is once seen to smile."

SHAKSPERE.

IN order that the course of our narrative may be clearly developed, it is necessary that we now briefly advert to the condition of Scotland at the period of which we write.

The jarring feuds that ravaged unhappy Scotland at length threatened a total subversion and ruin to her independence. Edward the First, of England, had long kept a watchful eye upon a country he had marked for his own, and he beheld with secret satisfaction the flames of discord that broke forth. It was the wished-for period of his hopes, and assuming the outward mask of a friendly arbiter, he artfully subjugated a noble race beneath his own sceptre.

Baliol, eager for the title of a king, had submitted, at the conference of Norham Castle, his right to the crown of Scotland to the sole decision of Edward; but Bruce, disdaining to acknowledge as a liege lord a foreign monarch, refused the enslaving offers of the English king. The award, therefore, fell upon the more tractable Baliol, whose spiritless nature promised to become subservient to the kingly power which had thus raised him to eminence.

But a very few years did Baliol enjoy his unsubstantial honours; his court was but the phantom of royalty, and his laws and statutes unenforced, for the subjects of Scotland, in open contempt of their king, appealed for redress to the courts of Edward of England, whilst that subtle monarch encouraged their disloyalty by giving sentence rather in favour of his rebellious people than of Baliol. From these repeated indignities the tame, inoffensive spirit of the latter recoiled, and unable longer to endure such insults, he boldly shook off the weakness of his fears, and publishing an edict throughout Scotland to that effect, soon found his way to the hearts of his people. The ravages of war again commenced, and King Edward saw with no little satisfaction that the moment had arrived when he might subdue the country entirely beneath his own control. Again he summoned Baliol to appear before him as his liege vassal, but the latter disdained a reply to this insolent demand, and Edward, seizing the opportunity, suddenly entered Scotland at the head of a numerous army, determined to chastise the contumelious behaviour of Baliol, and shake the powers of Scotland to their very foundation.

Defeated in every battle, the spirit of the nation sunk despondingly. Edward's fortune had made Baliol a captive, and together with the bravest of his friends, he was carried in chains to England, and died in banishment, ending his short-lived royalty in a foreign kingdom.

Bruce, the former competitor of Baliol, had also died, and the rightful claims to the throne of Scotland were at this time vested in his grandson Robert, yet a minor, from whom at present no apprehensions inimical to Edward's usurpation were entertained; for the latter, well knowing the justice of his claims, had bestowed upon him the Earldom of Cleveland, in England, and other rich possessions, in the hope that he might thus purchase his entire submission.

It was about this dark period that the Earl of Glenalvon fell a sacrifice to the ruthless cruelty of his savage enemy, who equally hostile to his native country, had grown afterwards into princely power and wealth beneath the English sway, to which he had been a firm supporter. But though nearly overthrown by her own intestine foes, unhappy Scotland still retained some bright sparks of her former animated fires. Headed by the dauntless Sir William Wallace, the hardy sons of Caledonia once more asserted their country's rights, and made a vigorous stand against their insolent invader. By prudent measures Wallace emerged from his obscure retreats, and as the numbers of his forces increased, he more openly declared his purposes, and gained ground upon the enemy. He was then declared sole guardian of Scotland, but, too nobly disinterested to profit individually by his own deserts, he secretly invited Bruce to escape from the hands of the English, and assume the government of that kingdom which he was the heir of.

At the head of a hundred thousand men, and accompanied by the captive Prince of Scotland, Edward once more entered that unhappy kingdom, and suffered the sword to lay waste every opposing barrier to his deadly rage, which nothing short of total devastation could appease. It was then that the fate of Scotland was decided. The activity and courage of Wallace had attracted the notice of Robert Bruce, who, compelled to fight against his own, and the rights of his native country, had pursued Wallace along the opposite embankment of the river, where, waving a flag of truce, he demanded a conference. Wallace acceded to this, and the generous sentiments he uttered sunk deeply in the mind of Bruce, and aroused in him a feeling of shame and awakened ambition. The greatness of his birth, and the justice of his claims to the throne of Scotland swelled in his bosom, and from that moment he repented his alliance with Edward, whose injustice he became aware of, and from whose power he resolved to release himself, and with the earliest opportunity embrace the cause of his oppressed country.

Edward, however, again compelled Bruce to return with him to England, with whom also he conveyed the Scottish Regent, John Cummin, Earl of Buchan, whilst the fate of the brave Sir William Wallace was soon afterwards decided, and he was basely betrayed by Edward's spies, when he was carried in chains to London, where his patriotism and magnanimity were rewarded with a death disgraceful as it was unjust, and brutal as the savage nature of his cruel judge.

Justly incensed at the ignominious fate of his intrepid countryman, Bruce determined to throw off the yoke of his captivity, and avenge the cruelty inflicted on the preserver of Scotland, and he now resolved to make known his intentions, redeem the crown of his ancestors, and shake off for ever the tyrannic power of the English monarch. The Earl of Buchan was the first who received his confidence, who seconded all his designs, and encouraged him to the enterprise. But the earl was deceitful and ambitious; he himself aimed at the throne, and had in secret plotted to restore himself to the dignity of Regent of Scotland. He now, therefore, betrayed to Edward the project of Robert Bruce, not doubting that the King of England would reward his baseness with the object of his ambition.

It was at this period that Lord Inverness, the father of Mackenzie, had been made acquainted with the designs of Bruce, with whose family he was connected in the strongest bonds, his son having lately married the Princess Matilda—Bruce's sister. The disposition of Inverness was bold and chivalrous, and his soul was devoted to the interests of his illustrious relative, whom he laboured to advance to the throne of his ancestors. He had early discovered the hypocrisy of the Earl of Buchan, whom he had seen at midnight steal towards the chamber of King Edward, and dreading the ambition of his restless spirit, he watched him till he found his suspicions justified.

Robert Bruce was now held rather as a state prisoner than treated with his former courtesy and freedom, and it was only by disguising himself that the Lord Inverness could gain admission to his presence. As one of his own vassals, he at length obtained an interview with the royal captive, and presented him with a purse of gold, and a pair of spurs, saying that his master, Lord Inverness, had commanded him to return them to him, as property he had lately borrowed.

He then hastily quitted the place, and Robert, not slow of apprehension, guessed the meaning of his errand, and trusting to a faithful servant the nature of his secret, ordered his horses' hoofs to be shod the contrary way, to deceive pursuit, and soon after midnight quitted the palace, and fled with precipitation to his fortress of Lochmaben, where Inverness had previously arrived, and convened as many of the chief nobles of Scotland as the suddenness of the event would permit. The Earl of Buchan was the only person present who offered any opposition to the accession of Bruce to the throne; but his voice was soon silenced in death, for his treachery was known, and he instantly fell beneath the daggers of those chiefs who were anxious for the liberation of their country from a foreign yoke. Soon after this Robert Bruce was crowned at Scone; the justice of his right to the crown was not disputed, but his views aimed at the welfare of his people, and the English were, therefore, soon made to feel that in the activity of such a leader, Scotland had a champion who needed no other support than the firm fidelity she was now manifesting.

At length the battle of Methven proved ruinous to Bruce, for though he himself fought nobly, he was compelled to yield at last to superior numbers, and quitted the field as a fugitive. Lord Inverness had fallen in the battle, fighting to the last by the side of his king, whose changing fortunes sometimes beheld him surrounded with every insignia of supreme authority, and then again plunged into the deepest abyss of wretchedness, and reduced lower than the lowest level of his meanest subjects.

During this long lapse of time, Lord Mackenzie had become a father, a widower, and again a husband. The meek gentle nature of the princess, his consort, unable to bear up against the tide of misfortunes that had for so many years afflicted her family, died in the seventh year of her marriage. Mackenzie mourned her loss with the truest sorrow, but though he had never made known the rankling secret of his heart, the royal Matilda had never been the object of his tenderest love. Long ere he had beheld the princess, his heart had been given to another, and even in the arms of Matilda he still sighed over his blighted affections, and fondly dwelt on the thought of her he prefered to all others of her sex.

Lord Mackenzie had been married some few years before the escape of Bruce from England, but his firm attachment to the captive prince needed no other incentive than that of chivalry to ensure his fidelity, for the generosity of his nature was incapable of an act of dishonour, and had not the Princess Matilda been his wife, he had been equally loyal to the cause of her royal brother. Mackenzie lived for the first six years after his nuptials in the constant struggles of a vain attempt to subdue the early impressions his heart had felt for another. His conflicts were dreadful, because concealed, and the inward agonies of his mind alone found consolation in the confidence of friendship.

The Princess Matilda had been the choice of his father, who saw only the increased consequence and grandeur to be derived to his family from an alliance so august, and though acquainted with his son's regard for another, he forbade his union on pain of his greatest hatred. The conflict in the soul of the young man was dreadful; every feeling seemed outraged in the necessity which thus forbade his union, and not till assured by the object of his passion that she would never become his but by his father's consent did he at length yield to the commands he had received.

Emmeline was the orphan ward of his father, whose birth, though noble, was not favoured by fortune's gifts. Her mind was gentle, and susceptible of every soft emotion ; she had been brought up under the care of her lover's mother, and was about two years younger than herself. Diffident and meek-spirited, Emmeline too often sunk under the acuteness of her feelings, yet shrunk from the enraptured gazes of her admirer ; and when commanded by his father to reject his hand, she implicitly obeyed his commands, and took an oath that for ever sundered her from the youth without the consent of his parent.

It was not till the last year of her life that the Princess Matilda too late discovered that she had never been the real object of her husband's love. It was revealed to her by chance, and from that moment it was evident that her health and spirits rapidly declined. In the hour of her dissolution she betrayed the inborn greatness of her mind. Her husband, as he leant over her dying form, was overwhelmed with grief for her loss, and admiration for the exalted heroism of her last generous actions. Emmeline stood near the couch, mourning her untimely fate, when Matilda, taking a hand of both, and placing them in one another, said,—

" Live for each other ! My dear Walter, the conflicting struggles you have endured for my sake are now rewarded ; say that you will not hate the memory of Matilda after her death, and thus she repays you the debt of gratitude and love she has so long usurped. Accept this hand from mine as a late but certain atonement of the wrong you have sustained, and of Matilda's penitence, but for whom, alas ! it had long since been your own. And you, dear Emmeline, refuse not to my dying entreaty the last boon I can ask, or that you can have the power to grant me. Promise that you will not delay the fulfilment of my wishes ; say that you will become his, and I shall die content. Do not deny me this boon, but promise me solemnly that you will suffer no unavailing regrets to protract this union."

Emmeline with some hesitation gave the required pledge, and Matilda, with a look expressive of satisfaction, smiled her thanks.

" Now I am happy," she exclaimed joyfully, and clasping the hands of her husband fondly in her own, she added,—" You, my dear Walter, will be blessed, and my Isabel will find a second mother as affectionate as Matilda. And oh ! Emmeline, love but my lord with half the ardour that I have, and you will be blessed also. Farewell, my dearest friends—I go to witness your felicity,"

And with a gentle sigh she fell back into the arms of her husband and expired. Walter's sorrow for the loss of the princess was genuine ; he mourned her as a being of a superior creation, and reflected on her virtues and exalted character with wonder and admiration. He reverenced her memory, and respected her commands ; nay, often accused himself of cruelty and selfish ingratitude in not feeling for her that fond regard which, however, was possessed only by the early object of his affections.

At length, when time had softened his regrets for the princess, he claimed the hand of Emmeline as the last gift so solemnly bequeathed him by Matilda, and with an ardour that overcame every scruple he at length received the rich reward of his love at the altar.

Soon after this period, Lady Ellen Glenalvon, the sister of Lord Mackenzie, accompanied her husband to their castle to defend it, if necessary, from the threatened invasion of an unknown enemy, who, under the English auspices, had several times attempted to surprise it. Shortly after this, Lord Mackenzie was compelled to head his forces against the foes of Scotland, and was absent nearly three years, during which period the melancholy news reached him that his sister, the Countess of Glenalvon, with her husband and children, had all been destroyed by the accident, as it was reported, which had involved the territory of Glenalvon and its unfortunate owners in a total dissolution.

Involved in warfare, and deeply engaged at the distance of nearly two hundred miles from the scene of action so fatal to his sister and her family, he could only give their unhappy memories a hasty tear of sorrow; and when afterwards a short cessation of hostilities permitted his return home, he made all the inquiries he could respecting the fate of the Glenalvon family, but without effect, and he was at length compelled to desist, with the melancholy reflection that no chance remained of unravelling the mystery.

At the death of her royal mother, the Princess Isabel had been taken from her father, and was placed in the monastery of St. Columba, whither the mother of Robert Bruce and Matilda had retired, accompanied by many Scottish ladies, as the only asylum that was held inviolable during the oppression of the times, amidst the warfare that had so long afflicted the country.

Reared to womanhood amidst the holy sisters of Columba, Isabel received from her earliest years the loftiest impressions of virtue and piety; surrounded by the greatest and most illustrious female characters of the age, and early taught to respect the honour of ancestry, her mind might perhaps have imbibed an unequal bias for the prejudice of high descent, had she not early rejected the sophistry of that pride of birth which sometimes misleads weaker minds to suppose that there is in life no good so advantageous as being born above the lowliness or humble worth.

She had never quitted the monastery of St. Columba till she was taken by her illustrious guardian to be a witness of the coronation of her uncle, Robert Bruce, at Scone, where her extreme beauty and modesty made her the admiration of every one, and from that period Bruce ever after entertained the most paternal affection for his niece, and on her departure from the court with his mother, the Princess Dowager Catherine, he saluted Isabel with every mark of love and friendship, and bade her remember that he was himself her champion and knight, and would be equally faithful over the guardian of her future fortunes.

It was a few years after the second marriage of the Lord Mackenzie, that having been some time absent in the wars, he suddenly quitted the camp, and bent his steps with eager haste towards his castle, once more to hold the object of feudal love. Entering at evening the interior of his mansion, the impatient husband waited not the coming of Emmeline, but passing through the silent crowds of vassals and domestics, he ascended towards the apartment usually occupied by his wife with all the eagerness of a lover. Dreadful, however, was his disappointment and the anguish it occasioned. Emmeline was not to be found—was not in the castle. A fearful dark tale of mystery remained to be developed, and not till Walter had himself searched through every well known spot which was her favorite haunt did the fatal intelligence reach him that she had, more than a month, been missing from the castle.

The accounts were so mysterious, so vague and uncertain, that not the slightest proof appeared to form a just conjecture as to the real cause of her absence. On the preceding day the Lady Emmeline had been seen in tears, a circumstance which had been observed frequently for some time before, and which was attributed to the grief she felt for her lord's absence.

All that could be gathered was that a strange warrior, habited in armour, and with the vizor of his helmet drawn over his features, had, on the night preceding her sudden departure, demanded admission within the castle, and instant access to Lady Mackenzie. He was alone, and though the castle was at this time much thinned of its inhabitants, yet a sufficient number of warriors remained to guard it against treachery or surprisal. The stranger was admitted to her presence, but the result of their conference appeared not till the following day, when it was discovered that she had, with Maria, her favourite attendant, quitted the castle in secrecy.

In the private closet of Lady Emmeline was found a sealed packet, directed to Lord Mackenzie, by a hand unknown, whose dark, threatening import was thus deciphered—a poniard was wrapt within the scroll :—

"Search is fruitless. She whom thou seekest is lost to Mackenzie's lord for ever. Dare to lift the dark veil that envelopes the flight of Emmeline, and this dagger declares the certain vengeance such conduct will provoke. Be silent, as thou hopest for length of life, and banish from thy thoughts every trace of her who is now nothing to Walter, or to the world. Thy every action will be watched, and if found hostile to this secret warning, will be punished with a doom as dreadful to suffer as it will be mysterious and unknown to all but to thyself. Tremble, therefore, to provoke the suspended fate that thus awaits thee, from one who, if aroused to revenge, will be the eternal foe to thyself and all thy race. Be silent, and remember !"

Regardless of this caution, Lord Mackenzie spent more than a year in the vain attempt to discover the dreadful secret of his Emmeline's mysterious retreat. Disappointed, and sunk in hopeless despondency and gloom, he became reckless of existence, and at length the paroxysms of his feelings ended in long, deep intervals of silent melancholy madness.

Five years from Emmeline's disappearance passed away, but the period weakened not his malady, and he continued wrapped in a hopeless state of sufferings which nothing could alleviate. The pangs of unrequited love rankled in his heart, and the image of Emmeline, amidst the wildest of his ravings on her supposed falsehood to him, reigned in his heart as supremely as at the first moment of his unfortunate passion.

Time afforded no balm to heal his lacerated heart, and peace was for ever after a stranger to him. To have mourned her as no longer living might in time have decreased the agonies of his mind, but to think that she was perhaps indulging in the gratification of a false love, triumphing in his sufferings, and mocking his despair, was a suggestion so terrible to his reason, that his mental faculties no longer retained their equilibrium, and madness usurped the throne of intellect, at once dooming him to all the horrors of the disorder, aggravated by the continued remembrance of a love that nothing could eradicate.

Yet there were intervals of reason, when he would fondly imagine his Emmeline still lived, faithful and constant to his vows ; and that perhaps the moment was not far off when the mystery of her conduct would be revealed, her actions honourably justified, and his every jealous doubt of her purity be annihilated.

Then again, he would suddenly start, as fancy reminded him that Emmeline's love for him had not a warmer motive than esteem, and that in absenting herself she had voluntarily bestowed her love upon some more favoured object, perhaps regarded long before her unwilling hand had been bestowed upon him, and was perhaps at that very moment triumphing in her guilt and perfidy, and scorning, with lost virtue, every sacred tie that bound her to an injured husband, whose greatest fault was a too excessive love.

Whatever was the inscrutable mystery of the fate of Emmeline, certain it was that her husband's tenderness and regard knew no abatement, but seemed rather to increase with the despair and wretchedness that every hour aided to undermine his health and constitution, and which at length reduced him to the deplorable condition in which the reader has seen him.

~~~~~~

CHAPTER XV.

Hast ever marked this man,
Or seen the deep hypocrisy and guile
With which he hides his purposes?
                                        THE RECLUSE.

At length, urged by tenderness and filial affection, the Princess Isabel resolved to leave the Monastery of St. Columba, and return to the castle, which was still the residence of the unhappy Mackenzie. She had been absent from it for many years,—had seen Emmeline but twice since the period of her first departure to the monastery, and her father but seldom.

At the appointed time, the escort sent by Mackenzie, and which was led by Sir Francis, Lord Morton, the ward of the former, approached the island where the convent was situated; and Isabel, bathed in tears of regret, bade a long and lasting farewell to the loved companions of her youth, and to those solemn quiet scenes she was now to exchange for a new and more splendid career. In silent sorrow she was conducted to the shore, where the pinnace waited to convey her over the waters to the mainland coast of Scotland, and to the mountain district that bounded the wide territory of Craiglynn, amidst whose stupendous precipices the lofty towers of her father's castle reared their embattled walls.

Isabel's memory of the scenes where she had first beheld the light had somewhat faded from her memory. She had never seen Craiglynn's romantic heights since the age of childhood, and when once more she beheld the frowning battlements of her future home, her heart bounded at the thought of once more meeting with a parent from whom she had been long separated. As she drew nearer and passed beneath the lofty rocks that rose above, the bright armour of the warriors parading the ramparts glittered in the sunbeams, and added life to the magnificent scene upon which she gazed. A signal horn from the pinnace was sounded by one of the escort, and a soldier, leaning over the walls, demanded who passed below.

"Friends," replied Lord Morton;—"the princess approaches!"

And immediately Isabel was saluted from above by shouts of loud and joyous welcome. She then landed, and, supported by her two favourite female attendants, began to ascend the steep acclivity, and after a wearisome lapse of time reached the huge towers of the principal entrance, which she passed through, and found the courts filled with all the warriors of Craiglynn, who waited with uncovered heads to salute her as she passed through to the interior of the building.

With an agitated mein Isabel bowed gracefully as she passed along, and was led towards the state apartments. Anxious to embrace her father, she hurried to his private chamber, but started back, shocked and afflicted, when she beheld him. The flush of health was gone for ever from the wan cheeks of the unhappy Mackenzie—pallid grief was stamped upon his brow, and a deep melancholy was visibly imprinted upon the countenance which once had worn nothing but smiles of happiness and content. His heavy eyes, dead to all worldly interest, were bent upon the ground, unmindful of any object on which to dwell with pleasing regard. The fixed, hollow look of speechless, uncomplaining sorrow, that shaded each finely-formed fea-

ture was, if possible, more dreadfully afflicting to see than the wildest burst. of woe; and Isabel's heart gushed forth the sympathetic anguish of her soul.

"Father! dearest father!" she cried, in tones of softest melody, kneeling before him and kissing his shrunk hands as she clasped them in her own. "Alas! is it thus, after so long an absence that we again meet?"

The hapless father had not beheld the entrance of the princess, but her endearing looks and manner immediately aroused his attention. Surprised into an instinctive feeling of nature, he soon recognised his daughter, and his whole frame underwent an instantaneous convulsive emotion. He trembled violently, grasped the hands of the princess in his own, and fixing on her a deep and mournful glance of doubt, exclaimed in tones of wildness,—

"Do not, oh, do not you deceive me."

"Never, never, my dearest father," she replied, fervently. "I must cease to exist ere I can cease to love the author of my being, and study to promote his happiness and comfort."

"Indeed!" exclaimed Mackenzie, with all the sudden eagerness of hope, but doubtful of her sincerity. "Beware of false promises, girl, for, trust me, they are the forerunners of misery, ending in the worst of guilt!'

Then, with a bitter groan, he added,—

"Emmeline was lovely, fair and virtuous: yet even she became a dissembler, and I am left to misery and despair."

Isabel shuddered as she beheld her father's hopeless state; till now she had been uninformed of his real condition, and to behold him thus created in her soul the most poignant grief. Without one selfish regret for the melancholy confinement of such a task, she from this time devoted every moment to soothe and comfort him, watching with tenderest

No. 12

care the various changes of his malady, and guarding him against re-collections that would but have increased his wretchedness.

Sometimes Lord Mackenzie knew his child, and at these periods he would clasp her to his bosom, and give way to tears of sorrow. Then, after a pause, he would murmur out the wretchedness of his heart, and repeat the tale of Emmeline's falsehood, to which belief he ever tenaci-ously clung, whilst every effort made by Isabel to soften these distress-ing scenes prevailed not, for, in addition to his first sorrows, her per-fect resemblance to his Matilda seemed to increase his distractions, and in their wildest paroxysms he would frequently accuse himself of murder, ingratitude, and cruelty.

These severe conflicts were, indeed, dreadful to encounter, and almost overwhelming to the gentle spirit of his daughter; for sometimes, sinking at her feet, and fancying her really to be Matilda, he would clasp her hands in his own, and, with all the moving eloquence of woe, beseech her pardon for his crime in loving another. Then, starting from Isabel, he would wildly call on Matilda to return once more, and see him die, and triumph in the fatal ruin that had fallen upon him.

By gradual degrees Isabel imperceptibly gained ground, and succeeded in relieving the misery of that derangement, which in a short time had else been confirmed beyond hope. Acquainted now by experience with each turn of his malady, she administered that only balm which in the end promised to repay her tenderness with a reward equal to her dearest wishes—his recovery. At those periods when the return of his disorder again appeared, she ever carefully concealed her face from him, wearing a thick veil, which she never withdrew but in his lucid intervals, and thus had wiled away many weeks, as yet unmarked by any peculiar event since the period of her first arrival at the castle of Craiglynn.

This calm, however, was suddenly to be invaded; war again broke forth more dreadfully destructive than at any former period. Robert Bruce had again emerged from his seclusion, and with a small army of hardy veterans, prepared to contend with Edward of England for the sovereignty which had been wrested from him.

A herald arrived at Craiglynn Castle with strong entreaties to its lord once more to hasten with his forces to join the army of the heroic Bruce. It was at a time when Lord Mackenzie had regained a longer interval of reason than since the continuance of his dreadful malady, and roused to action by a summons so unexpected, he hesitated not to obey it; nor would he yield to the earnest entreaties of Isabel, who heard his decision with dread, and besought him to remain at the castle, and leave the task of conducting his warriors to the field of battle to the ablest of his knights. To these fears, however, he replied that his fame would be for ever sullied and disgraced if he suffered any personal weakness to with-hold him from the glorious call of arms.

"Your pious love, my dearest Isabel," he said, "has imposed on your patience a long and painful task, and I am, perhaps, saved by your gentle care from a lasting affliction worse than the pangs of death itself. The delusive hours of happiness that once were mine are vanished, never, I fear, to return. My bosom has long been their grave, and my features the tablet of their buried memory."

"Alas! unfortunate Isabel!" cried our heroine, "to whom must you look for pity or regard? My father—my own dear father, rejects his unhappy child, and she will be left alone, unfriended, the singled object of a harsh world's oppression!"

Her entreaties were, however, in vain, and the scene of parting be-tween them was afflicting and heart-rending in the extreme; every feeling of the soul was awakened, and the afflicted Isabel clung round her father to the last, like one despairing over the dying moments of a beloved friend. Thrice her spirit failed to support her, and the dreadful apprehension that she should never behold her parent living, almost bereaved her of life itself, and as she parted from him, she cried in accents of despair,—

"My father—my dear loved friend, oh live for me—for your own Isabel ! Rush not with headstrong haste into the battle's heat, but think amidst its terrible ragings on your daughter ; think that in your life her only happiness is wrapt ! Oh, should you no more return to bless your child, forlorn and miserable must be her future days !"

Her father at length departed; his impatient troops once more with shouts of joy hailed the return of their brave commander, beneath whose conduct they again rushed eager to the strife of war. From the parapet of the great tower Isabel watched her father's receding steps, and whilst his arms gleamed in the sunbeam she traced his athletic form above the numerous warriors that accompanied him, still rising majestic above them ; nor did she quit the spot till not a speck remained upon the outline of the horizon.

As Craiglynn Castle was within a few miles of the seat of war, it would have been dangerous to have left it ungarrisoned during the absence 'of its numerous troops ; its defence was therefore committed to the young Lord Morton, the ward of Mackenzie, with five hundred men-at-arms, to protect it from any sudden attack.

Lord Morton had reached his one and twentieth year, the period that emancipated him from the wardship of his early protector. His mind, like his person, was bold and commanding, yet haughty, daring, and enterprising. His features were large and regular, but darkly expressive of slumbering evil passions. His step was firm and proud, and his demeanour and gait imposing and dictatoral, like his speech ; whilst the side-long roll of his black piercing eyes betrayed a darker meaning than the caution of his lips gave expression to, and seemed to scrutinize, whilst they could artfully fascinate, the object he meant to win to his purposes, if not sufficiently penetrating to discover his intentions before hand.

The youthful loveliness and perfect innocence of Isabel he. had beheld with an unqualified wonder and open admiration ; nor had many weeks elapsed ere she was herself informed of the sentiments she had inspired.

When addressed by Lord Morton in the impassioned language of his feelings, our heroine at first listened to him in confused silence, and forbore to express resentment, because she was too generous to insult or triumph in the disappointment of another ; whilst the lover, unacquainted with the refined cultivation of her mind and character, believed he had succeeded, and flushed with its presumption, firmly believed himself to be regarded by the princess, who, though she had not yet confirmed his hopes with an avowal of her sentiments, he doubted not would be prevailed on to declare them, were called upon by all the eloquence and persuasion he was practised in expressing, but which the long illness of her father had hitherto prevented him from urging with that vigour his impatience demanded ; for though he was in every way inferior in point of fortune and descent to the dignity of an alliance so far above him, yet the arrogance of his aspiring spirit, and the dauntless resolution of his character, taught him to raise his hopes to the highet pinnacle of human greatness ; and to obtain a prize so invaluable as the Princess Isabel.

The young knight had been bequeathed an orphan to the protection of Lord Mackenzie. The fortunes of his ancestors had never been great, and even the best part of these had been confiscated by the treasonable practices of his father; and, but for the humanity of Mackenzie, he would have been destitute, and a stranger to that superior station in which he then moved.

The sudden absence of his friend and patron, at a time so unexpected, was indeed a fortunate occurrence to the furtherance of his wishes and the deep laid plots their determined success had engendered. For some days after Mackenzie's departure, he devoted every leisure moment to the princess, and in all the bland, insinuating softness he so well knew how to assume at pleasure, he ingratiated himself into her society, and by his affected tenderness soothed her melancholy for the absence of her father, and took every advantage of an event so favourable to implant his own impression on her awakened memory.

Absorbed in her own grief and fears for the safety of her father, Isabel was in that condition of mind most dangerous to her peace, had her heart really acknowledged any other passion more fervent than filial affection. Her mind, pensive and weakened by sorrow, turned fondly towards every image that recalled the remembrance of a beloved parent, now exposed to the horrors of war, and the impending chance of a sudden and untimely death. The penetration of the Princess Isabel, not awakened to a suspicion of Morton's real intentions and artfully concealed wiles, and not harbouring a thought inimical to his honour and allegiance, too incautiously admitted him to her confidence, as a being worthy of the trust she favoured him with, and of a mind capable of feeling for, and partaking in her griefs.

On the other hand, Lord Morton, every hour thus exposed to the irresistible charms of a creature formed by nature to excite universal love and admiration, soon felt, in reality, all the jealous hopes and dreads inseparable from a lasting passion, and at the feet of Isabel, he at length revealed the fixed, unalterable affections of his heart, whose aspiring flame had first been lighted by the torch of ambition, but was now become a rooted, avowed love.

Too gentle to resent a presumptuous declaration she certainly was not prepared to receive from Lord Morton, Isabel, though astonished, and highly condemning the imprudence of her own conduct, was mild in the terms of her rejection of a confession so unlooked for; and while she forbade his ever renewing the subject, the delicate purity of her sentiments were couched in language too refined for his conviction; for his vanity and self-opinion led him to suppose that her refusal was but the effect of female caprice, and the blindness of his passion had so completely engendered the suspicion that she would one day become his own, that Isabel, from this period become more solely the object of his adoration,—to obtain whom, he now resolved to leave no means untried, however dangerous or unjust they might be.

Put upon her guard by the discovery she had made, Isabel no more suffered him to approach her in the solitude of her retirement, but for the future, confined herself wholly to the magnificent suite of apartments that had been allotted to her use; and seldom or ever, as formerly, did she now pace the embattled parapet that overhung the sea, ever her favourite walk at evening twilight. Maddened at the change which deprived him of the sight of the beauteous princess, and his passion inflamed by the difficulties that opposed him, Lord Morton's hardy and audacious spirit broke through every barrier of respect or delicacy.

Three days had intervened, and he had been unable to address, or even approach the princess, who now never quitted her apartments but when attended by the ladies of her suite, by whom she was always closely surrounded; and only at the banquet was she ever visible.

On the fourth evening, however, as Isabel was seated in the turret closet that overlooked the ocean, and was giving to past events many a tender, regretful sigh, her retirement was suddenly invaded and as she turned round her pensive glance she beheld Lord Morton advance towards her seat, and sink upon one knee before her. She was too much surprised to speak at the moment ; and in all the impassioned eagerness of his impetuous feelings, he again poured forth his soul, and thus concluded :—

" Scorn me not, dearest Isabel, nor disdain to avow for me your generous pardon for this involuntary intrusion, an intrusion that you may surely forgive since, if it be a crime of love, that crime can only spring from the dear object that has inspired its sentiments. From the first moment my delighted sight gazed on those matchless charms, their enthralling influence has alone possessed my mind, and reigned unrivalled and unmixed with every other passion, where the image of my adored Isabel will be for ever impressed, even though she should still doom my ardour to despair and wretchedness—an ardour and constancy that can never be extirpated but with life. Nor will I forego the fondly cherished hope that I may one day call for ever mine, her alone who can inspire my heart with genuine love. Say that you bid me not despair ; deign but to bless me with one favouring word of hope, and I will adore your goodness, and wait with patience the arrival of that happy, and let me believe, not far distant period, that shall crown our future days with a felicity as lasting and perfect as it will prove inseparable."

As he concluded he seized her hand within his own rough grasp, and would have borne it to his lips, but Isabel rose indignantly from her seat, and struggled to release herself from his hold.

" Unhand me, sir—unhand me, I command you !" she exclaimed, with a rising majesty of mien, and a severity of brow that surprised and awed Lord Morton into an instant silence and compliance, for he instantly relinquished his grasp, abashed and dismayed at the lightning glances that shot from her eyes. Then, somewhat recovering herself, Isabel added, with more composure,—" To steal thus privately upon the sanctuary of my retirement is an intrusion, sir, as offensive as is the presumptuous arrogance of the language with which you have addressed me."

" Pardon, dearest Isabel," he exclaimed, " and do not utterly condemn me till you have heard me sue for that mercy which it is in your power to bestow."

" Retire, sir," she replied with proud dignity, as she waved him from her presence—" retire, I say, and remember that if this insolence is repeated, my father shall be informed of the unworthy means you have resorted to during his absence. The Princess Isabel commands from you the reverence due to her rank and the unprotected situation in which she has been placed. And do not again oblige me, sir, to remind you, that only in the absence of my father would you have so far forgotten the difference of our stations as to provoke the justice of this well-merited rebuke."

Confounded, amazed, and at once convinced that he had deceived himself with false hopes, yet suffering under all the afflicting torments of the most violent passion, rendered the more desperate by its defeat and mortifying rejection, Lord Morton stood awhile transfixed, the statue of disappointment and confusion.

Meanwhile the Princess Isabel had quitted the apartment at the moment he had suddenly resolved on the last desperate attempt, either by force or entreaty, to soften her aversion. Maddened with rage, he uttered some inarticulate imprecations of violence, and was about to quit the chamber, when casting his eyes around, he beheld a rich purple scarf, beautifully enwrought in devices of gold and embroidery of silks, no doubt the labours of Isabel's own hand. With a burst of sudden exultation he seized it, and exclaimed,—

"Senseless captive! emblem of thy mistress's sure fate, thou art, as she shall be, safe in my possession. Omen of success! from this moment I date the blessed attainment of my firm resolves. Yes, lovely, but obdurate girl, thou shalt indeed be mine! Thy proud disdain shall yield to love's resistless force! My soul already sickens with impatience to possess the bright majesty of thy resistless charms. Beware, then, beauteous scorner, to repeat thy cruelty, lest, drawing my remembrance to thy haughty contumely, I avenge my slighted love and thy contempt at the moment that gives me the completion of happiness, and renders me the future master of thy destiny!"

He quitted the spot, whilst Isabel, disgusted and alarmed at the unblushing presumption of his manner and conduct, gave strict charge to her attendants never in future to quit the ante-chamber of her apartments. Returning in the evening to her favourite turret, she instantly missed the scarf; it was designed for her father, and had been the pleasing task of many a solitary hour. Her astonishment and resentment were not a little excited when, as she looked through the casement, she beheld this valued pledge of filial affection adorn the person of Lord Morton, who was at this moment deeply engaged in conversation with some friends upon the terrace of the rampart that ran beneath her window.

A deep glow of anger, never till now felt, because never so justly excited, flushed with alternate crimson the cheeks of the indignant Isabel, and hastily summoning one of her attendants, she bade her instantly demand the scarf, nor return to her presence till it was yielded up.

Catherine obeyed, and passing through the courts, reached the rampart, where Lord Morton still continued, smiling in the conscious triumph of his successful stratagem. The attendant made known the purport of her errand to him, and his lordship, with an air of insolent carelessness, exclaimed, with apparent unconcern,—

"The scarf, say you, my pretty Abigail; and wherefore, I prithee, do you make so unkind a request of me? Can my beauteous Isabel so soon forget the gratitude of her adoring lover for a gift so precious as the one she has been pleased to bestow upon me?"

"A gift, my lord!" exclaimed Catherine, somewhat confused, as much at the bold effrontery of Morton as at beholding herself scrutinized by a number of idle gazers who were assembled round the young nobleman.

"Aye, my fair messenger," he replied, with unblushing audacity and perseverance; "have I not said it was a gift, and would thy cruel mistress now recal the dear-earned treasure of my rich reward? Ah, no! It must not—cannot be. My heart—my life is her's: the one I cannot recal, and the other I will joyfully lay down if she commands it. All that is mine I dedicate to her service—all, save this sacred pledge, which I cannot part with, and which, should I lose, it would be a stain to knighthood and to chivalry, could I consent to resign a boon bestowed, whose worth a monarch's ransom could not redeem!"

"A boon bestowed, my lord!" cried Catherine, in accents of astonishment.

"Aye," he replied; "the princess gave it me with her own fair hands, and never can I part with it but with life. Is it not a proof of the triumph I have achieved, and shall I now give it up to your hands because my Isabel has manifested a woman's fickleness, and now demands back that which was voluntarily given? No, no—the Princess Isabel gave it me, and never will I resign it but into her own hands. Tell her so, good Catherine, and say that my love for her prompts me to prize, beyond all else, that which she bestowed upon me as a keepsake."

"A keepsake!" again cried Catherine; "your lordship surely mistakes, for my lady's hand never bestowed a grant like this to any but her own father. I beseech you, my lord, give back the ornament, for the commands of the princess were imperative, and I may not return without it."

Lord Morton affected to sigh deeply, as if injured by the sudden change of Lady Isabel's mind, and untying the scarf which he wore over his own shoulders, he cast glances of significant meaning upon the attentive observers, and exclaimed, with well-feigned emotion,—

"I live but to obey the Princess Isabel, and, though hard the duty she commands, I respect her will too devoutly—altered as it is since we last parted—to oppose the cruel severity of her request."

Catherine hastily retired as she received the scarf from his hands, and Morton, though disappointed in his aim, was too politic and crafty to risk a certain defeat to his high-raised hopes by persisting in a refusal.

His words, though false in their meaning, had been more than sufficient to stamp an impression on the minds of those present with a belief that the princess had really favoured his love in secret—a belief that he himself had instilled into the minds of the people of Craiglynn; it was, therefore, policy to resign the scarf, much as he wished to preserve it, lest Catherine's more open declaration should contradict his assertions; whilst the knights themselves, deceived by his words, hesitated not openly to avow their belief that the princess was merely desirous to conceal the affection she entertained for Lord Morton.

CHAPTER XVI.

" Misfortunes fall upon us with blighting power,
Destroying all before them.   Death and ruin
O'erwhelm our hapless country."   NEVILLE'S CROSS.

A FEW days elapsed after the events narrated in the last chapter, and the fears of Isabel were increased to an alarming height for the safety of her father. She had dismissed a page to the camp with the memorable scarf, and every hour awaited the expected intelligence his return would bring back. Four days more had passed away, but yet he appeared not. Every flying post that passed the castle walls brought the most fearful accounts. Robert Bruce, they stated, had twice made a brave but ineffectual resistance against the blood-thirsty legions of Edward; twice he had been vanquished, yet a third time he had advanced with redoubled vigour to the fight, resolute to conquer or to fall.

This ensuing battle would be decisive, and either the English would be entirely driven from the possession of Scotland, or, if the country should be conquered, it would be completely at the mercy of the invaders. Even the most remote fortresses were endangered by the event of this last struggle, and it was felt that in the defeat of their wronged sovereign their country would become enslaved.

Isabel's alarms now became nearly as poignant for herself as for her absent father. Should England prevail, a fortress so material as Craiglynn,—the inhabitants of which were known to be devoted to the cause of Bruce,—would become the next object of attack, and thus war and bloodshed would be brought beneath her very eyes.

The crisis of Scotland's fate approached, and the day that again rendered her a conquered nation, was in the end fatal to the princess. Her near affinity to the king, and the known attachment and firm allegiance that subsisted between King Robert and her father, were circumstances that must immediately turn the scale of danger against her future safety and repose, should the usurping King of England be successful. Yet, to quit the castle in such a state of uncertainty, was a thought too selfish ever to have entered her mind.

Recently she fancied she had not beheld in the garrison those appearances of zeal and affection for her welfare and security which the defenders of Craiglynn had so loyally displayed on the morn of her father's departure. The domestics of her suite had learned from the warders that many of the men who had been left the safeguards of the castle, had of late shown marks of dissatisfaction and impatience. Some of them had been seen at midnight assembling in parties in the outward courts, whilst unusual commotions of a dangerous tendency had twice disturbed the peaceful silence of the night.

From these circumstances it was evident that some pernicious schemes, inimical to the good order and welfare of the fortress, had been subtly engendered. Several broils and quarrels amongst the soldiers had reached the knowledge of the household;—the chiefs in command were either indolent or had neglected to enforce the necessity of strict discipline, whilst the variety of opinions and surmises that were darkly canvassed, often bore relation to some deep-concerted plot, which, while it confused the lower order of soldiers, could not be regularly traced to the fountain head, that had but too successfully disseminated some very dangerous tenets among the inhabitants of the fortress.

It was observed, too, that those marks of respect which till very lately had been shewn the princess were no longer displayed; the soldiery seemed rather to view their young mistress as the cause of their present inactivity from the more glorious strife of arms, and had therefore evidently altered their conduct, which was now become sullen and gloomy, though to what cause this sudden dereliction of their duty was owing could not be discovered.

The evening of the day that proved so fatal to Scotland's liberty passed darkly. Isabel had spent it in continual prayer and weeping, at one moment indulging the flattering delusion of hope, and at another, plunged in all the gloomy horrors of suspense and despair. She had not tasted food throughout the day; all within the castle was still as death itself,—no noise of approaching horsemen sounded on the air. Dejected and anxiously watchful, Isabel, till long after the close of day, continued to pace the battlements, and often ascended the loftiest tower, to descry at a distance the hoped-for approaches of messengers; but the gates were still closed, and silent from any signal sounds.

With her own hand Isabel placed on the pinnacle of the loftiest tower a flaming cresset, whose far seen light might speed the expected return of Lord Mackenzie. The more powerful rays of morning, however, at length began to render sickly the light she had kindled, and found the impatient Isabel vainly watching as she still hung over the parapet of the battlement.

At last, as the day advanced, a distant moving object was seen on the horizon, which soon after disappeared amidst the nearer woods that shielded the sides of the rising steeps. The heart of Isabel bounded, for not long after she saw the horsemen as they emerged from the thicket, and with tumultious joy she exclaimed :—

" It is my father !—he lives !—he lives ! Oh, bounteous Heaven, accept daughter's gratitude !"

The furious pace of the horsemen soon distanced the lower summits, and in a quarter of an hour they arrived at the platform before the castle gates.

Isabel darted from the place where she had been watching, and had reached the basecourt at the moment the gates had opened to admit— not the Lord Mackenzie—but a flying messenger, whose foaming steed declared the dreadful haste with which he had travelled. It was some few moments of torturing suspense ere the herald could recover breath to declare the ill-natured errand upon which he had come.

"King Edward is victor," he at length exclaimed; "our royal master is believed dead, and with his fall perishes the last surviving hope of our devoted country. The last words of your father were,—'Fly for thy life towards Craiglynn Castle, for I am wounded, and cannot leave the field of battle. Defend my daughter, for the foe hastens to the conquest of my fortress,—the last hope of Scotland.' "

"Great Heaven!" cried Isabel, in a paroxysm of terror; "will not my father return?"

"Alas! lady," answered the man, "I tremble for his safety, for should he have fallen into the hands of the enemy, his death is certain, such being the fatal edict of Edward against the leading chiefs of the Scottish army. The field was won by the English when last my lord's voice commanded me to hasten hither, and I fear he is either a prisoner or —"

"Dead!" cried Isabel, with trembling emotion. The thought was too terrible for endurance, and sinking into the arms of an attendant, she fainted. In this state she was carried to her apartment, and when again she was restored to animation, she beheld Lord Morton kneeling before her, but with a respectful solicitude of manner, that seemed to proceed from no warmer motive than the wish to behold her recovery. Isabel sat for some time in speechless despondency and tears, and at length Lord Morton rose, as she silently motioned for him to leave her.

No. 13

"I grieve, Lady Isabel," he said, "to be the messenger of further ill-news, but these papers which I have received, and which were sent by a special messenger from the English monarch, will instruct you in the truth of my commission, which, as governor of this castle, I must enforce.   King Edward now sways the Scottish sceptre, and with its high power rules also the fates of contending states and princedoms.   Let not my speech offend you, lady, when it thus unwillingly informs you of the necessity of preparing for the arrival of the conqueror, who means this night to sojourn within the castle of your ancestors ; and it were vain to oppose his entrance, since you are yourself become the ward of the victor,—for of the fate of your father little intelligence has yet transpired.   He was seen bravely fighting to the last beside his king, and when the latter fell —"

"Alas ! is the king, too, dead ?" cried Isabel.

"It is so reported, lady."

"And my father?"

"May yet be living, as his body has not been recognized among the slain," answered Lord Morton.   "Perhaps even now he may be journey-ing towards Craiglynn; and in case it should be so, I will instantly despatch a trusty messenger to warn him from the castle, and —"

"To warn my dear father from the castle !" interrupted Isabel, indig-nantly.

"Alas, lady !" exclaimed the hypocrite, "this castle is no longer his.; need I now inform you Edward now rules despotically over Scotland, and can dispose of princes and territories at his will.   These are his harsh man-dates.   Your sire is banished, and should he dare approach Craiglynn, his life must pay the forfeit of a trespass on Edward's sentence.   Behold, Isa-bel, the royal signature of England's king."

The spirit of our heroine sunk not under the dreadful severity of fortune's powers, but was suddenly awakened into the energy of its real character as these difficulties thickened upon her, and she replied undauntedly :—

"You forget, my lord, that the towers of Craiglynn are still unconquered, and, therefore, have not yet become the spoil of a tyrant usurper's plunder.   Let us still be faithful to ourselves," she added, with a scrutinizing glance at his countenance, "and we may safely scorn the vain boaster's attempts to sack our impregnable fortress.   Oh, should my beloved father have escaped the dangers of the battle's fury, he will bend his steps hither for shelter, and his hopes shall not be deceived."

"Think you, then," exclaimed Morton, "that it will be possible to defend the castle ?"

"In such a cause as this," answered Isabel, "I feel myself armed with more than a woman's fortitude and courage boldly to outbrave the ensuing con-flict.   I will for awhile forget my sex's weakness, and with Heaven's aid, and my own consciousness of right, will dare to hazard all, even life itself, to perform my duty to a beloved parent, and render myself worthy the illustrious line from which I am descended."

"Surely you will not hazard your life in this useless warfare ?" exclaimed Lord Morton.

"My father's mandates," she replied, "bade his people defend his child ; but not for herself does she now encounter the danger that threatens.   The cherished hope of his return has inspired my bosom with more than a woman's fortitude and resolution to meet unshrinkingly every dreaded evil, and every opposing shaft that fortune's malice may hurl against me.   Thus determined, I will abide with a dauntless firmness the shock of destiny, nor wince beneath the perils I may incur."

Amazement and confusion for a time held dominion over Morton as he listened to resolutions that, if put in practice, must defeat his secret plot; and should the princess discover their treacherous tendency, every hope of gaining her would also be annihilated. At length, having somewhat recovered himself, he said :—

"To oppose an arm so mighty and powerful as Edward's, will be to add the certain overthrow and slaughter of your people. The King of England's numerous hosts must soon overpower the handful of men that garrison the castle, and need I tell you that even many of these are disaffected, and have been withdrawn from their allegiance. Reflect, then, I beseech you, how vain the hope of resistance! Edward, once made a foe, is implacable in his resentment, and deadly in pursuit of his revenge. In that case, think how hopeless will be your own destiny!"

"I reflect only," answered Isabel, with calm dignity, "on the task my duty and affection both to the king and my father imposes; and it had better proved your fidelity, my lord, to their mutual interests, their honour and domestic peace, had your authority over the soldiers of Craiglynn more effectually sustained them in their obedience. I must remind you the absence of my father submitted to your lordship the command and guardianship of this fortress; but it yet remains to be discovered how well you have maintained a station so generously confided to your faith and honour!"

The pointed reproach contained in these words, together with the rising air of reserve and distance that marked her demeanour, abashed Morton's late assumed aspect of confident security, as well as filled his mind 'with the stings of conscious internal upbraidings and just rebuke. Rage burnt in his bosom, but prudence awed him into silence, though he inwardly felt galled, and uttered some half-expressed sentences indicative of the fury that consumed him.

The princess, waving her arm repulsively, put an end to any further conference at present. As he retired, she instantly issued a command to her attendants to summon the herald that had been despatched by her father, for she was still anxious to obtain that intelligence that was necessary for the shaping of her future course.

CHAPTER XVII.

"We command you, yield your castle to us,
Or with dread onslaught we'll attack the walls;
And force you to obedience."

COUNT RAYMOND.

OBEDIENT to the command of Isabel, the herald immediately entered the apartment, and kneeling at her feet, repeated the message with which he had been charged, and gave her fresh hopes, that after the battle of the preceding day, nearly four hundred men of Craiglynn had escaped unhurt from the English pursuers, and were journeying by secret passes towards the castle, with the view of aiding its present garrison against the too certain siege that Edward was preparing to make against it.

"But say, does my dear father yet live?" cried Isabel; "bless me, if thou canst, with a hope that he may yet return to his castle of Craiglynn."

"I hope and trust he may do so," answered Cameron. "I left him wounded on the field last night, but it may happen that his injuries are not mortal. I would have warned him thence if I had dared, but he commanded my absence, whilst he, to the last moment of twilight, still persisted in searching for the king. As I parted from him, his last words bade me cheer his daughter with a hope of his return as soon as he could with safety approach Craiglynn. At the same time he bade me to warn you to beware of secret treachery, and much, he feared, he said, the faith of Morton. More he could not add, for at that instant a party of English appeared in sight. He forbade me following, as he hastily retreated, and I trust has escaped by favour of the darkness, that by that time had set in."

Isabel trembled, but still retained some outward show of composure. The situation she was so unexpectedly thrown into, she felt would demand all the firmness of her soul to ward off the increasing difficulties that encompassed her; whilst the cheering hope, that should she, by her courage, and conduct, still preserve Craiglynn's independence, it would shield her father from the tyrant Edward's fatal edict, and in thus magnanimously opposing the lawless ravager of her prostrate country, some happier issue might ensue to rescue it from the slavery that again impended. Resolute in her patriotic determination, she hastened to put her projects into execution, and bade the herald instantly proclaim her will throughout the castle.

"Arm, arm, all ye warriors of our race," she cried; "tell them for once a feeble woman shall assume the spear of war. Remind the people of their duty and allegiance to their monarch and their chiefs; bid them trust in Heaven and the justice of their cause, and to rely upon the inaccessible strength of our battlements for conquest and security!"

Cameron hastened to obey his mistress, and Isabel, clasping on her shoulders her richest robe, prepared to inspire by her own presence and heroism, the hearts of her hardy people.

Upon her head she wore a light diadem, in the form of a helmet, sumptuously ornamented with precious stones. Her robe was crimson, of the richest texture, looped with ropes of silver, and magnificently adorned with clasps of jewellery. Upon her feet she wore gilt leathern sandals. Her pages bore before her the gorgeous standard of her house, displaying the splendid armorial ensigns of her father's ancestors, richly enwrought with the royal arms of Scotland.

Followed by the ladies of her suite and the household of the castle, she descended to the state hall of audience, and seating herself under the canopy of a raised throne, bowed to all the assembled knights and warriors present, who, with uncovered heads, respectfully saluted her, as with modest grace, but resolute purpose, she thus appeared amongst them.

Lord Morton was present, but shrunk within himself confounded and alarmed; for though his artifices had certainly succeeded in corrupting many of the garrison, he could not foresee or guard against the consequences an event like the present would occasion; and he now trembled at his own danger, as with envy and dread he marked the sudden and unfavourable change the conduct of Isabel had wrought in the minds of even the most factious of his partisans.

At length, rising majestically, she with undaunted firmness thus addressed the assemblage :—

" Warriors and friends, once the brave unconquerable defenders of your own and your chieftian's rights, if yet the memory of your former heroic deeds be not forgotten, revive again the hardy valour of your spirits, and scorn to yield ingloriously your hard-earned freedom to a haughty spoiler's usurpation. Commanded by his voice whom in battle you have so oft obeyed, the daughter of your lord relies on your protection, and, in her father's name, invites you to the glory of action. If still within your breasts reside the noble bravery of your warlike forefather's, the approaching crisis of danger will approve you the true descendants of their unsullied fame. Myself, though a woman, and unused to war's alarms, shall share in all your dangers, and contend for the glory of victory equally with yourselves, exposed to its conflicts. I will, encounter the shocks of opposing lances and barbed arrows, or meet, as becomes a freeborn spirit, the uplifted swords of the conquerers. My Lord Morton, to your charge is consigned the defence of these towers ; you will, doubtless, prove yourselves worthy the honourable task such a station imposes, and will well have deserved the thanks of your sovereign, and the praises due to a hero. Lead, gallant friends ! the daughter of your chief confides in your valour, and will, hereafter, reward the noble actions of her brave protectors."

Every sword was instantly unsheathed, and every voice shouted triumphantly the name of "Isabel." The assumed heroism of her character had acted like a talisman upon every heart, whose magic influence had inspired the spirits to action. The soldiers were enthusiastic, and shouted as with one voice :—

" We will conquer or die in the defence of our liberties and the safety of our noble chieftan and his daughter !"

With a heart agitated with the dread and uncertainty of her father's fate, Isabel had with difficulty supported the outward semblance of that fortitude she had displayed, feeling, however, the necessity of suppressing every appearance of fear equal to the undertaking, and which solely rested on herself; for should she discover any weakness all might be lost, since it was too certain the person she ought most to have relied on was an enemy in disguise.

Lord Morton had suddenly retired from the hall, and as Isabel passed onwards to the walls, a page hastily approached, and begged an instant's audience, and as she paused to hear him, he exclaimed :—

"The warden of the eastern portcullis, so please you, my lady, has withheld a passport to one of the heralds, who it is feared, demanded egress from the castle with no good intent ; he entreats your signet ere he suffers the courier to depart."

Well knowing that she had dismissed no messenger from the castle, but, on the contrary, had strictly forbidden the absence of any one, Isabel felt a new alarm, and hastened to the gate to trace the affair to its source. On arriving there, she demanded to see the man, but was astonished to find that he had, under a false pretence, passed through the postern. More alarmed as she reflected on the meaning of her father's words, which bade her beware of secret treachery, she felt the danger of her situation forcibly, but stifled her rising terror, remembering that this was not the moment to punish the treason, lest, in the chastisement of one offender, numbers might be aroused to disaffection and revolt ; for it was impossible to discover either who were the traitors, or what the result of their plottings, though it was now but too evident she was beset by such.

With strict orders not to suffer any one to pass without a signet from herself, she quitted the gate, the keys of which she commanded the warden to secrete in a secure spot, known only to herself and him.

Throughout the day Isabel continued to parade the courts and ramparts, and as each soldier was seen busily employed in preparation for battle, she conversed freely with them, and entering on the story of their domestic grievances, promised, as far as her power would allow, to redress those evils which the violence of the time had brought on them.

On this important and trying occasion, Isabel with wonder beheld herself casting aside the timidity of her sex, and acting with a firmness and decisive courage which is usually accounted the sole possession of man. Her motives she felt were just, and her feelings sanctioned the laudable actions they inspired ; for to herself the danger was infinite, since, if she failed, the rage of her conqueror against one who dared brave his might would too certainly expose her to the most severe evils that revenge and malice could inflict.

And her worst terrors were shortly to be realised, for the English commander was seen approaching with his hosts towards the decline of day, and it was whispered among the garrison that King Edward, disdaining a conquest so inglorious, remained at a short distance off, to look calmly on while the scene of destruction took place.

Thrice the English commander summoned the garrison to surrender, but the demand was sternly refused by those who well knew the fury of their enemies, who were mad with the triumph their recent successes had given them. It was evident the English monarch had expected unhesitating obedience, and not the brave resistance of a determined spirit, resolved to endure all the difficulties and dangers of a siege. But the first dart that was hurled from the castle walls declared the determination of those within; and the English commander, amazed at this unexpected proof of opposition, hastily retreated;—for the pass up the loft steep upon which the castle was situated, was so narrow, that its space was incapable of affording room for a sufficient number of men to carry on a successful siege. A brief pause, therefore, ensued; but soon the English, with incredible dispatch, pitched their camps in the hollow of the vale below the mountain, whilst King Edward himself, provoked at the disappointment this delay occasioned, gave orders that the castle should again be summoned to surrender, on pain of an ignominious death to every soul within its walls who should dare to hold out after this proclamation.

Once more the English heralds ascended to the gates, and loudly sounding a parley on their bugles, delivered their hostile message. The Princess Isabel, however, had armed her soul for the present conflict; for on herself alone its honour and success depended. Lord Morton, faithless to his allegiance, had suddenly cast off the mask, and openly vowed his resolution not to oppose King Edward, or risk the certain danger to his life the conqueror's edict threatened. Her only hope, therefore, now depended on the arrival of the troops her father had dismissed, and who only could be admitted within the castle through a private portal, concealed in the seacliffs beneath the western ramparts.

There was not a particle of masculine courage in Isabel's composition, yet in an event of so much importance her mind could display the most heroic self-command, and, compelled by the necessity, she shrunk not from the difficulties, but with firm courage ascended the battlements, and invited the conference with the English heralds, the foremost of whom, advancing, said :—

"King Edward was not with the feeble. He is sovereign of Scotland, and, as your liege lord, commands from you submission and homage. Yield, then, to his triumphant arms this fortress without delay, and you may expect such mercy as obedience merits; but should your people rashly brave his will, and disdain his clemency, the chastisement of war will quickly teach you the danger of resistance, and an ignominious death fall upon the offender."

"Say to your king," answered Isabel, firmly, "that as the fortune of war has not yet subjugated this castle, it acknowledges not his supremacy, and owns no other liege lord than Robert Bruce, for whom, to the last drop of our blood, we will defend it. Say also to King Edward that we solicit a truce till mid-day to-morrow, when our numbers will offer to his arms a foe worthy of his might. Let us this night rest from action, and be the event of the next prosperous to either army, as Heaven's justice shall direct?"

The party then retired, and Isabel, trusting to the success of her stratagem, ventured with confidence to hope, that should the succours from her arrive before the ensuing mid-day, she should be fully justified in her father decisive resistance, since the wondrous strength of the castle, and its naturally impregnable situation, were circumstances well calculated to inspire her hopes, whilst its defenders, if faithful, might well guard a spot almost inaccessible to the attacks of an enemy, even greater in numbers than those before the walls.

The twilight of evening soon darkened into night. The English heralds returned no more ; and after another hour of watchful anxiety, Isabel, wearied by her exertions, consented to quit the fortifications. She did not, however, retire till she had herself seen the sentinels pace the watch towers, and every postern strongly barred and guarded. All, indeed, within the fortress of Craiglynn; assumed the formidable aspect of a brave defence, and the most determined spirit of gallantry and resistance seemed to prevail throughout the garrison.

CHAPTER XVIII.

Thy bold defence hath forfeited thy life ;
Yet still doth mercy dwell within my heart,
And. upon certain terms, it is decreed
That thou shalt live.

DON RAFFAELLE.

ISABEL had been some time in her apartment, when sounds of sudden tumult ascended from the courts below, and disturbed the solemn quiet that had lately reigned within the castle. The door of the chamber was rudely thrown open, and Cameron, pale and aghast, rushed into her presence, as the loud blast of a war trumpet was echoed through the fortress, and answered by another at a greater distance.

" Treason !—treason !" exclaimed the soldier. " We have been basely betrayed !—Lord Morton, with a band of traitors, have opened the gates to the enemy, and King Edward and his legions have already entered the castle !"

At this instant Isabel's favourite page darted with a wild and disordered mien into the room.

" All is lost, dearest lady !" he cried ;—" fly, beloved mistress, to the sanctuary, for we are overpowered by thousands. The seneschal has lost his life in bravely defending his post, and—hark ! the clash of distant arms yet resound ! Our people are not all dastards, but their small ranks cannot, alas ! oppose whole legions. Fly, dear lady, to the sanctuary ; there only will you be in safety, for the edict of Edward is death and slaughter to all who have opposed him."

The noise grew louder, and evidently approached the interior courts, and ere Isabel could quit the chamber, a blaze of torch-light flashed brightly from the area below her window. With calm firmness she awaited the certain doom that she well knew was not to be avoided, and approaching the casement, beheld a full confirmation of her page's report. Beneath her she saw the majestic portly figure of a man of gigantic stature, clad in burnished armour of steel and gold, and wearing on his head a helmet of the latter metal, whilst a purple scarf crossed his breast, and a robe or surcoat of crimson hung from his shoulders. His gait was haughty and erect, and his features large, commanding, and full of dark and vindictive expression.

"Hail, hail, sovereign king and conqueror of Scotland!" shouted several voices, proceeding from a multitude of figures that surrounded him, whilst the red glare of the flaming torches, as they displayed the savage-looking features of many of the strangers, gave to their aspect a fierce and terrific outline, truly daunting to behold.

At this moment Lord Morton advanced, followed by two English soldiers, bearing the banners of Craiglynn disgracefully reversed; whilst himself, kneeling before the sovereign, said, as he laid two crossed swords at the conqueror's feet,—

"Hail, royal master!—Craiglynn submits to thine invincible command. Deign to accept our homage and obedience, and pardon the rashness of the misguided few who dared presume to resist thy sovereign mandates."

"Rise, my Lord Morton," exclaimed the king; "we are not unmindful of our royal promise, or of thy good faith, but will atone the evils that have befallen thy race, for their duteous loyalty to us at thy intercession; also, we pardon the folly of these misguided people, nor will we be slow to reward thy fidelity with the rich boon thou hast asked. Conduct the daughter of the traitor, Lord Mackenzie, to our presence."

"So please you, my liege, to withdraw awhile to the hall of state," said Morton, "and the Lady Isabel will there, doubtless, bend the knee of reverence to her sovereign."

The wily traitor, with low obsequious reverence, led the way towards the grand entrance, and Edward, not deigning to bend his proud looks to the earth, passed through the courts and entered the interior.

The feelings of emotion that at this moment filled the bosom of Isabel were so varied and tumultuous that language would faintly do justice to them. But grief and anguish for the fate of her father, now more than ever in the power and at the mercy of an inveterate foe, seemed the most overwhelming. The summons which she had distinctly heard given by her imperious victor, and which her page, as he now entered the apartment, again repeated, in an instant aroused the strong decision of her spirit to resolute action and firm resistance. The loose night robe she had assumed was again thrown off, and, assisted by her woman, she was soon attired in all the pomp and splendour of the most regal apparel. Her robes were of rich white satin, studded with pearls and diamonds, and looped with clusters of pendant amethysts. Her waist was clasped with strings of pearls and jewellery, in the form of a beautiful zone, while from her shoulder depended a long flowing mantle of the brightest purple hue, lined with ermine, and edged and spotted with an embroidery of gold. Upon her brow she wore a tiara of regal form, wrought with diamonds and precious ornaments, whose glittering lustre outshone not the sparkling radiancy of her eyes. The portrait of the royal Bruce was suspended from her neck, and those of her parents were braced with amulets of richest pearl upon either wrist.

Adorned for the splendour of a triumph, not the lowly abject submission of a captive, Isabel quitted her apartment, and was passing towards the outer corridor, accompanied by the ladies of her train, when the figure of Lord Morton met her startled view, who had for some time been parading before the door, anxious and watchful for her approach.

Advancing towards her, he addressed Isabel with a supercilious reverence that instantly betrayed the exulting confidence of a successful lover, and concluded with claiming the honour of conducting her to the presence of the sovereign.

Astonished at such open effrontery, she fixed on him a look of such bitter, pointed scorn and indignation, as for a moment nearly disappointed the triumph of his assured success; but disdaining to speak, lest the

abhorrence of her soul should betray her to yet greater indignities, she in silence gave her hand to her page, and bade him conduct her to the king.

Enraged at a contemptuous treatment so openly displayed, and still more mortified at his disappointed expectations, Morton impetuously seized the arm of the page, and throwing him from the princess, bade him at distance learn his duty.

" Shall an audacious slave," he exclaimed, " presume to enter the presence of majesty ! Can the Lady Isabel stoop to such vile indignity, when one who is her equal has offered his services to her ?"

" She will at least not stoop to resent the impotent presumption of Lord Morton," she haughtily answered. " Nor will she deign to use the language of reproach, where its faithless object is degraded even beneath her contempt. But although to your lordship's treachery I am made the subject of a hostile invader, you will do well to recollect that the Princess Isabel is still mistress of her actions, and can still proudly reject the insolence of an arrogant intrusion. Return, my boy," she added to her page ; " your office impels an implicit obedience to no other will than mine ; when *I* dispense with your attendance, then withdraw, but, till commanded otherwise, fulfil the duties of your station."

Isabel again gave her hand to her page, and without deigning to notice Lord Morton, instantly descended the gallery, whilst the traitor's rage could find no other present vent than ineffectual curses ; as at once he was compelled to love the proud beauty, though his galled spirit felt an alternate passion very like hate, to be obliged thus to resign the exulting triumph of presenting to the conqueror a captive so worthy the admiration of contending heroes.

The torches blazing in the hall below, displayed to the princess, as she advanced, the numerous assembled hosts of warriors that thickly lined its immense area. Her majestic figure attracted the admiring glances of those nearest to the entrance, and she sighed deeply as she remembered that but a very brief space had elapsed since she herself was in the chair of state, which now contained the form of him who sat before her as a conqueror.

Edward, leaning from the throne, was conversing with some of the surrounding warriors, whose vizors were removed; whilst many others of the English knights that were not admitted to the honour of the monarch's confidence, were seen in groups parading the hall, and descanting on the inspiring ardency of the late gained conquests, or some newly formed plan for acts of future triumph of cruelty and of bloodshed.

Isabel felt a gentle tremor agitate her frame, but at this moment her pride and delicacy enabled her successfully to suppress all outward appearance of weakness; for she was firmly resolved that the spirit of injured royalty, which had hitherto guided her conduct, should still maintain its rights and assert its own independence.

The king, as Isabel advanced towards the chair of state, viewed her in silent scrutiny, and before Lord Morton could make his way through the crowd, the page had announced, audibly,—

"Her Highness, the Princess Isabel, of Craiglynn."

"I attend to greet the *King of England*," said Isabel, bowing her head courteously, but not bending her knee.

Edward frowned angrily at the majesty of carriage, and loftiness of air, that ill accorded with his own pride. Isabel, however, bent not in prostrate homage and supplication before him; nay, she seemed to disdain the terrors his presence threatened, and to despise his power;—for in her air was apparent all the dignity and openness of an ennobled mind, and all the chastened grandeur of conscious worth and high born native greatness.

Though the king frowned he was fascinated, and with a something in his voice more harsh than his usual imperious speech to a fallen enemy, he said, haughtily,—

"Dost thou forget the reverence due to anointed majesty? Rememberest thou not before whom thou standest? Fearest thou not the terrors of that justice thy misguided zeal and treasonable practices to our rule and power have awakened? Are we not thy liege lord? How darest thou then encourage our subjects to rebellion? Presumest thou to hope the weakness of thy sex would save thee from our vengeance? Our edict is *death*, proclaimed through Scotland, to those who brave our arms and laws! —and such a sentence thou hast thyself incurred. Say, what canst thou urge to mitigate the rigour of our stern decree?"

"Nothing," answered the princess, firmly.

"Hah! thou dost brave us, then!"

"I have never acknowledged the power or the laws of England's sovereign," answered Isabel, "and, therefore, I hold not myself responsible to his tribunal, but still deem myself free, since our castle is unconquered, though the cowardice and treachery of a secret foe has betrayed it into your hands. In opposing the arms of a hostile monarch I obeyed only the dictates of my duty and the voice of nature; remembering that my father's allegiance was given to his rightful lord and sovereign. Nor can the King of England receive from me that homage which solely belongs to the illustrious Bruce, who has been driven from his throne by force of arms."

The heroic firmness with which this speech was uttered startled the English monarch, and roused in a moment all the natural ferocity of his soul, and all the proud, vindictive passions of his mind. He knit his dark, over-arching brows, and fiercely scowling looks of deadly silent meaning on the princess, recoiled on his seat, whilst the surrounding warriors trembled and shrunk from the gathering storm which Isabel, with unbending fortitude, awaited.

Lord Moreton, alarmed for the consequences of her fearless reply, advanced and said,—

"Lady Isabel, you are forgetful and disobedient. Sue for grace; for our royal master, if humbly entreated, will freely pardon the error of your too hasty words. I beseech you to remember the loyalty and reverence due to your lawful sovereign."

" It had been well, my lord," answered Isabel, " if you had done so, and practised the duties you affect to teach. In that case, the niece of your wronged sovereign, Robert Bruce, would not have been the victim of your base treachery and ingratitude."

" Peace, presumptuous girl !" exclaimed Edward, interposing, " Dost thou not tremble at the doom our nod can in a moment execute ?"

Isabel remained unmoved at this threat, and after a few moments the monarch continued,—

" Henceforth, at thy peril, dare not to glance a thought against the right we have gained by conquest; but learn to bend in duty thy stubborn spirit to our will. My word in Scotland is its people's fate, and death the reward of those that disobey. On thee its sentence hangs—thy life is forfeited; but submission and repentance may yet atone thy obstinate treason, and will best become thy age and sex. Learn, proud girl, that still to resist us, is but to pluck down the impending rigour of our avenging laws."

" My sovereign liege," cried Lord Morton, " upon my knee I humbly crave a boon."

" 'Tis granted, sir, almost before it is asked," replied the king. " Rise up and speak thy will."

" Vouchsafe, most gracious sovereign," replied Lord Morton, " to pardon the offence of Lady Isabel; misled by the ambition of Bruce, she has erred only from ignorance of the justice of your claims, and the strong attachments of family connexion. Hereafter these mistaken principles will yield to conviction, and with fidelity she will own no other sovereign than my royal master. For this I answer with my life, and will, so please you, sire, most cheerfully depend the issue of her future faith upon it, and still solicit your majesty's ratification of that promise which was given on a former occasion."

" You have prevailed, my Lord Morton," answered the king. " Your request is granted, and happy is it for her you honour with such preference that she has an advocate whose favour preserves her from our justly provoked wrath. Lady, receive this lord— your future husband —as a monarch's gift. She is yours, Morton; but did we not well believe we may with safety rely on your fidelity and obedience we should pause to trust you with an hostage whose regard to a ruined traitor might win your duty from us. Therefore, my lord, guard well the promise you have given in her behalf, for should your bride prove perfidious and disloyal to our interests, your life shall answer for it. Remember, too, that we forbid, on pain of certain death to both, that the banished Lord Mackenzie should find a refuge within your walls or territories. On these conditions alone shall we consent to remit the sentence on Lady Isabel, or grant the ratification of the boon you have asked."

Morton again knelt. " My gracious liege," he exclaimed, " deign to accept a grateful subject's homage, and his solemn tender of our mutual allegiance."

" 'Tis well, my lord," returned Edward ; " lead the way to the banquet, and let your fair hostage grace our festive carousal. In faith, my lord, you did wisely to secure, unseen by us, our royal assent to a prize so lovely, else had she been added to the number of our Scottish prisoners, and in England bid successfully for the prize of beauty against our high-born dames. We are your guests, fair lady, conduct us, I prithee, to the feast."

Edward rose, and descending from the throne approached the princess, who, with sensations of unutterable poignancy, was thus compelled to endure the mortifying humiliation of being present at the triumphs of those who had enslaved her unhappy country, dethroned her royal uncle, and driven her father from his native halls to banishment and wretchedness. And in addition to such tyranny the tenderest feelings of her soul were to be outraged, and herself doomed to the arms of a man whose base ingratitude had seized on the hour of adversity to betray those who had put their trust in him.

Isabel was placed by the side of Edward at the banquet, whilst opposite to her sat Lord Morton, whose eyes, filled with alternate joy and triumph, were frequently bent on the hapless princess with looks too plainly legible to be misinterpreted, though their expression varied to the deepest reverence as the king, at long intervals, deigned to address him.

The affliction that filled the bosom of Isabel, at length became so painful and overwhelming that her fortitude could no longer support her; her gentle spirit, deeply wounded, could no longer endure the dreadful occurrences of the night; and the varying colour of her cheeks declared the illness that pervaded her frame, and at length she fell back upon her seat senseless. The alarm her faintness caused did not subside till Morton had obtained the king's permission to bear her from the hall.

At length, recovering and finding herself alone with the man she most detested, she started from him, exclaiming,—

" Hence, villain !" for I am still unconquered, though my fortunes are degraded, and will not become your wife, even though the king himself should drag me to the altar."

" Isabel !" exclaimed the subtle traitor, " could you but read my soul, you would behold that deep repentance and contrition which your own virtue has there implanted. Would you then deign forgiveness of the past, every action of my future life should prove my gratitude, my devoted love, and obedience to your every wish."

" Forgiveness to thee!—never!" cried Isabel, with indignant scorn. "To have driven a noble father an exile from his home to wander forlorn and wretched, without a friend to soothe his sorrows, or a bosom on which to rest his aching head; desolate, and, perhaps, again the victim of insanity;—to have betrayed a powerless, helpless female, and to have exposed to the murderous sword of an inexorable and blood-thirsty foe the few generous spirits faithful to their duty, and willing to protect her from the miseries of captivity and outrage. These—these, my lord, are the proofs of love that I have received from one who thus dares profane the sacred name of virtue, and impiously assert that his crimes sprung from his love for me ! Villain ! destitute alike of honour and principle, presume no more to insult my ears with words so blasphemous; but begone, and amidst thy new-found friends seek a companion suitable to thyself to be the sharer of thy future hours, and the abject partner of thy guilt and treachery. Hence, dissembling slave ! and with thee go the knowledge of Isabel's abhorrence; for sooner than link my fate with thine, I will dare appeal to him thy treachery has admitted within our gates. The worst of evils Edward's tyranny can inflict will be but imprisonment, but should it compass even life itself, be assured the soul of Isabel can meet with fortitude the worst tortures that the malice of her enemies can devise."

At this moment a page entered the apartment to require Lord Morton's instant attendance on the king.

" I go," he exclaimed, and the messenger instantly retired. Then, after a pause of some duration, Lord Morton, with an ill-concealed scowl of anger and resentment, continued thus :—

" Ere I quit this chamber, Isabel, know that thyself alone has been the cause of all the mischief that has occurred, for, had not thy withering scorn and proud rejection of my suit rendered me desperate of consequences, Craiglynn would have cast wide its portals to receive its now banished lord, and my sword should have opposed to the last the entrance of the all-conquering Edward. And now the crisis of my bold attempt approaches. I have adored thy matchless perfections and wondrous virtue with a lover's tenderness which not even thy frowns could subdue. To-morrow, girl, yields thee to my arms."

" To-morrow !" cried the terrified princess.

" Aye, to-morrow," he replied ; " so deign to forget the past, and even here thy father should find security and shelter from Edward's revenge. Bury, then, in oblivion the memory of this night's transactions, and my never-failing love shall guard both thee and thine with tenderest care, and his future life shall atone for the errors he has this day committed. Thou shalt rule my destiny, and to win thy pity and esteem, I will become the soldier of thine uncle, Bruce, and with willing heart will fight his battles, and help to avenge his cause. But if, regardless of my power and thine own helpless weakness, thou wilt still oppose my wishes, and refuse to bestow voluntarily thy hand upon me, the moment that makes thee my wife by force makes me eternally thy deadly foe, and thyself my slave !"

" Villain !" gasped Isabel, horrorstruck at the perfidity of the man who thus addressed her.

" Aye," he said ; " I am prepared for thine anger, but the hour of triumph is now mine, and it depends upon thyself to avert thy misery, and make me still thy adorer—not thy tyrant husband. My speech is open and undissembled, and what my words now proclaim, my deeds shall hereafter testify. Isabel may still live happily as the wife of Lord Morton, and share equally with himself in honour and command. If she regards her future peace, she will, with prudent caution, shun the dangerous alternative. I now, however, leave her for a time, and ere to-morrow's sun shall set, will demand the final answer that decides her happiness or misery."

As he spoke thus he quitted the chamber, with a look so full of defiance and resolution, that the hapless girl recoiled from him with horror. Awhile she sat pensively meditating over the increasing miseries that now so thickly encompassed her. Her destiny, dreadful as it was, seemed indeed to be fixed irrevocably, and was not to be avoided by any means that she could think of.

Morton's successful treachery had evidently achieved its full accomplishment, and now, on every side hemmed in with hosts of foes, no dawning hope appeared to cheer the horizon of her destiny of the dark train of evils the future gloomy prospects presented to her view.

Disgracefully held captive within the walls that had witnessed her birth, and totally at the mercy of a fierce, inexorable victor; deprived of those whose loyalty and faith had been tried, and would have still done much for her safety, the alternative was indeed dreadful ; whilst her increasing terrors and distress on her father's account, gave a blow to the remaining fortitude of her former confidence and hope, that expelled every active faculty of her mind, and too certainly aroused the strongest fears of an inevitable destiny of approaching sorrow and misfortune.

For hours Isabel sat ruminating in melancholy solitude upon her altered condition. The morning of this inauspicious day, had beheld her strong in hope of a happier issue, and free from apprehension such as she was now become the victim of; but in a few hours how sudden and terrible had been the reverse! In one little moment she had fallen from her elevation to its lowest extreme, and the prospect of futurity was indeed forlorn and desolate.

At an early hour she had dismissed her attendants that she might, unseen and undisturbed, retire to weep in private over those severe misfortunes she was now alone to bear the whole weight of. She had passed into the small turret chamber of her suite, which opening on the terrace of the western rampart, overhung the rocky summit of the precipice, and was engulphed amongst the waves. She continued to watch from her casement the gradual stillness that had succeeded the late tumult, and had leisure to ponder on her approaching fate, freed from every observation. As this part of the castle was the most remote and unacceptable, the towers seemed to be totally unguarded by sentinels, and Isabel, assured of being uninterrupted, resolved to indulge her mournful ideas, by approaching nearer to the sea. The bell had tolled the departed hour of midnight, but its long echoed vibrations had passed by the unhappy girl. She now threw aside some portion of her robes and ornaments, and with a white flowing veil that quite enveloped her form, descended the narrow steps of the turret chamber, and opening the private portal, admitted herself on the lower terrace that hung over the white foaming billows of the ocean.

CHAPTER XIX.

" Say,
For what fell purpose dost thou visit me ?
Seek'st thou my life at this dark, midnight hour
When all around is silent loneliness ?"
                    THE INDIAN CAPTIVE.

KING EDWARD and his warrior knights sat till a late hour carousing in the splendid hall of Craiglynn, and revelling in the sumptuous feast of victory and triumph. At length, after midnight, the king retired, as did his nobles, to the various grand state apartments of the castle.

Throwing himself upon a gilded leathern couch, surmounted by a rich purple canopy of velvet and gold, the king soon yielded to the influence of sleep, when his pages and attendants retired to keep a watchful eye over the slumbers of the monarch in the adjoining ante-chamber.

The antique silver lamps that burned in the room, seemed to cast but a dim and bluish light on the heavy gothic walls, darkly lined with tapestry, once the labour of many a high born dame of Scotland, wherein were recorded the martial deeds of departed heroes, who, like the hands that had wrought this memorial to their fame, were long since mouldered into dust.

The chamber was spacious, and many of its arched recesses remained dark, notwithstanding the lamps that were burning in it. From one of these obscure alcoves, however, the tall figure of a man might have been seen emerging; he was tall, and the long dark cloak that he wore completely concealed his form, as with noiseless footsteps he passed down from the place where he had entered towards the centre of the room. Here for a few seconds he remained stationary as if in silent contemplation, but in a little time he again moved forward and approached the couch of the sleeping king. A lamp that hung suspended a little beneath the canopy, shone upon the countenance of the unconscious monarch, and the stranger again paused to gaze upon the sight before him.

The unknown intruder upon loyalty, wore upon his head a helmet of steel, that served completely to conceal the countenance of the wearer. Silently he advanced nearer to the couch, and raised with one hand the rich velvet hangings, and continued awhile to gaze intently on the sleeping, unguarded monarch of England. At length his voice found utterance, and in tones of command he loudly exclaimed,—

"Awake, Edward! blood thirsty and remorse king, awake and look upon thy foe!"

"Ah! who and what art thou?" cried the king, starting from his heavy slumber, and half rising from his couch.

"Thy mortal enemy! behold me!" exclaimed the other casting off his outer garment, which had till now concealed the figure of a warrior, encased in complete armour, and whose right hand upheld a naked dagger, which he held threateningly over the king.

"What, ho! there, my guards!" cried Edward, in tones rendered inaudible by the sudden tremor with which he had been seized. At this moment he snatched up a sword that stood by his bed-side, but this, with herculean strength, the other wrenched from his grasp.

"Make but one movement to escape me," he exclaimed; dare but to repeat that cry, and instant death awaits thee!"

"Who art thou?" again demanded the king.

"Behold me!" answered the other, removing his vizor, and revealing the pale, but still noble features of the unfortunate monarch of Scotland. "Ambitious King," he continued; "scourge of the innocent, and fell destroyer of the race of Bruce, dost thou not shudder and recoil with conscious guilt, to behold alive the kingly ruin of him thou hast driven from his throne?"

"Ah! I know thee now, presumptuous fool!" exclaimed Edward, with a scowl of deadly malice and revenge, "But thou art now in my power, and not all the glories of my former conquests could have presented me with a triumph such as this. My victim is at length within my grasp;—the traitor dies—and with him perishes the last hope of Scotland's freedom from my yoke."

"Within thy grasp, proud king," retorted the other, in a tone of contempt. "Prepare then thy tortures, rack every limb, and let the lingering agonies of suffering be mine, such as thy black soul only can delight to practice! Within thy grasp, thou man of death! Thinkest thou thy wrath can reach one who scorns and loathes thee? Dost thou suppose, unhappy Scotland's king, destroyed by the fierce love for universal rapine, will bend before thy proud tribunal, and meanly beg a life which thou canst never give, nor he receive from thee? Know that he scorns alike thy malice and the terrors of thy better fortune, which have indeed bestowed on thee greatness for a time, but not for ever, Hear, and thank me for thy life. Thou seest me here alone, deserted, powerless; cut off from every succour, and basely robbed by thee of this, my last retreat. In the midst of foes, Bruce is still invulnerable, and fearless of any evils thou mayest seek to execute."

"Art thou here to slay me?" demanded the king.

"No," replied Bruce; "thy life was at my mercy, and had not the ruling principle of honour, which thou knowest not, withheld the justice of the deed, with one avenging blow my steel had drank thy blood and freed unhappy Scotland from her usurping spoiler."

"How camest thou here?" asked Edward.

"I entered here unknown to all," answered the other ; "my accursed foe lay powerless at my mercy, and all his senses entranced in heavy slumber. Yet, though the retribution of my wrongs demanded thy life as an atonement for savage deeds against my friends, my country, and myself, yet the soul of Bruce is incapable of treachery, nor will he stab the foe that cannot openly resist him. Now then, I bid thee rush to thy revenge ; call forth thy myrmidons, and bid them rid thee of a foe thou so much dost hate. Edward is incapable of magnanimity, and will triumph in the blood of one who has dared to assert his country's rights and liberty."

"How gained you entrance here?" asked Edward; "and what is the purport of your midnight visit, if not murder?"

"Fate conducted me hither," answered Bruce; "to hurl on England's king poor hapless Scotland's curse! To blast thine ears, tyrant usurper of the rights of Bruce, with the repetitions of thine accursed deeds!"

"Begone! I'll hear no more!" exclaimed the king, casting a look of deadly hatred and smothered fury on his foe, who stood undaunted and unmoved before him. "Begone, I say; quit my presence ere my wrath rises to crush thee, and my voice pronounces the doom that will hurry thee to an ignominous death!"

"Not till thou hast heard repeated the wrongs of him thou hast dared to oppress," answered Bruce; "and till thou hast been made to tremble at the malediction I have come to hurl upon thee. To lay waste with fire and sword a valiant, but unfortunate people; to pluck from his seat of hereditary greatness a sovereign prince, were the early deeds of a ferocious, lawless plunderer; not incited to arms by the noble daring of a hero, or the justice of a legal claim, but rather the dark inspirations of an ambitious friend, goading on its ruthless votary to acts of cruelty and injustice. Yet, even triumph satiated not thy restless thirst of universal sway; to public injury, Edward, unmindful of his future fame, dared add private cruelty and murder; and the unoffending captives of his reckless conquests, fell the slaughtered victims of his malice. But Heaven's eyes are countless, and its arm of justice shall here, or hereafter judge between us. Thy dark malice is levelled only at the feeble and the helpless, and ages yet to come, when they shall record thy cruel deeds, will curse thy memory as the plague of mankind, and turn from the chronicle with disgust, amazed to read of characters once so great, clouded and blackened with crimes that sat at nought Heaven's delegated attributes, and outraged nature's laws. The orphan's and the widow's curses, mingled with their tears, shall ascend to the footstool of eternal justice, and draw down the bolt of vengeance on thee. Where is now my wife, my suffering queen? Where all that were most dear to me? Edward, ask thy restless heart the fate of those whose only crimes was being the friends of Bruce. Exposed to the tortures of an English rabble, encaged like common malefactors, and savagely borne through the streets to thy capital, a spectacle of disgraced majesty, the bleeding, heart-stricken captives of a relentless conqueror!"

"Avaunt! quit my presence!" cried the infuriated king; "or my voice shall doom thee to an instant and dreadful death!"

But Bruce heeded him not, and still mindful of the injuries he had endured, he continued,—

"Where, Edward, are my gallant brothers? Butchered by thy vindictive, rancourous hate and cold-blooded policy. But think not their unappeased souls shall long wander unsatisfied, or their blood sink unavenged in that lowly grave thy deadly malice bestowed. Scotland yet shall rise indignant at her injuries, to blast the ambitious workings of her destroyers, for her monarch survives her downfall, and with a voice prophetic, now greets thee, Edward, with his own and his people's curses. Sudden and speedy

be thy fate ! May the hells of conscious guilt rack thy dying moments and torture thy latest thoughts with the horrors of the future. Despair of Heaven's mercy for the blood of the thousands thou hast slaughtered in the wantoness of thy power, shall weigh down thy spirits, and ring in thy startled ear the terrific knells and shrieks of retributive justice. And when thy cruel and relentless soul shall dare ascend towards the gates of Heaven to receive its fiat, it shall be hurled to the lakes of eternal darkness, there to receive the punishment of thy earthly crimes. Remember the words of Bruce, lest their prophetic greetings be indeed accomplished ! Tremble, Edward, and depart *my land*, for my mind is yet unconquered, and I will still oppose thy tyranny and oppression ;—still cherish the hoped for moment when mine and my kindreds wrongs, and those of my oppressed country, may one day be avenged. Awhile thou art a victor, but soon will I tear from thy proud helm the laurel of thy savage triumphs. My spirit rises to the bold enterprize, and Bruce shall yet live to free his people from Edward's usurping yoke, and be it thy torment to know that thou hast still a potent, deadly enemy to contend against.

" Farewell !—In the battle's heat remember this my defiance, (casting on the floor a gage), and tremble to encounter me ; for my deeds shall still proclaim me thy rival, and the stern opposer of thy cruelty and ambition. Once more, farewell ; here thou art safe, but, in the battle's conflict, should we meet in arms, the justice of Heaven will decide between us, for then we part not till one or both of us is silent for ever !"

Bruce had been slowly retreating ; at the close of his words he paused majestically, and cast on the dismayed king a look so deadly searching and indignant, that Edward, who had never till now known the influence of fear, shrunk back recoiling, whilst Bruce, with measured pace, moved firmly across the chamber, bending, as he departed, his frowning glances upon Edward, who watched his receding footsteps till the figure became indistinct in the dark shades of the distant recesses of the apartment.

No. 15

At length the king roused himself. His fierce implacable nature had, indeed, for a time, shrunk from the sight of the unfortunate monarch of Scotland, and the sudden appearance of his rival had divested his mind of that command it had never till now ceased to practice. The dark passions of his soul again reigned despotic and wrathful, and he resolved to take advantage of the fortune chance had given him, to annihilate for ever the possibility of those threats being fulfilled, which had fallen from the indignant Bruce.

Starting from his couch, he loudly sounded an alarm bugle that lay upon a table near him, and in an instant the pages and guards rushed into his presence.

"How now, caitiffs!" he exclaimed wrathfully; "dare ye slumber on your watch, while a midnight assassin assails our rest? Fly, and instantly drag the intruding villain before me."

The guard, astonished and dismayed, fell upon their knees and solemnly assured the king they had been vigilant, and that no person had obtained admittance through the ante-chamber in which they watched. The king then recollected that Bruce had disappeared at a part of the room directly opposite the door they had just entered, and pointing towards the spot, he bade them search beyond for a traitor that he suspected was thereabouts concealed.

This command was instantly obeyed, but not the slightest opening appeared to warrant the belief that any one could have disappeared through a part of the chamber that contained no appearance of a passage, nor was there any other door in the room than that which led to the one in which the guard had been keeping watch.

"By Heaven!" exclaimed the king, "this is some deeply concerted device of treacherous malice! These Scots are faithless and still dare brave our vengeance. What ho, there!—call up the lords of our council, and bid forth Lord Morton. Meantime, go some of you and search through every hollow of the fortress for a secret enemy. Away! He that brings me the head of Bruce,—not long since departed hence,—shall receive ten thousand crowns of gold."

The alarm instantly became general—the whole garrison was under arms, and lights and torches blazed through every chamber and secret winding recess of the castle. Not a spot, however remote or obscure, was left unexplored; but the search was useless, for the departure of Bruce, like his arrival, was wrapt in mystery; and it seemed as if superhuman aid alone could have saved him from the destroying grasp of Edward's unrelenting fury.

Even Isabel had been disturbed and forcibly dragged to the presence of the king, though totally unaware of all that had occurred during the night. With stern anger Edward questioned and commanded her on pain of death to reveal her knowledge of the fugitive, and the means by which he had been admitted into the fortress. Amazed, and unacquainted with the purport of this sudden violence, the princess faintly declared her innocence, and disavowed the slightest knowledge of the means by which the stranger could have gained entrance to the chamber of the king.

Dissatisfied and gloomily lowering upon Isabel, the king more fiercely demanded if there were any secret passages leading from the apartment, hitherto undiscovered by the guards; and as he thus severely questioned her, he continued to watch keenly her every varying feature, in which he sought to discover in her air those marks of conscious confusion which might betray her to that fate he was desirous to involve her in. For Edward, remembering the undaunted firmness of her resistance to his might, and her adherence to the cause of Bruce, felt at the moment the most deadly rancour against her, which was still further increased by the dangerous adventure in which he had just now been engaged. And although his promise had been solemnly given to bestow on Lord Morton the princess and her fortunes, as a reward of the traitor's consent to deliver up the fortress of Craiglynn into his hands, yet the relationship that he had discovered existing between her and the oppressed royal hero of Scotland— a circumstance that Lord Morton had been careful to conceal—and the unbending firmness of her conduct, though his captive, had all aroused in his thoughts that deadly hatred and jealousy the king of England ever entertained against all those who had virtue and magnanimity to oppose him; and those sentiments of danger to the life of the innocent Isabel, which more than once had threatened her with a fate even more hostile to her life than her marriage with a discovered villain and traitor.

The unshrinking eye of Isabel, however, on this last occasion, fell not abashed beneath the penetrating scowl of scrutiny that was rivetted on her; nor could all the anxious search of Edward's guards pierce the mysterious veil that had favoured the retreat of the heroic Bruce.

"There is witchcraft in this dark, traitorous transaction!" exclaimed King Edward, fiercely. "Well we know Scotland's rebel practices and blasphemous incantations!" and he frowned fearfully on Isabel and the Scottish knights that were now assembled near him. "But," he continued, "we will defeat your hopes, and crush the subtle snake ere its venom can again engender its mischiefs. Prepare, lords, for our departure; treason still lurks beneath these mutinous walls, whose towers, teeming with factions against our state, we here seize on, lest they should again become a receptacle for rebellion, and a shelter to traitors from our justice. My Lord Morton, this instrument empowers you with full authority to conclude your nuptials with Mackenzie's heiress (giving the exulting traitor a parchment sealed with the royal signet). Remove her from hence speedily, lest the terrors of our punishment for treasons we still suspect originate in her, should decree her a doom such as her rebel deeds have provoked."

The Princess Isabel was again conducted to her apartment, and as she reached the interior, found herself no longer privileged to pass the postal of the ante-chamber, for a guard was instantly placed at the door which opened on the corridor, and restricted the freedom of her retainers.

CHAPTER XX.

" 'Tis joy to meet thee e'en midst fortune's frowns,
For I had thought thee dead, and in my dreams
Had seen thee, to my horror, lie before me
All festering in thy shroud."

THE RECUSANT.

In listless solicitude and dread of expected evils, still more fatal in their effect than those she was now the victim of, the sad hours of the day that succeeded this night of tumult and cruel humiliation, were passed away by the suffering Princess Isabel. Alas! the bitterness of regrets more poignantly increased, and the worst of miseries that would in a little space of time desolate every hope, at length rendered her the victim of the most harrowing despair.

Yet, rousing herself from these useless repinings, she began to reflect that should King Edward really have quitted the Castle of Craiglynn, something still might intervene to oppose the hated doom which impended; or could she delay the dreaded ceremony but a few days longer, there was a possibility that its completion might be totally defeated. It must, however, be admitted that her most terrible doubts hardly permitted her to calculate on this faint hope, since she could not forget what fatal power Edward's signet in the hands of her hated foe, gave him over the disposal of her person.

There were other causes, too, for the uneasiness of our heroine; the fate of her tenderly beloved father now weighed more oppressively than ever to her mind, and to her very natural alarms for her own security from the violence that threatened, was added the sickening dread of his unhappy destiny; and to the anguish of suspense was appended the horrible suspicion that he was perhaps at that moment a prisoner to the ruthless Edward, and might even now be condemned to death.

"His death!" she almost frantically exclaimed;—"oh, Heaven, avert that terrible blow, and the worst tortures that my evil destinies can inflict, will be cheerfully borne, rather than the lasting affliction of an event that is too terrible even for contemplation!"

The morning had gradually gilded over the western seas with a cloudless sky, whose bright glories Isabel had beheld, for the first time in her life, unmoved, nor did she as usual welcome his glad presence with the pious orison she was ever till now want to offer.

Buried in profound and pensive rumination she sat, or rather reclined on her chair, reckless of the fleeting time, and absorbed in misery and almost hopeless dejection; and not till the martial clangour of many instruments which echoed from the various courts, and were reverberated over the distant waves, did she wake to the occurrences of the present hour from the gloomy employment of her melancholy thoughts. The tumult arising from many voices resounded, whilst the neighing of eager steeds prancing in the spacious court-yard of the castle, declared some sudden event about to take place.

At mid-day her attendant, Catherine, with difficulty gained admittance to the apartments of the Princess Isabel. Her gentle, pitying heart felt shocked to view the ravages that sorrow had in so few hours effected. Isabel raised her tearful eye on her respectful attendant, and having somewhat removed her composure, she with a painfully assumed smile, welcomed her return.

"King Edward, madam," said Catherine, "has at length left the castle; but I grieve to say it no longer contains our own brave troops."

"Indeed," cried Isabel; "what has become of them?"

"They have all been sent away prisoners," answered the faithful attendant; "and the ramparts are now filled with sentinels chosen from the English archers; and they say the wards are garrisoned with more than a thousand men at arms."

"And Lord Morton?"

"Has gone to escort the king part of his way towards the north," answered Catherine. "He, however, soon returns, for purposes, I fear, most hostile to your highness's peace, since, before his departure, he gave orders that the chapel should be instantly prepared for his union with yourself, and has ordered litters and covered cars to be in readiness to convey you, with the females of your suite to another forfeited castle of your father's, granted to Lord Morton in right of his marriage with your highness."

"His marriage!—and with me!" repeated Isabel, recoiling back with a feeling of horror, that she could not suppress. "Yet, alas, girl!" she continued; "such I fear, is too certainly my allotted doom."

"I am, indeed afraid, your highness, there is no way of escaping it," exclaimed Catherine.

"Oh, Heaven!" cried the princess, in accents of the deepest despair, "are there no means to avoid a destiny so abject and hateful? Am I, indeed, to be made the sacrifice of the villain's successful treachery? Must I become so lost a creature—so despicable even to myself, and yield my liberty to a wretch my soul abhors? Tell me, Catherine, are there no means, no aid yet left me in Craiglynn, that may defeat the wretchedness and ruin that awaits me if I become the unwilling bride of Morton?"

"Alas! madam," said Catherine, "I have no hope to bestow, all that were loyal to your interests, and attached to your person and safety are removed from this castle. Every avenue is guarded with spies and sentinels; nor is the freedom of passing to or from your apartments permitted unquestioned."

"We have no hope, then?" replied the princess.

"I fear not," answered Catherine; "for vainly may we hope to oppose the will of those who possess such potent means of enforcing the utmost limits of authority, from which there is, unhappily, no appeal."

"Oh," cried the Princess Isabel, fervently, as her outstretched arms were raised towards Heaven; "oh! that the guardian angel of virtue, pitying my sorrows and my most urgent necessities, would once again conduct my wronged father hither. Then not vainly should the hapless Isabel implore assistance from his paternal arm, and once more should I be preserved from the artful snares that have been laid for me by this accursed traitor."

Catherine, with affectionate zeal, strove to divert the grief of her nearly subdued mistress, and by a thousand kind attentions, and occasionally changing the nature of the conversation, she sought, not only to chase away all dull thoughts, but to inspire a hope in the bosom of her mistress that she in vain tried to encourage herself.

The day passed slowly away in melancholy quietude, and the princess was suffered to remain undisturbed within her chamber; for warned by the report of her faithful attendant, she shrunk with timidity from the licentious insolence of the guard, who now lined the outward gallery of her suite, and carefully avoided exposing herself to a useless mortification. The privilege, however, of passing unnoticed upon the broad terrace, which extended along that portion of the ramparts, was still within her power, for as yet no watch had been placed there, and satisfied with the perfect security of this remote spot, it had, perhaps, on that account, escaped the notice of those who had forcibly taken possession of the castle.

Hither then, when evening approached, Isabel repaired, and was gratified at finding that there was no danger of discovery, for each end of the rampart was guarded by a lofty tower and portcullis; the latter being securely chained and bolted on the interior arch of these ponderous portals.

As she paced up and down the night grew chill and dark, except when the evening lightnings, at slow intervals of time, shot forth their faint bright flames, and displayed the melancholy waste of waters below, whose heavy rolling billows lashed fiercely the rugged frowning shores, and gave forth a sullen, threatening interruption to the solemn silence which usually marks the period of nature's repose.

The wind, as it swept the tall forest pines that waved high over the opposite mountain summits which were divided by the broad armlet of the sea from the western basement of the rampart towers, whistled mournfully to the responding sighs of the hapless Isabel, who continued for a length of time to lean over the heavy parapet, as her tearful eyes were fixed intently on the dark abyss, and reflecting upon the sad vicissitudes to which fortune has subjected her she could not forbear weeping at a destiny which each succeeding moment served to render the more certain.

At length, an object of an indistinguishable shape and form seemed to be slowly moving along beneath the overhanging precipice; but our heroine was raised at too great a height to be able to discover its real appearance, whilst the measured and slowly repeated dash of the oar, that now at intervals sounded from the ocean, seemed moved by cautious hands; and as the lightnings sometimes flashed a brighter gleam, Isabel was at last able to descry a pinnace with some human figures in it; but so diminished were they in size, from the vast depth of space downwards, that they seemed more like fairies then men, sporting on the shores, and half revealing their shadowy substance to mortal eyes. Isabel gazed upon the spot with surprise, and, scarcely conscious of what she was doing, she waved her veil over the lofty battlements, and then in tones of intense anxiety, exclaimed:—

"Who goes there? Speak, I implore you, and say, if you are friends of the hapless Isabel."

The fragile vessel glided on, and in a moment or two afterwards approached close under the ramparts where the boatmen drew in their oars, and the pinnace remained stationary. The figures appeared, by the extreme caution of their conduct, to desire secresy, and soon again their dim outlines vanished, as the gleaming lightnings ceased to dart forth their vivid flashes.

For some few minutes every trace was extinct, till the moon, bursting from a thick overhanging cloud, once more revealed to her sight the objects below, and displayed them before her more distinctly than ever. The boat still remained near the spot where she had last seen it, but as the signal displayed by Isabel was beheld by the men below, she heard their voices, and among them caught the sound of a voice that was familiar to her ear. Astonished, she started back, uncertain whether her senses deceived her or not, for her bosom was instantly filled with the most tumultuous and agitating feelings, and she scarely dared give way to the transporting hope that for a moment had found its way to her bosom. At length, however, the voice was again heard addressing itself to those in the boat.

"These ramparts and bastions," it exclaimed, "terminate the Princess Isabel's suite of apartments—and see!—some shining object glitters from that embattled parapet above."

"Oh, Heaven!" cried Isabel with joyful emotion, "it is my father!—He lives!—he lives! I know that voice; my ear was faithful to my heart's instinctive whispering, and it tells me that I am not—cannot be deceived! Speak again, oh, blessed sounds, and once more, dear father, recal your Isabel from despair to hope and joy."

"Be cautious, I implore you," cried Catherine, in accents of alarm, as Isabel, overcome with her emotions, sunk upon her bosom. "Suppress these tumultuous outpournigs of your frantic cries, should inquire their cause, and alarm the guarded watchfulness of your foes."

"Tell me, Catherine," exclaimed the princess, "did you not hear the well known tones of my father's voice?"

"I did, your highness," answered the attendant; "but your longer presence here may thwart whatever plans have been thought of for your release. Retire, therefore, I entreat;—I will, myself, speak to these strangers, and if so, as you suspect one of them should indeed prove to be your father, he will know me, and answer any questions I may put."

Scarcely conscious of what she did, the Princess Isabel fell upon her knees in speechless emotion, as Catherine, waving the veil repeatedly from the battlements, was distinctly seen by the strangers below, for the moon at this moment was entirely free from the clouds, and gave every surrounding object clearly and completely to the view.

"Isabel! dearest Isabel!" cried a voice in cautious, yet distinct tones, that rather startled Catherine, who looked round to see if any one was observing them. At last, satisfied that they were so far safe, she leant over the battlements, and exclaimed eagerly :—

"Who is it that calls upon the captive princess at this late hour? She is close at hand, but the danger of her situation prevents her giving any answer till she is assured that you are friends. If you come to rescue her, give some token by which she may know your faith."

Though speechless from excessive surprise and joy, Isabel could no longer remain inactive, and looking over the parapet, she was instantly recognised by her father."

"My loved Isabel," he exclaimed, "be not alarmed, for the hour of your deliverance is at hand. A secret entrance, unknown to all but me, and the former possessors of Craiglynn, will soon conduct me from this spot to your presence. Be prepared—be resolute, for I came to rescue thee from captivity and danger. Hush! no more; the watch are now parading round the walls. Adieu, my child—but ere long expect to see me again."

"Amazed, transported, and like one just waking from the stupor of a trance, the princess trembled so violently as to be unable any longer to support herself; with faltering steps she tottered from the terrace of the rampart, and, led by her attached and faithful attendant, she once more entered her own apartment, and sunk powerless from conflicting emotions upon a couch, where she awaited in pale and speechless expectation the promised blessing which was once more to restore her to the arms of a beloved parent.

Thus some few minutes elapsed, but all still remained silent, and Isabel's eyes were vainly bent in agonizing impatience towards the door : but it unfolded not, nor was she at last conscious of her father's presence till the sound of his voice startled her from the trance into which she had fallen."

"My child! my beloved Isabel!" he exclaimed, and in an instant she was clasped rapturously in his arms.

For a brief space of time she was unable to articulate a word. At last, she distrustfully raised her eyes towards his face,—the vision was indeed real,—her lips quivered, and with extreme difficulty, she faltered :—

"My father! Do I then behold once more the beloved friend, who I feared had been torn away from me by the ruthless hand of death ?"

Scarcely had she utterred this ere she slided from his embrace, overcome with the glad tide of happiness that was so unexpectedly completed. Excess of joy had been even more fatal than its opposite extreme; she had endured unshrinkingly, the severity of fortune's bitterest afflictions, but this unlooked for reverse at once overpowered her feelings, and it was some few moments ere the care of Lord Mackenzie restored her again to animation.

The ensuing scene between them can only be imagined by those whose feelings are keenly sensitive to the touch of nature's softest impressions, and for a long time the deeply oppressed father and daughter were alike speechless ; but every expressive look, and each fond endearing embrace that love and affection gives birth too, can alone declare the exstacy such a meeting must give birth too.

Isabel, when a little calmed, beheld with deep sorrow, the wan, shrunk visage of her father's looks, still furrowed with the lines of cureless grief and unextinguished passion. The loss of Emmeline was rooted in his heart never to be eradicated ; and the silent despair which now succeeded to his former wild ungovernable sorrows, was too legibly imprinted in his hollow sunken eye, to hope ever to be subdued from his constant memory and devoted affection.

Lord Mackenzie loved—fondly loved his daughter, and would have shed the best and last drop of his blood in her defence. He felt for her every paternal emotion of tenderness for her happiness and welfare; nor was his generous bosom less unmindful of her uncommon virtues and rare talents, although that bosom loved another even more devotedly than herself.

The dangerous situation in which Isabel was placed had been his constant meditation; nor would the consciousness of his own perils decrease the greater sense he had of her's. In the battle's furious rage her safety was his chief concern, and could he have reached Craiglynn before the hostile Edward became its imperious master, much of Isabel's present sufferings might have been spared, and the ancient fortress of his ancestors might still have proudly maintained its independency.

But to have risked his own safety by an open return to his lost domains would have been to expose himself needlessly to all the deadly fury of the victorious monarch, and might, in the end, have accelerated the fate of his child; who, robbed of her only support, would have become too certainly the victim of a destiny from which there would be no after appeal, and from the conviction of this certainty, Lord Mackenzie resolved to await the arrival of a more fortunate moment, since he had still a means of entering the castle of Craiglynn without even a fear or chance of being discovered.

Attended only by his dependent, Rupert, whom he believed faithful to his interests, he arrived at the shores that were engulphed under the vast rocky promontories of his princely territory, amidst whose wild solitary caverns he secreted himself and his attendant through the day, and at night ventured forth to snatch his child from the dangerous abyss, he was but too well assured the treachery and base ingratitude of Lord Morton had prepared to involve her in. He had, in fact, learnt from Cameron the chief transactions that had taken place in the castle during his absence, and from this man, whose keen penetration had sifted the masked designs of the ambitious Morton, he had gathered quite sufficient to assure him that haste was now absolutely necessary.

More than an hour had elapsed since the arrival of Lord Mackenzie, and the tolling of the heavy curfew suddenly proclaiming the lateness of the evening, awoke Isabel from the delirium of her silent joy. Her father, more collected now than he had been at the period of his first arrival, now proposed their immediate departure, since it was impossible to hope for security, or the liberty of action, in the now hostile towers of Craiglynn.

He had braved the wrathful edict of the relentless King of England, promulgated against himself, and every other heroic chief in Scotland, whose high rank and vast interests had been opposed against his savage, lawless arms; an event too frequent in Edward's usurped government to surprise Lord Mackenzie, or warp his generous adherence to an injured sovereign's cause.

The necessity of precaution, therefore, in his approaches to Craiglynn had delayed his earlier arrival; and it is not unlikely that Robert Bruce (to whom the noble towers of Craiglynn Castle had long been familiar) had departed by a leading avenue that branched into the very entrance by which Lord Mackenzie had gained admission.

Anxious to depart with her father as soon as possible, the Princess Isabel now retired to an inner chamber, to assume a dress less costly and more suitable to her present state, and which would better disguise her

person from the possibility of a discovery; whilst Lord Mackenzie, continuing to pace the chamber, passed the moments of his daughter's absence in melancholy meditation,—invariably ruminating on the long train of evils which had blighted his peace, and now successfully robbed his only child of that once exalted station and future prospect of honourable greatness she was born to inherit.

At times the moon was visible through the gathering clouds, but the wind had risen, and in hoarse, hollow murmurs swelled the lashing billows, and agitated their waters into threatening whirlpools, anticipating the symptoms of an approaching thunderstorm.

Anxious for the safety of his daughter, Lord Mackenzie passed through the turret closet, and descending to the terrace, approached the parapet, to observe if the tempest that lowered was likely to impede their projected escape; whilst Isabel was soon attired in a plain grey robe, whose only ornament was a trimming of sable, together with a veil which she wore to conceal her face from the gaze of impertinent curiosity. Plain as her dress was, however, every intelligent feature shone transparent, and was lighted by the cheering ray of hope, whose sweet serenity had already diffused its blessings, and recalled her depressed spirits to their wonted tranquillity,— for she felt assured that in a very short period the dreaded evils of the past hour would terminate, and she should yet escape a doom which she had trembled even to contemplate.

But she was fated to receive yet another shock, for scarcely had she passed the portal of her private chamber and entered the saloon, when the exterior door of the latter was hastily thrown open, and Lord Morton, unattended by any of his retinue, entered the apartment. Alarmed with every dreadful apprehension of discovery, the princess was unable to repel this insolent intrusion, but cast her eyes fearfully towards the seat on which

No. 16.

she had left her father on her previous retirement.   He, however, was not
yet returned to the saloon, and Isabel's looks, though she breathed again
more freely, sufficiently bespoke, by the death-like paleness of her countenance, the secret of her terrors.

As Lord Morton advanced towards the princess he beheld the change in
her attire with surprise and distrust.

"Are these," he said, "to be the nuptial robes that grace our union,
Lady Isabel?   I had fondly hoped," he continued, after waiting a brief
space for a reply, "that you would have given me a very different reception, and to have found my charming bride adorned, like her matchless
self, in all the triumphs of beauty, instead of being attired in robes that
would far better have suited a cloistered nun."

"My Lord Morton," she replied, in a commanding tone, "you can expect from the Princess Isabel no voluntary courtesy, since you deny her
even the privileges due to her sex, and insolently breaking down the ceremony of respect, thus insult her sight, and intrude, without permission, on
the sanctity of her retirement!"

"You are angry with me," he exclaimed.

"And not without sufficient cause," replied Isabel.   "I have, however,
but little to add, except to assure you that however the tyranny of a late
event may have operated, it cannot sanction your ill-founded expectations,
since you must be well aware that I have a voice, without which your delusive projects and vain attempts can never be fulfilled."

"Do you still reject me, notwithstanding the power I now possess
over you?" exclaimed Lord Morton, but ill suppressing the wrath which
consumed him.

"My lord," she replied, firmly, "I cannot stoop to the shallow artifice
of dissimulation, or disguise that too justly aroused abhorrence your actions
and yourself have created in my soul.   You will do well, therefore, to
understand my fixed determination, from which neither force nor threats
shall move me."

"Have you forgotten how much you are in my power?" exclaimed the
traitor, trembling with inward rage.   "Know you not that here you are
without help, and that my commands bear sovereign sway within this
castle?"

"I am but too well aware of what treachery has done for you, my lord,"
she replied.   "It has raised you to temporary importance here, but be
assured the time is not far distant when you will meet the just punishment
of your crimes.   I regard you with loathing and disgust, and be assured
the Princess Isabel will never become the degraded wife of the false Lord
Morton, or suffer any further continuance of his insolent presumption."

"Have a care, proud girl!" exclaimed Lord Morton, with ill-concealed
rage;—"have a care, I say, lest you arouse the powerful resentment of a
sleeping lion, and draw upon yourself a fate more terrible than the alternative you have thought proper to reject."

"This is well worthy of you," cried Isabel, scornfully.   "You have
failed to attain your base purposes by hypocrisy and deceit, and would now
try to intimidate me by your threats of vengeance."

"You mistake me," answered Morton, "and forget the utter impotency
of your present situation.   It has escaped your memory, I suppose, that
you are no longer the haughty mistress of Craiglynn, but the prisoner of a
conqueror, and the affianced wife of Lord Morton, who is armed with a
power supreme, and royally gifted to enforce his claims, and bend a weak
resisting woman to her doom."

"I have not forgotten it," answered Isabel, "for deeply do I feel and remember the cruel degradation to which I have been reduced. Nor can I forget, my lord, the dissembling hypocrite, and the base means he used to betray the daughter of his early friend and benefactor."

"These reproaches are in vain, and only serve to make me your foe instead of a friend," exclaimed the traitor. "It is true I admitted King Edward and his victorious troops into this castle, but by so doing I saved the slaughter and destruction that was otherwise threatened. You would have fallen a sacrifice had the castle stood out after being summoned to surrender by the English monarch, and you have therefore to thank me for your life, rather than heap reproaches upon me that I do not deserve."

"Lord Morton need not fear," answered Isabel, " that his *honourable* deeds are recorded everlastingly among the heroic, valiant actions he has performed. And, doubtless, such *unsullied* fame as he has acquired, must crown him with the palm which only the truly noble can receive. You speak of your actions, my lord, as if I ought to regard them with admiration ; yet the truth you have forced me to speak, and thus with my scorn do I repay the deeds you have done against me. Insolent intruder, begone, and never again dare to shew yourself before her who can only abhor and execrate your villany !"

"Girl !" he exclaimed, fiercely, "your words would drive me to acts of violence, even though I might be disposed to treat you with mildness and moderation. But, beware how you taunt me farther, for the tiger in his wrath is not more terrible than am I when once my fury has been aroused."

" Nay," cried Isabel, unmoved by his insolence, "presume to threaten only where your dastardly power can command, nor dare again forget the reverence to one who was born in a sphere far above your own, and who, still superior to the ruin of her fortunes, shall yet retain her soul's entire freedom, and disdaining the degraded level of your own ignoble standard, will be the mistress of her own actions, though, unhappily, no longer of Craiglynn. Yet still am I conscious of my unconquered free will, and thus again do I command your absence from this room."

" 'Tis well, my Lady Isabel," he exclaimed, with quivering lips, whose ashy hue betrayed the violent emotion that shook his soul. " You have defied me, but will soon be taught to fear, if not respect the power of him who in a moment becomes the master of ,yourself and your future destiny, and repent the haughty insolence with which you have defied my present superiority over you."

"And have you never reflected, my lord," demanded Isabel, "that the triumph you now boast may be snatched from you as suddenly as it was obtained ? Scotland is not yet subdued, fallen though she may be through the successful villany of men, who, like yourself, have sold her liberties for your own advantage. But it is in vain to reproach one who is as destitute of honour as he is of feeling, and, therefore, I desire you will quit my presence."

" You have mistaken me, Lady Isabel," exclaimed Lord Morton, " Softness might have won me to forbearance, and the patience of a love gained you a respite from the doom you affect to think so far distant, but which you will find I possess here indisputed power to control."

" Indeed !" exclaimed the princess with disdain ; " you would have me humbly submit myself to your tyrannous decree, and beg upon my knees that respect which I have a right to command. But you know not the spirit that actuates me to this resistance, and rather would I perish by the slowest and most cruel tortures than give my hand to him whose deeds have earned for him utter contempt."

" I again warn you, Isabel, to urge me no further to desperation," he exclaimed. " Love for you has made me what I am. You knew my passion long since, and rejected my offer without giving a satisfatory reason. I thought your conduct might have arisen from the caprice of girlhood, and resolved to wait till reflection should teach you the justice of rewarding my constancy with your hand. With what success I have met, you yourself are the best judge. I am called a traitor, and no one should better know than Isabel, that whatever fault I have committed, has been instigated by the cruel doom she has thought proper to pass upon me."

"You can find no excuse for the baseness of your conduct," cried our heroine, " and before Heaven I swear never to yield to the solicitations of a villain who has basely sold his country to a foreign enemy."

"Isabel," he exclaimed, with an ominous scowl of rage, "you have disdained my love, and must therefore prepare for the justly-merited severity you have drawn upon yourself. This night, girl, beholds you my bride."

"Monster!" cried our heroine, "dare you add violence to your other crimes?"

"Aye," he replied, "and you may thank yourself for the evils that have thus been brought down. Struggles and resistance are unavailing; in Craiglynn remains not a single arm that dares oppose my purposes. Destitute of every friend, bereft of all, and at my mercy, you will soon learn to value what you now seem to abhor; nor do I despair to soften that obduracy which now provokes your destiny, and shall not retard the fixed purpose of my soul."

"This is indeed worthy of a villain like yourself!" exclaimed Isabel. "You believe me to be powerless and unprotected, and would meanly take advantage of it in furtherance of your own base designs. But the hour of vengeance may not be so far off as you imagine. My father yet lives, and be assured he will never rest till he has had full and ample satisfaction for the injury you seek to do his daughter."

"Your threats are uttered in vain, Isabel," returned the other in a tone or self-confidence. "From the traitorous Lord Mackenzie no expectations injurious to my success can now be entertained, as he dares not approach these walls; nor do I fear the impotency of his revenge, for on him will I wreak the deadly resentment your scorn has aroused; and though he were kneeling before me to implore his forfeit life, I would execute on his banished head the justice his sentence awards him, and force his proud daughter to yield herself even in his very presence."

"I will perish rather than become the wife of such a villain!" cried Isabel.

"Nay, it is in vain you resist me," he replied; "numbers of my people fill the gallery without, and wait but my signal to bear you from this place. Yield, therefore, and accompany me voluntarily to the chapel, or thus will I enforce your compliance!"

Isabel had caught hold of the open door, as the bold, resolute villain was dragging her from the chamber; but the gigantic strength of her opponent rendered resistance perfectly ineffectual, though it convinced him that from her voluntary consent to the nuptials he had nothing to hope for. Resolutely determined, however, to compel her to be his, he now lost every remaining feeling of respect and delicacy for her distress or condition, and snatching her from the ground, was bearing her through the room with rapid strides, when, no longer mistress of her reason, or conscious of the result that might ensue, she, in her terror and distraction, gave forth a shriek, which the conviction of immediate and pressing danger prompted, and the next moment Lord Mackenzie rushed into the room to save his child, and punish the audacious miscreant.

"Turn, false, audacious ingrate!" he cried, pointing his sword at the breast of Lord Morton, and fiercely opposing his passage towards the door. "Turn, villain, and meet the vengeance of an equal foe, who will perish in the defence of a beloved daughter !"

Aghast and pallid with the effect of conscious baseness, the traitor, loosening his hold of Isabel, drew forth his sword to ward off the furious blows of the friend he had so deeply wronged. They fought—but the injuries of Lord Mackenzie weighed down the determined vigour of his opponent's blows, and after a short contest, Morton fell to the ground, nerveless, and utterly vanquished.

Mackenzie was about to take the forfeit life of the guilty traitor, but pity moved his heart, and nobly disdaining his advantage over a humbled foe, and still mindful that the offender had once been dear to his regards, he exclaimed with tremulous emotion :—

" Thy life is in my power, ingrate, but take it from my hands, and by an early penitence learn to atone the errors of thy past misdeeds, and the practice of that humanity thou hast forfeited in thine ingratitude and falsehood to thy early benefactor. The memory of a crime so heinous will be its own avenger, and needs no greater scourge than those which an evil conscience will awaken."

Having uttered these words, Lord Mackenzie awaited not the issue of this rencontre, but supporting his almost fainting daughter again into the interior apartment, he made fast the door, so as to prevent pursuit till after it would be of no avail; then giving Catherine directions to meet the princess either at Glenroy Castle, or the Convent of St. Eustatia, led the nearly unconscious girl towards the secret pannel, known only to himself, and passing through it, guided her steps towards the place from whence they were to escape.

CHAPTER XXI.

" Where have our wandering footsteps brought us, child?
Wild desolation here has found a throne,
And all around us bears a trace of woe
The heart must sink at."

THE PILGRIM'S REST.

No time was to be lost, for the slightest delay might prove death to himself and ruin to the unfortunate Isabel. In silent haste, therefore, they pursued their flight, but Lord Mackenzie sank into his accustomed melancholy gloom; he spoke not, but led his daughter through many long winding avenues, that were completely obscured in the deepest shades of darkness. With cautious terror Isabel advanced; the novelty of her situation, and the fatal evils she had been rescued from, absorbed for a time every mental faculty, and, but that she knew herself to be in the protection of the only being likely to secure her safety, she would have shrunk appalled from the present dismal enterprize. Still she could not help feeling a constant horror and sickening dread to find herself traversing unfrequented ways, without even the small cheering comfort of a light to guide their uncertain footsteps; a precaution which her father was obliged to adopt, lest the rays of a lamp, shining through the crevices and loop-holes of this secret pass, should betray their progress, and render the attempted escape ineffectual.

Every step they trod was well known to him, and though assured his guiding arm would safely conduct her through the dangers of such an undertaking, yet Isabel could not resist the thrilling alarm which ever sways the mind when encompassed by the unknown dangers of darkness, and traversing the unfrequented spots of which no conception can be formed, but of which the apprehension is generally more poignant than the reality. At length the voice of her father was heard in whispers, as he said :—

"We have now reached the upper basement of the platform; these deep-hewn steps, which we must descend, have no impediment to retard or endanger our progress; be, therefore, courageous, my Isabel, and our danger will soon be at an end."

"Ah !" she sighed in reply, " let me but once more see my dear father restored to peace, and his Isabel will then be blessed even beyond her hopes."

" Restored to peace !" groaned the unhappy nobleman; " alas! 'tis a vain hope, child, for my peace has for ever flown. Never more shall I know happiness on earth till that wished-for moment arrives which shall terminate a joyless existence, and free my wearied spirit from the bondage that enthrals it."

The cold, freezing shudder that chilled the heart of the unhappy Mackenzie, and vented itself in an inward groan of agony, communicated not itself to his daughter, for still no ray of light gleamed on their dreary progress, or revealed the settled frenzy and deep despair that at this moment of revived remembrance distended the death-like features of the sufferer.

Still they continued gradually to descend, till at length, from a small perforated opening of a lofty, overhanging cliff, Isabel was startled by the sudden loud roar of the sea, which in an instant became visible, as the aperture of the rock admitted a prospect of the heaving waves, rolling in huge mountain billows towards the base of the rocks, whilst the lightnings darting from the clouds over the immeasurable space of waters, produced a scene at once startling and magnificent. Isabel continued to gaze through the aperture, for her father had descended the remaining steps to prepare their little bark, and watch the moment favourable for their departure. His speedy return awoke her from the meditations the scene inspired, and leading her down the steep descent, they groped their path along a narrow excavation, which abruptly terminated in a small outlet that opened upon the interior of a rocky cave, from whence they could obtain an uninterrupted view of the troubled ocean.

It seemed almost dangerous to trust the furious elements, and the father paused in some alarm as he observed the angry waves heaving their foaming heads towards the sky, and most keenly did he feel for his Isabel, thus about to be exposed to all the fury of a tempest. His eye was bent in sadness on her, then awhile raised with indignation on the lofty battlements of Craiglynn. His soul swelled with resentment as the mortifying reflection crossed his mind that only a few hours had elapsed since those towers were the undoubted right of his daughter, and that now they afforded shelter and protection to a deadly foe. But little time, however, was allowed for the indulgence of these unavailing reflections, for at this period voices from above, calling from the embattled ramparts, harshly mingled with the roaring blast that swept by them, and as Lord Mackenzie lifted Isabel into the bark, he beheld several torches flash their light from the summit of the castle, and reveal those who now manned the walls.

"To arms! to arms!" shouted a confusion of voices; " the castle is beset; discharge your arrows, and let not the fugitives escape alive!"

Fortunately the tide and wind favoured their flight, and the short interval of murky darkness that obscured the moon, rendered the discharge of the enemy's darts ineffectual; whilst the bounding vessel, driven with resistless swiftness by the winds, needed little assistance from the pilot, and soon distanced the random shot of the foe. A few arrows only had fallen on the deck, whilst the impotent rage of the archers was spent on the waves which bore the fugitives from the threatened danger.

Isabel shivered in the keen nipping air, and though she felt most sensibly the difference in her present situation, she was but too happy at her escape to complain of the inconvenience to which she was exposed. The wind still roared with an increasing violence, and the sky became even more lowering and terrific, for the moon in vain strove to struggle through the clouds, and at length totally disappeared, and only when the gleaming lightning shot forth, could Isabel distinguish the horrible picture with which she was surrounded.

Her father intended to reach, if possible, the distant shores of Argyle, amidst whose mountain summits his castle of Glenroy reared its gigantic towers, for there only could he and his daughter find shelter during the period that Scotland lay prostrate at the foot of a conquerer. For hours, however, the little vessel was tossed about at the mercy of the tempest, and every hope had yielded to despair. Isabel now lay speechless in her father's arms, who hung over her with an agony impossible to describe. The sea washed over the deck, and had with difficulty been prevented from penetrating the little cabin in which Lord Mackenzie and his daughter had taken shelter. The pilot had resigned his office, and either could not, or would not guide the vessel to its destined harbour, but left it to the fury of the elements, which drove the bark wide of that haven which his lordship was most anxious to anchor in, and the day had dawned before a change in the weather permitted them again to hope for preservation from the danger that impended.

At length the vessel stranded on a sand bank opposite a cluster of rocky headlands, and it was then discovered that they were among the western isles, far from the shore where Lord Mackenzie had intended to land. To put to sea again was a danger not to be risked, for, as the morning cleared, a vessel was seen on the verge of the horizon, and might too probably be an enemy sent out in search of them. The present alternative, therefore, alone remained, and might for a day or two secret the fugitives till the rage of pursuit was abated, and their return to the mainland of Scotland become again secure. For it was but too certain the dastard spirit of Lord Morton would never relinquish the hope of obtaining Isabel, whilst his revenge would assist the power of Edward, by destroying the man who had been his friend and benefactor.

Lord Mackenzie had, beside his attendant Rupert, but five men on board, who, though devoted to his service, could not guard him and Isabel from numbers, and he therefore immediately landed at a creek, and saw the vessel placed in such a situation as to elude the search of any enemies that might arrive at the place.

Supporting the harrassed Isabel, he now traversed the beach to find an ascent that might lead up the rock, and at length, through a cleft of black rocks, a narrow defile presented itself. Followed by Rupert only, the father and daughter proceeded onward; whilst the pilot and the others were to keep watch on the shore, and defend the vessel in case of an attack. At last the gloomy pass opened on a rough ascent, presenting a long track of mountains to the view; whilst, at the distance of a league, the lofty towers of a castle terminated the prospect.

Irresolute how to act, Mackenzie paused to reflect whether it were less dangerous to return and remain in the vessel, or to advance and make known their present situation, and claim from the residents of the castle the assistance and protection they so much needed. Isabel, worn with terror and fatigue, yet sustained herself rather by an effort of fortitude than by the natural strength of her frame. It was not unlikely that, could she still bear up sufficiently to reach the castle they had observed, they might obtain assistance till they could venture to put to sea again.

Isabel, though exhausted, displayed no repining weakness, but yielding to necessity, cheerfully accorded with her father's proposal, and after an hour and a half spent in wearisome toil, they succeeded in penetrating the intervening forest, and beheld at no great distance the grey embattled turret, peeping from amidst a long avenue of trees.

"At all events," exclaimed Lord Mackenzie, "yon noble pile doubtless owns some hospitable chieftain, from whose courtesy my beloved daughter may receive relief and repose. We will there to-night recruit our exhausted strength, and on to-morrow's early dawn again pursue our way towards the castle of Glenroy."

The lofty ruins of a once magnificent building now burst on the admiring yet disappointed gaze of Lord Mackenzie, who now began to fear his former hopes would deceive his expected welcome. The castle was moated, but its waters were become a stagnant pool, and their sources completely dammed up. The lower portcullis offered no impediment to the progress of the wanderers; no chained portal forbade free entrance to the interior courts, whose spacious, solitary areas were choked up with rank weeds, and the melancholy bird of night here hoarsely hooted, and seemed the only thing that lived within the ruins.

They, however, still pressed onwards, and entered through an open portal into a large gloomy hall, where he called loudly, and demanded assistance, but not a sound, save the echo of his own cries, was heard in reply. Rupert was now desired to ascend the broken staircase to look for human aid, whilst Isabel, silent and oppressed, reclined upon a bench, and almost gave way to the terrors which their situation had inspired. In a short time Rupert returned:—

"There are chambers, my lord, of great extent on the upper stories," he said, " which still retain vestiges of former habitation. But surely you mean not to pass the night in a place that may be the resort of robbers?"

Lord Mackenzie made no reply to this latter observation, but desired Rupert to conduct him to the apartments he had discovered; whilst Isabel, unwilling to remain alone, hung on her father's arm, and ascended with him. At length, they came to a chamber, though which, desolate and comfortless in the extreme, was still adapted to afford them a temporary shelter.

It was the ruined castle of Glenalvon, that had thus, by a singular fatality, received the banished Lord Mackenzie and his daughter, though both of them were totally unaware of the fact. The former knew that the husband of his sister claimed the title of an earldom from the domain of Glenalvon, but it was a residence seldom inhabited on account of its remote and insular situation; and as the possessions of the Earl of Glenalvon were numerous, his lordship had never visited his sister here, or at any other of her husband's territories, except one at some distance off.

The remainder of the day was passed by Mackenzie and his attendant in penetrating the northern wing of the castle, during which Rupert discovered the panel that led from the angle chamber, through nearly the whole suite, where he prepared two of the nearest for the use of his superiors, and himself occupied another, that opened from a long gallery which branched off towards the opposite end of the whole. Rupert then returned to the vessel, and brought thence the choicest provisions that were to be found on board.

Hitherto Lord Mackenzie, occupied too much by the necessity for vigorous action for his own and his daughter's safety, found little leisure to brood over the anguish of his soul. Night, however, again recalled his memory of the past, and Emmeline, though now certainly lost to him for ever, still as firmly occupied the same place in his heart as she had done in the happier periods of his life.

The returning day found Isabel revived and invigorated, and casting aside the dignified character of her birth, she became the gentle artless child of nature. Her plain robe was regarded with satisfaction, for it assured her she was far away from the splendid misery that had lately been her doom ; and she now quitted her chamber to join her father, and, if possible, withdraw his thoughts from those subjects which tortured and afflicted his mind. His heavy eye and worn countenance assured her but too well that the night had been a sleepless one to him, and throwing herself in his arms, she cried, affectionately,—

"Alas! my father, why do you thus give way to griefs that are beyond the power of mortal cure? Yet if these sorrows must be indulged in I will in silence share them with you—will mingle tear with tear, and still seek to divert your sad memory from the past ; and, oh ! should my cares steal, each passing hour, a something from the weight that presses on your heart, I shall indeed be happy !"

"My child, my beloved Isabel!" he exclaimed, "you are indeed the solace of my heart—the balm that cools the raging fever of my brain. Oh, could I behold you safe and happily secured from dangers, all that now binds my weary spirit to its bondage would be accomplished, and the rest would soon be peace and eternal quietude."

"Think not too deeply on the past, my dear father," cried Isabel. "Despair not, I entreat you, for the evils of the past may end in a rich futurity of happiness to reward the sorrows with which you have been chastened."

"Aye," he murmured, " the *future* alone can realize the joys of peace. and peace is in the sleep of death !"

The second day of their arrival here was passed in the most fearful alarms. Rupert, returning from the vessel, had seen, as he reported, several

No. 17

armed men, whose helmets sustained the English ensign; whilst the figure of their leader bore such strong resemblance to the treacherous Lord Morton, that it was almost impossible to doubt his identity. Maddened with grief and alarm, Lord Mackenzie quitted the castle to watch the movements of the enemy, whilst Isabel, guarded only by Rupert, sat fearfully trembling for her father's safety, and praying for his return."

"These dismal ruins, lady," said Rupert, at length, "are dreary and forlorn, and must, I fear, create melancholy reflections. As I reached them some time since a peasant started from my path, and when I bade him conduct me through the mazes of a wood towards these towers, he, shuddering, crossed himself, and turning to run away, exlaimed,—

"'Not for the joys of paradise would I approach yon haunted castle. If you are indeed mortal, avoid the horrors of the spot; and if in need of present shelter, there is an ancient fabric, not three leagues distant, where you may find rest and shelter.'

"The man then hurried from my sight, but I can well believe his fearful report; and, might your servant, lady, counsel you, you would seek the ancient mansion the stranger warned me to repair to. Doubtless, it will afford a shelter more suited for the purpose than this place, to which an evil destiny has driven you."

Isabel had been for some time deeply buried in a profound and pensive meditation, but the harsh tones of her attendant, as they thus grated on her startled ear, created an alarm that dismayed her fancy with the terrors of an expected enemy's approach; and, unmindful that Rupert was the speaker, she turned round fearfully, believing herself again in the power of her dreaded foe. There was a dark, subtle expression in the features and aspect of this man, that had often filled her with alarm. His large penetrating eye was generally half closed, as if to conceal the deep meaning expression of cunning and ferocity, that were his usual characteristics; his broad forehead was prominent, and his black bushy brows were ever contracted by an habitual scowl, which he sought to conceal under the helm he constantly wore, and which was always drawn close over his upper features.

In the height of her happiest prosperity the Princess Isabel had ever been mild, gentle, and condescending, to the lowliest of her father's vassals; but there was in this man's appearance a daring character stamped in every gesture, that all his apparent servility could not soften or remove. Isabel's penetration had early discovered the traits of cunning his unguarded demeanour sometimes displayed; her suspicions of his fidelity had more than once been assured, for she had herself experienced of late a presuming confidence, and want of respect in his manner towards her, that had been received with anger though overlooked with silence, because her father had more than once expressed his entire satisfaction of this man's fidelity and zeal in his service. The freedom of his present discourse, however, could not be repelled by the coldness of the princess, and having in vain waited for a reply, he resumed,—

"The castle of which the peasant informed me is but a short distance hence; and, with the aid of horses, your ladyship might with ease reach its hospitable refuge before the sun sinks behind yon range of western hills. My lord's return is uncertain, but even his protection is insufficient to ensure your safety here."

The stress laid upon the last words aroused the attention of Isabel, and she answered reproachfully,—

"If you were acquainted with any foreknowledge sufficient to warrant these alarms, wherefore did you neglect to reveal them to my father?"

Rather startled by these words, Rupert half raised the lid of his full dark eye on the princess, as a glance of insolent freedom and expressive meaning was rudely bent on her.

" 'Tis not for me to interfere," he muttered; "doubtless, my lord has his reasons for preferring to remain in a spot so remote and desolate, and which will indeed well conceal those whom the state has banished from their territories. Pardon, then, lady, the perhaps too officious duty of your servant, if he seeks to withdraw you from a place so comfortless. It were unjust the innocent should suffer for the crimes of the real offender."

"How is this?" cried Isabel, with anger; "have you forgotten that your lord is an injured, not an offending man? How dare you thus presume to speak of him in this disrespectful manner?"

Rupert artfully contrived to pervert the real meaning of his words, but could not dissipate the inward alarm which the princess—assured of his hypocrisy—felt increasing, and during the ensuing pause, he said,—

" 'This spot, I fear, is the secret haunt of outlaws, and should my lord and yourself be discovered, the event will be indeed to be dreaded. It is lonely, and shunned through the day by the *living* inhabitants of the island, but at night its dark hidden recesses teem with untold deeds and fearful sights of appalling horror. Had your ladyship vouchsafed to have departed your father, informed by my care of your safety, would doubtless have followed, and in witnessing your security have made certain his own."

Isabel started up wildly; it was nearly dark, and her heart palpitated with a tumultuous terror never so severely experienced as now. She trembled at the dangers of the place, thus alarmingly increased by Rupert's account, and felt alarmed at the intrusion of a man whose style of familiar address had a something in its manner that betrayed the immediate presence of danger.

She was alone, and completely in the power of a being who, if really the villain her alarmed fancy had pictured him, could execute any bold scheme the present crisis of danger would favour; and whether her surmises were just is uncertain, but the powerful impulse of fear urged her flight, and ere he could intercept her purpose, she rushed in speechless alarm from the apartment, resolving to find her way if possible to the outward courts of the castle, and await on the drawbridge the period of her father's return.

Heedless of the path she was pursuing, Isabel, as she flew along the dark vaulted avenues, passed the only turning that would have conducted her to the staircase. The further she penetrated these dreary passages the more she became lost and bewildered in their gloomy labyrinths, till, exhausted with fatigue and terror, and agonised with the most dreadful surmises for her father's safety, she sunk exhausted and nearly fainting upon a broken window seat.

Here, as the vivid lightning revealed the horrors that surrounded her, Isabel tried to discover some passage or other way of communication that might extricate her from her terrible situation; but with an impatient feeling nearly bordering on despair, she continued for more than an hour to wander through the darksome galleries in vain, till at length a shriek of torturing disappointment escaped from her lips, as with wild dismay she saw that all hopes of escape were now in vain, and that she must remain where she was till the morning's dawn assisted her escape.

Actuated by despair, however, she again traversed a vestibule which led into another corridor, where she beheld in a niche a burning lamp, which had no doubt been placed there by Rupert. As she joyfully hastened towards its friendly rays, the cry of Angus Glenalvon reached her ears, and gave rise to the dreadful supposition that it proceeded from the murderous pursuers of her father. Terrified with this dreadful belief she hastened back again to the north chamber, where Lord Mackenzie had but the instant before arrived. He also had heard the sound of voices in the hal when he entered the castle, and not doubting that they were foes, he rushed on the unguarded Angus, who, this night conducted by chance to the ruined house of his ancestors, had received from the hand of his unknown relative a wound which was nearly proving fatal in its consequences.

The rapid occurrences of the two following days need not be repeated; they at once amazed and bewildered, whilst they left an interest on the mind of the gentle Isabel, that neither time nor cirumstances were ever likely to obliterate.

CHAPTER XXII.

" Again fate threats us, love, and we once more
    Must quit our place of refuge;—again must seek
    Another home to shield us from the foes
    That hunt us e'en to death."—MORGANA.

THE dagger which had been the equal cause of [suspicion to Lord Mac-kenzie and Angus, and which the latter had so singularly in his bed-cham-ber, was the very weapon which had been so mysteriously conveyed to the father of Isabel in the threatening letter which forbade him to seek after his lost wife. The means by which it could have been conveyed to a place so remote, can only be conjectured, but not traced, and like the mystery it enveloped, was still inscrutable. The sight of it again had harrowed up afresh the dreadful mystery of the appalling transaction; when, rushing from the presence of Angus, he had intended instantly to quit the ruins, could the necessary preparations have been accomplished, for at this mo-ment he believed that Angus was in some way implicated in the mystery of the dagger, and that he was sent to remind him of the secret malice of that warning evil he had been taught to avoid and expect, whilst, with a seve-rity of tone and manner never till now experienced, he forbade his daughter to speak to the strangers, or approach their chamber; the harshness of which command Isabel promised to obey, though grieved at its necessity.

To quit the island that night was, however, impossible, for it was nearly certain the ruin was now the last, only resource that could shelter him and his daughter from the number of lurking parties that throughout the day were seen on the heights. Still the prejudice Mackenzie had conceived towards the youthful strangers could not be eradicated by the recollection of their helpless condition, or the injury Angus had received from his hands. He still believed him to be a spy over his actions, employed by some un-known foe, and he therefore determined to disappoint the treacherous malice he suspected.

For this purpose it was he had obliged Isabel to confine herself through the day to the chamber beyond the exterior apartment; and thus it was she saw no more of the strangers till Angus came to her rescue in the moment most fatal to her future peace and honour, and save her from the brutal violence of a wretch, who, privileged by the misfortunes of his master, (for it was Rupert), and the pressing danger of the times, had aimed at the destruction of the unsuspecting victim he had ensnared.

When led from the castle, Isabel shuddered as her eye traced, through the sombre twilight of evening the gloomy exterior of the castle; for though the sad narration of the horrid deeds perpetrated within its walls had been but slightly mentioned, yet she could not view it without dread, remembering, as she did, that the story involved the murder of her nearest and dearest relatives. For the first time, she now remembered with keenness the severity of her own and her father's fallen state; she remembered, with the bitterness of regret, the altered condition of her parent. Long did she ponder on this melancholy theme; and Angus, the noble, generous offspring of her father's tenderly loved sister, found an interest in the heart of his beauteous cousin as deeply rooted and sincere as if the acquaintance had commenced at the earliest period of infant memory.

At length not a vestige of the ancient pile remained perceptible, save only a twinkling light that glimmered through the shades of night, still marked the spot, till increasing distance faded its lessening rays, and the next moment it was out of sight.

"May Heaven protect them!" sighed Isabel, as she thought of the dangers that threatened the orphans of Glenalvon, and to whose destinies she felt so deep an interest.

The night was dark and dreary. Lord Mackenzie's melancholy was, if possible, greater than ever, and as Isabel guided her horse by his side over the pathless waste they were journeying, she often listened with an aching heart to the frequent sighs that were uttered by her father. She, however, restrained her emotions, and attempted not to obtrude an unavailing sympathy for those lately added sorrows which were too certainly beyond the feeble strength of human pity to alleviate or subdue.

Some hours had elapsed in traversing the whole extent of the island, a precaution her father had thought it necessary to adopt to prevent discovery. He had, therefore, resolved to embark at the opposite extremity, where the vessel had been previously taken. For, in addition to the enemies he had fled from, he had now to guard against the treachery of his servant; and lest, in revenge for his defeated hopes, Rupert should betray the retreat of his daughter, he now felt the danger of exposing her to such a risk, and therefore determined to decline, for the present, visiting Glenroy till the search he was well aware Edward's creature would make, was abated and defeated.

The necessity of caution had compelled the fugitives to progress through the desert and unfrequented tracks, and Isabel often trembled as she passed over the precipitous summits of huge mountains, whose unexplored regions presented only pictures of inhospitable solitude and desert, and gloomy woods that might be the resort of bandits.

By and by, however, they reached the shore, and Isabel, when about to descend to the beach, cast back a glance of tenderness and dread; but her feelings were checked from open expression by some internal motive, and with a half suppressed sigh, she suffered the guides to lead her down the steep and winding defile.

Not a moment was now to be lost; it was still night, and only at this late hour could the fugitives pass safely to the opposite shores of Scotland, where, in less than an hour, Isabel was re-landed beneath the walls of the convent of St. Eustatia, which, deeply embosomed amidst trees, reared high its lofty front.

For the first time since their departure from Glenalvon, Lord Mackenzie broke the long silence that had been observed. Isabel's heart died within her as she listened to the orders he gave for the vessel to be held in readiness for his immediate return to the place from whence they had come; for at that moment deep concern for the safety and presence of her father made her unmindful how necessary it might be for him to return to the two youths, who it was likely would there wait for his arrival with much anxiety.

"Alas! dear father," she cried, mournfully, "and must we then part so soon?"

Mackenzie in silence then led his daughter towards the venerable walls of the convent.

"Here," he at length said, "till the danger of the times abates, and the pursuit of our foes has become exhausted, you will be safe. These sacred walls will at least afford protection till Heaven's arm again restores unhappy Scotland's freedom, and humbles the haughty pride of our usurpers. Till then, my Isabel, we must separate. Your father, despoiled of his inheritance, banished his native land, and even a price set upon his own head, is, alas! powerless to defend you from the insolence of a presuming traitor. To me, all fortunes are now alike indifferent; let me, then, but behold my only treasure secured from further violence, and that assurance will be the only cheering balm remaining to reconcile the sad necessity which compels us thus to part."

"And why should we be thus sundered?" asked Isabel. "If these towers will afford a refuge to your child, oh, why may they not shelter you? Think, I pray you, on the anxious moments I shall spend in wretchedness and uncertainty, when no longer blessed with your presence and the knowledge of your safety. Ah! should my dear father leave me now, he will never more behold his Isabel."

"This weakness should be conquered," exclaimed her father; "the danger may not be so pressing as you may imagine, and I doubt not we shall meet again ere long."

"Would that I could think so," cried Isabel; "but a sad oppression, like the forewarning admonition of destiny, hangs on my sunken spirit; its prophetic meaning is the inspiration of truth, and I shall never, never more be happy,—never again be pressed in a loved father's arms. Oh, do not,—do not leave your Isabel!"

"Daughter!" exclaimed Mackenzie with solemn fervency, and struggling inwardly to suppress his own deep regrets, "mark my words, and let them sink deep into your heart. I have hitherto, my child, seemed too regardless of your happiness and welfare; grief, that has so long weighed down my spirit, has absorbed every mental faculty; the injured shade of the sainted Emmeline has mourned the neglected fortunes of her suffering child;—do not oppress—do not thus humble me with a tenderness I feel I am unworthy to receive. You have had little cause, Isabel, to lament a parent (even were he no more) whose wayward destiny so long has divided him from nature's paternal rights, and who has so ill deserved the love of such a heart as yours,—whose selfish feelings have excluded him from those gentle endearing affections your generous nature breathes. Severe were the trials my erring heart imposed, but your tenderness, my child, with steadfast constancy, shrunk not from the task; and that I still survive, is a debt wholly owing to your filial love. But here these trials terminate! think of your father hereafter but a lost friend, once slightly known, and but slightly to be remembered. But it grows late, and I must now begone. Honour and fame forbid me to remain inactive when my country should be struggling for the restoration of her rights. Nay, a yet nearer motive calls upon me, for the wronged sons of my murdered sister claim the hand of friendship to sustain their hopes, and restore them to their rights. Let them, my Isabel, dwell kindly in your thoughts, and when to Heaven you address your prayers for a father's peace and safety, forget not to sue for those who in future will claim your sisterly regards. And should, hereafter, a brighter sun dawn on our benighted Scotland, these deeds, which I now resign into your hands, will establish your rights to the vast domains of your ancestors. Adieu, and may the saints of Heaven keep you in their care."

Subdued, and almost speechless, Isabel clung round the neck of her parent in a vain effort to detain him.

"Farewell—a last farewell, my father!" she at length cried. "Alas! I feel but too painfully assured that never more will my eyes behold you living!"

Lord Mackenzie, deeply afflicted with the anguished despair of his daughter, and yet weak with his own internal misery, again pressed her in silent agony to his heart. Then, after a painful pause, he said,—

"I trust, my Isabel, your words will not be prophetic of my fate. We may yet meet again, even here—at least, I hope so."

"Do you indeed hope so?" cried Isabel, raising her tearful eyes towards the half averted countenance of her father. "Thanks, thanks, my dearest father, for that kind wish—that little treasure of comfort. Oh! if indeed you hope again to behold your Isabel, she will yet venture to believe this parting not eternal! Yes, I see—I feel assured that I am beloved—still dear to a father's heart, and, for my sake, he will yet be careful to preserve his life from the foes I so much dread."

"Yet, dearest girl," answered Lord Mackenzie, "for your sake I will endeavour to preserve an existence that may be of such importance to yourself. And now, my love, retire with this assurance, thus solemly given, that while my senses continue to submit to the governance of reason, I will treasure your affectionate fondness in my own heart, and guard my life and safety as I fear for the welfare and continuance of your existence; and, at least, if not firmly, yet submissively, I will bend to whatever fate may impose upon me."

"Nor shall your example be lost upon me," said Isabel; "for though our lot is a hard one to bear, yet will I endure all, in the one fond hope that a termination of our miseries will yet arrive."

"It will," answered Lord Mackenzie; "and recollect, Isabel, that if your father's afflictions have rendered his mind imbecile, they should impress on your's a necessary lesson, that may teach you how absolute is the duty incumbent on virtuous spirits to acquire firmness, and endure those severe trials to which life is heir, and which even the noblest and greatest cannot escape from. Once more, then, dear Isabel, adieu; remember the instructions I have given you, and should any unforeseen event destroy the security of your retreat, hasten to the Castle of Glenroy, where I will seek you, and where you will find that honourable protection its aged chieftain will joyfully afford. Adieu!"

Lord Mackenzie now gently released himself from the ardent embrace of his weeping daughter, and placed her in the arms of the attending sisterhood, several of whom had by this time approached to receive her. Isabel, however, to the last sorrowfully watched the receding form of her beloved father, and hung over the summit of the high embanked beach, as she watched in speechless agony and tears his gradual disappearance. At length the vessel diminished to a speck upon the waters, and was in an instant lost amidst the dark bounding waves, and the dim glare of the torches no longer shone on the bark which had bore away her father.

Catherine had already reached the convent, and now came forth to the assistance of her sorrowing mistress, through whose attention Isabel found a balm which the officious, but well-meaning consolations of the holy sisterhood would have rendered irksome and intrusive.

Isabel's grief was silent, and demanded the sacred privilege of solitary indulgence. She was then conducted through the heavy, sombre portals of the convent, and received by the lady abbess with all the dignified respect her high rank and station demanded.

The meeting between them was cordial in the extreme, for Isabel had, in her general demeanour, a suavity and gentle courtesy that never failed to impress favourably the minds of those she conversed with. It was now the first hour of matins, yet, though worn with grief and weariness, she refused to retire, but at her own entreaty was conducted to the church of the convent, where, bending herself before the high altar, in fervent prayer and supplication, she piously besought for her father and her late-found relatives the merciful protection and support of Heaven.

CHAPTER XXIII.

"His form
Assumes the air of true nobility;
And e'en a transient glance must soon declare
The high-born station that belongs to him.'
                                        THE WANDERER.

WE must now return to the aged Ronald, who, though senseless, was not, as the fears of Angus presaged, dead; and after a short suspension of animation he recovered. Angus, with divided grief, and mingled sensations of rage and sorrow, hung over the good old man whom he supported in his arms, as he exclaimed,—

"Alas! what ruin has not our ill-fated house occasioned thee and thine. Inhuman savages! must fidelity like Magdalen's also fall your victim? Do not shrink from me, Ronald; but, if you can, forgive the afflictions my own sorrows have brought on you."

"Do not increase them, son of my beloved master," cried Ronald, faintly, "or wrong an old man's love with ill-deserved suspicions. My daughter has, indeed, fallen a prey to her enemies, but it was in a righteous cause, and, therefore, must not be deplored. She has nobly performed her duty, and her reward will be in Heaven."

He paused, for tears choked his utterance, and it was some few seconds ere he could add,—

"Magdalen has been long torn from my sight, and, till I beheld you, I had taught myself to forget and to believe her dead. But she has proved herself worthy of a father's fondest blessings, and, therefore, let not her memory want a tear, for willingly, I know, did she perish in a cause so virtuous as that she was engaged in."

"She shall be lamented in tears of blood!" exclaimed Angus, with a burst of anger that he could not suppress. "Come, old man, let us go forth and avenge this barbarous deed. Conduct me, Ronald, to the place where the hated foe of our family has found concealment."

With long and earnest entreaties Ronald endeavoured to divert the sorrowing youth from a purpose so likely to prove ruinous to him, but in vain; till suddenly recalling to his memory the idea of Lord Mackenzie, from whom alone a real benefit might be derived to the lost Edwin, Angus paused. The frenzy of a too hasty decision gave place to the arguments of reason and truth; whilst a secret impulse, unknown in its source and spring, seemed to dictate the necessity of preserving a life which had yet so many charms, and which it was a duty he owed to Edwin's safety not carelessly to throw away. The image of Isabel, too, became a powerful stimulant to his caution, and was at this agonizing moment a soothing balm to the wild distraction of his despair.

"Edwin is lost to us for the present, but may still be recovered," continued Ronald. "His life too certainly depends on your security, and while the tyrant's power is incapable of compassing your freedom, he will not harm the unoffending captive he now holds. To murder him while you still live would be a wanton excess of cruelty which even the chief of Bade-

noch will not dare to practise, since his death will yield him nothing, while a greater and more potent claimant to the dignities of Glenalvon survives. Let us, then, my dear young lord, rather secure our safety in immediate flight."

"And whither, old man, can we flee?" demanded the youth doubtfully.

"King Robert Bruce," answered Ronald, "receives with open arms his faithful countrymen who are still attached to the cause of liberty and independence. The call of glory now invites your sword, and 'tis time you signalize yourself as your great forefathers have often done in the cause of your injured country's freedom—a cause for which so many valiant heroes have freely fought and bled. Should we at last be conquerors, the restored rule and sovereign power of our good king will soon enable us to rescue the sons of Glenalvon from the grasp of his enemies, and amply afford the means of vengeance and redress to those who are resolved to seek it."

Thoroughly convinced by the old man's persuasive eloquence, Angus silently acquiesced, and, conducted by Ronald, he descended the Watch Tower, and quitted its forlorn and desolate interior. On the dawn of the second day they reached, unmolested, the island of Arran, whither, as rumour reported, Ronald had on the way learned the King of Scotland had retreated after his late defeat.

The shores of Arran were bold, lofty, and, in some parts, inaccessible, but possessed, amidst their melancholy wilds, some excavated causeways, remotely concealed from general view, and only known familiarly to those who had visited their deep recesses. Ronald had, with his late lord, more than once traversed every corner of the island, and was well acquainted with its sublime and romantic scenery.

With little difficulty he led the silent, dejected Angus through many a wild caverned pass, and at length entered a deep-hewn cave, whose long,

No. 18

winding mazes were lighted from the ceiling by the breaks and fissures with which it abounded, whilst the ground was rendered smooth by the sea-sands, that at high-water flowed from the ocean in shoals, and which, when settled, became a hard bed, strewed with dried leaves, that were whirled by the winds from the inland extremity of the cavern.

At last the pass widened, and became enlarged into a wide, spacious amphitheatre. Surprise and admiration took possession of Angus, as, bending forward, he plainly beheld several armed men busily employed in military evolutions; whilst many more were looking to their arms, as if in expectation that they would soon be required in an engagement with the enemy. The youth had not yet reached the extremity of the narrow pass that opened on the amphitheatre, and, therefore, could only receive a partial glance of the wonders that attracted his bewildered attention.

A figure of noble and warlike appearance, with arms enfolded, and looks bent in pondering meditation on the ground, slowly pacing through one of the numerous avenues, was now discerned at some little distance from the spot where the weary travellers had paused awhile to recruit their exhausted bodies. His air was peculiarly martial and athletic, his mien noble and commanding, and his step firm and majestic. In speechless suspense Angus and Ronald continued to remark his advancing progress, and not till he was close beside them did the warrior perceive the presence of strangers, when pausing, as he eyed them with steadfast scrutiny, he demanded,—

"From whence come you, and what seek you here? Know you not these recesses are sacred from the intrusion of strangers, and all access denied but to those whom duty and willing service brings hither? Declare your purpose quickly, lest, in being found secreted in these concealed passes, we suspect you to be enemies that have come hither to betray us into the hands of our enemies."

"So please you, noble knight," answered Angus, "I entreat that you will believe us guiltless of so base a design. We shall be found, in truth, that which we here proclaim ourselves, honourable, though humble men. We seek the royal champion of our injured country, and if service so poor in number may proffer itself with loyal duty in our monarch's cause, then may we trust his clemency will deign to accept the humble tender of our services, nor scorn the zeal which lacks fortune's prouder ensigns to stamp a value on its services."

"Your zeal is apparent," replied the unknown warrior, "in the modesty and candour with which you offer your services. But say, come you unattended, and with a firm determination to hazard the dangers and difficulties that must beset those who dare to draw a sword in Scotland's behalf? There is yet time to avoid the perils I speak of, and should you resolve to quit this island, it shall be my care to convey you to a place where you will be safe till the present scene of strife has been brought to a close."

"We are unfortunate, but not guilty fugitives," answered Angus. "We love and reverence with due allegiance our rightful sovereign, nor could we, to have gained a kingdom, have sought the opposing camp of our country's insolent invader. Duty now promps us to assert the right of the king, and the love of arms inspires our bosoms to aid the righteous cause. Our own evils we seek not at present to redress, but should the royal Bruce succeed in regaining his throne, then will we claim his aid in the punishment of those that have injured us."

"Fear it not," exclaimed the warrior, "for you behold before you him whom you seek,—him who once was Scotland's supreme ruler, and, let me add, one that never closed his ears against the cries of the oppressed or disdained to share his people's wrongs, and, as his power permitted, to redress them. Speak freely all your griefs, for a king's best prerogative is to live in the hearts of his people, not less their governor and lord than their friend, and protector. I will possess the love of my subjects, or resign a sceptre no longer valued, if I receive not the free assenting voice of those my fortune has called me to rule over. Assured that my sway shall know no other end than justice, and the entire freedom of the country, the meanest of my countrymen shall not lack a king's redress to right his injuries, and Bruce will not fail hereafter to remember, good youth, those who have been base enough to wrong you. For the present I will not urge you to reveal their names, but I would fain hear who it is that has thus presented himself before me, that when I present you to my gallant warriors, they may receive you as becomes your birth, which, if my conjecture deceives me not, is noble."

"August sovereign," exclaimed Angus, "the story of my wrongs would be too tedious to enter upon at present. My father was lord of Glenalvon's princely domains, but his son inherits not the privilege to command his many hundred warriors, nor has he a second arm to add weight to the wish which has urged him to offer his services. Stripped in infancy of his birthright, and now a wanderer from foes that seek his life,—unknown and unhonoured, Glenalvon's son claims no pre-eminence of greatness, nor must receive other honours than those which his sword may chance to win, if permitted to serve with loyalty where duty and true glory calls, beneath a leader so renowned and glorious."

"Thy suit is granted, noble youth," answered Bruce, with a smile of approving satisfaction. "I respect the nobility of soul which disdains to plume itself on the mere chance of illustrious birth, for the lustre of great actions, when the spontaneous offspring of virtue can alone bestow that real dignity on man which is above the titled greatness of ancestry and splendid descent."

Then assisting to raise Angus from his knees, he added with kindness and condescension :—

"Though thy modesty forbids thy tongue to utter any further explanation, one favour shall be bestowed upon thee, and as thy deeds hereafter declare thee noble, so shalt thou meet from my hands a noble recompense. Behold, my lords of Douglas and of Randolf," he added, as two martial figures clad in armour advanced,—"behold a youthful warrior, whose eager and active spirit, soaring above his ruined fortunes, and long panting for fame in arms, is come hither to tender his services. Receive him, my lords, as joint partner of your toils, and trust me, if my judgment deceives me not, you will find him not unworthy your confidence. Declare your name, young stranger, that when you rise the honorary badge of knighthood may grace your deeds, and render you equal with our gallant friends."

Stepping forward, and kneeling at the feet of the king, Ronald briefly declared the lineage of his young master, together with the dreadful transactions that had destroyed the noble family of Glenalvon ; and in conclusion, he related the loss of Edwin, and the fears he entertained that the youth had fallen into the hands of the enemy, whose evil deeds had procured the ruin and destruction of all who bore the name of Glenalvon.

The two lords were visibly affected with the old man's dark tale of horror and cruelty. Angus, unable to hear the repetition of his house's wrongs, turned aside his head to conceal the starting tear he could not suppress. The keen eye of Bruce was, however, upon him, and stretching forth his hand, took that of the unhappy Angus, and with a mind of deep feeling, he said :—

"Blush not, my young friend, that we have witnessed this testimony of native worth and reverence for the memory of those thou art bound to lament and to redress. I honour these tears of affection, and should account thee less than a soldier, couldst thou remain unmoved when filial impulse prompts the soul to sorrow. Look up with confidence, should our arms again restore our native land to freedom, for thou shalt rejoice with her monarch in the restoration of thy possessions, and largely partake the blessings which thy valour may assist in securing. Meantime, rise up Sir Angus of Glenalvon," he added, laying his sword gently on the head of the youth as he knelt to receive this high honour from his sovereign, " whose future fortune we, from this period, become the guardian of."

" My liege," exclaimed Angus, with emotion, " the honour you have been pleased to bestow upon me shall never be tarnished by any unworthy act of my own. My country's wrongs must be avenged, and happy shall I be to die in my efforts to release your kingdom from its foes."

" Heaven's eye is upon us," said the king, " and justice, with slow but certain pace, seems hastening to atonement. Scotland still is faithful and unsubdued, and the inherent valour of her warlike sons shall yet achieve her freedom. The invading English, embroiled in constant acts of cruelty, rapine, and injustice, have at length roused the souls of our hardy countrymen to vengeance; our forces increase hourly in number, and my brave people, no longer misled by the wild ambition of our disaffected nobles, now seek their king, impatient to redeem their lost honour, and avenge their country's wrongs;—whilst Edward, sickly and aged, now lies inactive on his couch, incapable of remorse, yet a prey to conscious guilt, and his brain troubled with horrible dreams, that disturb his slumbers, and harrow up his soul. We will, therefore, no longer give a respite to his arms, but again bravely rush to the fight, and obtain a victory over our foes. Follow, friends, to the camp;—let us hasten to cheer the spirits of our soldiery, and with our voices inspire them to deeds of noble daring. To Heaven we leave the issue, whose arm is omnipotent, and can decide for oppressed Scotland, and again restore its native character to all the glory of its ancient splendour."

With a gracious smile, Bruce again bade the youthful warrior welcome, and taking the arm of Lord Douglas, advanced through the archway. As he disappeared, Lord Randolf, with a brotherly kindness, took the hand of Angus, and said as he led him forth :—

" Receive, my young comrade, this hand, whose friendly grasp assures thee of my esteem and love. Together we will rush upon the foe,—together conquer, or together bravely fall."

" And when I prove unworthy thy confidence," answered Angus, "let thy hand be the first to plunge a dagger in my heart, that I may not survive lost honour, or outlive my fame."

" Nay, it is impossible you should do either," replied Randolf, with generous ardour, " for thou art of the race of the valiant, nor was thy father's renown in arms unknown, or unacknowledged. Scotland mourned his untimely death as the setting of its brightest star. But his son yet survives to emulate the valour of his noble deeds, and aid in the restoration of his country's rights."

The heart of Angus swelled with grateful pleasure; he would have spoken, but the emotions of his soul rendered him for a time speechless. The praises of a man so famous in chivalry and honour as Randolf were indeed stimulants to heroic actions, and his heart blessed, though his lips could not, the words that had fallen from his new-found friend. Hand in hand they quitted the cavern, though not till Angus had paid the grateful tribute of commendation to his venerable conductor.

" He was the only friend that survived the downfal of Glenalvon," he

said, taking the hand of Ronald. " His faithful love has preserved the offspring of his lord from assassin violence, and he must share with me the
happier fortune that Heaven has now vouchsafed."

"Fidelity and love like thine," said Randolf, addressing himself to the
aged attendant, " is above all price of recompense, and Sir Angus would
forget himself could he ever cease to remember it. Attend us, good Ronald,
to the camp, and equal with ourselves shall be your place of honour."

Lord Randolf was of a mild and courteous aspect, as were his manners
and deportment impressive, honourable, and knightly. He was not yet
more than five and twenty years of age, but from earliest youth had been
trained up in the exercise of arms. He was nephew to the king, and had
for some time fought against him in the English army, but being made the
prisoner of Bruce, the gallant and generous conduct of the latter soon won
his entire esteem. Shortly after he renounced the English interest, in
which from his youth he had been admitted, and with the conviction of the
injustice he had hitherto committed in fighting against the liberties of his
native land, resigned for ever an unnatural allegiance to the usurping
Edward, and endeavoured by his future deeds to atone his former error.

Strongly attached to Bruce, more for the worth and greatness of his mind
and character, than from the connecting tie between them, Randolf became
his ally, and solemnly linked in a lasting compact of sworn friendship with
Robert Bruce, and the equally noble Douglas, these three illustrious heroes
became inseparable, and famous for their mutual love and unbroken faith
towards each other; whilst Randolf, just to the cause he asserted, became
at once the glory of his own nation, and the terror of that whose commander had sought, and nearly completed, the overthrow of his princely
rival.

A friend so potent and skilled in arms as Randolf, Earl of Murray, so
warmly enthusiastic in his professions, and equally steadfast in their con-
clusions, was a fortune the most ardent wishes of Angus could not have expected to achieve, whilst the flattering reception of the king for a time
divided his thoughts and cheered his heart with better hopes. Melancholy,
however, still weighed upon his mind, and the loss of Edwin was a blow
that no circumstances would overcome. Magdalen, also, was nearly as
deeply lamented, whilst the secret whisperings of his silent thoughts, too
often for his peace, presented another object whom no sorrow could banish,
and the soft enchanting loveliness of Isabel yielded neither to time or the
great scene of shifting actions that now engaged so much of his attention.

It was near the decline of day when Lord Randolf conducted Angus to
the spacious amphitheatre of the high surrounding rocks that on every side
enveloped its extensive circumference. The last yellow streaks of the setting sun danced on the purple heath that crowned the summits, whilst the
darker objects of the plain beneath their bases displayed a melancholy
shade, strangely contrasted by the active moving figures that filled it.

Around this vast space, open to the skies, were ranged, in regular lines,
the hardy Scottish soldiery, whose glittering spears and bright armour
flashed a gleaming radiance, as the slanting beams of the sun glanced over
the rocky heights, whilst on the fortified summit of a precipice above wer.
seen, in dark majestic grandeur, the grey outline of a rugged Danish tower,
whose ponderous battlements, though they frowned terrifically over the
Scottish army, afforded a strong retreat to its valiant chieftains and monarch, and was the principal surety of their general safety.

By this time Bruce had declared to the eager soldiery his royal purpose
soon to abandon their present fastness for the glories of renewed hostilities.
The listening veterans, with shouts of triumph and joy, received the welcome tidings; each countenance suddenly brightened into pleasure, each

man seized his battle-axe and raised it on high, in token of their impatient readiness for the encounter. The spark of animation shot like a flash of lightning through every breast, and each individual was, in thought, a hero and a conqueror.

Angus beheld their warlike evolutions; his soul caught the enthusiastic fire of action, nor did his first essay disgrace the noble confidence his king and friend had reposed in him. Active, vigorous, inured to toils and dangerous hardships, disdaining all relief, and boldly resolved to conquer, Bruce looked, spoke, and moved like the royal hero he was, and it is therefore little to be wondered at that he was regarded by his soldiers and warriors as a being gifted with a divine spirit, and a person invulnerable from all mortal harm and injury.

It was not till dark that the warlike evolutions of the troops were finished, when Bruce, accompanied by Douglas, Randolf, Angus, and the illustrious train of chiefs, whose tried fidelity and long service had rendered them dear to their injured monarch, departed. Thus attended, he quitted the camp, and lighted by his pages, ascended the rocky steep that led up to the fortress above. It was built upon the summit, and strongly enclosed by a high rampart of immense thickness, and well guarded by watchful sentinels, who day and night paced the walls, and from their lofty stations had a far extending prospect over the island, sufficient to descry and forewarn the army in case a sudden surprisal should be attempted by the enemy.

Bruce passed onwards towards the interior of the gloomy edifice, where the nightly feast awaited to recruit the heroes for their daily fatigues. The king disdained the stately distinction of gorgeous titles, and their formal privileges of pre-eminence; he remembered only that his warriors were men, illustrious for the worth of their actions, and equal with himself in the glory of arms. The lowest of his knights, therefore, were ever admitted to his society, and partook with their royal master the banquet prepared for himself. Angus sat by the side of his friend, the noble Randolf, and the night passed away in moderate enjoyments and earnest talk of warfare.

In a few days Angus profited so well by the instructions of Lord Randolf, that he soon became versed in the military tactics of those heroic times; but, alas! the bright dawning horizon of his opening prospects could not cheer his mind, or withdraw it from those causes of melancholy dejection that corroded and cankered the bloom of youthful hope. The domestic sorrows of his house dwelt ever foremost on his saddened thoughts, and Edwin, writhing under the agonies of a cruel oppression, and perhaps wearing away his wretched hours in a loathsome dungeon, was the gloomy image that haunted his fancy.

Love, too, divided and equally distracted his bosom with its fruitless images and soft enchantments, and Isabel, the all accomplished, beauteous Isabel, became the sole, first object of his youthful adoration and most enduring affection. Often when the lonely hour of night had given a respite to the martial duties of his new employment, would he steal from the camp, and wandering amidst the upland lawns and heights, would he ponder on his secret, and sigh over the defeated hope of his devoted love, and of the late terrible events which had bereft himself of peace, Edwin of liberty, and Magdalen of life itself. Lord Mackenzie, too, became an object of inquietude to his mind; some days had elapsed, but he had not yet arrived to join the army of the king.

The dreadful catastrophe which had compelled Angus to forfeit his engagement of waiting his arrival at the ruined castle of Glenalvon, might perhaps have offended the father of Isabel; yet still Angus doubted not being able to appease his resentment when they again met. He was unable to account for his absence any other way than by hoping Mackenzie was still with his daughter, and would shortly join the army, a project he had himself planned when the former was to have been presented in person by his uncle to the monarch of Scotland.

Ronald, worn with age and grief for the horrible fate of his daughter, declined apace. The shock had been too much for his spirits, enfeebled and sinking with a blow that he was so little able to endure. The dreadful outrage of his daughter's death hung oppressive on his memory, and weighed down his remnant of life to a premature dissolution. His last moments approached, and were terminated in the arms of Angus, who mourned his loss with a regret that was almost filial. The death of the good old man was placid and tranquil, and to the last his wishes and prayers all centred in the happiness and welfare of his beloved young master. Again he reminded Angus of the spot which contained the treasures belonging to his house, and the papers that related to his future rights; and when in the act of praying for his lord, he heaved forth a gentle sigh and gave his spirit to eternity.

On the night succeeding Ronald's death, Angus, forgetful of himself, and only anxious to hide his griefs from every eye, wandered forth, alone and unseen, far from the fortress. The frequent sighs he uttered declared his unhappiness, and on this evening a deeper gloom of melancholy hung upon his spirits. All that he had loved seemed one by one torn from his sight; Magdalen, his first, best friend, was too surely murdered; her aged father, to whom he was become attached by the strongest ties, was gone; Edwin's fate was still wrapt in fearful mystery, and it was but too probable the high rank of Isabel would prevent every prospect of their union, and thus condemn him to a life of misery and despair.

For more than an hour Angus wandered about, through trackless woods and over frightful precipices, and he would have continued to proceed onwards, forgetful of the distance he was from the camp, had not the loud echoes of a shrill whistle very near him startled and aroused him from his meditations, as a voice, commanding and deep toned, exclaimed,—

"Desist, ye murderous traitors; or if I fall, be sure my people will not fail to avenge me!"

The voice was at once familiar to the ear of Angus, and swift as the lightning's flash he rushed from the place where he had been standing, and beheld by the twilight, that had not yet quite darkened into night, five fierce, gigantic-looking men in the act of surrounding a sixth, whose figure our hero instantly recognized for that of the king, who, like himself, had this evening strayed too far beyond the boundaries of the camp, a custom frequent with Bruce, to meditate and ponder over his vast deeds, and had been thus waylaid by hired ruffians, whose murderous designs were now aimed at the life of the defenceless monarch, and he must in an instant have yielded to his impending fate had not Angus plucked an arrow from his sheath, and with certain aim directed the weapon to the breast of the foremost ruffian, whose axe, uplifted with a mighty force, was about to cleave the devoted Bruce, when its master fell lifeless to the earth, nor ever again beheld that world his villany had justly forfeited.

Thus freed from the deadly grasp of the ferocious regicides, the king seized the offered bow of his deliverer, and stood undauntedly upon his guard, prepared for the approach of his murderers; who, when they found they had no greater number than two unarmed men to encounter, recovered from their mometary panic, and with deadly purpose rushed to the destruction of their intended victims.

With a bravery unequalled, and almost superhuman, Bruce valiantly repelled the furious attacks of three of his foes, who at the same instant fell desperately on him, whilst the fourth, of gigantic form and strength. darted on Angus. Scarcely could our young hero draw forth his sword ere he felt the heavy strokes of his powerful adversary, and long the double contest raged unequally, though with uncertainty as to what would be the result.

With no other weapon than the bow Bruce warded off the deadly aim of his three antagonists, who all attacked him with a determination that it was almost impossible to resist. The blows of the royal combatant were mighty, and eventually he maimed and disabled two of the ruffians, who fell, unable any longer to continue the strife. At that moment Bruce picked up a spear from the ground, and hurled it at the breast of the remaining assassin, who was in an instant pinned to the earth. Seizing the ruffian's battle axe, the king instantly despatched him, and with generous ardour paused not, but hurried to the rescue of his brave young deliverer, who, though he fought valiantly, was wounded, and sinking under the unequal combat.

Seeing the total defeat of his companions, and the advancing person of the king, the surviving ruffian quitted his unsubdued antagonist, and darting through the thick tangled wood, had nearly escaped, when the well-directed aim of Bruce laid him breathless in the very act of flying.

"Generous youth!" exclaimed the king, embracing our hero ardently. "Thou hast, indeed, well acquitted thyself in the first action thou hast been c lled into. Not more for life than for the justice of my former prophecy, do I thank thee. Henceforth thou art dear to the soul of Bruce, and hast well deserved his confidence. He shall himself declare thy gallant bearing in the dangerous strife, and reward thy heroism with a monarch's highest favours. Remember, Sir Angus Glenalvon, we are from this moment friends ; be ever nearest to my person, and when again Scotland shall have enthroned me as her king, fail not to demand whatever boon thy wishes may have formed."

At that moment a loud blast upon a bugle was sounded at no great distance off.

"Hark!" cried the king, "that signal bespeaks that we have friends at hand;" and soon after the Lords Douglas and Randolf, with many other chieftains and warriors, rushed with eager haste towards the spot where the king and Angus were standing.

"Said I not rightly, gallant friend?" exclaimed Bruce, as the others approached. "Behold your monarch's preserver, whose timely presence alone rescued me from the villains that attacked me!"

"My friend," cried Randolf, taking the hand of Angus, "fortunate and enviable was the proud triumph of this night dearer than my own. I prize that life which thy valour has preserved; and most heartily do I rejoice that the honour of saving the king has fallen to thy share. Thou hast ensured the eternal gratitude of Randolf, and early acquired that glory which will for ever stamp thy name with noble worth, and render thee pre-eminent in deeds of arms and great renown."

"Forbear, my lord," replied Angus, modestly. "Behold where lie the proofs of our king's gallantry (pointing to the dead bodies of the ruffians), and then give the honour to him who but deserves it."

"Receive him, my lords," said the king, "as one that is equal with yourselves in honour and martial enterprize; and as you value my friendship and life, esteem him my preserver from an inglorious death."

Randolf now discovered, as Angus leant on his arm, that he was severely wounded and faint with loss of blood. He was, therefore, supported on a

litter that was hastily constructed, and in that manner conveyed back to the fortress.

The news of the king's late encounter and imminent danger had reached his hardy warriors, who, mistaking Angus for their king, hung down their heads in silent dejection, but when assured that Bruce was unhurt, and the youth, as he declared himself, but slightly wounded, the shout of tumultuous gladness rang on the silence of night, and a hundred torches were thrown high through the air in triumph for the safety of their royal leader. To quiet this tumult, Bruce found it necessary instantly to proclaim his fixed purpose of soon quitting Arran, and commencing hostilities. The wound received by Angus was soon staunched ; indeed he made so lightly of it, that not one hour's delay on his account interfered with the orders which had been given for getting everything in readiness.

The remains of Ronald were committed to the tomb with all the solemnity and honour of military ceremony. Angus was deeply affected at the scene, and turning away from the spot, he exclaimed, in agitated tones of painful remembrance :—

"Farewell, thou good old man ! In the regions of eternal peace, thou wilt behold my father, who living, thou didst faithfully love and serve ; and there also wilt thou be received by that daughter whose loss has hurried thee to thy grave. At the throne of grace solicit favour for the orphans of thy generous care ; and, oh ! may thy guardian spirit be permitted to watch over the helpless Edwin !"

The future must reveal the actions of Bruce and his illustrious heroes. The Scottish monarch, his chief, and warlike veterans, once more emerging from the shores of Arran, England's usurping sovereign felt in proof that the threats of his heroic rival were not made in vain.

No. 19

CHAPTER XXIV.

"The tombs and monumental caves
Of death look cold, and shoot a chillness
To my trembling heart; the horror of this
Place and silence will increase my melancholy."
CONGREVE.

WE must now return to Isabel, whose days were passed in solitude and listless suspense. Her mind had received a dreadful shock in the late disasters that had so powerfully called forth all the tender sensibilities of her nature. Hitherto, passing her time in calm, unbroken ease and retirement, surrounded by beings enlightened and refined by superior intellectual endowments, beloved by all, and sheltered securely in the royal sanctuary of Scotland from every danger that had so long afflicted her bleeding country, the transactions of the foregoing events had been so rapid, and so violent in their effects, as to threaten an almost total destruction of her happiness.

Uncertain of her father's destiny, she in secret shed bitter tears of doubt and dread; whilst at times a kind of prophetic sensation, like the internal conviction of approaching misery, seemed to oppress her reason, and weigh her spirits down with feelings of morbid melancholy, that effectually destroyed the serenity she might otherwise have enjoyed.

Not daring to quit the convent, lest she should betray the secret of his retreat, (for of late several strange figures had been seen lurking beneath the walls,) she confined herself to her own remote chamber, except when, to wile away a pensive hour, she sometimes crossed its mazy galleries, and seating herself in the niche of the iron grate, which was fixed in a small round turret that overhung the screen, she would try to amuse her thoughts with the lute, as her eye wandered over the huge mass of waters, or watch in anxious expectation the hoped-for arrival of each distant sail, fondly imagining it might perhaps waft her father once more to her longing eyes in safety, and with him the youthful Angus, whose early misfortunes she had so often wept over with the truest sorrows, and for whom she had felt the deepest interest, and the warmnst sentiments of pity, regard, and dawning love.

It was one night, when all within the convent was sunk to rest and quietude, and every sacred function of the holy sisterhood had ceased, and not a lamp remained burning, save those which constantly illumined the sacred shrine of the sacred patroness of the community, and all was solemn silence around, when Isabel was on a sudden startled from a deep slumber by a loud repeated knocking at the principal entrance of the outward portal. Alarmed at this unusual occurrence, the princess fearfully raised herself on her couch. A number of incoherent conjectures assailed her mind; and with a sudden exclamation of joy, she at length exclaimed :—

"It is—it is my father! and with him, perhaps, the generous preserver of Isabel's peace and honour. Happy moment! Oh, be propitious, Heaven, and once more restore to me a loved but persecuted father!"

In impatient agitation she continued to wait the expected summons; and so confident were her hopes which had been thus excited, that hastily clasping the zone of a loosely flowing robe around her, she prepared herself for the happiness so fondly anticipated. She listened eagerly for each sound, and presently a signal at the door confirmed her hopes :—

"'Tis he!" he eagerly exclaimed; "my dear father has at length returned! Holy mother, receive a prostrate suppliant's thanks!"

Isabel bowed before the image of the virgin as she quickly passed the niche where it stood, and with trembling steps approached the portal; which having unfastened, she admitted, not, as the impatience of her wishes expected, her father, but an elderly stately nun who, with a lighted taper in her hand, stalked slowly, and with form erect, into her presence.

Too eager for information to notice the pale, affrighted looks of sister Mary, our heroine impatiently demanded if Lord Mackenzie had arrived at the convent. But the nun was not to be diverted from her purpose by any questions that might be asked, and with a reproving frown, she delivered a summons from the abbess to attend her immediately in the sanctuary of the convent.

"The sanctuary!" cried Isabel, with tones of alarmed surprise and disappointment. "Heavens! what cause of sudden danger can have rendered its holy retreat necessary to our superior?"

"I was enjoined to conduct you thither in silence," answered sister Mary, "and must not be detained by ill-timed questions. Our holy mother forbids me to commune with those who are not professed. Ah! my daughter, hadst thou, like us, been favoured with a call from Heaven, our sacred shrines had thus afforded thee a shelter from all thine enemies."

Too impatient to behold once more her beloved parent, Isabel attempted not to question the import of sister Mary's allusions, but following the steps of the nun, she was passing the shrine, when sister Mary, with a forbidding look of silent consequence, held up her shrivelled finger as she pointed to the tomb in solemn reverence, then crossing her arms in her bosom, with a devout air, she sighed forth some inarticulate sentences, expressive of her homage and submission to the blessed saint; then, rising from the humble posture in which she had thrown herself, she again moved forward in the same silence as before. Isabel followed her with wonder and anxiety, and at length found herself within the sanctuary of the convent, where she found the lady abbess kneeling reverently before a small altar, and who, rising from her devotions, said, with some solemnity:—

"My daughter, the prayers I have just offered up were for thee. May they be found acceptable, and may our gracious Lady vouchsafe to inspire in thy bosom that divine spirit which will, I trust, conduct thee to our sacred altars, a pure and spotless vestal, devoted to her services."

Isabel looked surprised, unable to comprehend the extraordinary purport of the superior's words, whilst her feelings became suspended between the dread of defeated hope and the anticipated explanation of these words.

"I see," continued the abbess, "thou art ignorant of the purport of my words. Retire, good sister Mary; your silence and obedience to my words have well merited my praise and commendation."

The shrivelled countenance of the nun softened into a look of pleasure, as she bowed lowly to the superior, and retired to the sanctuary; and Isabel, as she noticed the varying features of the nun, could not help inwardly remarking that even the aged votary of religion had passions to be gratified which her sacred profession ought in youth to have subdued; nor was sister Mary's mind inaccessible to the attacks of vanity. Scarcely had she disappeared, when the lady abbess, with solemn emphasis, thus went on:—

"Thou hast seen, my daughter, the peaceful joys which reward those who take shelter beneath this roof. A mind so good and rational as thine, my dear child, can no doubt justly estimate the lasting reward and benefit of devoting itself thus early to the service and worship of Heaven. Thy pure thoughts, I am sure, will reject with pious horror the vain transitory parade of earthly pomps and empty sounding grandeur, whose wiles but lure us to destruction, and betray, ultimately, our souls to purgatory. I see my prayers for thee have not been offered in vain, and that I shall soon have added another to the faithful flock that here pass their lives in peaceful entertainment."

Isabel, no longer able to endure the torturing suspense and dread of evil this long speech teemed with, now interrupted the lady abbess, as, with strong emotions of distress and increasing terror, she exclaimed :—

"Is, then, my father dead? Oh, gracious Heaven am I indeed, bereft of that one worldly hope, and stay, my fallen state had left me!"

The lady abbess frowned indignantly at this interruption, and casting upon our heroine a piercing glance of anger, she answered, upbraidingly:

"Is this, daughter, the reverence our speech and presence should exact from thee? I would have set before thee all the joys of Heaven,—have taught thee how to secure its inheritance, and led thy youthful fancy, entranced in delightful rapture, up to the very gates of paradise. Nay, I would have rendered thee eager as myself, to shake off the vanities of life, that thy freed spirit might have looked anxious to the joys of another state of existence. But, alas! vain are my endeavours to save thee from the delusions of the tempter, for thy wayward thoughts wander after wordly vanities, and only long penitence and earnest prayer can save thee from impending dangers."

"Forgive me, holy mother, the unconscious offence I have been guilty of," cried Isabel. "Remember, you yourself were once a daughter, and, like me, fondly regardful of the welfare of a beloved and absent parent, and, perhaps, as eager to behold and embrace him as I am."

Restraining the asperity of her temper, which she began to see would be of little avail, the lady abbess affected to be softened by these words that had been addressed to her. At least she was too proud to deny the passion of a feeling, which, nevertheless, she had not at any time cherished; and to Isabel's repeated inquiries and pathetic appeals to be informed of her father, she at length vouchsafed to acquaint her that Lord Mackenzie had not arrived, nor did the present disturbance originate in any tidings from him. And with a still more solemn look, and gloomy contraction of brow, she continued to address the drooping Isabel, as she held forth a vellum manuscript sealed with the royal arms of England and Scotland united.

"Your person, my daughter," said the abbess, "has at this late hour been demanded by King Edward's commissioners, nor dare I risk the peril of disobeying his commands, lest the sacred sanctuary of our house should be outraged by unlawful footsteps, and our holy altars profaned."

"My father, madam," answered Isabel, firmly, "placed me beneath your care, confident of your power to afford me an honourable retreat from the insolence of his own and his daughter's persecutors. If, however, the charge was too heavy, or beyond your ability to perform, wherefore did you unnecessarily stoop to deceive his faith in your honour, or receive me to your protection, since, in any other, such a doubt could not have been apprehended?"

The abbess frowned, and became confused, but after some hesitation, she replied:—

"Imprudent girl! I have not said I was unable to fulfil my promise to your father; and it remains with yourself only to secure your safety. The commissioners of King Edward of England are at this instant within the abbey walls awaiting your deliverance into their hands. At present this sanctuary is the only spot that can shield you from their search, and should you consent immediately to receive the monastic veil, you are then secure from outrage, nor will they dare insult our holy shrines by dragging a vestal from these altars, otherwise I have no power to refuse you to their high commission, nor can I risk my own and my convent's safety longer to harbour the foes of our present governors. Say, therefore, my daughter, and let yon image receive your vow, that you consent to embrace our holy profession, and this instant I will dismiss the commissioners with an assurance that you have already become a nun of our holy order."

"Say, rather," answered Isabel, resolutely, "that you know your power, and, therefore, have presumed to urge the utmost limits of its extent, to force a helpless female to yield to your own will. For the present you will do well to reflect on the hazard to yourself; and remember, that as I now *demand* a safe refuge in your house, and the unquestioned privilege of freedom of action, you are bound to afford me the shelter I require, till with safety I am able to remove to another, less interested in the cause of a usurper, and steadfast in its allegiance to the rightful monarch. Till tonight only shall I remain in the abbey, and it will be for the interest of its inmates to protect the niece of King Robert Bruce from violence or insult, since a strict account will hereafter be demanded of its superior, who alone must become responsible for her safety!"

Awed, confounded, and defeated in her artful projects, the abbess stood irresolute and undetermined. She felt enraged at her baffled hopes, and still more provoked and indignant at the severity of reproof and manner with which she had been addressed by our heroine. Imagining the princess to be too youthful and passive to be much experienced in worldly knowledge, she had resolved to take advantage of the present momentous crisis, and prevail upon Isabel to take the veil, and thus secure for the convent the vast wealth which belonged to the family of Mackenzie. Defeated, however, in this hope, and completely silenced by the resolute spirit and decisive energy of Isabel's rejection to her terms, the wily abbess softened the asperity of her former manner, and with more kindness of tone, said :—

"My daughter, since you reject my offered love, and with language illadapted to our meek order, have forgot the reverence due to the person of its superior, I will convince you no malice harbours in our holy society, though the right to inflict penance might authorise me to impose it in an instance like this. Await, therefore, with confident security beneath our roof, for Heaven knows I would fain save your innocence from the tempters of this wicked world ; and should our pious sisterhood consent to my ardent wishes still to retain you an inmate, be assured I shall rejoice to fulfil the duties of my station, and will, at any risk, resist the threatening evils that may befal our house's welfare to ward off the dangers that encompass you. Farewell, daughter ; expect my return soon, and be assured I will unceasingly labour for your good."

With a frown of disappointment the abbess then quitted the sanctuary, and Isabel, left to her own heavy ruminations, experienced the alternate emotions of sorrow, disappointment, and strongly awakened terror. Lord Morton, it was but too evident, had traced her flight, and now no longer guarded from his insidious machinations by a father's presence, everything was to be dreaded from the known claims the fierce resentful Edward had empowered him to fulfil. She sighed bitterly to the memory of the past.

"Ah !" she cried, as a tear stole down her cheeks, "had not adversity thus fallen upon me, I should not thus have had to seek an asylum within these walls. But fate still pursues me, and Heaven only knows when I shall again know the blessing of security and repose."

After about an hour's absence, the abbess returned ; her brow was still clouded, and her look disturbed, and seemingly sorrowful. For a moment she cast on Isabel a look of scrutiny, and with a sigh, exclaimed :—

"Alas! my dear daughter, I grieve to find my power unequal to my tender care and anxiety to preserve you from impending dangers. Edward's will is absolute in Scotland, nor dare we resist his sovereign edicts. Since my last departure hence, a second mandate, more peremptory than the first, commands us, on peril of our lives and the total ruin of our house, to resign you to the state commissioners appointed to receive your person, and should we refuse obedience to these decrees, the sacrilegious plunderers are armed with full powers to burn to their foundation our venerable walls, since no other terms will save it but your deliverance, or an assurance that you are become a sister of our holy order."

With steadfast gaze Isabel looked firmly at the abbess.

"I see," she exclaimed, "that your convent cannot protect me from the dangers with which I am threatened. I will not, therefore, subject myself to the offered indignites, nor will I, by any act of my own, involve you in the perils of my own wayward destiny. Let me, however, owe to your generosity a last benefit, and I shall depart with a sense of gratitude due to those who only from want of power are unable to protect me."

"Speak your wishes," answered the abbess; "yet wouldst thou make choice of our house, and secure to thy future days that serenity and tranquil happiness its peaceful inmates possess, then might we with holy zeal guard thee from harm, and the church have a sacred right to resist the sacreligious violence now offered against its repose and safety."

"On that subject," answered the princess, resolutely, "I must not be importuned; for unless the express injunctions of my father sanctioned and commanded the step, be assured no earthly persuasion should induce me to consent to such a sacrifice. Had you granted me a safe retreat beneath your roof, much happiness had probably been spared me; but I submit to a destiny that cannot be avoided, and have only to entreat you to provide me with guides and horses necessary for my departure this night, when, in obedience to my father's wish, I shall in future sojourn at the castle of Glenroy. Such are my present purposes, nor can I doubt your willingness to aid me, remembering, as you must, that your faith is already solemnly pledged. You have assured me of present security here, and the time is but short that can render uncertain your endangered repose, since upon my departure the convent will be released from the threatened fury of its invaders."

"Holy Virgin!" cried the abbess, in a tone of alarm; "mean you then, my daughter, to tempt the violence of these distempered times, and encounter all the difficulties of a journey perilous and dreary, and full of snares that are almost certain to bring you to destruction? What shall I say,—what reason can I give Lord Mackenzie when he demands you of my hands, should I suffer you to depart?"

"My resolution is unalterably fixed," answered Isabel, "and my father will approve it, and exonerate you from blame, when he learns the necessity that has forced me to retire from your protection."

Provoked, yet not daring openly to express her resentment, the abbess muttered some unintelligible words as she quitted the sanctuary, and Isabel, now confined within its narrow precincts to avoid discovery, awaited the slow, lingering hours, impatient for the moment that would terminate the difficulties of her present irksome situation, and free her from the persecutions of the infamous Lord Morton.

At length the day declined, and the abbess appeared to prevail on our heroine to remain where she was for the present. Isabel was, however, firm in her resolve, and opening the lid of a small casket, she took from it a purse of gold, which she laid at the foot of the altar, begging of the abbess to accept of it as a tribute of her gratitude for the protection she had received. The offering was not refused, and having found that all further persuasion would be in vain, the superior once more prepared to depart.

"Adieu, my daughter," she said, "and may Heaven guard you from every harm. At nightfall, sister Mary will conduct you from our sanctuary, for I have prepared all things for your departure, and when the vespers are ended you shall set forth. Trust me we have hazarded much to ensure your safety, and should the troop that guard the gates discover your escape before all things are prepared, our danger from the vengeance of King Edward would be dreadful, if not fatal."

After solemnly bestowing her blessing upon Isabel, the abbess retired, and the princess, once more alone, continued to pace the chamber with thoughts fevered by doubtful fears and sorrowing conjectures. As the moment grew nearer, her alarms increased, for she knew the step she was about to take would be attended with danger and extreme difficulty; and much she grieved that she was not permitted to remain in the otherwise peaceful seclusion of the convent, where she had hoped to have found a secure asylum from the rude violence of the times, and those domestic grievances which had thus driven her forth a wanderer from home.

At length the sister Mary's hasty signal was heard, and Isabel, trembling with alarm, could scarcely withdraw the bolts of the little portal.

"Hasten, hasten, daughter," whispered the nun, hurriedly; "not an instant is to be lost, for the commissioners, joined by another troop of horsemen, lately arrived at the convent, have more peremptorily demanded you from the hands of our superior, who, frightened by their threats, was compelled to use a stratagem to prevent their entrance into the chapel. A moment's delay, perhaps, may involve our whole community in destruction."

"Heaven forbid!" earnestly ejaculated Isabel, alarmed as much for the safety of the sisterhood as her own.

"Truly, daughter, your prayers are needed, for the event to us may be sacrilege, if not violation," exclaimed sister Mary, in a sharp tone. "I tremble to reflect on the consequences that may ensue, should the fierce soldiers profane our holy sanctuary. Alas! what, then, will become of us poor helpless lambs, devoted to the ravenous wolves that will shortly beset us? They will shock our ears with vile professions of love—nay, our very honour may be endangered and assailed!"

Isabel suppressed the smile that curled her lip in spite of her alarm, as her eye glanced on the shrivelled features of sister Mary, who, almost palsied with age, seemed particularly to anticipate evils of which her very aspect was an antidote. The aged nun, however, continued to descant largely on a string of improbable suggestions, full of the most dreadful events, and impending ruin to every soul of the holy community.

"We shall all be murdered, or, perhaps, worse," she went on; "our very altars, to which we may vainly fly for refuge, will be outraged. Oh, Blessed Virgin, what can save us from these dangers if thou dost not put forth thy hand to aid us?"

"Do not doubt, good sister, the care of our holy patroness," answered Isabel, with a smile. "She has heard your petition, and will shield your innocence and unexampled virtue with her own arm; nor will anything of harm or guile dare approach those her Heavenly influence guards."

Sister Mary's fears yielded to the pleasure of being thought an object of that danger which she affected to believe herself liable to; and with an air of less severity she smoothed her ruffled brow into what she imagined a graceful, meek resignation, and then led Isabel forth, as with a lighted lamp she conducted her through several unfrequented passages, and descending the vestibule, they, in silence and gloom, gained the cemetery—for the lamp gave but a feeble gleam on the damp, black walls, and Isabel's foot more than once became infirm, as she continued to pace the narrow descent that opened upon the farthest catacombs of the vaults. She shuddered as her eye encountered several dismal objects and coffined relics which strewed the sides of this antique repository of the dead. Drawing her folded veil still closer over her face, she tried to avoid the sight of those dreary spectacles that every step she trod presented themselves to her startled view.

"I am wandering through the house of death," she inwardly thought. "How awful—how impressive is the lesson it teaches!—How futile does it render all the vain distinctions of worldly greatness, and with what a silent sternness does it not remind proud mortality of its frail, uncertain tenure here. Oh, let but a few transitory years, perhaps moments, elapse, and I shall be for ever silent and forgotten!"

Isabel sighed heavily as she remembered her father, and her eyes swam in tears as she thought of their parting, and the uncertainty whether they should ever meet again in this world.

"Alas!" she murmured to herself, "must I live, dear father, to mourn thy early loss!" She shuddered at the prophetic image her fancy had created, and with a struggle tried to shake off the influence it had upon her. "I am to blame," she continued, "thus to anticipate so much additional wretchedness. 'Tis the silent horror of this appalling spot, which has conjured up the phantasies of a disturbed imagination, and rendered my mind imbecile, and thanklessly mistrustful of Heaven's merciful goodness."

Still the images of her awakened fears continued, and unknowing that she was observed, she gave way to the silent grief that afflicted her bosom.

Sister Mary noticed and attributed its origin to the terror of the lonely place they were then traversing. Harshly she rebuked the childish weakness, as she termed it, and, with a self-important air, bade her imitate her pious example of confidence and trusting reliance.

Isabel's thoughts, too deeply abstracted in pensive meditations, permitted her to give but little attention to the observations of sister Mary, who, uninterrupted, she suffered to continue her long harangue, till, quitting the winding passages of the vaults, our heroine on a sudden beheld herself arrived at the abrupt termination of the lower portions of the convent, whose outward aperture, guarded by an iron grating, opened upon an adjoining wood, where, as had been planned, she recognized her faithful Catherine, and two men with horses, ready caparisoned for the journey.

Taking from her arm a rich bracelet, Isabel presented it to the well-pleased sister, who, with a long drawn sigh, prayed the saints to guard the hapless fugitive; then kissing her cheek, she again retreated behind the dark vaulted avenue, and closed its heavy portal.

Isabel, seated on her palfrey, and feeling a revival of hope that presented a prospect of approaching safety, free from the late persecutions she had endured, gave the necessary directions to the guides, and, aided by a dim streak of twilight that yet marked the western horizon, she began her perilous journey.

CHAPTER XXV.

" Foul, treacherous fiend, I know thy purposes ;—
Again thou would'st deceive me with fair words,
But, loathing thee beyond all other men,
I bid thee hence for ever !''

THE WIZARD'S CURSE.

THE ancient castle of Glenroy, to which Isabel was now journeying, was situated amongst the mountains at the further extremity of Argyle, and its venerable earl was the brother of Lord Mackenzie's mother, to whose protection he had long since intended to consign his daughter. Our heroine had never seen the noble chieftain, nor had her father of late years maintained a personal intercourse with the aged earl of Glenroy, whose infirmities had long since confined him to the retirement of his own princely domains, and who, amidst the long and sanguinary war that had raged in his unhappy country, and deluged her once fertile valleys in her people's blood, had remained unmolested and free from the consequences which had involved so many illustrious families in ruin and decay, whose valour and hardy courage in the rescue of their native country from the tyranny of the English yoke had been hitherto unconquerable, and was now become valued and famous in every court throughout the civilized world.

The earl of Glenroy, though permitted with an easy and serene quietude to decline gently into the vale of years, had not been totally exempt from the attacks of private, though not public, calamity. There was a mystery, involving some branch of his connexions, which had long since disturbed the venerable warrior's repose, and not a little aided the constant melancholy that of late years clouded the former lustre of his prospects.

Lord Mackenzie had early planned the favourite wish of placing his
No. 20.

daughter beneath the safe guardianship of this, his nearest and only relative; and but that the great distance of Glenroy from the ruined castle of Glenalvon somewhat interfered with his present duties, he would himself have conducted her thither. He, however, reflected that such a step would greatly retard the eager expectations of his newly found nephews, who must be obliged to remain a day or two longer in their dangerous retreat—a measure, he foresaw, perilous to their welfare, if not to their liberties and lives, since their secret enemy might too probably be now at Badenoch, and if so a secret spy over the actions of the wronged sons of Glenalvon, whom, too fatally, he might, in such an interval of time, secure beyond the reach of every effort of discovery.

From such motives as these, joined with those already stated, Lord Mackenzie changed his first intentions, and not doubting the sacred recesses of a house devoted to holy worship would protect his daughter from every threatening danger, he had, as has been seen, unhesitatingly placed her where, alas! no security was destined to confirm the assurance of his anxious but mistaken hopes.

Conducted by her guides, Isabel now hurried swiftly from the convent walls, and penetrating a thick embowering avenue of the forest, soon felt herself comparatively secure from the fear of pursuit or discovery.

It was a dark dreary night, for as yet the moon had not risen, and it was therefore absolutely necessary for the guides to light their torches. Isabel, however, regarded this circumstance with alarm, for she feared lest the glaring reflection of the flambeaux should reveal their position to any of the unrelenting persecutors, who might even now be searching after her through the deep mazes of the wood. The guides that attended her were but two in number, and in case any attack should be made very little assistance or defence was to be expected from them.

At length the woods being traversed, the moon, which by this time had risen, rendered the torches no longer serviceable, and as Isabel reached the opening of a dell, she beheld, with sensations of wonder and ecstatic delight, the sleeping beauties of the romantic scenery, which, softened by the shades of night, yet rendered distinct by the moon, displayed objects of admiration that till now our heroine had never beheld.

Descending the precipitous steeps that terminated this portion of their journey, Isabel breathed forth the thankfulness of a bosom fraught with gratitude for her escape, and shortly afterwards they entered a deep valley, whose picturesque landscapes exhibited images at once sublime, varied, and strikingly grand and beautiful. Huge masses of basaltic rocks rising into stupendous acclivities, surmounted by extensive colonnades, whose rugged forms were wildly scattered by the hand of nature in almost all her varying forms of tremendous horror and fearful sublimity, were the principal objects that attracted the eye; whilst the lower steeps displayed the deep obscured glens, hollowed by the convulsions of former ages, and laying open to the sight deep yawning chasms, beneath which a narrow causeway conducted the travellers over these dangerous but romantic solitudes, whilst in the deep-bottomed hollow the rock-streams from the cataracts above rolled their agitated waters, and glittered through the clefts and fissures, amidst which the moon-beams at intervals danced upon the clear surface of the current, and partially revealed the dark sombre objects of the surrounding scene.

As they continued to advance the scene varied into a thousand grotesque and romantic objects, whilst the road at times became more difficult of access,—for in many parts vast massive fragments, decayed through age, had fallen into the vale, and lay in scattered heaps across the pathway, whose rugged exteriors still afforded a thin layer of earth, and were here and there crowned with dwarf shrubs of various kinds; whilst the waters, that had lately been swelled by the continued floods, overflowed their banks, and forcing for themselves a passage over the steeps, descended with a stunning violence in huge cataracts into the lower vale, breaking, with melancholy reverberations, the solemn stillness of that lonely hour.

The moonlight, when slightly overcast, gave to each surrounding object a deepening misty tint; and Isabel, drawn from the contemplation of her own sorrows by the beauties of so enchanting a scene, slackened her pace. At a distance, when she cast her eyes behind her, the wild steeps of Ben Lomond were beheld, the towering monarch of the scene, whose hoary head rose high above the surrounding summits; and as our heroine, after long labour, reached the top of a lofty causeway, she beheld several distant rivers, lochs, and mountain torrents, all dimly traced in the glitter of the moonbeams, whilst the magnificent waters of Loch Leven were descried,— and as she continued to advance towards its rising banks, darkly shaded with forest woods, the deep sombre shapes of its woody islands, like huge specks, reared their high tangled groves and indented shores, presenting to the meditative mind a scene so wonderfully wild, romantic, and variegated, as to render feeble the most fervid description of memory, and only to be justly estimated and known when viewed by minds capable of enjoying the grand sublimity of Nature's stupendous productions.

From these reflections Isabel at length awoke to a recollection of her own melancholy state, and to her demand of how far distant was the castle of Glenroy, one of the guides replied,—

"Many miles, and that they could not expect to reach it till some hours after sunrise."

Isabel had already began to feel weary, and this information but ill-cheered her drooping spirits, or accorded with the expectations she had formed. The heights of Inverness were here, indeed, to be plainly distinguished, but their lofty summits were far distant, and she had yet to travel many a rugged steep ere she reached the promised haven of rest that it was anticipated the castle of Glenroy would afford. The pathway now wound round the pinnacle of a huge overhanging rock, and Isabel found herself entering under the deep hollow of a double embankment, whose high ridges were thickly lined with mountain ash, birch, and tall pines, entwining their branches over the narrow defile, so as almost to exclude the moonbeams, which in vain endeavoured to penetrate their leafy coverts.

The further they advanced the more gloomy and darksome became the way; and their progress was rendered more difficult and slow from the steepness of the rugged ascent. The guides now evidently advanced unwillingly, and at length Isabel discovered, from the hesitation of their manner, that they had lost their right road, and were traversing a wild and desert country, remote from every near habitation or human aid, and only visited at times by the hordes of freebooters that occasionally sheltered in these nearly inaccessable passes from the pursuit of justice.

Scarcely had this fear-inspiring account been given by one of their guides, when their worst apprehensions of danger were verified by a loud, shrill whistle, which at this crisis suddenly echoed near the spot, and in an instant the affrighted travellers heard the quick galloping of horsemen approaching. To retreat was impossible, for there was no opening through which to escape, and before they had time to deliberate they were surrounded by a troop of about twenty horsemen. The guides were then seized, and others of the ruffians securing Isabel and her attendant, Catherine, they were forcibly lifted from their horses and placed on those belonging to the strangers, who, deaf to every remonstrance or entreaty, galloped forward, and presently were out of the reach of the terrified guides.

The ruffians had separated Isabel from her attendant, for Catherine, bitterly lamenting the fate of her beloved mistress, by the clamour of her grief provoked the anger of her fierce conductor; whilst our heroine, disdaining all complaint, in silent resignation yielded to the hapless necessity of her adverse destiny, and wrapt in the sad employment of her reflections, spoke not at all, nor even opposed the violence of her enemies, for she felt convinced that she was in the hands of the English commissioners, and that she had been betrayed by the treachery of the abbess, who had doubtless revealed her flight to save herself from the vengeance of King Edward.

For some time the horsemen continued to goad on their jaded steeds through the most dismal solitudes and frightful wildernesses, whose terrific aspects dismayed the heart of Isabel with the most alarming suspicions, and it was not till the grey dawn of day again returned that the travellers quitted the forest shades, and Isabel, at a distance, traced the blackened battlements of some stupendous towers, loftily seated on a rocky promontory that overhung the waters of Loch Leven, to which they had been for some time gradually approaching.

The strangers were all masked, but as the increasing light of day displayed their figures, the foremost, who led her horse, made a signal to his attendants, who immediately drew back to a respectful distance. He then withdrew the mask from his face, and revealed to the terrified Isabel the features of the treacherous Lord Morton. He observed the indignant fire that shot from her eye, but without appearing to take any notice of it, he said in a tone of affected courtesy,—

"The lovely Lady Isabel will, I trust, vouchsafe forgiveness to the violence which has thus impelled me to oppose her designs, when she is informed that only by this means she could have been preserved from the dreadful malice of her implacable foes."

"What mean you, my lord?" she asked coldly.

"That your life is at this moment forfeited," he replied; "King Edward, rankling with the resistance you offered to his arms, has condemned you and your father to meet an ignominious death. Had you not fortunately succeeded in escaping from the convent of St. Eustatia, you must have been at this moment his prisoner; nay, I still tremble for your safety, for his people even now scour the country round, eager in the pursuit, and should we not reach a place of strength ere they discover the track we have taken, my own life, equally with yours, must pay the penalty of his revenge for opposing his decrees."

"If your speech deceives me not again," answered Isabel, "I am not only your prisoner, but devoted to swell the lists of those unfortunates whose whose fidelity and loyalty to their lawful sovereign have been rewarded by a usurper with death. It may be that I am indebted to you for a life which else had thus terminated, and in that case I shall not forget the obligation your service demands. Perhaps you will convey me to the castle of Glenroy, to which place I am journeying, and, if really sincere in your repentance for the indignities I have sustained through your delinquency, you will merit my future forgiveness of the past; conduct me, therefore, to my place of destination, or desist from detaining me in my flight."

"Such an attempt, Lady Isabel," replied the hypocrite, "would be fruitless, and can only expose you to the certain consequences of impending destruction. The last arrived troop, who demanded you at the convent of St. Eustatia, have doubtless discovered your retreat from thence, and will pursue you, as they dread to provoke the rage of the disappointed Edward. I have bribed an English soldier, who revealed to me the certain ruin that awaited you if once again within the ruthless grasp of your royal foe, and by stratagem have thus gained possession of the royal warrant issued for your seizure. Deign, then, to owe to me your present safety, since, acquainted with the perfidious designs of Edward, I have provided the means to baffle his deadly purposes, and in the castle of your ancestors will conceal you from the fury of his hatred till some future opportunity, favourable to your interests, may again restore you to your illustrious rank, and all the splendour of which you have been unjustly deprived."

"It is in vain, my lord," cried Isabel, "that you seek to convince me of your good intentions. My retreat in the convent of St. Eustatia was unknown to all unless to you, and you must bear with my candour, if I tell you, that only from the most dishonourable causes would you have dared thus again betray a helpless female to the relentless power of him whom your base arts have rendered my foe. Remembering the dark treachery of your actions at the castle of Craiglynn, you cannot wonder if I withhold my belief to professions so boldly avowed, and equally distrust the report of that hazard to which you say my life is exposed. If your designs in thus violently impeding my free progress were really the result of an honourable wish to secure my tranquillity, wherefore are my guides thus torn from me, and even the slender protection they could afford me denied?"

"That they may not reveal the place of your retreat where alone you can hope for security," he replied. "It would have been madness to have trusted them with a secret of such magnitude, who, for a bribe, would have betrayed you. Glenroy is more than fifty miles distant, and to reach it almost impossible. Trust me, Lady Isabel, I have mourned in penitence the injuries you so bitterly reproach me with; they are the last I can ever be hurried into committing, and my future actions shall amply atone my past transgressions. A suppliant, and your devoted slave, I live but to obey your commands."

"And have you, then, forgotten," asked Isabel, "the miseries your crimes have inflicted on my family?"

"It is true," he replied, "that I betrayed your father's castle to the foe, but only from the conviction that to oppose was to sacrifice the lives of our brave defenders, did I unwillingly comply. It is true, also, that Edward believing me devoted to his cause, has heaped on me honours and titles I never accepted, but in trust, to render them back again to their lawful inheritors. I will owe nothing but to the Princess Isabel, and with my existence, if she demands it, I will sign away all that was her's, so lately possessed by myself. Ah, Isabel, happy had it been for your ill-judging father had he deigned to have trusted me. The wound he inflicted opened my eyes to the conviction of my misdeeds, and I hastened to throw myself at his feet and implore oblivion of the past. It was for this purpose alone that I followed you to Glenalvon, whither my people had traced you, inspired by the glory of rescuing you from certain destruction."

"Whither are you now taking me?" demanded our heroine.

"You now behold before you the towers of Stratheden Castle," answered Morton, "the ancient seat of your forefathers. Its portals open wide to receive and welcome you with loyalty and homage, for with pleasure I resign their possessions to you, claiming only the envied distinction of guarding the object of his respectful duty and submission from the hostile foes that seek to invade her repose."

It was indeed, and Isabel, even before she was aware of the near conclusion of her journey, found herself within the heavy embattled portcullis of Stratheden Castle. Morton had thus effectually secured his intended victim, and though his smooth deceit had beguiled and confused the judgment of the devoted princess, his real designs were thus artfully accomplished, and not even an alternative allowed her to choose or refuse the destiny he had laboured to achieve.

Never till now had Isabel beheld this once famed mansion of her ancestors; it had been seized, some years previously to her quitting the monastery of St. Colomba, by the cruel depredations of the English, and had since that time undergone many severe sieges and changing fortunes. King Edward had bestowed it, lastly, on the treacherous Lord Morton, who had now approached it with the certain prospect of securing it for ever in his own possession.

Isabel, the true and only living heiress of Stratheden's wide domains, was at last in his power, beyond the reach of aid to oppose his designs; and though he affected to receive her with all the honorary homage due to the representative of an independent chieftain, he took care early to convince her that her title was only nominal, and his power undisputed.

The tear of filial affection bedewed the cheek of the princess, as, passing into the grand entrance hall, she found herself recognized by a few grey-headed domestics, (evidently prepared to expect her arrival,) that once belonged to her father's household, and still were permitted to retain their stations, as emblems of the ancient consequence of the family.

For awhile nature's impulse suspended the nearer interests of her own present alarming situation, and giving way to the fancied security which the protection of a beloved home is expected to afford, Isabel forgot that she was rather the prisoner than the mistress of the venerable fortress. The trophies and emblazoned arms that floated solemnly in the gale, suspended from the vaulted roof of the hall, declared them the standards of her forefathers; but all around was desolate and decaying, for the castle of late years had seldom been inhabited, except when suddenly seized on by the opposing factions as a place of refuge during a temporary danger, or a retreat from a pursuit, whilst its grandest apartments, now dismantled, had been nearly stripped of their once magnificent furniture.

The old domestics beheld the entrance of Isabel with strong, but silent marks of distress. Their attached hearts, faithful to the race of a beloved chief, indignantly saw torn from his descendants the rights they had bled to defend; but remembering that perhaps the princess was a voluntary captive, they retained within their bosoms their secret thoughts, lest the usurper of her fortunes should discover their unwillingness to acknowledge his ill-gained possession of a princely domain that they well knew was the inheritance of Lord Mackenzie.

CHAPTER XXVI.

" 'Tis vain thy pride rejects my offered love,
  For thou art now my captive, and a word
  Brings forth my willing slaves to end thy life
  And woes together."   LORENZO.

ON the third morning after her arrival at the castle of Stratheden, Isabel, as she was slowly pacing her apartment, was startled by the sudden appearance of Lord Morton. The respect and distance which had marked his deportment on the previous day was no longer visible; his entrance was free, familiar, and even boldly commanding, and Isabel, displeased at the intrusion, stretched out her arm to forbid his presence; but her action was not heeded, and Morton, with an insolent air, unhesitatingly approached her.

"My lord, this infringement is unwarrantable," she exclaimed in angry tones, and retreating from his approach. "Remember, I will be amenable to no usurped authority, or constrained to receive your visits, nor must you presume to think yourself privileged to treat with insolent freedom a female by rank superior to your hopes, and alone the disposer of her own destiny. Unhand me, my lord ; I will not be detained ! Attempt again to repeat this intrusion, and I will instantly quit the castle, and seek elsewhere that protection I am now too well convinced I was deceived when I suffered myself weakly to entertain a belief Lord Morton's honour could afford me."

"Stay, Isabel," he said peremptorily, and still detaining her ; "you quit not this castle without my special permission ; the fortunate chance which restored you to my power shall not be neglected, and he is but a coward who dares not claim his own, when fortune invites him to assert his rights and brave the dangers of the enterprize. I have never deceived you, Isabel, with a hope that I should resign those claims, nor could you doubt a love so fervid as mine would yield to time or the cruel scorn of its object."

" My lord, you are presumptuous !"

" Nay, frown not," he exclaimed ; " you cannot awe me into silence, and must hear me once more thus ardently repeat my declarations of love. Resistance to one so determined can little benefit your obstinacy, and will but enhance the blessing of possession ; and trust me, obdurate girl, you have acted wisely in accepting protection where the power of rejecting it was denied you. I come not now to waste time in idle parley or resentful speech, since, far removed from all that can oppose my firm resolves, my deeds must now declare my intention. You are in my power, and must therefore unhesitatingly yield the necessity your fallen fortunes impose. They may yet be fortunate if shared with me, but, rejected, the alternative will be speedy destruction. Behold !" he added with a look of dark ferocity, displaying a death-warrant signed by Edward ; " your very life is mine, and by this instrument I am empowered to end it or to save you. Gratitude to him who alone can preserve it should teach you to reward the hazard I have, for your sake, dared to encounter. Say, then, that in three days from this you will accompany me to the altar, and I will now depart, nor again intrude but as the happy husband, privileged to guard his treasure from the dangers that encompass her."

" Monster !" exclaimed the indignant Isabel ; " I cannot express the deep abhorrence with which your words have filled me. I am but too well aware of my unprotected condition to need your base repetition of my dependance on your forbearance, but this is the only humiliating acknowledgment your usurped power can force from me ; nor will I upbraid the lawless violence of that injustice and outrage which has thus betrayed me, and triumphed on the ruins of my father's destruction. But know your arts have failed, since they have raised in the bosom of your victim a spirit capable of action, and dreadless of every evil that malice and oppression can inflict."

" Girl !" exclaimed Morton, fiercely, " have you forgotten the peril I just now warned you of ?"

" I reject with scorn and aversion," she replied, "your proffered protection and vaunted mercy in saving me from the axe of the usurping King of England, and utterly disdain your alliance, together with the security it may afford me. I can meet death with resignation, but will not yield to your presumptuous hopes that freedom of the soul which I will rather sell with my heart's blood than purchase its bondage of life if shared with you. Thus resolved, it is needless to repeat, my own consent shall never sanction your detested purposes."

A contempt so rooted, so openly avowed, startled the traitorous Morton, and seemed at once to exclude every hope for ever. Isabel, as she concluded, had retreated into an outward apartment, for, astonished, and thrown completely off his guard, he had suffered her to retire before his confusion had sufficiently evaporated to permit him to interrupt her departure. But now, maddened with rage and disappointment at his defeated projects, he at one instant felt almost fatally resolved to break down every opposing barrier, and either violently enforce his wishes, or resign her to those he knew were in search for her, for it was true that Edward, though lying on his death-bed, had broken faith with Morton, and had actually resolved to break off the projected union of Isabel to a thirst of hatred he had conceived against her,—a hatred that perhaps originated in the midnight visit of Bruce, on which his mind dwelt with deadliest resentment, and delighting to torture and destroy every relative connexion of that oppressed prince, he resolved to seize on the open resistance of Isabel to his forces as a pretence on which to impeach her of high treason to his government, a crime always punished by him with immediate death to the offender.

Morton knew this, and also knew that Edward, once deceived, kept little faith with even those Scottish allies who had been most favourable to his invasion, and had so greatly assisted to render his power over Scotland despotic. He still, however, had carefully treasured the royal warrant which gave him a right to force the princess to become his bride, and also a title to the lordship and demesne of Stratheden. But Morton's politic and wily subtlety easily foresaw that unless Isabel became his wife, his claims to these treacherously obtained riches would be but of short duration, since, should the daring spirit of Bruce and his heroes recover Scotland from the English yoke, Lord Mackenzie must be restored to his despoiled dignities, and his own treachery would in that case draw on himself the vengeance of the Scottish monarch to his utter ruin, if not powerfully upheld by a union which alone could exalt him to that pinnacle of greatness his ambitious views aspired to.

From these causes he had been regardless of the wound inflicted by Lord Mackenzie, and having traced Isabel from the ruins of Glenalvon to the convent of Eustatia, he had pursued her thither, and by bribes sought to betray her from her retreat, that he might compel her to yield to his wishes before the envoys of King Edward should again have traced her flight. The abbess, not daring to avow the deceitful part she was acting, had forged her tale to mislead the princess, who she dared no longer detain, though for a large bribe she almost immediately revealed the departure of our heroine to Morton. Meantime Edward's party arrived at the convent, who, equally distrustful of those he most seemed to favour, was not uninformed of every trivial occurrence that pertained to his Scottish allies, among whom he maintained spies, who constantly watched their movements, and revealed every circumstance to their employer.

It was thus, through Morton's own unguarded means, that the retreat of the princess was made known to Edward's commissioners, who reached the convent on the night of Isabel's retreat, empowered to drag her from its sacred seclusion to the seat of Edward's government, where he held his tyrannous tribunal of justice, and retained judges suborned to his will, who obsequiously pronounced whatever sentence himself should dictate.

Morton knew that King Edward was hastening to his final account, and he trembled lest his prize should escape ere the monarch's death should render invalid the warrant which confirmed the ratification of his nuptials with Isabel, who in such an event would be no longer amenable to its control, and might, without danger, claim undisputed privilege to reject him, or appeal to the protection of the state, in case her father was either no more, or had contrived to make his escape from the kingdom.

It was for these reasons that Morton again threw off that appearance of courtesy so foreign to his fierce and restless mind, and, bent on the accomplishment of his designs, he now sought to terrify the hapless princess into the artful snares he had prepared for her. But with dismay and rage he

found her abhorrence of him was more confirmed than ever, since she knew but too much of the baseness of his character ever to surmount its feelings. The pangs of unrequited love, awakened jealousy, and mortified pride, by turns, raged fiercely, and at length worked him up to a resolution fatal to Isabel, and he now became determined to enforce the power he had acquired, and at all events compel her to yield to his purposes, though at the expense of incurring her lasting hatred.

The spirit of our heroine yielded the moment she was again alone, and as the tumult of her thoughts disordered her fancy with anticipated images of terrible suffering and future misery, every prospect of hope seemed to disappear, and the only alternative to prevent yet greater wretchedness seemed in submitting patiently to a doom from which there appeared to be no possibility of escaping.

At length Catherine once more presented herself; she had been long absent at the desire of her mistress to try if there were no means of interesting the old domestics of Stratheden in her behalf. But, alas! they could only afford ineffectual pity and their prayers for her assistance, being too weak from age, and too few in numbers, to give the assistance she stood so much in need of.

"Every gate of entrance," said the attendant, "have within this half hour been closed, and the outward ramparts, though decayed and falling into ruins, are now manned with sentinels; whilst Lord Morton, secure in his hopes, has appointed the confessor of the castle, to-morrow, to perform the nuptial ceremony of your union with himself."

"That event shall never take place," cried Isabel, starting indignantly as she heard these words. "I will resist the power of my persecutor even at the hazard of my life, and would rather welcome all the terrors of King Edward's vengeance than submit to become the unwilling bride of the man I loath and abhor."

No. 21

Catherine made no reply, for she had no consolation to offer. She, however, saw with resentment her beloved mistress ensnared by the treachery of a dissembling villain, beyond all chance of rescue or redress, and trembled for the almost certain accomplishment of the morrow's threatened events.

The remainder of the day passed in listless solitude, and Isabel peremptorily refusing to comply with Lord Morton's request for her presence at the banquet, refreshments were served in her own apartments. These were large and desolate, but had once been splendidly and richly decorated, though their superb trappings were now defaced or removed, and much of the beauty of their tapestried hangings destroyed by the neglect and damps to which they had been subjected.

At length she retired to her sleeping apartment, but there also reigned a solemn vacuity and stillness that cast an additional gloom over her spirits. She had dismissed Catherine at an early hour to her own chamber, and as she paced her remote apartment a stealing fear began to overpower her senses. She was unable to sleep though the hour was late, and, therefore, to divert the melancholy of her thoughts, took from a shelf a manuscript which in the day time she had cursorily looked into. It had struck her fancy, for it was an old romance, which, though defaced by time, was still legible enough for perusal.

The narrative which thus engaged her attention was long and terrific, and its impression upon her mind too dismal to be then concluded. She therefore threw it aside for the present, and throwing herself once more upon her couch, endeavoured to forget in sleep the afflictions and troubles which just then were so heavily pressing upon her.

CHAPTER XXVII.

" Resistance to my will is now in vain,
  For thou art now a captive in my hands,
  And all the hopes that e'er have fired my heart
  Shall now be realized."
                              DON RAYMOND.

UNEASY as was the mind of Isabel her slumbers were not of long duration, for mournful images of death disturbed their tranquillity, and passed in dreams of horror over her sleeping fancy. The pale melancholy form of her long mourned mother, clothed in robes of flowing white, appeared by her bedside to warn her of those evils which she was unable to teach her how to avoid. Thrice she moaned over her hapless daughter, whilst a melancholy strain of sweetest harmony filled the air, and then gradually faded away, whilst the last dying cadence of the music sunk from the ear to the heart of Isabel, and as it floated upwards in long solemn sounds of harmony, its response awoke the sleeper to a consciousness of her real situation, and to all the fearful evils it threatened.

It was by this time morning, and the sun shining brightly through the casements served to chase away some of the terrors that had been inspired by her dreams. Awhile she mused on the magnificent prospect that lay spread before her window, the broad surface of a lock was seen beneath, whose lofty embankments were skirted by a verdant sweep of tall pines, shelving themselves in gradual ascents up to the summits of the more distant mountains in all the grandeur of alpine scenery.

The rich beauties this romantic country afforded was enlivened with all the variegated tints of the young summer; all nature seemed harmonized, serene, and sportive ; the majestic eagle flapped his dark wings, and as he mounted, basked joyous in the genial warmth of the sun, and awed by his flight the inferior winged subjects of his imperial rule. Isabel sat awhile deeply pondering on her present alarming situation ; her strong mind taught her nature's chartered privileges,—to resist oppression, and assert her own right to be the guardian of her own freedom, since an unhappy mischance had thus early torn her from the parental protection she so much needed.

For a long time she remained in her apartment undisturbed by any intrusion whatever, but on entering the adjoining chamber she found that everything had there been prepared for her morning's repast. It was luxurious, and under present circumstances quite superfluous ; and scarcely had she seated herself ere the hasty opening of the door displayed the form of Lord Morton, who entered, and was followed by three of his retainers, nearly clothed from head to foot in armour.

This sight was enough to assure Isabel that the crisis she so much dreaded had arrived, but disdaining to suffer any weak terrors to lessen her firmness, or betray her from her guarded self-security, she continued seated, as she bent on the intruder a stern commanding look. But Morton, with a bold, undismayed air of insolent familiarity, approached, and attempting to seize her hand, he exclaimed, in a tone of ill-concealed triumph,—

" I am come, Isabel, to tell you that the hour for our nuptials has arrived. This happy morn, the most blissful period of my life, bestows on your fortunate lover the brightest of Scotland's peerless maids. This day makes Isabel my wife, and ratifies for ever the contract of our mutual love."

" Hear me, Lord Morton," she cried, indignantly, " and dare no longer to entertain hopes that I have long since told you were in vain. You already know my unalterable determination, and it is now only necessary for me to say that no power which you possess shall ever force me to become the bride of the man I can only regard as a tyrant and oppressor.

" How !" he exclaimed ; " am I to be resisted by one whose very life is at my disposal ?"

" Take it," she replied, " for never will I yield even though the dagger were pointed at my breast !"

" Vain girl," he muttered, " you little know the man whose will you thus seek to frustrate. The ceremony which shall this hour be performed, and which makes the haughty Isabel the wife of Lord Morton, will dissipate the severity of her dislike, and upon that hope I am well content to rely ; nor fear I but hereafter she will relent from the sternness of her hate when once she has been bound to me by that ceremony which makes her mine for ever."

" We shall see, my lord," she exclaimed ; " and perhaps too late you may be made to repent the base cowardice that has prompted you to this act."

" Nay, may I not hope?"

" All hope is futile," answered Isabel, " since no forced obligations can ever fetter the free spirit to an unacknowledged duty ; and be assured, my lord, my tongue shall never dissemble the abhorrence it has so frequently expressed against one whose actions have declared him to be my enemy."

" You have forgotten, then, it seems, the injunctions of the King of England," said Morton. " I have his permission to make you mine, and that alone is sufficient warrant for the decided course I have taken in this affair."

" Nay," answered Isabel, " I cannot but remember an act of which I have every reason to complain ; nor do I admit that there is any power that can constrain me to submit to a decree which you thus insolently seek to enforce. You will also do well to recollect that I am the undisputed mistress of my own actions, and will not yield to the usurped power of the monarch who has rendered desolate our unhappy country."

Lord Morton could not suppress the fury with which he heard those words, and he bit his lip as the ungovernable passion rankled in his heart. At length, however, subduing his feelings in some degree, he said with an affectation of calmness,—

"You have suffered your pride to deceive you, Isabel, and have thus compelled me to remind you that your boasted freedom of action is lost in the captivity of your person, which now belongs to your conqueror, King Edward. Hitherto you have been treated with the forbearance and respect due to your former station and rank, which, being lost, the conquered must bow to the yoke that has been imposed. And let me remind you that I am now the indisputed master of your fortunes, and can enforce that compliance which I have thus far sought to obtain by gentle means.

"Insolent braggart!" exclaimed Isabel, as her eye shot flashes of resentment upon the audacious object of her wrath; "hast thou no sense of shame to awe thee into silence? Art thou as destitute of truth as honour? Tremble to think of the future consequences of thy bold treasons, and henceforth learn to respect those who have not involved themselves in shame as thou hast done. Presumest thou to hope an outrage so daring will escape unpunished? Hast thou forgotton, traitor, the kingly Bruce is my guardian, and that he will chastise the injustice she sustains from thee? Henceforth avoid my presence, nor provoke me to bring upon thee that avenging wrath thy insolent conduct demands, and as thou fearest the peril of thy sovereign's anger, presume to offend me no more!"

Till this moment Isabel had never so absolutely exerted the prerogative she derived from her royal birth. She now felt the necessity of doing so, but Morton also knew his power, and though he trembled at the consequences of the future,—should Bruce regain his throne, he still persisted in the object he had resolved to attain. Enraged at a scorn so determined, yet coveting the royal maiden who thus repulsed him, he said,—

"Must I again remind you, Lady Isabel, that Scotland no longer acknowledges the banished Bruce for her sovereign, or his adherents for her sons? Edward now rules the fates of her proudest nobles, and prudent will they be who yield submission to his will. What vengeance, I ask you, while thus protected, have I to fear from those you have spoken of? or why should I not triumph whilst all goes on so smoothly in my behalf?"

"Yet still," she cried, "do I warn you of the danger your base acts will bring upon you."

"You are mistaken," he replied with his usual effrontery; "for in me you behold no cowardly or spiritless adventurer. I have weighed well each probable circumstance, nor need I tremble at whatever event befalls, for, should Bruce ever chance to be victorious, your person must become the hostage of your lord till my pardon be secured and ratified, and you must thus share in my danger or mourn my liberty. Ambition and love reign in my soul,—their inspirations have impelled me to this act, nor shall any human opposition divert me from the completion of my bold achievement. What ho! there," he added, beckoning a figure who was advancing from the inner chamber, and who, clothed in priestly vestments, came forward at the summons of his imperious master. "Welcome, holy father," added Morton, "your aid is needed, and I entreat you to proceed with dispatch in the performance of those sacred rites which will for ever render this lady mine."

His frowning eye was now bent sternly upon Isabel, but its anticipated effects were impotent and disregarded, for his dark looks failed to awe her to his purposes. She rose above the severe trials and indignities of her falling fortunes, nor could the threats of her insolent persecutor subdue the firmness and composure of her mind. Passion, or the meakness of tears she alike disdained, and with calmness and dignity she awaited in silence the moment favourable to her purpose.

The aspect of the monk had no reverence in its appearance, but he seemed wrapped up in his own contemplations, which evidently partook not of the present scene, though he could not behold without wonder the flushed and varying looks of Lord Morton for the immediate performance of the ceremony; whilst the settled majesty legibly traced in the countenance of the princess, failed not to impress him with an interest and respect which he had not expected to yield.

At length he opened the sacred volume, and in a solemn tone began the marriage ritual. Still Isabel continued silent, but when desired by the monk to present her hand to Lord Morton, she with peremptory decision refused. The priest paused and regarded with astonishment a proceeding so singular and unprecedented, whilst Morton, impatient and resentful, bade him proceed and finish the ceremony.

Again the monk began, and with more earnestness of manner, repeated his former demand.

"Will thou, lady," he said, "with all thy heart's free will, give to thy espoused lord thy hand, thy love, and thy duty?"

"Never!" she replied firmly.

"Nay, reflect I implore you," exclaimed the priest; "for thine obedience in this instance can alone save thee from those dangers which I tremble to think of."

"You have heard me, holy father," answered Isabel, undauntedly. "From my heart,—yea, from my very soul I swear to reject and renounce every tie between us; nor is there a power on earth, save the authority of a parent, that shall compel me to acknowledge Lord Morton as my husband."

"Wherefore was I summoned hither?" demanded the priest in a tone of impatience.

"To complete the rites you have commenced," answered Morton, with an angry frown.

"And how can I do so?" asked the monk; "for, since the consent of Lady Isabel is wanting to ratify this holy contract, I have no power to proceed further."

"Old man," exclaimed Lord Morton, with ill-dissembled rage, "hesitate not in your task, but conclude the ceremony without the delay of another instant. Behold! I possess a warrant whose sovereign commission is all-powerful, nor will any priest of Scotland's church refuse to obey its absolute injunction. Read there the authority which gives you the power to make me the husband of Lady Isabel."

The trembling monk took the warrant from the hand of Lord Morton. Its signature was that of King Edward, and gave a legal, undisputed title to Morton, to seize on the person of Lady Isabel Mackenzie, and enforce her, as a ward of the conqueror, to accept the hand of him upon whom the warrant had been bestowed.

The priest read the royal mandate, and perceived that its decrees were too absolute to be disputed, and he no longer hesitated for the third time to begin the ceremony. All hope now seemed to vanish, and Isabel beheld herself with horror on the point of becoming the bride of her more than ever detested persecutor. Collecting, however, all the fortitude that remained, she commandingly bade the monk to pause ere he rendered himself a party to so scandalous a proceeding.

"Hold, father!" she cried, wildly, "lest, by aiding the tyranny of Lord Morton, you become the partner of his crimes, and bring upon yourself the punishment that ere long awaits him. Upon my knee I solemnly adjure you to protect me from this hated marriage, which here, in your presence, I avow is forced and illegal, nor will I in any form whatever submit or consent, or ratify. And you, Lord Morton," she continued, addressing herself to the traitor; "at your peril I command you to desist. I have never deceived you with a hope of ever becoming your wife, and, be assured, no mockery like this shall ever render lawful the union you seek to enforce."

"It is in vain that you appeal to me, Lady Isabel," answered Morton, coldly. "I have resolved to make you mine, and no prayers or entreaties shall ever turn me from my purpose. Proceed, I command you, holy father," he added to the monk, "or expect to meet that punishment which my anger will be certain to inflict."

—"Let me entreat you, my lord, to grant a few days' respite," said the priest. "In that time I shall be able to reflect upon the demand you have made, and perhaps Lady Isabel will yield to your desire, if a brief interval is allowed her to consider the danger of a refusal."

"I will grant no time," answered Lord Morton, resolutely, "and you have yet to learn that, to oppose the decrees of King Edward, is death to the offender, nor will even the sanctity of your office secure you from the vengeance of an offended monarch. It is sufficient for you to know that his warrant authorizes your willing compliance, and the future perils, if any there are, will fall on me. Therefore, once more, I command you to proceed with the ceremony."

These words were uttered with a commanding tone and aspect that awed the priest into submission; and, turning towards the now trembling Isabel, he said, with more decision than he had hitherto displayed,—

"This warrant, lady, is peremptory, and confirms the demands that have been made upon us by Lord Morton. It were vain to resist its mandate, since you are now become a ward of Edward, King of England, and your destined husband is hereby fully entitled to claim your hand in marriage whenever he may think proper to do so."

As he concluded, the monk held forth the warrant towards Isabel, and, with his finger, pointed out those passages that rendered it imperative for him to proceed.

Suddenly a thought to save herself from a doom almost more terrible than death itself rushed through the brain of the unhappy Isabel;—she, with frenzied haste, snatched the paper from the hand of the monk, and in an instant scattered it in a thousand torn fragments on the floor; then, seeming to be relieved from the peril that had been so much dreaded, she exclaimed, joyfully,—

"Behold how readily I have freed myself from this boasted power of the king! The death to which I am condemned by his tyranny, will be less fearful to my soul than the present alternative of lasting misery. I can behold with pleasure and resignation the tortures his malice may inflict, and my last consolation will be in knowing that I have at last escaped the snares that were laid for me by the artifices of a villain."

The royal mandate law strewed upon the ground, to which they had been thrown by the indignant Isabel, and she stood proudly gazing upon the fragments with a joyful satisfaction that she had not experienced during many a month before. For a time at least she felt that the power of her oppressor was weakened, if not altogether destroyed; and, as some interval must elapse ere Lord Morton could communicate with the king, there was a chance that Bruce might succeed in asserting his right, and thus she would be released from the degradation and captivity to which she was at present obliged to submit.

The fury and rage manifested by Lord Morton were in vain, for so sudden had been the action of Isabel, that he perceived not the threatened destruction of all his cherished hopes until it was too late to avert the mischief. For a moment or two he stood gazing upon our heroine with a look of vengeance, and then, unable to control his passion, he was about once more to order the priest to complete the ceremony, when one of his men at arms rushed affrighted into the chamber, proclaiming the sudden arrival of King Edward's commissioners, who had already passed the outer court, and were impatiently awaiting the delivery of the Princess Isabel, who had been demanded as a prisoner by the person that had been appointed to command the party. The rage of Lord Morton was unbounded when he heard this death-blow to his hopes; and, drawing his poniard, he would have slain the bearer of these tidings, had not the man foreseen his danger, and avoided the blow that was struck at him.

"Villain!" exclaimed the wrathful baron, "I have been betrayed, and thy death alone can appease the indignation thy cowardice has excited."

"Indeed, my lord," cried the terrified retainer, "we all of us did our best to prevent this intrusion of the commissioner's into your castle."

"Did I not issue commands," asked Morton, "that no one should be permitted to pass in or out without my orders?"

"You did," replied the man; "but we dared not disobey the summons of the king's commissioners. I therefore entreat you to spare my life, since to have resisted the will of our sovereign would have been to incur his wrath, and ensure a certain and dreadful death."

"Begone from my sight," exclaimed the incensed lord, "lest in my indignation I trample thy worthless carcase in the dust. Begone, I say, and never let me see thee again till thou hast repaired the mischief thou hast this day done me."

The man shrunk dismayed from the chamber, when Isabel, with an air imposing and majestic, addressing Lord Morton, said, resolutely,—

"I now demand to be conducted into the presence of the king's commissioners. You have no longer even the shadow of a pretence to detain me here; and I myself demand to be instantly surrendered to those who have come to seek me."

Internally cursing the sudden and unlooked-for defeat of all his daring projects, Morton regarded her with a look of surprise, and gloomily exclaimed,—

"Can it be possible the Lady Isabel means to resign herself voluntarily to the impending ruin King Edward's ruthless hate engenders, and all the dreadful consequences of his terrible power to inflict certain misery—perhaps death?"

"Aye, to any fate, however great its danger, and to any power will I cheerfully resign myself rather than remain where I am," answered Isabel, fearlessly. "And now, old man," she continued, addressing herself to the monk, "I commit myself to your guidance, and my desire is that you instantly conduct me to the presence of these English commissioners."

Thus saying, she gave her hand to the priest, and, without deigning any further notice of Lord Morton, quitted the apartment. The resolution she had betrayed seemed utterly to confound the guilty baron, who remained for some time motionless with surprise, and unable to determine how to act under the unexpected situation in which he had been involved. He, however, resolved not to be defeated, and upon becoming more composed, began to devise fresh schemes to attain the object of his wishes.

CHAPTER XXVIII.

"When will my sorrows cease?
Alas! each day brings fresh ones to my heart,
Till dark despair has seized upon my soul,
And I am crushed."
                                        THE CAPTIVE.

WITH an undaunted step Isabel advanced towards the leader of the English party, and with a firm air surrendered herself as a captive in his hands.

The person to whom she had thus committed herself had in his aspect an air of manly openness and humanity, and with a courtesy that our heroine had not prepared herself to expect, he compassionately and respectfully declared that he would wait her leisure before they set forward on their journey to the capital, assuring her of such indulgencies on the way as his limited power could venture to extend towards her.

It was not without considerable pain that Isabel learnt she was to be sent a prisoner to England; her heart sighed responsively to the afflicting prophecy of its fears, and with agony almost insupportable she believed that her departure would be the commencement of an eternal separation from her father. The spirit which oppression had so lately roused into action and resistance was now evaporated into grief, and Isabel, but a brief time previously so steadfast and unyielding, was now subdued to the weakness of anguish and despair.

It was, however, impossible to pause on these mournful reflections, for suddenly a scene of tumult and confusion resounded through the castle. Lord Morton, determined not willingly to yield his prize, had by threats, commands, and promised rewards, collected his troops together, and was thus enabled to forbid the departure of the captive princess. The leader of Edward's forces, with calm but resolute speech, reminded the treacherous Morton of his homage to the king of England, and bade him desist, lest he should provoke the heavy consequences of his disobedience. But the imperious baron was not to be subdued by mild terms, and giving free vent to his unbounded rage, he exclaimed,—

"I scorn alike the power of Edward and the thunder of his threatened wrath. Your haughty sovereign, once faithless to his royal promise, made by solemn contract, to bestow on me the hand of the Princess Isabel, can no longer demand my homage or obedience. Nor must even the sway of majesty itself infringe on the just rights and privileges of a free-born subject. From henceforth, therefore, I renounce him and his government over Scotland, and will act unquestioned for myself alone, without any control from kingly authority. The treachery your English sovereign has stooped to practise shall be repaid with like sincerity. Isabel is my affianced wife, nor will I suffer her to quit this castle till a superior force drags her from the shelter it at present affords."

As he uttered these words, Morton drew his sword and aimed a tremendous blow at the head of the leader. The signal for action thus boldly given was sufficient for both parties, and the combat instantly commenced with vigour, so that the clangour of arms raged dreadfully through the ancient halls of Stratheden.

Isabel was led from the scene of affray and bloodshed by some of the terrified domestics. Shocked to have been the cause, though innocently, of the scene that was then taking place, her soul died within her, and she retired to weep over the hapless destiny, and felt assured that, let who might be victors, she must alike be doomed to misery and despair.

The adherents of Lord Morton fought well, but not with willingness; their numbers were somewhat greater than the English, but the dread of the consequences of such open rebellion to the power of Edward's authority damped their ardour, and rendered their overthrow by no means difficult. Lord Morton himself fell to the ground disarmed and slightly wounded, for passion had overpowered the usual prudence of his conduct, and rendered him an easy conquest to the cool, deliberate attacks of the captain. His fall was the end of the affray, for his people dropped their arms and hastened to hide themselves from an enemy they had so much reason to dread. The English, on the other hand, paused to rest themselves, and after the lapse of an hour prepared to depart.

It unfortunately happened that Catherine had been seized with a sudden illness, too severe to admit of her being removed from the castle, and thus deprived of her last remaining friend, the prospects of our heroine seemed to blacken with increase of misery. She, however, uttered no complaint, but having crossed the drawbridge with a heavy heart, was quickly seated upon a horse, that was there waiting for her service. The party then goaded and urged their horses forward, and soon the narrow winding of a close defile excluded all view of the ancient fortress of Stratheden.

Scarcely had the silent troop and their sorrowing captive wound through these passes, and gained the main road which led towards the capital, when they were met by a flying courier, who, breathless, and with a countenance filled with alarm, could not at first declare the cause of his alarming speed. At length Isabel, with emotions too various to be described, learnt that the foe most powerful and dangerous to her future peace was for ever rendered harmless. In fact, the news conveyed by the messenger was that King Edward, the conqueror of Scotland, had just expired, and that, consequently, she was released from the oppressive yoke of her fate, and must now be set free from the bondage in which she had been held.

No. 22

In silent dismay the troop received these melancholy tidings, whilst Isabel addressed herself to the leader, claimed her immediate freedom, and entreated to be conveyed to the castle of her uncle, the Earl of Glenroy. This request seemed to startle the person to whom she had spoken, and he remained musing for some little time; but, at length, resolving upon what course it would be proper to pursue, he said:—

"I cannot, lady, resist the force of your entreaties, for I am myself a father, and know what it is to fear for the welfare of a beloved daughter, and to feel the thrill of nature at the thought of again folding her in my arms. I will, therefore, myself, be your conductor to Glenroy, if assured that you will not quit that residence, or conceal yourself from me should I return to claim you as my prisoner."

"Alas!" cried Isabel, "am I still to consider myself as a captive, when the death of Edward is alone sufficient to give me the liberty I have unjustly been deprived of?"

"I am still responsible for your safety," answered the leader; "and though the death of my royal master has somewhat changed your destiny, it has, perhaps, only for awhile suspended its fulfilment, and, should you be demanded of me by Edward's successor, my own life would pay the penalty of your escape.

Moved by these words, Isabel pledged herself to abide whatever doom might be issued against her by her foes, nor did she hesitate to give her solemn promise to appear when called upon to do so. This done, she soon had the satisfaction of seeing the English soldiers,—except the captain and two of his men, proceed on their way towards the capital, and shortly afterwards, with her guard, she took the road that led to Glenroy.

Her thoughts now recurred to the late scene of peril, and the near completion of that misery which her crime with Lord Morton must have produced. Doubly did she feel relieved from a fate so full of wretchedness, remembering, that since she had now no longer a foe so powerful to contend against as the haughty Edward, she was thus secured from the tyranny of princely hatred, and she resolved that, should Glenroy not afford her that protection her present unfortunate situation demanded, she would again return to the venerable cloisters of St. Columba, and there wait the termination of her destiny as well as that of her oppressed country, with whose welfare and freedom that of her own and her father's were too closely connected.

In that convent she felt assured she should find a shelter and a tranquil retreat from the weight of those additional cares, which originated in her near relationship to the brave but wronged monarch of Scotland; against whom, and all his connections, the most cruel rigour of Edward's hate was ever levelled, but to whose blood stained usurpation and tyrannous power her spirit rose indignant and disdained to bend.

It was not till evening that Isabel and her escort gained, through the gloom of twilight a faint view of the lofty battlements of Glenroy, embosomed in mountain woods, whose thick, clustering recesses bespoke retirement and almost total seclusion from the world, and secured the haunt of melancholy and the seat of silent contemplation.

Darkness had completely set in, when, wearied and exhausted with fatigue, she at length reached the ivy crowned seat of her venerable relative, and was conducted up the steep windings that led to the broad base of a promontory on which the castle reared its colossal bulwarks. As she ascended this rugged pathway, and reached the principal gate of entrance, she was surprised to observe several rough looking men at arms pacing the court-yard, and as the torches they held, displayed their figures clothed in iron mail, she could not suppress the sudden terror their uncouth forms and fierce aspect created, for she had always heard that the castle of Glen-roy was seldom or never in a state of warfare, since its chief, unable through age, to take an active lead, had been suffered to remain undisturbed in his retreat.

She felt almost unwilling to advance further or quit the security which her escort afforded,—for the English officer was now retiring, having per-formed his duty, and placed her, as he doubted not, under the guardian-ship of her friends. Isabel would have fain persuaded the captain to rest one night at the castle, but this he was compelled to decline, and having again promised not to leave Glenroy without informing him whether she went, she bade adieu to her escort, and reluctlantly entered the abode she had sought with so much eagerness.

The heavy portal soon closed the English soldiers from her sight, and, conducted by the principal warder, Isabel ascended the steps which led to the grand hall of entrance, and was received, not by the venerable earl, himself, but by the chief seneschal and two female domestics. Surprised at this, she requested to be taken to the presence of their lord; but they replied not to this, and there was an expression of terror in their counten-ances, from which our heroine anticipated a foreknowledge of unwelcome intelligence, which, for some reason or other, they dared not tell her of. The seneschal then led the way through numerous apartments, and Isabel at length entering an open parlour, threw herself in silence on a seat, un-able to hide the emotions that her forlorn condition gave rise to. For some little time she gave way to the melancholy thoughts that crowded through her mind, and then suddenly rousing herself, she enquired whether she could not see the earl. This question was not immediately answered, but Marianne, one of the female attendants, after some hesitation, said :—

"The Earl of Glenroy has been informed of your ladyship's arrival, but for the present declines seeing you. Lord Robert, our good chief's nephew, *as he calls himself*, has also been told that you have reached the castle, but, he says, his uncle is too ill and too closely confined to his chamber, to be seen by strangers.

The heart of Isabel sunk as she heard this, and, at a loss to conceive what the mystery could mean, she exclaimed :—

"Is it possible, the Earl of Glenroy can, by this coldness, refuse me the shelter and protection I so much need? My father, I am sure, was not aware of such a change, or he would not have desired me to risk such a re-ception as I have received."

"Ah! my lady," exclaimed Marianne, "you must not judge too much from appearances, for the earl, I am sure, would be rejoiced to see you, and it's only the fault of,—that is, we fear——"

"Silence, daughter!" interrupted the seneschal, with a frown that in-stantly cut short her speech; and then addressing himself to Isabel, he continued :—"The shortness of the notice, my lady, has, I fear, but ill enabled us to make preparation for your arrival. My Lord Robert, how-ever, has instructed us in the performance of our duty, and he will, himself, take an early opportunity to apologize for any inconvenience you may have been put to. If it is your ladyship's command, I will go and say it is your wish to see him."

"Not to night," replied our heroine, for she felt her bosom chilled with a reception so unwelcome, and as Lord Robert was unknown to her, and indeed, a connection she had never before heard of, she was not at all inclined to accept from him a reception to her uncle's castle.

"If I am not permitted to see the Earl of Glenroy," she added, "I will now retire to my apartment for the night; I am fatigued and weary with the length of my journey, and must, therefore, decline the visit of Lord

Robert. You can inform the Earl of my arrival, and my earnest desire to be admitted to his presence with as little delay as possible."

The seneschal bowed submissively, and Marianne, conducting the princess through the halls towards the grand staircase, ascended to the corridor above, and passed onward till she entered a small but elegant room, beyond which was the sleeping chamber assigned to the use of Isabel. Having entered this, Marianne closed the door, and gazing upon the female she had conducted thither, seemed as if anxious to speak upon a subject that was forbidden. The princess was pleased with the countenance of her young attendant, from whom she hoped to learn the meaning of that mystery which she had observed since her arrival, and to ascertain the cause of the earl's confinement. These demands Marianne seemed ready enough to comply with, and having first assured herself that no other persons were present, she said:—

"There have of late arrived so many strangers at the castle, whom nobody knows, or from whence, or for what purpose they came, that it is quite impossible to remember half of them, and truly this great wilderness of a place is as intricate, and has as many turnings and windings and underground chambers, that one may wander in it for days and not be able to meet with the person one is in search of. And then my lord has been lately confined, shut up, I may say, in his own chamber, where none of the domestics and old attached servants of the household are ever permitted to see him, or even to approach the gallery leading to the room where he is."

"This is, indeed, strange!" cried Isabel, with surprise, "and I fear some villany is at work which all our efforts may not be able to prevent."

"I don't know what to make of it," resumed the attendant; "for all on a sudden the castle has been filled with fierce looking men and strange warriors, who are admitted, the new lord says, to guard it in case of an invasion. But pardon me, my lady, for I fear I am too presuming thus to address you, and my father would chide me, were he to know I have said anything about the goings on here."

Isabel saw that her attendant was a simple, honest child of nature, and she was far from wishing to maintain the distance of her own superior rank unless when urged to do so by the insolence of unprovoked offence. She, therefore, requested Marianne to remain in her apartment, for feeling bitterly the forlornness of her situation, she was unwilling to remain alone in a strange place, whilst necessity compelled her to take advantage of the only present means to penetrate the mystery in which she found herself involved. With such considerations as those she felt she resolved to make a friend and confidant of Marianne, and finding that she was disposed to reveal some of the secrets of the castle, enquired who was this new lord of whom she had spoken in such doubtful terms.

"Ah! my lady," answered the girl, "nobody can tell who he is, but not long since he arrived here quite a stranger, and then all of a sudden he proved himself to be my lord's nephew, and has ever since taken up his abode in the castle, and has ordered and domineered over the household with as much authority as if he were indeed our lord. But," added Marianne, in a lower and more cautious tone, "since that day the Earl of Glenroy has drooped, and never held up his head nor smiled as he used to do, but seemed always sad and dejected, as if he pined inwardly over some heavy grief that he feared to reveal. And, for that matter, he had no one to tell it to, for the new lord took care to remove from his presence his most faithful attendants, and no one has been suffered to approach the door of his chamber, where Lord Robert has placed spies to watch that nobody gains admittance to him.

" Spies placed on the actions of the Earl of Glenroy ;" cried Isabel, in a tone of indignant surprise.

" It is, indeed, true, my lady," answered Marianne, " and Lord Robert not unfrequently takes that task upon himself. All the old domestics, as I said before, have been debarred from attending him, and their places are filled up by strange, fierce looking people ; nor can any one gain admittance without leave of him who reckons himself the future Earl of Glenroy."

Isabel was more and more amazed, for she knew that her father was the nearest heir to the title, and whoever might be this unknown claimant, his title was unfounded and usurped, though it appeared he was resolute to assume and contest its legality.

The account given by Marianne went no further than to state that Lord Robert was the nephew of the earl, but his title had never been acknowledged by the latter, who seemed to regard him with horror and alarm. Isabel knew that her grandmother, the Countess of Stratheden was the eldest sister of the present Earl of Glenroy. She also remembered to have heard that the earl had another sister who followed her husband to the Holy Land, and had died of grief, lamenting over his corse, which it was reported had been brought from the field of battle where he was slain. Isabel, however, never remembered to have heard that any offspring had been left ; and, indeed, had there been any they could have no claim to the estates of Glenroy whilst the elder branches survived. It was with wonder and alarm that she listened to the dark surmises contained in the narration of Marianne, and she felt an interest in the fate of the earl, totally divested of every selfish view, that powerfully incited her to the attempt of discovering his real condition, and the dark mystery of the actions of the unknown Lord Robert.

Somewhat mortified at first with the coolness of her reception, Isabel had resolved to quit the castle on the following morning, and by apprizing the English captain of her future residence, still adhere to the promise she had made him. But now a nearer interest had been awakened in her bosom, for more than half convinced, by the hints and words of Marianne, that the aged Earl of Glenroy was, in reality, a stranger to her arrival, she determined not hastily to quit the place till assured that her presence was not wished for; a doubt she could not very well entertain, as her father, she well knew, had sent messages to Glenroy to apprize the earl of her intended visit, and had received in reply, an invitation, even more pressing than had been anticipated. In fact, the earl had expressed himself with all the warmth of a fond father, truly gratified at having so important a trust confided to him.

Anxiously did our heroine reflect upon this affair, and having at length formed a resolution in her own mind, she exclaimed, in a tone of decision : " The mystery which clouds this business shall now be dissolved ; it is a duty that I should see the earl, and receive from himself that welcome which I should have had ere this, had he not been restrained by one who has assumed an authority over him that he had no right to exercise. I hold not myself responsible to Lord Robert, and, therefore, Marianne shall demand to see the real lord of this castle without delay. Hasten then to those that are out to watch over him, and inform them of my intentions, for I cannot suppose they will presume to refuse admittance to one who is the daughter and representative of their master's heir, and the future inheritor of these towers. Whatever may be their authority, mine is paramount, and in making this demand I will take all blame and peril upon myself."

The girl looked as she really was, terrified, and falling upon her knees before the princess, she with tears in her eyes exclaimed :—

" I shall be murdered ! my father will kill me ! He will discover that have told you what he with threats and imprecations forbade me ever to speak about!"

Pitying the violent distress she saw depictured in the girl, Isabel endeavoured to re-assure her, though she was not now to be turned from her determined purposes, and Marianne, finding her immoveable, at length said with more composure :—

"Since your ladyship is resolved, if for my sake, and to save me from my father's and Lord Robert's fury, you will wait till midnight, when all in the castle are at rest, I think I can venture to conduct you to the Earl's apartment, and should he recollect your ladyship, perhaps all in the castle may be well again, and then I shall have no need to fear my father's anger, nor the frightful looks of that gloomy Lord Robert. But indeed, my lady, I have done wrong in disobeying his command, as I dare say you will think; but never again will I incur such a reproach from my conscience, though one can't help opening one's lips when one sees such bad goings on, and I could tell of such things, if I durst, as would frighten every soul out of the castle. But if some folks can live in it, 'tisn't for others that are innocent to be afraid, though I'm sure I would not have such a load on my mind for all the riches Scotland can bestow."

"You have forgotten," said Isabel, smiling, "the subject upon which you began to speak."

"Why, so I have indeed, my lady," she replied. "I was going to tell you there is a little private door which leads from an unfrequented passage to the ante-chamber of the earl, through which we, that is your ladyship may gain an entrance to the room occupied by the earl, though I fear to very little purpose if it be true that he is speechless, which they report he is, and in that case all this risk will be fruitless."

Compassionating the girls terror, and too considerate to involve her in the consequences she seemed to dread, Isabel assented to her last proposal, and Marianne promising to return as soon as the clock struck twelve, quitted the apartment to make inquiries respecting Lord Mackinzie; for Isabel had previously charged her attendant to execute this commission, not doubting but that her father had either been at Glenroy since last they parted, or was perhaps on his road towards it, in which case Marianne was the only being she had met with since her arrival, who seemed willing and happy to oblige her, and who would, she doubted not, the sooner convey Lord Mackenzie to her presence on his arrival at the Castle of Glenroy.

For some time after Marianne had quitted her apartment, the Lady Isabel sat reclined on her chair in the deep abstraction that her reflections had given rise to. Her thoughts at this period were varied and tumultuous; for herself she rejoiced, yet trembled, and felt alternately tranquil, yet inwardly uncertain of its durability, in being relieved from the weight of a bondage so oppressive as of late she had endured.

She felt also somewhat reconciled to her present situation, since from Marianne's account it now appeared the strange and discourteous style of her reception at the castle was the result of some as yet undiscovered cause, but in which the earl was evidently not implicated; and whenever might be this new-sprung claimant for the future honours of Glenroy, for whom she felt sensations anything but favourable, and something very like alarm, perhaps excited by the exaggerated yet confused accounts she had just received.

In her own mind she resolved not to see Lord Robert, whose conduct was quite sufficient to fill her with alarm, and to postpone, if possible, any interview with him till the arrival of her father might render such a step safe. The Earl of Glenroy, however, she determined to seek that very night, but the step she was then taking convinced her more than ever how difficult was the conduct she must practice in the absence of her parent, who, had he accompanied her to Glenroy, would not only made its residence to her peaceful, but have insured from its venerable chieftain that honorary, and, no doubt, affectionate welcome that she had felt herself so greatly disconcerted by the want of.

From these and other even more perplexing meditations, she was soon afterwards aroused by the appearance of Marianne, followed by a stranger habited in a suit of armour. The heart of Isabel bounded with joy, and darting forward, she threw herself, not as she anticipated, into the arms of her father, but into those of Angus Glenalvon. The flame of Marianne's lamp revealed the features of the youthful hero, and immediately afterwards the attendant quitting the chamber, left the lovers to a free indulgence of their joy at so unexpected a meeting.

Confused and blushing at the error she had been betrayed into, Isabel withdrew herself hastily from the fervent embrace of the wonder-stricken Angus. He, however, quickly apologized for the abruptness with which he had entered the room, and having succeeded in composing the agitation of the Lady Isabel, he informed her that having learnt from Marianne how she was to behold her father, he had hurried to her presence to inquire whether he could be of any service in seeking out the present abode of the persecuted and unfortunate Lord Mackenzie.

CHAPTER XXIX.

" Let not my love be withered in its prime,
  But grant the fervent prayer that I have offered up,
  And a whole life of ardent gratitude
  Shall recompense thine act."

THE KNIGHT'S REVENGE.

THOUGH disappointed in the person she had expected to behold, Isabel would not repress the rapturous joy she felt at, a meeting so little looked for, and it was without anger that she regarded Angus sinking at her feet, as in language ardent, glowing, and respectful he revealed the secret of his heart, and with the eloquent language of truth and nature, pleaded all his hopes, while he besought her pardon for having thus abruptly presented himself before her.

Too much astonished, and perhaps too much gratified in again beholding the object of her constant memory and secret regard, Isabel remained speechless, and from the effect of sudden surprise, or, it may be, from real unwilling to chide a visit which, though unexpected, afforded a pleasing enjoyment to her long-surpressed feelings, replied not. The expressive sorrow of his fine, noble countenance, spoke in language too congenial to her heart to be rejected, and not a little aided the interest his appearance so strongly revived.

His helmet concealed not his features, for its vizor was unclasped, whilst his glossy hair waving on his forehead, softened the sternness of his martial mien, and his eyes, sombre, large, and penetrating, beamed with an expression that showed the depth of his ever-enduring passion.

He was still uninformed of the occurrences that related to the Lady Isabel. He remembered to have heard Lord Mackenzie declare his intention of placing her under the protection of the Earl of Glenroy, whither the inspirations of love had thus impelled him, and chance and good fortune favoured his designs.

Isabel could not give expression to her words, but as she sat wrapped in amazed silence and listening attention, Angus felt encouraged to proceed; and in all the suppressed agony of his feelings, he narrated the dreadful occurrence of Edwin's loss, and the principal events which had succeeded. Isabel's tears flowed for the fate of her lost cousin, but at length recovering herself, she exclaimed :—

"Oh, my Lord Angus, could ineffectual wishes restore your ill-fated brother, need I say how fervent mine are, or how deeply I feel and mourn with you over his hapless destiny. But, alas! I have woes equally great with your own, and tremble with apprehension as I think of the dangers to which my persecuted father is exposed. Think me not selfish for thus obtruding my sorrows upon you, but I had fondly indulged a hope that he might have been the companion of your journey hither, and it only remains for you to say how far my expectations may be realized."

Grieved at having given rise to a hope that had been so fondly indulged, Angus endeavoured to reconcile her to the possibility that Lord Mackenzie, though not the companion of his journey, might be on the road to Glenroy, and in that case his arrival might be expected in a day or two. He, however, occasioned the most agonizing alarm when he informed her that he had never seen her father since they last parted at the ruined castle of Glenalalvon. Angus, however, changed the conversation, and taking advantage of their present solitude, he ventured to divulge those hopes and fears which had filled his heart from the first moment of their meeting together.

"Disconsolate for the loss of my brother," he said, "yet devoted to love the only being whom fate had hitherto thrown in my way, I felt my passion to be at the same time the ecstacy of bliss and torture; and though my presumption may bring its own punishment, still must my soul for ever dwell upon its defeated hope, though fatally assured the Princess Isabel is a being beyond my level, and to whom it may be deemed presumption to aspire; since, though of noble birth myself, it must ever be far distant from the standard of her rank, and the still more exalted claims of her merit, which render her fit only for the contention of princes. To know this was sufficient to have taught me how unavailing was my love; how vain the ambition of its hopes, and believing that it became a duty to resist the impulse of my soul, I dared to think I could eradicate the fatal impression those charms had made upon my heart. Eager to fulfil this intention, I sought in the field of battle that death which would have added honour to my name, and relieved me from a life of which I had begun to grow weary. Yet have I escaped all perils, and now, trembling at my own destiny, I await your answer. Dare I, Lady Isabel, suppose you do not scorn and disdain the presumptuous Angus, or hope you have ever vouchsafed to remember the hour when first I saw and loved her?"

He paused through excessive emotion, and upon recovering himself added,—

"Alas! too well do I read in those averted looks the fatal hopelessness of my heart's fondest wishes. Let me then remove myself from the chance of ever again offending; and thus terminate those anxieties which at present oppress me. Yes, Lady Isabel, I will this instant be gone, for your silence, more eloquent than words, condemns me to despair, and forbids me to repeat the subject I have thus ventured to mention. Farewell, then, dearest Isabel, and let my last wish be, that you will not despise though you cannot love me. My heart may have erred involuntarily, but it shall cease to beat ere it ceases to respect and reverence the object its devoted homage, and in the eternal silence to which I banish its despairing but constant feelings, shall it expiate the ambitious presumption of such an avowal as I have made.

As he concluded, Angus turned aside to conceal the emotion he could not suppress, and Isabel, confused at the declaration he had made, sat for some time speechless and agitated. They were both the children of nature, and the first impressions of minds so sensitive as theirs, were stamped with an energy no after occurrence could ever erase. They had mutually resigned themselves to the gratification of loving each other, almost without knowing from whence sprung an impulse too pleasing to be resisted, and of which they were too uninformed to judge correctly.

Their first meeting, under circumstances so singular and interesting, was an event that kept alive the memory of their fancy, and assisted to mature its growing and natural propensity; nor had Isabel been less constant in her remembrance of her cousin Angus, than he had been devoted to the fascinating indulgence of cherishing his fondest hopes. The princess was, indeed, possessed of so many rare excellencies, that not only Angus and Lord Morton had felt the power of her charms. Many were the lovers who sighed for her smiles, whilst the generous nature of her mind impelled her to feel grateful for their good intentions, though she could not yield her heart to any but the one object of her constant thoughts. Angus was, indeed, the lover of her choice; but there were many difficulties in their way at present, and it had been her endeavour to conceal every symptom of partiality, till the moment arrived when she could accept the offer of his love, and bestow upon him those vast estates of which she had been deprived through the violence of the times, and the convulsion which at that period shook Scotland from one end to the other. At length, however, with the most perfect confidence in the honour and generosity of her lover, she, in timid accents, said,—

" You have spoken, Angus, as if there was a difference in our stations; but are you not the nephew of my beloved father, and my own adopted friend and brother?   With charms like these, should I not be doubly ungrateful to despise one who has only been unfortunate from the cruelty and oppression of a secret foe?   And oh, Angus! can my heart, think you, ever cease to remember with esteem and gratitude him whose arm snatched me from the destruction meditated by a villain?"

Angus, as a being rescued from some apprehended danger, was on a sudden recalled to light, life, and hope; and, once more prostrating himself at her feet, he repeated to her the declaration of his love, and sought to draw from her a more explicit acknowledgment of her own feelings towards him than she had hitherto given.   But the diffidence of Isabel's disposition, though it generously disdained every mean artifice to conceal a passion she could not restrain, resisted the ardent eloquence of his words, and, in trembling accents, she said,—

"At present, Angus, it is necessary that we suppress the emotions with which we are both inspired.   As a brother you shall possess my affections, and willingly will I share the troubles in which you are involved by these unhappy times.   More I cannot at present grant, nor must you, Angus, attempt to urge me further, lest I deem you unlike the picture my fancy has painted.   Hereafter, should peace return to our land, a happier issue may appease the long buried wrongs you have sustained from infancy, and in that case a father's blessing may sanction the love you have but just now declared.   Till then I must entreat you to forbear urging me upon a subject so painful, and rest satisfied with the assurance that you possess a sister's fondest regards, and that upon her constancy and lasting fidelity you may repose the most boundless confidence."

"I will cheerfully yield myself to your commands, dearest Isabel," he replied; "yet deign to assure me that you will retain for me alone that place in your affections which will admit no nearer interest, no rival contest in another's behalf.   Say that you bid me hope, should life be spared me, that at some happier time I may aspire to the dear privilege of openly declaring my ardent passion."

Yielding to his persuasive eloquence, and somewhat thrown off her guard, Isabel, with some emotion, gave him a solemn assurance that, though she now forbade him to encourage the passion with which he was inspired, she would never receive the addresses of any other person unless she had reason to believe that he had transferred his affections to another.

"I have been surprised into making this confession," she added; "but do not lessen me in my own estimation, Angus, by seeking to prolong an interview which, under circumstances, it is to be regretted, has taken place between us.   Remember, too, that I am but just arrived among strangers, whose evil conjectures and remarks might give rise to much unpleasantry."

"Nay, do not leave me yet," cried Angus, earnestly.   "Stay but a little longer, and I will promise never to return to this subject till I have your own permission."

"It may not be," she replied, "for I have already acted with imprudence, and it is time that I break the spell with which you have bound me." Then, giving her hand to him, she added :—"Let this be a solemn pledge between us, Angus, and rest satisfied that my heart will ever be unchanged whilst you remain constant to the avowal you have just made.   Leave me, I entreat, and forget not, dear cousin, that my happiness is bound up in your future safety."

Unwilling to depart, Angus would fain have prolonged an interview that afforded him so much pleasing hope.   Compelled, however, to yield obedience to her request, he tried to bid her a reluctant adieu, yet still lingered as unwilling to tear himself from an object so beloved.   Isabel observed his reluctance to depart, and, assuming an air of resolution that she could but faintly express, she exclaimed,—

" You must not forget, Angus, that the fame of a woman should be pure and spotless. Our present meeting has been private, and its further continuance would but expose me to suspicions that I tremble even to think of. Our most innocent actions are but too frequently misjudged, if they wear but even the semblance of mystery; and I fear lest this long visit should have been observed. Once more, then, farewell;—may Heaven guard you from the dangers of battle, and forget not, should my father join the legions of Bruce, that he may need your saving arm to snatch him from destruction !"

" Rely on it, Isabel, he shall be my first care," answered the youth, " and doubt not but the day will yet arrive when we shall return as victors to the castle of Glenroy. Yes, dearest lady, I will fondly cherish the idea which, ere long, may be realized, and this hour shall ever be hallowed to the gratitude of Angus Glenalvon."

With lingering and unwilling footsteps he now forced himself to quit the presence of ,the Princess Isabel, who, to the last, fixed her eyes upon his receding form ; and, when he was no longer to be seen, she sank back upon her seat, and, giving way to the emotions of her heart, exclaimed,—

" Farewell, dear adopted brother of my heart ; and, oh ! may the moment speedily arrive that shall restore you, my father, and the lost Edwin, to my longing sight. Take with thee, dear youth, my love, and the fervent prayers of a sister, for thy safe return from the battle's furious storm ; and, oh ! may you sometimes think of me, and for my sake avoid the dreaded perils into which your own ardour for military renown may lead you."

Overcome by the violence of her emotions, a temporary dizziness seized upon her brain, and for some time she was unconscious of the melancholy circumstances into which an adverse fate had plunged her.

CHAPTER XXX.

" Speak, dread form;—
What is thine errand here ? Why dost thou come
To chill me with thy presence ? Let me hear
The purpose of this dreaded visit.'
ROMANZI.

IT was not till some time after the departure of Angus that the princess recovered from the stupor into which she had fallen, and she blushed with confusion as she thought of the scene that had taken place between them. The image of her lover still flitted before her imagination, and her spirit seemed entranced in a more delightful serenity than she had enjoyed for many previous months. Rousing herself, however, from these pleasing thoughts, she removed her hand from her eyes, and, as she did so, was startled by an object that instantly put to flight the sweet images that love had depicted in her mind. Before her she plainly saw a tall shadow lengthen in the glimmering rays of the lamps, which shone from a distant arch, and, raising herself from her half-recumbent posture, she with dismay beheld the figure of a gigantic form that for a moment stood stationary before her. It was that of a warrior cased in complete armour, and his vizor, half concealing his features, displayed only his lips, and the lower portions of a dark and ferocious visage. His whole appearance was' threatening and alarming, nor could the dismayed Isabel summon resolution enough to break the fearful silence that reigned throughout the apartment.

Presently, advancing towards the lamps which lighted the chamber, the alarm of the princess increased into astonishment. and dread, for in an instant they were all extinguished, and no other light remained but that imperfect one which the moon reflected through a large casement opposite. It was sufficient, however, to reveal the heavy form of the mysterious intruder, and gave to his outline a more than mortally terrific appearance, whilst a deep voice, harsh and discordant, exclaimed in her ear,—

"Listen to me, lady, and observe my words :—Beware of curiosity, and presume not to make inquiries into things that are to be hidden from earthly knowledge. Slight not my warning, for, should'st thou rashly dare to tempt the dangers of discovering a hidden mystery, thy fate will be misery and despair. No earthly power can save thee from its certain doom, which is awful, sudden, and irremediable, if once provoked ; shun, therefore, its dreadful fiat, as thou hopest for peace on earth, and happiness in the world to come. Remember, girl, these fearful forewarnings, for they involve thy life and safety, and will be repeated to thy lasting horror and ruin, should'st thou neglect to profit by the warning you have received. Be silent and obedient ! Should we meet again, which alone depends on thy submission, the encounter may prove fatal to thyself !"

As he uttered these last words the fearful intruder slowly retreated, and the fixed eye of the Princess Isabel pursued the retiring figure as aghast, with fear and doubt she watched the departing form, and at length lost all traces of it in the obscurity of the further part of the chamber. A slight noise succeeded as of a closing door, and Isabel, with an emotion of terror, convulsively exclaimed :—

"Great Heaven ! what means this horrible phantasy, and whither, oh, whither have my erring footsteps betrayed me ?"

A low hollow voice in whispering, but audible tones, immediately answered—

"To the mansion of a nameless deed, thyself perhaps the victim of a powerful foe ! Hasten then from the horrid spells that will shortly engulph thee for ever in ruin, or with resolute courage and contempt of danger, rely on the saving arm of Heaven, and boldly dare this instant to save the injured innocent !"

"Mysterious forewarner," cried Isabel, with forced courage ; " if mortal, and as thy words impart, a partaker in the secret deeds from which thou hast cautioned me, dare openly reveal their hidden terrors, and instruct me how they may be avoided."

"Hark !" exclaimed the voice ; "the sounds of music float upon the breeze. Prophetic omens of death ! my mournful spirit responds your solemn strains as they ring a knell that portends the dissolution of the feeble and helpless !"

A strain of sweetest harmony did indeed resound as it swept along the exterior of the chamber, then for a moment remained stationary, and soon afterwards died away in melancholy soul-absorbing notes of the most rapturous music. Entranced at this, Isabel was unable to move, and at that moment she beheld the tall figure of a female, who, clothed in long flowing garments, stalked slowly and solemnly by, and then in an instant vanished ere she could tell by what mysterious means it had disappeared from the chamber.

A death-like stupor, the effect of terror and long-endured fatigue, now overpowered the faculties of Isabel, and in this helpless condition she was found by her attendant, Marianne, who returning soon after the late wonderous events, beheld with affright the total darkness of the apartment and the situation of the Princess Isabel, who lay fainting and powerless on the ground.

At first Marianne knew not what steps it would be best for her to pursue, but after long care and watching, she succeeded in restoring the exhausted spirits of her mistress to animation, who, opening her eyes and gazing wildly round the room, demanded where she was.

" In the castle of Glenroy, my lady," answered her attendant.

" What hour is it ?"

" About half an hour to midnight," replied Marianne. " Almost all in the fortress have retired to rest, and I came to ask if it is still your ladyship's determination to visit the chamber of the earl."

The princess answered not immediately, for her thoughts were directed to far different subjects. The late terrific occurrence, a second time so solemnly repeated, had for a while banished the recollection of Angus, and in its room created a thousand wild fantasies of alarm and bewildering thought, and she now almost felt inclined to forego her purpose till informed by Marianne of the helpless condition in which she had found her. Her ideas then changed, and she seemed to experience an uncertain conviction that the foregoing events were not real, but the frightful conjuration of a disturbed slumber, impressed on her dreaming fancy by the forlorn loneliness of her present situation. At length, addressing herself to Marianne, she anxiously inquired whether any stranger was in the chamber when she entered it.

" No one but yourself," she replied.

" Are the casements closed ?"

" They are all secure."

" Know you the reason of this room being enveloped in darkness ?" asked Isabel ; " or is it possible I have slept so long that the tapers have burnt themselves out ?"

The superstitious fears of Marianne were aroused, and being unable to answer the questions of her mistress, she turned to another subject.

" Will your ladyship be pleased to retire to rest ?"

By this time Isabel had recovered some of her usual firmness ; her countenance, it is true, was still wan from the effect of terror ; but she remembered that she had appointed to visit the earl's chamber, and was therefore unwilling to display less resolution and perseverance in the fulfilment of an engagement which she perceived her attendant was very desirous of though she pretended to offer obstacles to it.

In some degree the presence of Marianne had served to recal the energies of our heroine's mind, she felt an irresistible impulse, urging her to the enterprise, and she now resolved, that since she could only put the design into execution at the silent hour of night, she would not delay the difficult task, and if once she gained admittance to the apartment ot the earl, to be guided in her future conduct by the circumstances the undertaking would produce. For since Glenroy was now become the only remaining home that could shelter her, she felt bound to reject every other welcome, but such as had been promised by the earl himself, without whose personal assurance of safety and protection it was impossible to rest satisfied.

At length she was roused from her meditations by hearing the solemn hour of midnight tolled from the deep-toned castle bell. The moment for exertion had therefore now arrived, and Isabel, with a throbbing sensation of alarm, that she knew not how to account for, arose to commence an adventure, the termination of which it was impossible to foresee. She was, moreover, deeply mortified at being thus obliged secretly, and, at so late an hour, to force herself on the presence of a man, oppressed with years, and afflicted with a long and painful illness. Still, however, she could not continue to accept a refuge so forbiddingly yielded, though she felt unwilling to quit a place which had inspired a hope that here she could with certainty expect to realize the anticipated blessing of again beholding a beloved father whose sufferings had filled her with so much uneasiness.

The countenance of Marianne betrayed an expression of mingled fear and curiosity. Her remarks, though respectful, when addressed to the princess, were, at times, ambiguous and obscure in their meaning, and it seemed evident that she was labouring to conceal the difficulty she inwardly struggled with, in order to prevent her tongue from revealing some secret that she had been enjoined to keep.

Proceeding through the corridor, the Princess Isabel, occupied by her own perplexing thoughts, observed not the singularity of her attendant's demeanour, which was a mixture of blended terror and apparent reluctance to proceed, yet an equal desire to have her awakened curiosity satisfied. Following her pale and affrighted guide, Isabel at last turned hastily beneath a long arcade, exactly in a line with the principal portion of the castle. Marianne then walked nearer to her side, and said in an undertone :—

"These melancholy passages, my lady, are much less frequented and more remote from intrusion than the grand galleries that lead to the principal entrance of my lord's suite; and though all the inhabitants of the castle are, I dare say, by this time sleeping, yet I did not dare to risk the danger of entering them lest any stragglers should chance to be loitering about. The Holy Virgin shield us from harm; for it must be confessed my spirit fails me, and I cannot help trembling for our safety. Oh! should any mischief befall this perilous adventure, I shall never again know peace or quietness."

"Of what mischief are you thinking, Marianne?" inquired the princess, anxiously. "If any real peril, known to yourself, but unrevealed to me, remains to be explained, you will, indeed, have committed a grievous wrong should your apprehensions be well founded, and must, at a future period, become answerable for any harm your culpable silence may have betrayed me into."

"Believe me, my lady, I have no fears on your account," replied Marianne; "for I think,—nay, I am quite sure they will not dare to harm— Ah! what is it I am thinking about? how ridiculous, to be sure, do these groundless terrors make me appear. But this dismal old building is so particularly gloomy at this midnight hour, and, as they report, is so full of hobgoblins and horrible apparitions, that I wonder how I can venture thus to walk its lonely galleries and dark passages. I'm sure nothing but my respect for your ladyship's commands would have induced me to leave my own comfortable room to — But holy Mary be praised! we have, at length, gained the end of our journey. That little door, my lady, that you see yonder, will take you into the antechamber, and lead you immediately into the one occupied by his lordship. I will now return to your apartment and wait your return there, lest my presence in this place should excite suspicion."

As she said this, Marianne placed one of the lamps she carried in the hand of the princess Isabel, and hastily retreating, was going away before the calls of her mistress could arrest her flight; for she had run from the spot with all the speed she could, and it was plainly evident that no persuasion could prevail upon her to return.

Isabel watched the receding form of her attendant till she had passed through the corridor, and gained the door of the vestibule leading to the chamber she had just quitted. Somewhat awed by the loneliness of her present situation, the princess seemed, for a moment, almost inclined to postpone her present difficult task till some other opportunity, for to proceed without a guide to introduce her to the object of her search appeared highly improper, and awhile she paused, irresolute, whether to advance or retire. At length directing her eyes towards the door leading to the apartment of the earl, she perceived that it was partially open, and before she had well determined what to do, she mechanically passed onwards, and entered the adjoining chamber.

The lamp she carried gave but a partial view of the objects contained therein, and she paused, for a solemn feeling had crept over her senses, and for a moment she stood motionless with the strange effects her present extraordinary situation produced. Presently, however, she recovered from these emotions and advanced a few paces forward. All around was silent as the grave, and collecting all the fortitude she could, she exclaimed within herself :—

"What have I to fear, doing no wrong and obeying only the voice of instinct and humanity? Those fearful warnings were but the first images of a frightful vision, and shall they then have power to terrify me from the accomplishment of a laudable purpose? No, let guilt tremble and shrink back appalled, for if the innocent are not dreadless in a just cause, the criminal may without remorse be permitted to perform his evil deeds without shuddering at the punishment he merits. Hark! what means that dreadful cry?" she added, as a low, heart-rending groan came upon her startled ear; "it was a sound that proclaims mortal anguish, and yet my limbs refuse their office, though my heart prompts me to lend what poor assistance is in my power."

The solemnity of the hour, together with the forlornness of her situation, again nearly overpowered her courage, as a deeper sensation of fear crept through her heart at the dismal sound she had heard. She felt convinced that the groan she had heard, and which had so much startled her, proceeded from the venerable Earl of Glenroy, who was said to be confined from ill-health and growing infirmity, and perhaps the anguish of pain had occasioned the sound that had caused her so much alarm. Hastily passing to an opposite door from whence the groan seemed to have issued, she softly unclosed it, but stood petrified with horror as she plainly heard a feeble voice in tones of supplication and terror, exclaim :—

"Save me; oh, save me, Heaven, from the fell murderer's grasp. Alas! I am lost! 'tis done! the deed that robs me of life is accomplished."

CHAPTER XXXI.

"Hast thou no pity in thy heart?
Look on the grey hairs of a weak old man
And let them stay the vengeful, murderous blow
Thou aim'st against his life."

THE VESPER HOUR.

HORRIFIED at the words which she had heard, the princess no longer hesitated, but wildly rushed, unmindful of her own danger, into the room, but too late, alas! to prevent the cruel deed that had prostrated the earl upon the floor in the last agonies of death. Convulsed and deluged in his own blood lay the aged form of Glenroy, as a man of terrific aspect, encased in armour, buried at the instant she rushed into the chamber, his blood-drenched poniard a second time into the body of his hapless victim. Horror-struck at the sight, Isabel staggered towards the dying man, and with a courage inspired by desperation and frenzy, stood over him, as with pallid, bloodless features, and wild despairing looks, she opposed with outstretched arms the repetition of the assassin's blow.

"Insatiate bloodhounds, avaunt!" she frantically cried, "desist villains, I command ye, from your fiendish deeds, for the blood of the innocent shall rise to Heaven's avenging tribunal and cry for retribution on your heads. Away, monsters! begone from the scene of your enormities or I—woman as I am—will yet find means to bring upon you that dread punishment your crimes have so justly merited, both from Heaven and man!"

"All aid is hopeless," cried the dying man, "life ebbs apace, yet fain would I have been spared a few short days that I might have revealed a tale of horrors that has thus far been concealed within my own bosom. But it may not be; the hand of death is on me, and denies me even the respite of an hour. I die a guiltless death, and may its inhuman perpetrators never experience that mercy which they have denied to me. The last act is finished, and I die by the hands of villains that have been employed by —"

He could utter no more, and a single glance served to convince the distracted Isabel that the old man had yielded up his last breath. Dreadful was the doom that now awaited herself. She had fallen fainting on the bleeding body of the murdered Glenroy, and when again recalled to life she found herself still in the dreadful chamber of horror, supported in the ruffian grasp of the ferocious murderers, whose dark, vindictive looks afforded a dreadful presage of the sufferings to which she was doomed.

One of the assassins held to her bosom a dagger still reeking with the blood of the former hapless victim, whilst his companion, with threatening gestures, held to her lips a cup of deadly poison. Urged by terror and despair, Isabel made one faint effort to escape from them, and as she did so her eyes encountered the stern features of the nearest ruffian, and, in an instant she recognised a face that she remembered once before to have beheld at the castle of Craiglynn, when King Edward so treacherously obtained possession of that fortress, and had been accompanied by this mysterious and unknown being.

She shuddered at the recollection, and without a hope of mercy closed her eyes on the terrors that surrounded her. Powerless to resist her doom, and lost beyond all earthly aid, she was now completely at their mercy, whilst from the taller of the two villains she heard with trembling dismay the following words :—

"Presumptuous girl! wert thou not commanded to avoid the dangers of curiosity, and forbidden to search into the mysteries of this castle? Hast thou not incurred the fate forewarned? and having dared to brave all dangers, bear thy sentence, for thou art lost past all hope of pity or forbearance! Drink of the cup, girl, and meet the death to which thou hast doomed thyself!"

"Merciful Heaven!" faintly ejaculated the princess; "save me from the hands of these ruthless men!"

"Neither Heaven nor earth can now protect thee from our wrath!" muttered the villain. "Aye, thou mayest well tremble, for all hope of aid has forsaken thee. Pronounce thy last farewell to all in life, and then drink the bitter potion, for it is decreed thou art to die."

"Again do I call upon thee, Heaven, to hear my cries!" murmured Isabel in frantic tones; then falling prostrate at the feet of the remorseless ruffian she sued for mercy, in tones that none but himself could have resisted.

"If you are deaf to pity," she cried—"at least, be warned by me of the terrible retribution that will follow the ruthless deed you contemplate. Forbear, then, this savage act, and purchase pardon for your past crimes by listening to the voice of mercy. Spare me, and when thine own awful hour comes thou wilt not plead in vain for the mercy of which thou hast so much need."

"I will be trifled with no longer," he exclaimed; "drain off the fatal
cup to its very dregs, for no persuasion shall ever urge me to change thy
doom. Thou hast brought all this upon thyself by thine own folly, for I
would have preserved thee, and even warned thee of the danger that would
surely follow thy ill-timed curiosity."

Then holding the poniard threateningly in one hand, and presenting the
poisoned cup with the other, he continued,—

"Drink, girl, or meet thy death by the more lingering tortures inflicted
by the dagger, for no soul that has ever dared become a witness of the deeds
I execute in secret ever yet escaped with life to tell the world of acts that
would bring upon me an ignominious punishment. Thou hast obtained a
fatal knowledge of a deed that should have been secret, and, therefore, art
justly doomed to expiate thy folly at the expense of thy life. Once more I
command thee drink, or thus will I enforce obedience to my will!"

Threatened by the dagger which he held to her bosom, and held firmly
in the grasp of the other villain, the unhappy Isabel was powerless to resist
her horrible doom. Her spirits sunk exhausted—her frame shivered and
became dreadfully convulsed, and life itself seemed to be rapidly fleeting
away as the terrible unknown held to her lips the fatal cup from which
she was to drink. Thus compelled she had no alternative, and shuddering as she complied, the poisoned draught was swallowed to its very
dregs.

"Ha! ha! ha!" laughed the monster demoniacally; "the deed is done,
and now that *she* is my victim, fortune and greatness are mine. No eye
witnesses my acts, and all is safe. Glenroy sleeps to wake no more—
Mackenzie is alike my victim. The fiend of darkness favours my bold designs, and ambition's thirst will be slaked by the accomplishment of all my
purposes. And thou, too, girl, the last of my victims, will never awaken

with the memory of this night's deeds, nor wilt thou tell the dark tale that has laid thee low. Such ever be the fate of those who dare oppose my will, and search into the mysteries that are forbidden to be known."

The senses of the princess began to leave her, and mis-shapen objects of confusion and failing sight floated wildly before her; her eyes became heavy, and fixed in the rayless inanimation of fast approaching dissolution. The fearful unknown with eager eyes impatiently watched the rapidly approaching strides of death. On the floor, at some little distance, lay the blood-stained form of the murdered Earl of Glenroy; a feeble lamp dimly threw a melancholy tinge around the chamber of death, whilst the principal ruffian supported in his arms the sinking Isabel, whose form was still and motionless. Her long flowing robes swept the floor, and her hair hung unconfined over her bosom, and half concealed the death-like wanness that spread over her once beauteous countenance.

The other ruffian stood fiercely watching over the forms before him, and his lowering eyes glared terribly as he beheld the last gaspings of expiring nature, whilst his dark outline, half obscured in the deepened shade where he stood, gave to him the semblance of a fiend exulting over the dreadful deeds that had been committed. At length a heavy sigh was uttered by the princess, and with a convulsive shudder she sunk back motionless into the arms of the villain that supported her.

At this instant the chamber of death became on a sudden more dark and dismal even than it had been previously; but the fiend-like assassins were bold in their guilt, and for awhile triumphed in their murderous deeds; they laughed at the crimes that had that night been committed, and congratulated themselves upon the certainty that no human eye had witnessed the accursed acts they had so remorsely executed. In the midst of this their lamp expired, and for a moment they were involved in utter darkness; presently, however, the wind suddenly rose in fearful violence, the lightnings darted in angry flashes from the clouds, and the rolling thunder, with appalling reverberations, loudly sounded, as if proclaiming the vengeance of Heaven against the monsters who had been revelling in human blood. Even the usually fearless hearts of the two ruffians quailed in this moment of terror, and they stood paralysed at the terrific storm that seemed to increase in violence with each succeeding peal of thunder.

CHAPTER XXXII.

" And will my sufferings never find an end.
But thou, remorseless fiend, must still pursue
And crush me with thy hate? Begone from me,
For I do know thee for a fiend incarnate.''
THE BETRAYER.

THE draught administered by the ruffians was not of the deadly nature that had been expected by the Princess Isabel; for after many hours had elapsed she awoke from the deadly stupor into which it had thrown her, and as her wandering faculties returned, she once more fixed her eyes upon the gigantic form of a man, whose grim features were too forcibly impressed upon her mind to be easily eradicated. She observed also that she was in a gloomy chamber that was totally unknown to her, and quickly rousing herself, she eagerly exclaimed,—

" Whither have I been conveyed, relentless fiend, and for what purpose have I been taken from the Castle of Glenroy, where I had once fondly hoped to obtain shelter and protection? Oh, memory, will you never shake off the fearful visions that afflict my mind, or must I ever be the sport of those cruel misfortunes that so long have persecuted me ?"

"Lady," exclaimed her base persecutor, "restrain these feelings, and learn that you are now with one who can alone shield you from the miseries you so much deplore."

"Monster! I know thee now," cried Isabel, with startling vehemence, for she had already recognized in him the murderer of Glenroy, and the present usurper of the titles and honours of the late earl. "Thou art the fiend that slew the good old man, whom I, alas! could not save from the merciless daggers of the assassins. But beware of the punishment that awaits thee, for Heaven knows thy guilt, and already is its arm bared for the retribution that surely awaits thy many heinous crimes."

"Of what do you speak, Isabel?" demanded the usurping Earl of Glenroy, with well feigned surprise. "Your senses still wander, and your tongue discourses of some terrible vision that has visited your mind."

"A terrible vision indeed, and most dreadfully is it realised to my waking fancy!" answered the shuddering Isabel. "Alas! I remember all that took place in the Castle of Glenroy, and he who was the chief actor in that dreadful tragedy now stands before me."

"Your brain wanders, girl!" he exclaimed fiercely. "Who do you take me for that I am thus to be charged as the perpetrator of some crime that I know nothing of?"

"I remember you too well to be mistaken," answered the trembling Isabel. "The foul crime will never be obliterated from my mind, and even though death may be the reward of my boldness, I denounce you as the midnight assassin of the aged Earl of Glenroy."

"Be more guarded in your speech, girl," exclaimed the other, with a threatening scowl, "for you know not yet the fierce, vindictive wrath of him you have thus boldly taxed with crime. You are deceived, and some fearful vision still cheats you with its mockeries. Again I say you know me not, and the deeds you speak of are nothing but the delusions of a disordered brain."

"Do you deny, then," she asked, "that the Earl of Glenroy died from a wound inflicted by your dagger?"

"I do deny it," exclaimed the other. "The earl expired two nights since, but not by any act of mine. His death was a natural one, and, therefore, the words you have addressed to me are cruel and unjust."

"Nay," she replied, "you cannot persuade me against the evidence of my own senses. I saw the deed committed, and it may yet be in my power to proclaim your monstrous villainies to the world."

"Beware, girl, how you urge me to desperation!" exclaimed the other. "I would fain spare your life, but another threat such as you have just pronounced might urge me to an act that I had hoped to avoid."

Isabel regarded him with a look of mingled hatred and disgust, and gathering all her fortitude for the effort, she said, firmly,—

"I am not to be terrified into silence by the threats you may be pleased to utter in the presence of a defenceless girl. It is true I was compelled to swallow a stupifying draught which for awhile entranced my spirit, but it has failed to deaden the sickening memory of the past. I ask thee, then, inhuman monster as thou art, dost thou not tremble whilst my lips reveal the fearful secret thou hadst hoped was for ever buried in oblivion ?"

The ruffian did indeed quail beneath the steady gaze with which the princess regarded him. It is true his designs aimed not against her life, or he would have taken instant vengeance; but he had hoped that by administering the subtle potion to produce oblivion of the past, and thus, without shedding more blood, to destroy the only evidence that he had to dread.

But he now discovered that his scheme had failed, and with secret dismay he felt that he had yet to dread a being, who, if once freed from his power, would take the earliest opportunity to bring upon him the doom he so much feared to think of. For a moment or two, therefore, he remained silent, but at length, with a stern and frowning aspect he once more approached her, and exclaimed, threateningly,—

"Isabel Mackenzie, I see thou art, indeed, acquainted with the past, but thou hast not yet reflected upon the consequences that may follow that fatal knowledge. Thou art now a captive, and powerless to oppose a destiny which no earthly means can ever avert; dearly, therefore, hast thou purchased thy boasted knowledge of my secret, since henceforth thou must remain here the prisoner of the man whose power you affect to despise. Removed hither by my commands, there is not the slightest chance of thy place of retreat ever being discovered, and after the search of thy friends has for awhile been fruitless, they will naturally give thee up for dead. Here thou art condemned to linger out the remainder of thy days, and must submit to the dark fortunes which thine own rashness has produced."

"If it is Heaven's will I yield myself to my sad fate without a murmur," answered Isabel; "and yet," she added, "I warn thee of the consequences of thy base deeds, for, be assured, the time will arrive, ere long, when thou wilt be made to repent the injustice thou hast done to one who never injured thee."

—"Ah," he replied, indifferently, "I am content to abide the danger thou dost threaten me with. And now listen to me, proud girl, and know that it is in my power to mitigate thy sufferings, on condition that thou wilt accept my terms, and bury the remembrance of the past in oblivion. Such are the conditions which may yet recal thee to existence, and to oppose them will be vain, since it will only provoke a harsher decree, and make an eternal foe of the incensed Chief of Badenoch."

"The Chief of Badenoch!" cried the now terrified princess; "is it, then, true that I have fallen into the power of that ruthless destroyer of all that is good and innocent? Alas! alas!—I stand, then, in the presence of the murderer of Glenalvon, the heartless plunderer of his orphans' rights!"

"Curses on thy words!" exclaimed Badenoch, fiercely; "what voice is it that recalls the memory of the past, and blasts my ears with sounds that weigh down my soul to perdition!"

"Ah! thou dost repent, then?" cried Isabel.

"Hark!" he exclaimed, without heeding her words, "that fearful sound seems echoing from the grave of the murdered! Helen Glenalvon's pale and threatening ghost shrieks the knell of retribution, and my soul recoils with horror, as she recounts my deeds, and abandons me to all the tortures of despair. Yet why should I despair?" he continued, upon recovering somewhat from his frenzy; "let weak souls start back with dismay when conscience reminds them of the past. 'Tis for the brave alone to despise her cries, and to crush the gnawing worm that eats like a poisonous canker into the heart."

Uttering these words, he flew wildly from the chamber; and Isabel, with speechless amazement and terror, reflected upon the perilous situation in which she was now placed. How long she had remained in this state of unconsciousness she knew not; but at length she was aroused by the voice of Marianne, who, falling at her feet, exclaimed. in piteous accents,—

"Ah, my lady, can the guilty being, thus prostrate before you, ever hope for your forgiveness?"

Isabel regarded her with surprise, as a frown of displeasure passed over her countenance.

"You have, indeed, betrayed me, girl," she answered angrily, "and are, therefore, the best judge of what lenity you can expect from me. Leave me, Marianne, for never more can I take you to my confidence."

"Alas! my lady," cried the despairing attendant. "Do not, I implore you, drive me hence in displeasure. I have done wrong, very wrong, indeed, in suffering you to go to that frightful chamber of death, when I almost suspected what was going forward there. But indeed, my lady, my conduct has not been so very bad as to deserve all this anger."

"It is in vain that you endeavour to excuse the treachery of your conduct," answered Isabel; "did you not betray me to the scene of murder?—and knew you not that I should there behold those horrors, the remembrance of which have almost driven me mad?"

"I cannot deny it, my dear lady," answered the attendant, "yet Heaven is my witness that I disobeyed my father, in warning you to avoid the chamber; and although, as I have already confessed, I suspected there were foul deeds performing, I knew not you would endure so much suffering; but rather hoped that, should you see the late unfortunate Earl of Glenroy, the dreadful event that has occurred would have been frustrated. Ah! if I had only known what has since come to pass, I would have refused to obey your commands, and nothing should ever have induced me to conduct you to those terrible apartments."

"I may believe, then," said the Princess Isabel, "that your penitence is perfectly sincere?"

"Indeed, indeed it is, my lady."

"If so," answered Isabel, "you will convince me of it by instantly sending a messenger, upon whose fidelity we may rely, to the convent of Jona, informing the Lady Abbess of the peril in which I am placed. Or, if that cannot be done, some other means must be thought of that will ensure my liberation from this dreadful place. Assist me but in this, Marianne, and rely upon it I will make any sacrifice to reward the service."

"Ah! my dear lady," cried the attendant, "could I but afford the assistance you need, you know not how happy it would make me; but it is impossible, for you know not what you ask, since I am as much a prisoner here as your ladyship is, for having disobeyed the commands of the new Earl of Glenroy. We are now, indeed, confined in one of his gloomy fortresses, and, I fear, beyond all hope of escape or rescue."

"Then Heaven defend me!" cried Isabel, despondingly; "yet speak, Marianne. Tell me all, I implore you; and, whatever my peril may be, fear not to let me know the worst, for suspense does but increase my misery, and I can endure anything rather than the uncertainty that at present involves my lowering fortunes."

The attendant advanced, and, after some little hesitation, proceeded to recount the events of the last few hours in the following words.

CHAPTER XXXIII.

" O'er mountain steep, and rugged plain,
We'll bear the maid away,
For we must reach the fortress gates
E'er comes the close of day."
                                FAIR EDELINE.

"AFTER you had left me," Marianne went on to say, "I waited in the great corridor of Glenroy Castle about half an hour; and, becoming alarmed at your lengthened absence, I determined to seek you, and for that purpose, after much hesitation, entered the dreadful scene of outrage at the moment when you were lying convulsed in the arms of the remorseless murderer. My shriek of horror and alarm betrayed me; and, before I could flee from the spot, I was seized and dragged back to the apartment where, with horrid threatenings that I can never forget, the ferocious ruffians terrified me into silence. The foremost of the two men then regarded me with a look of the fiercest malignity, and, flourishing a dagger that he held in his hand, exclaimed, in a voice hoarse with rage,—

"'Thou hast dared presume to become a witness of the deed we have this night committed, and thy life has become forfeited. On one condition, however, thou may'st save thyself from death. Swear to reveal to no mortal the scene thou hast this night witnessed; swear it, I say, or the poniard that now glitters in my hand shall be buried in thy heart.'

"Terrified at his words, I fell upon my knees, and readily swore never to reveal anything that I had seen or heard, though every minute I expected nothing else but that I should be murdered, for I saw blood on the floor, and knew but too well what would be my fate, if they had the least suspicion that I would break the oath I had been forced to take. I, however, could perceive that you were not dead, and the fierce-looking Fergus said you were not, but had swallowed a sleeping potion, and that if I meant to preserve my own life, I must do as he commanded, and never presume to utter a syllable to anybody of what I had been so presumptuous as to witness. So, after I had again promised silence, my lady, they seemed to be better satisfied; and, when I began to recover from my fright, I tried gently to raise you from the ground, and to wake you from the death-like torpor into which you were lying. At one moment I thought I could perceive a faint sign of returning life; and, placing my hand close to your heart, I felt it beat slowly, which satisfied me that my worst fears for your safety were without foundation. I then begged for means by which to revive you; but his lordship, with a ferocious frown, bade me be silent, or expect the death he had before threatened me with.

"'She is not dead,' he added; 'but will revive when the potion she has drank ceases to operate. In a few hours the effect of the narcotic will have worn off, and it will then be for her to decide whether she will accept my terms, or pass the remainder of her days in solitude and imprisonment.'

"Then addressing himself to his equally ferocious companion, he continued,—

"'It is now necessary that we bear her to the fortress I have spoken to you about. Its sea-girt towers will admirably serve to conceal her from all impertinent inquiry, and there she shall remain till liberated by her own conduct. She shall not perish yet, Fergus, but be there detained my prisoner till her haughty soul has been subdued.'

"These words of terror filled my soul with fright," continued Marianne; "and, unable to restrain myself any longer, I called loudly for help. But this only served to provoke them the more; and, with another exclamation of vengeance against me, he lifted you in his arms, and bore you rapidly away through a dark opening, at the same moment Fergus threw a cloak over my head, and I could neither see nor hear anything more that went on for some time afterwards."

The blood of Lady Isabel chilled at this recital,—her heart sickened, and her frame shuddered convulsively; but she was unable to find utterance for her words. Marianne observed this, and would have left the remainder of her narrative till another time; but the princess was anxious to hear it all, and by a sign commanded her to proceed.

"Well, your ladyship," resumed the attendant, "I saw no more, for Fergus forcibly seized my arms, and dragged me forward; and then, giving myself up for lost, as well as your ladyship, I prayed forgiveness of our sins, not doubting that we should soon be plunged into the lake where I knew they intended to convey the body of the unfortunate Earl of Glenroy. It proved, however, that we were not to die then, for soon afterwards I felt myself lifted into a vehicle, and Fergus, having removed the cloak which he had thrown over my head, I found myself placed by the side of your ladyship in a covered car, and we were immediately hurried forward with impetuous speed, and every moment I expected we should be hurled down the dreadful precipices, along the sides of which our road lay.

"At last the long wished-for morning came, and, through a hole in the vehicle, I was able to see the wild, dismal country through which we were travelling. At times our way passed through wild mountainous districts, then by lakes and torrents, or amongst woody dells, where, at some periods, we seemed to be involved in all the darkness of night. It was a sad journey, indeed, my lady, and I tried to waken you ; but the effect of the sleeping draught had not yet lost its power, and I was doomed to see all my efforts thrown away.

"Again night came upon us, but the moon shone brightly ; and, hearing voices, I ventured to look out—saw that our vehicle was guarded by a party of men at arms, one of whom saw me, and asked so many strange questions about your ladyship, that I was glad to get away and lie down by your side, in order to see if I could get any repose. This, however, was quite impossible, and, rising once more, I found that we were travelling over a very hilly country, which, becoming impassable, the horses were unharnessed, and poles being affixed to the carriage, we were carried by men, whilst a party on each side kept guard in case of a sudden surprise. Of course the bearers were frequently changed, and we proceeded with tolerable rapidity, till at length the men came to a house, when the loud notes a bugle once more filled me with apprehension.

"What to make of this I knew not ; but presently afterwards I could plainly distinguish the clashing of swords, and voices in dispute, at which period our vehicle was placed upon the ground, and, once more having recourse to my little loop-hole, I saw a few strange warriors engaging fiercely with our people, in spite of the numbers that were against them."

"Did you recognise any of those that came to our rescue?" demanded Isabel.

"Indeed I did, my lady," answered Marianne ; "for, would you believe it, in the principal warrior I plainly saw the young knight that had so earnestly entreated me to conduct him into your presence only the evening before."

"Merciful Heaven!" cried Isabel, with mingled emotions of dread and rapture, "are you certain, girl, that the person you saw was Sir Angus Glenalvon?"

"I am as certain of it as that I now stand in your presence," answered the attendant ; "for the moon was shining brightly at the time, and I could have sworn to him among ten thousand others."

"And did my captor see him ?" asked our heroine.

"Indeed he did, my lady," replied Marianne ; "and a terrible effect it seemed to have upon him, I can assure you, for his countenance turned deadly pale, and in a trembling voice he exclaimed,—

"'It is the shade of the murdered Glenalvon which has thus risen from the tomb to blast the guilty Badenoch with its presence ! Such were the arms he wore when living, — such the stern look he fixed upon me at the moment when my poniard was struck to his heart !'

"As he uttered these words, my lady, he fell to the ground, and Sir Angus rushing forward, seized him by the throat,

"'Murderer!' he exclaimed, 'arouse thee from this womanish fear, and look upon no ghostly visitant, but upon the son of those whom thou didst sacrifice in thy boundless hate! The heir of Glenalvon still survives to hurl upon thee that terrible retribution which has been but too long delayed!'

"'Mercy! mercy!' groaned the conscience-stricken wretch.

"'Aye,' answered the young knight, 'such mercy as thou didst show thy victims will I bestow on thee. Murderer! I have long and anxiously looked for this moment; and now that thou art thus thrown in my power, I will avenge the blood thou hast so remorselessly spilt!'

"As he uttered these words, he would have plunged his sword into the heart of his prostrate foe; but the other had foreseen his intention, and springing upon his feet, he avoided what I imagined to be a certain death. Then addressing himself to his followers, he pointed towards Angus and exclaimed, in a voice of thunder,—

"'Hear me, slaves, and obey! Seize upon yonder impostor, and suffer him not to escape as you value your lives!'

"Well, my lady," continued Marianne, "I became so alarmed, that I could not look any longer, though I could hear a great noise and confusion that immediately followed. What induced me to do it I know not, but with a loud scream I called for help, declaring that the Princess Isabel was in danger, and would fall a prey to her enemies unless instant assistance was given. These words, I have no doubt, must have reached the ears of Sir Angus, for directly afterwards he rushed towards the caravan and would have rescued us had he not been overpowered by numbers; and as he was dragged away, I could once more hear the crash of arms, and I suppose a desperate fight took place; for when I could again venture to look forth, I saw the young knight still engaged in combat; but out of all the followers that had been with him, only two or three remained. At length Sir Angus fell wounded to the earth, a shout of victory was raised by his conqueror, and—and——"

Here Marianne paused abruptly, for the head of the princess sunk upon her shoulder, and it was some little time before any signs of life appeared. At last, however, with a heavy sigh, and a burst of anguished tears, she again unclosed her eyes; and, having in some degree recovered herself, she eagerly inquired of her attendant whether she was certain Angus had fallen in the manner she had described.

"I thought so, my lady," answered Marianne, with a well-meant endeavour to allay some of the anguish she had occasioned; "but the truth is, Fergus hurried us away just at that moment, and we were carried forward with such speed, that I had no time to ascertain whether Sir Angus had really received any injury."

"Alas!" sighed the princess, "I can but too well judge your motive for thus concealing the worst from me. You have but too much reason to believe that Angus Glenalvon is dead, and have forborne to tell me all lest my spirits should sink beneath this accumulation of misfortunes."

"Indeed, my lady, I have all along been hoping the best," answered Marianne; "for, as I before observed, it was quite dark when the combat took place, and I've been thinking that though they might have left him for dead, he may afterwards have revived, and in that case we may expect that it will not be long before he takes some means or other for your release from this place. Or he may have been made a captive, and in that event he will perhaps contrive to escape and take you with him to some place of safety."

"Your words, girl, do but add to the grief that presses with such dreadful weight upon my heart," cried the princess, "since in either case I can

have no hope of ever seeing Angus Glenalvon again. There is but too much reason to fear that he has fallen by the hands of his ruthless and implacable foe, and even should he be a captive in the hands of his enemy, the Chief of Badenoch bears him too much hatred to spare his life, even on condition that he passes the remainder of his days in a state of miserable and hopeless captivity.''

"Nay, my dear lady," cried Marianne, "do not give way to despair, but rather look forward with hope, and endeavour to yield with submission to your present trouble."

"Alas!" sighed Lady Isabel, "the duty of submission is a hard and difficult one when all in life that is dearest is torn with savage violence from us. Angus Glenalvon is for ever gone, or his gallant soul would ere this time have prompted him to attempt some means or other for my rescue. His captor well knew that he could obtain safety only by the death of his foe, and I fear there can be little doubt that he has revenged himself upon the youthful knight who dared to step forward to frustrate his base designs against a helpless woman."

Overpowered and subdued in spirit, the Princess Isabel wept in despairing anguish over the melancholy thoughts that crowded upon her mind, whilst Marianne, alternately weeping and entreating, sought to arouse her mind from this anguish by continuing her narrative from the period of their arrival at the castle to the present time.

Nothing, however, could rouse the mind of the princess from its despondency and grief, for the idea of Angus having perished by the hand of his implacable foe seemed to be confirmed, and she felt as if torn for ever from one of the few beings she had ever loved, and whose loss was a calamity that was deeply to be deplored, and from which she felt she should never entirely recover.

No. 25

CHAPTER XXXIV.

" A barren and detested rock it is,
The trees, though summer, yet forlorn and lean,
O'ergrown with moss and baleful missletoe.
Here never shines the sun, here nothing breeds,
Unless the nightly owl or fatal raven."
                                        SHAKSPERE.

THE island, or rather rock of Rothellan, was scarcely a mile and a quarter in circumference; its lower base is perforated into deep excavations by the constant rushing of the billows with which it was on every side surrounded. Its nearest point to the shore was about a league distant, the other portions being bounded by a number of small rock islands that appeared at one period to have formed a portion of a tolerably spacious island. The nearest of these was Glenalvon, considerably larger than the rest, and the scene of the deeds of violence and bloodshed with which this narrative commenced.

As we have observed before, the strait which divided the shores of the latter from Rothellan was a narrow, dangerous whirlpool, which could only be passed at certain times, and not even then without considerable risk of being swallowed in the raging waters. Above this fearful spot rose the gigantic bulwarks of Badenoch's chief residence; its gloomy towering battlements, formed out of the solid hewn rock, were of cumbrous shape, large and irregular, but possessing a degree of strength that could be found in few other fortresses in the kingdom.

On every side the rock was inaccessible, for not a sloping declivity favoured the possibility of reaching its lofty summits: its height was far beyond the reach of scaling-ladders, nor was there even a foundation of shelving rocks on which to rear such a means of ascent had there been any place of ingress within view: indeed, the only access to the castle was by means of a crane and pulleys, having a strong rope, to which was affixed a seat in which those who had business in the castle were either raised or lowered as occasion or pleasure demanded; and by a similar process stores of all kinds were received, whilst even the boats could at will be drawn up and secured from sudden surprisal by means of the same contrivance.

Rothellan had formerly been a royal fortress, and was only to be subjugated by the treachery of its garrison or inhabitants, a fate it had sustained some years since, and which had rendered it the property of an individual; for King Edward had bestowed it wholly on the Chief of Badenoch, as a reward for his base services, in assisting the English monarch in his ambitious project for the total conquest of Scotland.

Badenoch was the son of the Earl of Glenroy's younger sister; his father was of noble descent, but a younger branch, and had died in the field of battle, leaving a widow, who, however, did not long survive him. The youthful Badenoch had been brought up by his uncle till he reached his seventeenth year, when he suddenly took his departure, resolving to embrace a military life, but undetermined whether to take up arms in favour of Robert Bruce, or to take part with the ambitious Edward, who at that time was carrying on a fierce war with Scotland. A very brief time, however, served to decide him in the course he was to adopt, and in Edward he willingly recognized a master, who would amply reward his degenerate baseness and faithless desertion of his oppressed country; and who had promised to raise him shortly to that pitch of grandeur that had ever been the summit of his hopes, and which he would have made any sacrifice to acquire.

A feeling of revenge, too, had no inconsiderable share in urging him to the step he had taken, for, as we have before had occasion to observe, Lady Helen had been his first love, and dreadful were the imprecations he breathed against the Earl of Glenalvon, after he had wooed and won the fair object upon whom he had set his heart. These deadly vows of vengeance were at length but too successfully accomplished, for the domain of Rothellan eventually became his, and thus gave him the power to put his horrid purposes into execution.

The victories gained by King Edward over the Scottish armies were fatal to the life and greatness of Glenalvon, for by those events Badenoch had risen highly in the estimation of the usurper, and, secure in his iniquity, he determined to satiate the secret hate of his soul against the man who had deprived him of Helen's love, and thus rendered him a prey to feelings of the most bitter disappointment.

King Edward of England would gladly have obtained the assistance or the Earl of Glenalvon and his numerous retainers, but he knew well the connecting ties which bound that nobleman to the interests of Bruce, and consequently despaired of ever seeing him become a traitor to his country. The Chief of Badenoch, therefore, found no difficulty in obtaining his sovereign's consent to his deep-laid schemes, which, to give a colouring to, he pretended only originated in his wish to punish Glenalvon's obstinacy in resisting the English king in his attempts against Scotland, and to hold the earl a prisoner, as a traitor to his liege lord, the victorious Edward. Thus the monarch was deceived by his specious representations, and the remainder of the task became comparatively easy.

When the tragical death of the Earl and Countess of Glenalvon had been accomplished, the King of England was imposed upon by Badenoch with a false representation of the occurrence, and the sovereign was too well satisfied at hearing of the death of a powerful antagonist to express any anger at the means which had been taken to rid him of the man he had long regarded as the chief obstacle to his acquiring full possession of the country he was resolved to conquer. Nor did Badenoch's hypocrisy terminate here, for, skilled as he was in dark stratagem, he found means to deceive the too credulous Lord Mackenzie by a story that he had invented to turn all suspicion of treachery from himself.

Shortly after the murder of the Earl and Countess of Glenalvon, the Chief of Badenoch married a rich orphan ward, whose person and fortunes the King of England had seized upon to bestow upon his unworthy favourite. This unhappy girl was rather a passive sacrifice than a willing bride, and within twelve months from her marriage she died, after giving birth to a daughter.

Rosalind, the child in question, was brought up in the castle of Rothellan, in total seclusion, strict orders having been given never on any account to permit her to wander beyond the walls of the place which had been the scene of her birth. At this period of our narrative she had just passed her seventeenth year, and, as may imagined, was the child of simplicity, nature, and innocence. Her heart, unlike her fierce and relentless father's, was gentle, timid, submissive, and benevolent. In short, she was the only being in his power whom his tyranny had not yet afflicted, for her sweet complying meekness of disposition at once disarmed his rage, and thus deprived him of all excuse for harshness or severity, except so far as regarded the orders which had been issued to confine her within the limits of the castle walls.

Innocent, and totally unacquainted with the world, Rosalind thus lived remotely from all social intercourse, save that which she found in Rothellan, nor did she ever sigh for the pleasures of a world that she had been artfully taught to believe were full of dangers. In fact, Rothellan, totally unconnected as it was from the mainland, seemed to her to comprehend the whole space of inhabited earth ; and with the society of her nurse, her lute, and the freedom of the ramparts, she lived contentedly, without seeking to make inquiries into affairs that she little cared about. Resignation to the will of her father, she conceived to be her first duty, and never having known a change from the dull round in which her life had been passed, she could not regret the want of those pleasures which it had been the object of Badenoch to keep her in ignorance of.

Marianne's account of the occurrences of the journey had not been exaggerated in any one particular. Angus, after quitting the presence of the Princess Isabel, hastened from the Castle of Glenroy, on his way to rejoin the forces of Robert Bruce, anxious to reach the camp before his short absence should either be missed or noticed ; for he was now more ardent than ever in the cause of his injured sovereign, and relying upon present appearances, he believed that the issue of the next battle would serve to replace Bruce upon the throne from which he had been driven by the ambitious King of England.

Journeying onwards, and excited by these newly-awakened hopes, he was at length overtaken by a party of Badenoch's troops, and conducted to the very spot where the hapless Lady Isabel was lying, to all appearance, dead from the effect of the potion she had been compelled to swallow. Badenoch saw the youthful knight, and the instant his startled eye caught a view of Angus, the very image of him who, a few years before, he had so ruthlessly destroyed, he staggered and fell to the ground. Conscience, at a moment least apprehended, had awakened his memory with a knell of horror, and all the past came with terrible distinctness to appal his guilty soul, and weigh down his spirit with the enormity of the crimes he had committed.

But this feeling was only a temporary one, for he shortly recovered himself, and, when convinced that he had no supernatural foe to contend against, a deadly fury took possession of his soul, and his thoughts were instantly directed to the means by which he might best revenge himself upon the youth who had been thus unexpectedly thrown into his power. A fiendish triumph was manifested in his looks as he gazed upon Angus Glenalvon, for the only being on earth that he had cause to dread stood helpless and unprotected before him, and his fate might be decided by a single word which would thus rid him for ever of a hated foe.

Judging the thoughts of their master by his dark and malignant looks, two of the attendants had fallen upon the young knight, when a skirmish ensued, which terminated in Angus and his followers being made prisoners, except one of the men who contrived to effect his escape, in the hope that he might be able to reach the camp of Bruce, and thus give intelligence of his young master's perilous situation.

CHAPTER XXXV.

" He is in blood
Steeped so far, that sin will pluck on sin ;
Tearfalling pity dwells not in his eye."

SHAKSPERE.

DAY had not yet dawned, when descending from a long chain of rugged mountains, the Chief of Badenoch, with his captives and bands, reached the shores of the ocean, and soon after the still unconscious Angus and Isabel were conveyed to the interior of Rothellan Castle. At length when the youthful knight was restored to sensibility, he found himself upon the highest point of the rock, and gazing round, he with astonishment beheld a female form, beautiful as fancy could depicture, stationed upon a low terrace and watching him with a countenance in which might be portrayed the softest feelings of pity for the cruel destiny that awaited him. Her long flowing robes were agitated by the winds, her golden tresses waved sportively, and displayed the shape and transparent whiteness of her neck; her full, expressive eyes swam in tears of melting sensibility, and her soft-toned voice breathed forth the compassion of her gentle heart at beholding the unfortunate Angus thus thrown into the power of his enemies.

At length she approached, and blushing deeply, as her eyes met those of Angus Glenalvon, she said :—

"Droop not, good stranger, for my father will, I am sure, do all he can to soften the severity of the hard destiny it is your fate to endure; nor shall the care of Rosalind be wanting to heal the wounds which you have received in this night's conflict."

"Your father, fair girl;" exclaimed the startled Angus, in a fit of surprise; "is it possible then that one so fair can belong to a race so merciless and cruel as is he who has brought me a captive to this fortress?"

"You wrong him, Sir Knight," cried Rosalind, in a tone of gentle rebuke, "for my father, though terrible in war, is kind and merciful to the feeble. I will entreat him to spare your life should it be forfeited, and you shall yet have it to confess that you have wronged him by the words you just now uttered."

Angus was about to express the indignation of his soul, when a sentinel approached and said respectfully :—

"Pardon me, Lady Rosalind, but it is my duty to bid you retire from the terrace, for your father approaches and I have received orders to convey the prisoner to his dungeon."

"It is impossible my father can be so unjust," exclaimed the maiden, "for this knight, though unfortunately a captive, is no criminal that he should be thus harshly treated. He is unfortunate and commands our respect and commiseration."

"Nay," interrupted Angus, "I am in the hands of my enemy, and therefore look not either for favour or mercy from him; already have I suffered deeply from the wrongs he has inflicted upon my family, and I would rather perish than owe my life to one I have so much reason to execrate."

"Again do I say you wrong him," answered Rosalind; "I, therefore, pray you tell me your name that I may obtain that respectful treatment which you no doubt have a right to demand. And you, my friend," she continued, addressing herself to the sentinel, "will convey your charge to one of the chambers in the west tower where he will await the further commands of my father."

"That part of the castle is never used for prisoners," muttered the guard, and beckoning to one of his comrades he desired him to assist in removing the prisoner to his dungeon.

"Aye," exclaimed Angus Glenalvon, haughtily, "lead me to the dungeon, for I know my fate, and disdain to sue for mercy or justice to a tyrant that I loath and execrate. The son of the wronged Glenalvon will never stoop to beg for favour from the murderer of his parents."

"The murderer!" cried the horror-struck girl, but ere she could repeat the question, Angus turned to follow his guards, exclaiming tenderly:

"Farewell, sweet lady; I thank thy gentle commiseration, though it cannot soften the agonizing sorrows of my soul, or avert the assassin's dagger, which has already drank the blood of the innocent, and is again uplifted to slay the offspring of those whom he has destroyed in his ruthless hatred. I must fall the victim of remorseless rancour, but my curses shall descend upon my assassin and embitter the remainder of his days."

Angus could utter no more for he was now violently dragged from the spot by his guard who forced him through the portal towards a long flight of steps that led towards the dungeon to which he had been doomed. Rosalind heaved a pitying sigh for the sufferings of the captive, and retired for the first time in her life, seriously unhappy and discontented with all around her.

In the solitude of her chamber she continued to ponder on the late occurrences, for she could think of nothing but of the youthful hero who had appeared before her under such afflicting circumstances, and whose doom seemed to be sealed by the remorseless hatred of her father. Restless, pensive, and eager to learn more concerning his fate, she had thrice dismissed her attendant to make inquiries, but the accounts she received were varied and unsatisfactory, and all she could gather was, that the youthful stranger had been placed in close confinement in one of the secret dungeons beneath the foundation of the castle, and her heart trembled and sickened as all hope seemed to be thus cut off for ever. She, however, resolved to make an effort for his rescue, by imploring the mercy of her father towards one whose sad misfortune it was to incur his deadly rage.

Light of foot as hope itself, and deceiving herself with an expectation of success, she descended the stone gallery, and without difficulty reached the chamber usually occupied by her father. She had not seen him for many months, and his features she now thought had, during that interval, acquired a fiercer and more reckless character. She had ever feared him and shrunk from his frowns, but now she could not resist the tremor which agitated her whole frame lest the purpose of her visit should be frustrated, even at the moment when she had most expected to meet with success.

With stern, forbidding silence, the Chief of Badenoch listened to her earnest petition, and having heard her to an end, he bade her, as she feared his wrath, to retire, nor presume again to tempt the consequences of his severe displeasure. Alarmed and struck dumb by the stern severity of his manner, she dared not repeat her request, but hastening from the presence of the frowning chief to the refuge of her own chamber, threw herself into the arms of her faithful nurse, and wept her disappointment, as she thought upon the harshness with which she had been dismissed from the presence of her father.

Till now she had never ventured to oppose the vindictive passions of the Chief of Badenoch, and therefore had never experienced the rage which was so frequently exhibited towards others with whom he came in contact. Now, however, she saw how little influence she possessed over him, and her heart sank with apprehension for the unfortunate youth whose fate seemed to have been resolved upon. Angus was, in fact, the first congenial being, of either sex, that she had ever seen, and the impression his appearance had implanted upon her heart was fervent and indelible.

Katherine, the good old nurse, to whom Rosalind related all that had passed, listened with sorrowful attention to the narrative of her mistress, and sighed heavily as she exclaimed :

" Alas ! my lady, may the saints be his protectors, for if my lord be not merciful to him, his fate will, I fear, soon be decided by a doom that I tremble even to think upon."

" You know something then I suppose," said Rosalind, " that induces you to believe he will perish ?"

" Listen, dear daughter,' exclaimed the old woman, " while I relate some fearful events which occurred some few years ago, and which will serve to show how little ground there is to hope for mercy from your father. Alack! alack! 'tis a dismal tale, and if all I have heard whispered is true, my Lord Badenoch has much to answer for."

Rosalind listened with breathless attention, for the nurse was relating the fall of Glenalvon, and with indescribable horror she for the first time heard of deeds which, though but partially known to Katherine, were sadly confirmatory of the real character of the Chief of Badenoch. The unhappy girl could no longer doubt the extreme peril which threatened the life of Angus; and at length, dismissing her attendant, she gave way in solitude to the afflicting thoughts which she in vain endeavoured to subdue.

In the meantime the vindictive Chief of Badenoch was occupied in devising his schemes for the accomplishment of that vengeance which he darkly meditated. To destroy Angus Glenalvon was now his firm determination; for should he suffer him to live, it was possible he might find means to escape, and, in the event of that happening, the foul enormities of his former wrongs against his captive's parents might find a future avenger, from whose wrath there would be no escape. Yet, on the other hand, should it be known to the world that Angus, the son of Glenalvon, was still alive and in his power, he might have to dread the alternative of a public scrutiny into his conduct. But these doubts soon gave way to others that were scarcely less perplexing, and at length a decision, fatal to the life of his victim, was determined on, and be the consequences what they might, he was resolved no longer to endure the suspense which at present tortured him.

We must now return to the Princess Isabel, who passed the solitary hours of her first day's captivity in a distraction of mind not to be described; for, in addition to her own misfortunes, was now added the terrible doubt whether Angus had not already fallen beneath the hatred of an implacable enemy, nor could she gain any certain intelligence that might confirm or dissipate the fears with which she was distracted.

Herself a prisoner, beyond all hope of ever being restored to liberty, and her future destiny involved in mystery, she trembled to reflect on the approaching event, and in vain strove to fortify her heart against the evils which she foresaw awaited her. She was now alone, for her attendant, Marianne, had been absent for some time, and even that circumstance served in no little degree to increase the despondency that afflicted her. At length, however, Marianne returned, and with looks full of terror, exclaimed:—

"Oh, my dear lady, what will become of us? I have just heard that Sir Angus is still alive, but one of the fierce men that belong to this castle has told me he is a prisoner, and confined somewhere in a deep dungeon among the caverns of the rock upon which this place is built."

"He lives then!" cried Isabel, in a tone of grateful surprise.

"Oh, yes, my lady, he still lives, to be sure," answered Marianne, "but, then, who shall say how long he will be permitted to do so now that he is unable to help himself?"

"Alas! I have myself feared the worst," sighed the princess, "and my worst anticipations are, perhaps, about to be realized."

"The man I have spoken to," continued Marianne, "says he will never come out of his dungeon alive; and then he shook his head so significantly, and shrugged up his shoulders in such a fashion, that though he didn't say much, could leave very little doubt that there's everything to fear from the violence of the terrible chief of this castle."

"Peace, girl, and torment me no more with these words of evil omen," cried Isabel, in an agony of terror. "Do not, I implore you, deprive me of all hope, for while I know my beloved brother still lives, I would fain cherish a thought that he may survive the peril that threatens him."

" Your *brother*, my lady!" exclaimed Marianne, with surprise.

" Yes, girl," answered the princess, scarcely conscious of what she uttered ; " he is most dear to me, and whilst life lasts I shall never cease to regard him with tenderness and affection. His imprisonment in the castle affords me more grief than do my own troubles, for though I have every reason to fear the Chief of Badenoch, yet for the present, at least, I believe he does not meditate taking away my life."

" That just reminds me, my lady," exclaimed Marianne, " that I have been charged to bring you a message."

" A message to me !" cried the Princess Isabel, with surprise ; " and from whom, I pray you ?"

" From the chief himself," answered the attendant. " As I was crossing the gallery to join the corridor which leads to this chamber, his lordship suddenly came out of an opposite doorway, and seizing my arm, bade me, with a frown, acquaint you that he desired to see you without delay."

" And what did you tell him ?" asked Isabel.

" That you are ill," answered the girl, " and will not see any one till you have quite recovered."

" Did he seem satisfied with that ?"

" Not at all, my lady," replied Marianne, " for he frowned terribly, and I could see by his looks that he was getting into a towering passion."

" What answer did he make ?"

" Not a very civil one, you may be sure," replied Marianne. " 'Hence to your lady,' he said, 'and tell her that matters of great import demand an immediate interview between us, and that she must admit me to her apartment without delay.' Then letting me go, I ran from his presence, frightened enough, for I could not help thinking he must be Satan himself, and I trembled from head to foot lest he should take it in his head to follow me."

" He is, indeed, a man of terror," cried Isabel, shuddering.

" Oh ! you would say so, my lady, if you had seen as much of him as I have," answered the attendant; " and then to think of the strange manner we were conveyed up here to a place so solitary and remote, so full of armed men, or captives, and, as I heard from one of the pages, oftentimes the scene of strange frightful sights, witnessed at midnight, and of dreadful deeds and secret murders, perpetrated amongst the caverns, that nobody knows anything about, enough, as the youth says, to scare the senses out of one. I'm sure I shall never enjoy a moment's rest here ; and when I go to bed of a night, I shall fancy I see ten thousand ghosts and goblins dance in the chamber. Oh ! that I was but once more in the lowliest hovel of Glenroy, for never can I know happiness in this terrible abode of crime."

Lady Isabel was reclining upon her couch, too deeply absorbed in her own sorrows to attend to the loquacity of Marianne. The dreadful injury her frame had sustained from the strong effects of the subtle potion she had drunk left her almost powerless to sustain the additional misfortunes with which she was threatened. It was only in this reduced state that, as the twilight darkened into night, the gigantic figure of the dreaded Chief of Badenoch entered her chamber.

Isabel shuddered, and felt her soul recoil at thus again beholding the destroyer of her own and Angus Glenavon's peace, and the murderer of his unfortunate parents. A foe so deadly and so hardened in the practice of every enormity of guilt, so determined, and so soon discovered, left her without a doubt as to the dangers of her situation ; and when thus she silently regarded him, and thought on the probable fate of Angus, her heart sickened with the fearful presage that they were now for ever sundered, and tears of anguish were fast gathering in her eyes, when pride came to her aid, and she sufficiently commanded her emotions to suppress

them for the present. At length the Chief of Badenoch spoke, but on this occasion he did it with more gentleness than he was accustomed to observe :—

" I have come, Lady Isabel," he said, " to hear from your own lips what course you mean to adopt with respect to the propositions I have already made. Your destiny is in your own hands, and I hope you will not urge me to an act of violence, when by a single word you can make me your friend."

" My lord," answered Isabel, firmly, " it were needless to dwell upon the past, or to repeat the dreadful occurrences I have so fatally been a witness of. Those deeds of horror and outrage, which I now forbear to repeat, will receive their punishment hereafter, and to heaven's eternal justice I bequeath them. I seek no favour, my lord, but such as you have no just title to withhold."

" What is it you would ask of me ?" he demanded.

" That you suffer me instantly to depart," she replied, " and rely upon the assurance I give you, that I will pledge myself never to make known those events, the discovery of which you have so much reason to dread. But if I am longer detained here against my will, I shall, when released from your hands, consider myself no longer bound to secrecy, but will pursue such measures as may draw on the assassins of the venerable Earl of Glenroy the just punishment their horrible crimes demand."

" The power," he replied, " which made you my prisoner, will be sufficient to keep you here in safety. That, at least, you should have learnt in the course of your brief stay here, and, also, how vain it would be to oppose a destiny that no earthly aid can possibly avert."

" You mistake, my lord," she replied, " or, at least, seem to forget that I am not destitute of powerful friends who will not fail to punish your conduct towards me ; nor is my father, though basely plundered of his for-

No. 26

tune and high honours, without the means of avenging the captivity I am at present forced to endure. You will, therefore, do well to reflect on the danger to yourself in persisting to keep me here, since I was a witness of the horrid deed for which your life may hereafter be made responsible."

The Chief of Badenoch started back aghast, and a dark frown instantly passed over his countenance. He bent his angry eye upon Marianne, who, at Isabel's request, had remained in the room, and, pointing towards the door, motioned for her to depart.

" Leave us, girl !" he exclaimed, fiercely, " and dare not to return again until after I have taken my departure."

Marianne, however, was not to be thus intimidated by the threats of the imperious chief; but perceiving that it was the wish of Lady Isabel, she remained firmly where she was. Badenoch frowned more furiously, and bit his nether lip with ill-concealed rage, as he continued to address himself to his unfortunate captive.

" It would have been well for your peace, my lady, had no curiosity tempted you to pry into the hidden deeds of him who, by that error, is now become the disposer of your liberty, and even of your life. But since the past is yours to ponder o'er, let its acts teach you how terrible can be the hatred of the Chief of Badenoch when aroused, and the necessity of submission, when to resist is only to endanger your own security."

" Why do you still persecute me thus," she cried, " when you know how impossible it is that I can ever regard you with any other feeling than abhorrence and disgust ?"

" Lady Isabel," he exclaimed, " you have long been the prize upon which my heart is set, and it was not to secure your silence alone that you were brought hither from the castle of Glenroy. Nay, frown not upon me, for your anger cannot turn me from the object I have been at so much pains to accomplish, and which nothing shall now prevent."

" Have you no mercy," she demanded, " for one who is helpless and in your power ?"

" In Badenoch," he replied, " you will find no whining boyish lover—no Morton, whom a look could awe into silence and submission. In vain may you hope to elude my purpose—in vain with scorn reject me, for still will I assail thee with my love, nor cease my importunities till persuasion or force compel thee to accept my terms."

" And yet," she replied, " you may find that I am not so utterly at your mercy as you imagine."

" It is in vain to look for assistance now," exclaimed the Chief of Badenoch, " and I, therefore, throw off the useless mask for ever. And while my lips avow the deeds my soul has and can still execute, let them tell thee also that I glory in my guilt, and will continue in my pursuit till you have consented to become mine for ever. With resolution to execute the thought which inclination prompts and love inspires, my fair captive will soon learn to reconcile herself to her destiny, and then, by according to me her love, may secure her own future tranquillity and safety ; and, as the wife of the Chief of Badenoch, again be released from that bondage which she must endure till she deigns to adopt the only means that can liberate her from a confinement that must soon grow irksome."

" Leave me," exclaimed Lady Isabel, " and dare no longer to insult me with your hateful presence !"

" Say that you will think seriously upon this subject," he replied, " and I will then leave you for a time. You shall be my wife, Lady Isabel, and be this the pledge of future amity between us."

As he spoke thus, he seized her hand and pressed it to his lips ere she had power to resist him.

"Away, my lord," exclaimed the indignant girl, "and dare no more to enter the presence of one who never can forget the crimes of which you have been guilty."

"Till to-morrow, Lady Isabel, I will bid you farewell," he replied. "I leave you to reflect on my speech, and, as you value your own happiness, yield to the wishes I have so openly given utterance to. Remember my words, and it will be your own fault if, at our next interview, you are not restored to liberty and happiness."

He then hastily quitted the chamber, but the increasing darkness of night obscured the deep malignant traces of cruelty and baleful resolution that lowered on his gloomy features, and the awe-struck Isabel, transfixed with horror and amazement, remarked not the deadly lurking malice that dwelt upon his countenance during this conversation; for the openly avowed purpose for which she had been ensnared, left her no other faculty unoccupied than the dreadful certainty of hopeless wretchedness and despair. At length, with a transport of agony, she wildly clasped her hands upon her bosom, as in anguished tones she uttered,—

"Merciful Heaven! am I indeed so lost that not a hope is left me! Must I indeed become the wife of a murderer—of him whose relentless hatred destroyed the noble race of Glenalvon, and has driven forth the hapless heirs to become wanderers, whilst he triumphs in the villany that has been but too successfully accomplished?"

"My dear, dear lady," cried Marianne, with intense anxiety, "do not thus utterly despair, for though things have come to a bad pass, something may yet happen to amend them. Surely, when all is considered, your highness would not rather die than live."

"To live," answered Isabel, mournfully, "when life becomes valueless and hateful, is to drag on in hopeless misery a galling chain of existence, torturing to myself and all that approach me."

"But you surely will not think of becoming the wife of that dreadful man?" cried Marianne.

"No," replied Isabel, "never shall my fate link its eternal welfare with that of a being so hateful as the Chief of Badenoch. For my father's sake I will yet repel with courage whatever trials may await my safety, and the dear hope that we may again meet in peace hereafter, shall stimulate my heart to fortitude, and my spirit to resistance. For the sake of Angus, too, I will reject the offers that have been made by this tyrant chief, and perhaps the time may yet come when both of us will be rewarded for the heavy trials we are at present compelled to endure."

The affection Marianne had conceived for the princess had become a source of the greatest comfort to the latter, for in a place so full of lurking dangers, and remote from every connecting tie, Isabel's fate would perhaps have been less tolerable, without the attentions of a person whom accident and the beauty of her appearance had first attracted, and misfortune rendered mutual in its cause, had now completely confirmed.

Marianne's heart was really affectionate, and when compelled by the lawless power of Badenoch to share the imprisonment of the devoted captive, she had watched over her with an interest and care which, though Isabel was insensible of, had much contributed to alleviate her former forlorn condition, the long continuance of which was not only designed to stagnate every after recollection of the dreadful deeds she had witnessed, but also to render her an easy prey to his arts; for Badenoch was aware that a female of her illustrious rank and character would not want defenders if she was able to make known her situation.

Thus the horrible potion she had drunk, and which Badenoch hoped had had the desired effect, was doubly the means of insuring him success; and though the screams of Marianne, on discovering the persons of Angus and his attendants, had at first excited his fears, and afterwards harrowed up his soul with conscious dread, yet he was soon recalled to the accustomed ferocity of his nature, and with a demoniac joy, he triumphed in the double conquest chance had thus conspired to give him, for, once secured within the impregnable fortress, there was no chance that his victims would ever have it in their power to escape. Here he and his band resorted, for it was a place of inaccessible strength and security, and thus became the receptacle of the very refuse of mankind, who had for many years with sullen satisfaction submitted to the Chief of Badenoch, beneath whose protection they were concealed from the just vengeance their former atrocities had merited. Hardened to all sense of shame or remorse, they ever delighted in deeds of violence, and the practice of every species of cruelty to their fellow men, and were only to be satisfied when employed in acts of rapine, blood, and massacre ; savage propensities which their no less ferocious leader never denied them.

The fortress and its rock-hewn ramparts stretched entirely over the base of the cliff, awing the surrounding islands, on which it proudly looked down in towering altitude. Its terrific and gloomily buried chambers, vaulted within the rock itself, were of immense number and spacious extent. Its winding galleries and long vistas had each a dismal and terrific aspect, and Marianne feared to traverse alone their obscure and dark-shaded gloom ; nor, indeed, was she permitted to do so, or to pass further than the adjoining corridor, that led to the chambers occupied by the Lady Isabel. At the end of this gallery a sentinel paraded, and to him Marianne was directed to make known whatever demands were necessary to be supplied ; and she soon found that her mistress was indeed a prisoner, for beyond the place she was prohibited to pass.

The departure of Badenoch left Isabel to her own saddened reflections and bitter regrets. Marianne, as the night advanced, often trembled and turned pale, but did not venture to break in upon the meditations of her mistress, who, however, worn with long fatigue, found herself unable to resist the attacks of sleep, and having been assured by Marianne that the doors of both chambers were secured, she dismissed her attendant to her couch, and herself, after a fervent prayer to Heaven for protection, sunk with reluctance upon her pillow, and after long watching, yielded her exhausted frame to that repose which the recent fatigue and exhaustion she had undergone rendered imperatively necessary.

CHAPTER XXXVI.

" How vast the battlements
That here, in frowning majesty, surmount
The lashing waters of yon raging sea.
Here crime and rude disorder reign supreme,
And virtue scarce knows entrance."

THE BONDSMAN.

At an early hour on the following morning the Princess Isabel quitted her couch with a mind somewhat more calm than it had been of the preceding day. Her spirits now began to recover from the stupifying effects of the late horrible occurrences, and once more restored to the elasticity and firmness of her character, she ceased to weep despairingly, and with rising energy prepared her mind for the worst that evil fortune could inflict.

She was, however, convinced that she had but too much cause to dread the dangers of that situation into which she had been betrayed ; for a cha-

-racter such as Badenoch's, at once cruel, subtle, and relentless, and stained with crimes, which none but the most hardened in guilt could have perpetrated, was a foe not easily vanquished, whose usurped power to oppress and torture his victims was protected from all human appeal or retribution, whilst defended in the commission of his enormities by legions of fierce and savage minions, all linked in bonds at once adverse to the rights of justice, and the devoted instruments of destruction to every moral goodness, and every social and endearing tie.

But the soul of Isabel, thus prepared and guarded, taught her the reliance she might place in her own firmness; nor had she ever sunk under the difficult and afflictive circumstances that had so unexpectedly overwhelmed her. She had been taught the necessity of supporting with becoming dignity the consequence which was attached to her high descent, so that she felt at once all that was due to a virtuous superiority, but disdained the littleness which plumed itself only in the chance of possession of splendid descent, yet wanting every other attribute to render itself really noble and worthy of the world's esteem.

The knowledge that Angus Glenalvon was the prisoner of his mortal foe, was to her even more afflicting than the tyranny which had caused her own captivity; for though she had at first despaired, yet with returning calmness of mind she was enabled rightly to reflect that Badenoch would be fearful and cautious not to proceed to any acts of further violence against her, since her near affinity to the heroic monarch of Scotland must be a present security from any dark project he might else have formed against her life.

This consideration had served greatly to tranquillize the terrible apprehensions which the bold and insolent professions of his hateful love had the night before so fearfully aroused. She reflected also that, as she had so wonderfully become acquainted with Badenoch's most fatal secrets, she was possessed of a power to awe him from any dreadful act his rancorous malice might form against Angus Glenalvon; since, as he knew she was well informed of his hatred, he would not dare to practice against the life of the already too deeply-injured youth, so long as the terror of its discovery must rest in herself, who, when again released from his power, would become ultimately his accuser, and the avenger of the enormous deeds of violence of which he had been guilty.

These reflections were somewhat consoling, and Isabel no longer dwelt with dread or horror on her captivity, but now resolved to exert all her energy, and to adopt any course that might appear most likely to rescue herself and Angus from the restraint which at present held them.

In the hope of chasing away the thoughts which had been too long indulged, she rose from her seat, and opening the door of her apartment, found herself in another room of larger dimensions, and furnished in a style of greater magnificence. Its walls were dark wainscot, grotesquely carved with ponderous figures of various forms and shapes. The roof was supported by lofty pillars of oak, the basements of which were highly ornamented. The whole of this extensive apartment was lighted by one large window at the further end, near which she beheld a small lyre, which, it appeared, had recently been left there. She passed her fingers over the strings, and for a few moments diverted the melancholy of her mind by the dulcet notes which her skill in music enabled her to produce.

The prospect from the window was sublimely grand, but not much diver-sified, for its only view was the ever restless ocean, bounded by an horizon of sky and water. Turning from this, she perceived near the window recess a small empannelled door; it unfastened to her touch, and passing onwards, she observed a few stone steps which wound in a spiral ascent upwards, and mounting them, found herself on the summit of the battlements, from whence was obtained a magnificent and widely-extended view. Isabel stood transfixed for a few moments in speechless amazement as she gazed fearfully downwards upon the deep fathomless abyss below, and paused in wonder to observe the stupendous scenery which on every side met her view.

The account given by Marianne of the rock on which the castle stood, was nearly correct :—This solitary, insular crag, romantically embosomed on every side by the ocean, rose into a steep and alpine precipice, unconnected with any land and verdure, except on the northern side, where only a few hardy yews shed forth their dingy foliage. No other part showed signs of vegitation, save the lower steeps, amidst whose broken fissures the sea moss, and other long straggling aquatic plants hung down the almost perpendicular sides of the rock, or scantily fringed the extreme edge of the lofty summit, of which the castle ramparts were composed.

The interior of this aerial structure was scooped, as it were, out of the middle of its ridgy platform, and reared with its rocky granite, spread its dark frowning bulwark over the whole of its circumference, looking haughty defiance, and proud sovereignity on the ocean, which rolled its billows beneath.

The edifice was but slightly injured by time, though much blackened by its long inflections, and had alike withstood the attacks of centuries and the attempts of hostile armies to subdue it. Its lofty acclivities, perpendicular to their summits, were many a fathom above the level of the ocean, and the prospect from its loftiest pinnacles was magnificent in the extreme.

Isabel, at first, could not forbear shuddering, and she clung fast to the battlements, till by degrees she became assured of the certainty that she had no danger to apprehend. Then, with feelings impressed with awe and solemnity, such as scenes so sublimely grand must ever awaken in the mind, she ventured to gaze over the tremendous steeps, and to look around her with mingled sensations of regret and admiration. The islands of the west displayed a rich diversified scenery, rising in rocky heights, and between which the scarcely ruffled sea glittered brightly in the sunbeams. Tears of tender recollection started to her eyes as she made an effort to distinguish the loved venerable shades of Isna's sacred groves, amidst whose tranquil seclusion she had passed some of the first and happier portions of her life, and had received the earliest impressions of that religion which now enabled her to endure with patience the misfortunes which threatened her future happiness.

"Dear, beloved scene of my heart's fondest memory," she exclaimed, fervently, as her eye rested upon the isle she had so anxiously sought "my fancy hails and embodies thy blessed abode, though distance thus separates me from thee ! Alas ! how painfully pleasing it is even to trace thy remote solitudes, where so oft, in happy security and buoyant youthful joy, I have wandered delighted amidst thy awful glooms, and solemn painted aisles, happy in an unconscious disregard of every worldly snare or danger to my repose, and of spirits as elastic as the most ardent hope could render them. And now, sad reverse! how changed and gloomy is the scene I look upon! How is the morning of my youthful anticipations blighted, and every blossom blasted in its opening bud. Thy venerable and hallowed towers, once my home and secure refuge from every ill, are now far beyond my reach ; and my heart, lacerated with misfortune, and jarred with dread of apprehended evil, yearns vainly with fond regret towards the spot endeared to it first affections. Yet why do I give way to thoughts which do but add to the sorrows I have to contend against ? For the present I am a captive in the hands of a harsh inhuman tyrant, and unless Heaven aids me, the remainder of my days must be passed in this gloomy fortress, a prey to the bitter griefs which the memory of my wrongs must ever give rise to."

Isabel sighed bitterly at the afflicting recollection of past felicity, as she compared it with the cruel reverse which had now befallen her, and her heart became indignant at the tyranny to which she was compelled to submit. Unable to bear the cruel contrast of such painful retrospections, arising from the objects which had thus occupied her mind, she precipitately quitted the battlements, and again retired to her prison chamber.

Here she found Marianne, who, during her absence, had prepared the morning's repast, and Isabel having sparingly partaken of the meal, took up her lute, and returned to the melancholy employing forth those songs of sorrow which circumstances now reminded her of. Whilst she was thus occupied, the castellan entered the room, and great was the surprise of the old man at discovering that she could find even this solace amidst the afflicting trials it was her hard lot to endure. In his admiration at the firmness she displayed, he threw himself at her feet, and declared his readiness to do all in his power to render her present situation as comfortable as possible.

"Rise, my good old man," exclaimed Isabel, "and accept the thanks of one who has nothing but gratitude to offer for the kindness you have expressed in my behalf. Should I, however, live to see happier days, I trust it will be in my power to reward those who have pitied me in my misfortunes."

"I do indeed pity you, my lady," answered the castellan, "but at present have it not in my power to offer you any effectual aid. My master is cruel and vindictive, and my purpose in now visiting you is to encourage you to resistance, since it is likely that in a short time your friends will attempt your rescue from this fortress."

"Heaven grant it may be so," cried the princess, "though much I fear all efforts to aid me will be made in vain. The Chief of Badenoch is as vindictive as he is cruel, and never whilst life remains will he suffer me to be torn from the grasp with which he holds me in bondage."

"Give not way to despair, lady," exclaimed the old man, "for the deeds of evil men cannot endure for ever, and something tells me that a period of your sufferings is fast approaching, and I think my lord himself is rather afraid of it, for orders have been given to put every part of the castle in a state of defence, and that looks if he expects an attack to be made very shortly."

"And why should I wish such an effort to be made," cried the Princess Isabel, "when I know that the castle is considered impregnable, and that consequently my friends will be exposing themselves to danger without benefit to myself? Besides, King Bruce requires the aid of all who are able to bear arms, and why, therefore, should they waste their time in a vain effort to release me from captivity?"

"It is your father, I believe, that will lead them on," replied the old man, "and as he knows more about this fortress than anybody else, it is likely he may succeed in forcing an entrance into it. At any rate he has my good wishes in his favour, and should have my assistance if I could only find an opportunity of affording it."

"You can perhaps serve our cause better," exclaimed Isabel, "by carrying a letter from me to my friends."

"That I'm afraid will be impossible," answered the castellan, "for I am suspected of having no great liking for the Chief of Badenoch, and for some time past I have been forbidden to quit the castle on pain of death. Not but what I would risk anything to serve your ladyship, but as it seems you have not many friends in the place besides myself, it would be better that I should be at hand in case of any sudden emergency arising."

" Know you of another prisoner," asked Isabel, " who was brought into the castle when I was ?"

" You mean the young knight, Angus Glenalvon ?"

" I do."

" He is in one of the dungeons, I believe," replied the castellan, " and I fear his life is in danger."

" I fear so too," sighed our heroine ; " but know you whether any orders have yet been given respecting his destiny ?"

" Everything upon that subject is kept a profound secret, my lady," answered the old man. " I, however, know that the Chief of Badenoch regards him with the utmost hatred, and for that reason I'm afraid he will not lose so favourable an opportunity to wreak his vengeance upon him."

" May Heaven avert so diabolical an act !" cried Isabel, shuddering with horror. " Angus Glenalvon has already suffered much from the unrelenting tyranny of his oppressor, and fearfully would he have retaliated those injuries, had he not unfortunately fallen into the hands of the Chief of Badenoch, through his generous interference in my behalf."

" Poor youth !" exclaimed the castellan ; " his is indeed a hard destiny, for there seems little chance for him now that he has unfortunately fallen into the hands of his enemy."

" But you say the castle will shortly be attacked," cried the princess, " and in that case he may yet be snatched from the dreadful destiny with which he is threatened."

" That, I am afraid, is hardly likely," answered the old man, " for no sooner will my lord see his danger, than he will pronounce sentence of death against young Glenalvon, in order to prevent all possibility of his rescue."

" Alas !" cried the princess, " then the efforts which are making to snatch me from the den of horrors, will hasten the death of him for whom I would willingly sacrifice my existence."

" I fear there is no help in for it," he replied, " for the chief is terrible in his wrath, and hating young Glenalvon as he does, he will not hesitate for a moment to carry out his deadly intentions. You, however, may be saved, because he still has hopes of making you his wife, and a skiff has been ordered to be in readiness to convey you away to another of his castles, should it appear that the enemy is likely to gain possession of this fortress."

" There is yet one resource left, even in the worst extremity," said the Princess Isabel, firmly. " I have taken care to arm myself with a dagger, and rather then suffer myself to be dragged from hence by the Chief of Badenoch, I will bury the weapon in my heart, and thus rid myself of a life that has now become a burden to me."

" Be not too precipitate in the commission of such an act," exclaimed the castellan, " for even in the moment of your utmost need, Heaven may work your deliverance from the hands of your enemies. Your friends are powerful and numerous, and strong as this place is, it may yet yield to the force with which they will attack it. But I must remain here no longer, my lady, lest my absence should be discovered, for should it be known that I have visited you, suspicions would be formed of the object that brought me, and thus all hope of your rescue might be for ever cut off. So, farewell, and remember that your chief safety consists in the firmness with which you await coming events."

The old man disappeared as he uttered these words, and Isabel snatch-

ing up the lute which he had put aside, again attempted to forget her miseries in the sweet melody she produced. Marianne watched her for some few seconds in silence, and then suddenly exclaimed,—

"Ah! my lady, that instrument was last played on, I suppose, by Lady Badenoch, for these were her very rooms, as I have heard one of the pages say, and in yonder apartment, I think he said, she died; and a happy release it must have been for her, poor soul! to get away from such a monster of iniquity as her husband seems to be. Ah! could we but once manage to get on the outside of this horrible place, nothing in the world should ever tempt me to come back to it again."

"It is, indeed, a hard destiny to be compelled to remain here," sighed Isabel, "and the more particularly so as there appears to be but few to whom I can look for kindness."

"Very few, my lady," answered the attendant; "to be sure there's the sentinel that keeps watch to prevent you from escaping, is tolerably civil and talkative whenever he and I meet together, and, to speak the truth, he seems rather to have taken a liking to me, which is more than I can say in return just at present."

"Has he ever spoken to you about me?" asked Isabel.

"Why, he always seems to avoid the subject as much as possible," answered Marianne; "but I have taken care to tell him a piece of my mind about matters, and that I thought it no better than treason to force your highness from your own castle—as Glenroy must have been if everybody had their rights—and thus burying us both alive in this dreadful place. And who knows if some stormy night or other the sea may not rise up through the subterranean caverns and overwhelm us all, or, perhaps, swallow up even the whole rock itself."

"Peace, girl!" cried the Princess Isabel, "and let us now speak on a

No. 27

subject of more importance to us both. You spoke just now about the sentinel, and a thought has struck' me, that upon advantageous terms being offered he might be induced to assist in our escape."

"Why, I don't know much about that, my lady," answered Marianne; "because there is danger of his being punished with death, if it should happen to be discovered that he is engaged in a plot against his master."

"But he may assist us without the circumstances becoming known," returned Isabel. "Tell him, girl, from me, that should he consent to undertake our release from this place, I will reward him to the utmost extent of his desires."

"Well, there's something in that, to be sure," exclaimed the attendant, "and I don't know but he may be prevailed upon to give us his assistance upon such terms as those. He seems to be of rather a greedy disposition, and knowing as he does that, in the event of our escape, you will have it in your power to reward him with a large sum of money, he may be induced to lend us a helping hand. But then he may chance to think of the danger and hazard of such an undertaking, and if that should have the effect of frightening him, we shall be doomed to remain prisoners here for the rest of our lives."

"At least, Marianne, the attempt must be made," exclaimed the princess, "for without the trial we may chance to lose an opportunity of escaping from the power of the haughty Chief of Badenoch."

"But has your highness considered the dangers we may be exposed to, even if we should contrive to get beyond the walls of the castle?" asked Marianne.

"I have," she replied, "and am resolved to undergo every hardship and peril rather than remain here any longer a voluntary captive. From the malice of my enemy I have everything to dread, and, therefore, no time must be lost in seeking to extricate myself from his power."

"You wish me then, my lady, to sound him upon this subject?" said the girl.

"I do," replied Isabel; "but in speaking to the sentinel, you must be cautious not to trust him with too much confidence till assured that he has not only the power but the will to assist me."

"That you may depend on," replied Marianne; "but how am I to convince him that his services will meet with such a reward as he will expect?"

"Give him this purse of gold," said the princess, "as a pledge of my intention to reward him more liberally should he be inclined to assist me. And most of all, good Marianne, beseech him, if possible, to learn the fate of Angus Glenalvon, without whose freedom my own cannot with safety or pleasure to myself be achieved."

Marianne took the purse which had been offered her, and promising to do the best she could towards bribing the man, she hurried away full of hope and joyful anticipation as to the result of her attempt.

CHAPTER XXXVII.

" Oh ! yet, ye dear, deluding vis'ons, stay !
Fond hopes of innocence and fancy born,
For you I'll cast these waking thoughts away,
For one wild dream of life's romantic morn."—LONGHORNE.

ISABEL, now no longer desirous to quit the precincts of her present apartments, since she was not denied the privilege of access to the outer battlements, resigned for the present her former design of penetrating the long corridors that led from her place of confinement to the more habitable portions of the castle. When Marianne left her, therefore, she threw over her head a long, thick folding veil that almost enveloped her figure, and once more ascended to the exterior of her prison, and continued with anxious gaze to look upon the distant heights of Scotland, whose rugged shores and lofty promontories, washed by the ever rolling waves, were traced with eager wishes by the hapless girl, as she frequently sighed for permission once more to tread the romantic and well known spots she gazed upon.

Towards another direction she beheld a towering rugged cliff, whose lofty brow, butting far over the gulf, nearly overlooked the vast isolated rock upon which stood the ancient Danish Watch Tower. As she gazed on its colossal battlements, Isabel little imagined that there Angus and his brother had lately lived in seclusion; for it was the headland point of Glenalvon, whose dark wooded mountains waved their pine-clad foliage along the straggling summits, embosoming the lower steeps that surround the rocky foundation of the tower's precipitous base with its thick mazy woods.

At such divisions of the granite where the craggy point of the headland gradually declined into a lesser altitude, Isabel could with perfect ease distinguish the verdure of inland pasturage, and now and then descry the smoke of a lowly cabin, perched midway on some inhospitable barren shelving of a lower promontory, whose beetling head hung threatingly over the humble roof of the hardy mountaineer, at once his shelter from the rude northern wintry blasts, yet the constant memorial of his dependant state.

"Ah!" sighed Isabel; "with even a habitation so desolate, and Angus and my beloved father for my constant companions, I could be contented and happy, nor repine at the scanty gift bestowed upon me by fortune, since in their loved society everything would be comprised that could render life a blessing to me. Ah! why did cruel fate ordain us to sustain the heavy burden of oppressive greatness, whose richest title is, at best, but splendid vassalage, and the aim of envied brightness for the tongue of calumny to point its malignant shafts against; and in the hour of depression and misfortune rewarded the prey of lawless, but too successful villany!"

Nor were these bitter feelings of Isabel without foundation. Stripped by the cruel hand of wanton power of that pre-eminence and regal dignity she was born to inherit, she had thus suddenly fallen from her high station; and by an event, as unforeseen as fatal, was become the victim of treachery and triumphant villany. And fearful, indeed, was the unavoidable doom that now awaited her; whilst at times not even all her fortitude and heroism could enable her to suppress the apprehended train of evils her reason sometimes conjured up. Frequently did she, with an almost foreboding conviction of impending misery, dwell on the too certain probability of her own and the ill-fated Angus Glenalvon's ruin. Every circumstance that occurred to her mind forbade the indulgence of hope; whilst only the strongest efforts of her mind could at times resist the growing phantasies of despair which her melancholy train of thoughts suggested.

She now reflected with trembling suspicion that her present thraldom was effected with such secresy and determined dispatch, that no trace, she feared, was left by which to lead to the discovery of her real condition. Catherine, her attached attendant, and, indeed, the only faithful servant the sudden downfall of her state had left her, was separated from her; for as the commissioners of King Edward, who had pursued her to the very gates of Stratheden Castle, had no right over any other than her own person, she had forbidden her favourite servant, as well from the affectionate wish of her heart to preserve her from the danger she was about to encounter, as from her illness, to share in her mistress's forlorn destiny; whilst her arrival and removal from Glenroy had been the result of a moment too sudden to preclude the possibility of insuring for herself any assistance in her defence or rescue in a place where she was soon convinced Badenoch had gained the most absolute and preremptory control.

The gulf, or strait, which parted the western point of Glenalvon from the rock on which she then stood, was a rapid whirlpool, in continual agitation, at all times dangerous to ford, though the distance between them was not greater than two or three hundred fathoms except where the shores of the first named island retired into deeply indented bays on its southern side.

Isabel in vain tried to trace an outline of the ridgy steeps of Craiglynn, the princely seat of her ancestors; but, though in a direct line, not the faintest shade was she able to distinguish, perhaps from the great haziness which had now spread over the intervening space. The bold stupendous mountains of the thickly scattered isles, upon whose lofty summits were seen many a frowning fortress, were the chief features that characterized the scene upon which she gazed with so many varying emotions. Our heroine sighed heavily as she thought of former happy times, and contrasted them with the misery it was her present lot to bear; yet her spirit was not entirely to be subdued, and reflecting how much adversity might yet be in store for her, she aroused herself to exertion, and resolved to awe her persecutor into respect by the firmness with which she could endure the tyranny he exercised against her.

The parapet whereon she stood was of long and irregular extent, often impeded by turrets which had been erected for the purposes of defence, and in other places overtopped with towers of greater magnitude than those which she had seen in the vicinity of her own apartments, but with which her's had no connection or communication whatever. Passing round as far as she could, she anxiously directed her gaze into the wide courts below, but they were filled with armed soldiers, whose fierce demeanour and savage ferocity of character were calculated to inspire her with renewed alarm, both for the safety of Angus Glenalvon and herself.

It was not till the fall of evening had rendered the smaller objects indistinct that she again ventured to approach the barbicans, for on one occasion she had been observed by a lonely sentinel, or rather, as his coat of mail seemed to declare him, an inferior officer, who, as he leaned on his battle spear over the rampart, had been some time watching her, as she was almost unconsciously gazing upon the prospect before her, and, though the visor of his helmet partly obscured his face, she could perceive that his attention had been attracted towards the spot where she stood, and that he made a slight motion as if with the intention of saluting her.

Uncertain whether this man might be the guard of whom Marianne had made so favourable a report, she scarcely knew whether to return his salutation or not. The circumstance, however, gave some slight hope that she was not without one friend in the castle, and as the man again looked up towards her, she slightly waved her handkerchief in token of recognition, and then instantly retired from the spot.

In the solitude of her own cheerless apartment Isabel remained for some time, for even Marianne was obscure, and the circumstance, slight as it was, gave rise to a feeling of uneasiness for which she found it impossible to account. At length, however, the attendant again made her appearance, and the princess, anxious to learn whether she was the bearer of good news, inquired what had occurred in the castle during the time that she had been away from her.

"Oh! my lady," replied Marianne, full of importance, "the whole castle is in a foment, and the garrison and men-at-arms are running about the wards and courts and armouries as if they were all mad together. I tried to question some of them as to the cause of so much bustle, but none of them thought proper to give me any explanation, and it's only by picking up a little here and there that I've been able to get at anything like the real truth of the matter."

"Keep me no longer in suspense, Marianne, I entreat you," cried the princess impatiently; "but, be the news good or bad, let me know it all without further delay."

"Well, then," exclaimed Marianne, "the old castellan was quite right in what he said about there being some fear lest the castle should be soon attacked by an enemy."

"Indeed!" cried Isabel, "and who is it, I pray you, that has taken upon himself the almost hopeless task of attacking the fierce Chief of Badenoch in his own stronghold?"

"No less a personage," answered the girl, "than King Robert of Scotland, who has already once more exalted his standard and struck terror to his foes."

"Alas!" sighed the princess, "then I fear he is but hurrying on the destruction his foes have meditated."

"I rather think, from what I can learn, that matters are not quite so bad as your highness imagines," answered Marrianne. "His army, no longer disheartened or weakened by the loss of numerous allies, are every day gaining ground and making a more determined stand against the enemy."

"But the English," replied Isabel, "will only become exasperated, and soon, I fear, they will send their legions to oppose our gallant monarch and crush the noble ardour that has excited the spirits of our brave countrymen to rescue their native land from slavery and debasement."

"I am in hopes matters will not come to so bad a pass as that, my lady," returned Marianne; "for the English king has begun to discover that our people are not to be conquered quite so easily as was at first thought, and his soldiers are growing tired of a war in which they seem likely to meet with nothing but defeat and disgrace."

It further appeared from the account given by Marianne, that confirmation had been received of the death of King Edward of England, at which time a summons came from his successor, inviting the Chief of Badenoch to join his forces to those of the new sovereign in opposition to the heroic Bruce, who had proved that he was not yet conquered, though fortune had not at present smiled upon his efforts to cast off the fetters with which it had been attempted to bind his country. It seemed, also, that the Chief of Badenoch was not well pleased at the message which had been sent to him, and with ill-dissembled unwillingness he was compelled to depart from his inaccessible fortress, ere the bold and lawless projects he had formed could be executed.

Isabel listened to the narrative of her attendant with some doubt, but deeming it prudent to remain silent upon the subject at present, she suddenly changed the conversation by inquiring whether she had seen the sentinel of whom they had spoken in their last conversation.

"I have, my lady."

"And does he seem favourable to my wishes?" asked the princess, "or am I still doomed to remain a helpless captive in the hands of my relentless enemy?"

"I believe, your highness, he may be trusted," answered Marianne, "though, of course, there's no telling how far we may believe a man that is employed against us."

" What said he to the proposition I charged you to make to him?" demanded Isabel.

" He was careful enough not to say anything that might afterwards get him into trouble," replied the attendant. " He, however, bade me say that if your ladyship will deign to admit him this night to your presence, he would propose such terms as perhaps may secure your escape from this place in the course of a very short time."

" What means he by proposing terms to me?" demanded the princess, doubtfully.

" That is more than I can undertake to explain," answered Marianne; " but, if it is your pleasure to give him an audience, he will be able to afford all the information your highness may require."

" Did you tell him," asked the princess, " that the reward should be commensurate to his services, and that he should find a secure refuge in the camp of Robert Bruce, who will not fail to heap honours upon him should he procure my escape from this hateful place of imprisonment?"

" I did, my lady."

" And did you also tell him how necessary it is that he should keep this affair a profound secret?"

" Yes," answered the attendant, " I told him all that, and he seemed quite to agree with me in everything. But still, he said, nothing could be done towards making arrangements for your escape without a previous interview to concert proper measures to ensure its success."

" And yet," cried the princess, " how do I know but I have revealed this important secret to one who may betray me to his vindictive master? This man has, doubtless, been long connected with his present associates, and there is therefore too much reason to fear that he will seek to find favour with his master by informing him of the hopes I have formed of effecting my escape from the fortress."

" And in my opinion it's very natural that you should have done so," replied Marianne, " and, as for the chief, who has thought proper to make you his prisoner, I should think even he must admit that you have a right to get away if you can."

" At all events the attempt shall be made," exclaimed the princess, in a tone of resolution; " here I am deprived of liberty, through the base stratagems of a detested tyrant, and if necessary my life shall be sacrificed in making an effort to extricate myself from the power of the Chief of Badenoch."

" Aye, my lady," answered the attendant, " anything is preferable to staying here, and so, with your permission, I'll go and tell the sentinel that it is your pleasure to see him at as early an hour as it may be convenient."

" Do so," returned the Princess Isabel, " and tell him that I shall remain here till he finds an opportunity of coming to me unseen. You will say, also, that I am willing to pay a liberal price for any service he may do me, and that his future advancement shall not be forgotten, should he contrive to take me in safety to the camp of our Scottish king."

Marianne once more retired, and the princess, with more confidence, began to indulge a hope that during the absence of Badenoch, not only her own, but Angus Glenalvon's liberty might perhaps be accomplished. The hope, feeble as it was, inspired her with more cheerfulness than she had for some time before, since an assurance had been given her, that in obtaining her own liberty, she should be enabled to give freedom to him to whom she felt her heart was indissolubly allied by mutual sentiments and endearing affections, over whose apprehended death she had despairingly mourned, and now deeply grieved for, as she dwelt with commiserating tenderness on the severity of his sufferings, and also on the unhappy circumstances posed, through the hatred of the Chief of Badenoch. But a faint beam of sunshine illumed the darkness she had been involved in, and she began to look forward with some slight degree of hope to the future.

CHAPTER XXXVIII.

" Her grave rebuke,
Severe in youthful beauty, added grace,
Invincible:—Abashed the tempter stood,
And felt how awful goodness is, and saw
Virtue in her shape, how lovely."

MILTON.

To the Princess Isabel, this evening had seemed longer than usual, and had been passed in restless reflection, for Marianne had been long absent, for the purpose of conducting the sentinel into her presence. The strictest caution was, however, necessary, lest his absence from his post should create alarm; for the jealous fears of Badenoch permitted him not to confide on any of his people, and almost every four hours the different watches were relieved by others, lest any should be tempted to desert his duty, or mislead his comrades. At length, however, Marianne appeared in the chamber, and said in a whisper :—

"He is come, my lady; I have been watching in the great corridor beyond your apartments, for the last hour, fearful lest I should betray either of us to a stranger; for the guard is often changed, and they wear the vizors over their faces when on duty, to prevent their being known when employed on their secret expeditions."

"Are you sure, then, that the one who has accompanied you here is the right person?" inquired the princess.

"Oh, yes, I'm quite sure about that," replied Marianne, "for he made the sign agreed upon between us, and is now here ready to obey your orders."

A soldier, habited only in a breastplate of armour, now entered the chamber. Isabel slightly bent her head to his salute, for she saw he was apparently the same person she had beheld from the battlements some little time previously. Marianne retired almost instantly from the apartment; when kneeling before the princess, the stranger threw up the vizor of his helmet, and as the lamp shone upon his features, she started back in dismay upon discovering that she stood in the presence of Lord Morton!

"Be not surprised," he exclaimed, "but deign to forgive the prostrate supplicant before you. Distracted for your loss,—hopeless of your regard, and convinced that my former violence and passionate conduct had robbed me of a chance of possessing your much covetted esteem, yet feeling myself still devoted eternally to adore the deeply-injured Isabel, and confess myself her slave for ever, my soul become at once torn with remorse for my past guilt, and my mind the seat of agony and despair."

"Let me hear no more of this, my lord," cried the princess, as soon as she could recover from the surprise and indignation his presence had excited. "Already have I learnt the hypocricy which governs your conduct, and yet you have now followed me as if to prove that all my former opinions of your baseness were but too well founded."

"You have wronged me by these thoughts," he exclaimed, "for love alone has urged me to the madness of which I have been guilty. I followed and arrived at Glenroy in time to be a witness of the mysterious manner in which you were betrayed from its towers; and to gain access to your presence, and become the guardian of your safety, if endangered, I become a volunteer in the troops of the Chief of Badenoch, and by the aid of a bribe, have gained an entrance here unknown to all, and my rank and person totally unsuspected."

"It had been better that you had left me to my fate," answered Isabel, "for never will I accept any assistance from one whom I so much despise as Lord Morton."

"Am I then still doomed to live without hope?" he asked in a tone that scarce concealed the rage that was rankling in his heart. "Can I expect no pardon from Lady Isabel, for those wrongs which were urged on by the potency of an unconquerable passion, and which I have in vain endeavoured to subdue?"

"My lord," answered the indignant girl, "I will not listen to the artifices with which you seek to conceal the villany that has added so much to my cup of misery. Your offered services I reject, as I do the pretended contrition with which you have endeavoured to deceive me, because your penitence has been assumed too evidently for the base purpose of ensuring a second time an intended victim to your purposes."

"Do you then believe me guilty of a falsehood?" he asked.

"At least, my lord," she replied, "I can place no confidence where I have once been so basely deceived. The motive which you say induced you to follow me to my place of imprisonment, your own words betray as selfish and designing, since you are already assured that there is not the shadow of a claim to my attention which can warrant a presumption of any nearer interest or connection between us."

"Am I still to be reproved," demanded Lord Morton, "when I have expressed my sorrow for the past?"

"Reproof from me were needless, for I cannot stoop to relate the numerous reasons I have for regarding you with scorn and detestation. I can forgive an injury when assured that it is sincerely repented, yet cannot dissemble that strong aversion which I have concealed, and which you are aware originated in your own violent conduct, and the treachery with which you betrayed my father's castle into the hands of a ruthless invader."

"These recollections of the past," he exclaimed, "can only excite my anger, without in any way serving your own cause. That I have acted blindly I admit, but surely my conduct has not been so bad that it may not be palliated by circumstances."

"My opinions in that respect can never be changed," cried the Princess Isabel, "for he who is capable of revolting from his allegiance to an injured sovereign, can challenge little confidence from man or woman; and I must cease to live ere I can forget that to Lord Morton's ingratitude and treachery the friend, father, benefactor, and guardian of his youth, now owes, perhaps, with his child, the ruin and destruction of a name that once stood amongst the most honoured in the country."

"Nay, you wrong me, Isabel."

"That is impossible, my lord," she replied, "and with the conviction in my mind of your utter worthlessness, and the humiliating recollection that to yourself only I am indebted for the oppressive calamity that has now befallen me, I can scarcely be expected to accept assistance from a being who has fallen beneath my contempt."

"Have you reflected," he sternly demanded, "on the consequences of your refusal to accept my terms?"

"I know the worst," she proudly replied, "and can meet unshrinkingly the severest inflictions of destiny, but never will I humble myself by receiving service, however needful for my safety, from one whom I know to be

a villain, and whose presumption at any other time would not have escaped its well merited punishment."

The determination and calm severity with which this reply was uttered, confounded Lord Morton, and for a moment rendered him incapable of making any answer of it. But again he recovered himself, and having by this time discovered that violence would but serve to defeat his purpose, he said, with an air of hypocritical repentance :—

"If mercy ennobles and purifies the soul, will the deeply wronged Isabel refuse pardon to him who thoroughly repents his evil deeds? Can no penitence atone for past transgressions, and soften the rigour of your indignation? Oh, my lady, cannot the danger with which you are surrounded in this place, induce you to forget the injury you have received at my hands? At the hazard of my life I have ventured to obtain this interview, not as a lover, but as a penitent, forlorn of every hope, yet devoted to your safety and service, and for ever faithfully obedient to whatever commands you may be pleased to charge me with. Reject not, I implore you, the only means which now offers itself for your deliverance, which now solely depends on the use we make of the present opportunity to effect our escape."

"Your conduct, my lord," she replied, "has been sufficient to induce me to take the step I have. I know you, and the base purposes which have induced you to make this proposition, and I therefore reject your terms with a request that the subject may not be again alluded to."

"You wrong me, Isabel," he exclaimed, "and, when removed from the unknown, but terrible effects of Badenoch's power and despotism, you find yourself again in honourable safety and protection, you will acknowledge that my repentance is sincere, and then, perhaps, I may hope to find forgiveness where most I have offended. When that happy moment arrives,

No. 28

I will make ample reparation for the past, and redeem my lost honour by joining, heart and soul, in the cause of Robert Bruce."

These words, artful as they were, had not their expected effect on the princess, who at once saw through the hollowness of his professions. She knew that he sought only to deceive her, and directing towards him a look of firm determination, she said :—

"My resolution, Lord Morton, is as immoveable as my sentiments of your principles and character are unchanging. You will therefore do well to consult the means of your own safety, by withdrawing from a spot so dangerous to yourself, since I have only to add that, though my present imprisonment here is painful and irksome to endure, yet it is preferable to the liberty you have proposed. Nor need I remind you that as King Edward of England is no longer living to sanction the violence of your conduct, I hold myself free from further persecution of this degrading nature, and, for the dangers to be apprehended here, they are of a nature that must soon terminate, since my retreat will ere long be discovered by my father, whose power will be sufficient to effect my release."

Isabel could not forbear internally trembling at the conviction of her danger, for in her own mind she knew that the castle was impregnable to the attacks of an enemy. She, however, possessed too much self-command to betray the shudder of terror that passed through her frame, as she thought of the peril to which she was still exposed. Besides, she doubted the boasted power of Lord Morton to release her from the fortress, and not choosing any longer to encourage a conference every way repugnant to her feelings, she would have rose to quit the chamber, had he not suddenly opposed her passage, and with an angry look of determination, seized, and detained her hand, as he exclaimed with an affected tone of respect :—

"Forgive me, Lady Isabel, if I presume to detain you to urge one other argument, that may serve to alter the cruel determination you have expressed. Need I remind you, that in this place, not even the forbearance of a single day can be expected from the stern Chief of Badenoch. Despotic power, passion, and a determination not to be thwarted, all conspire to render your further stay in this place utterly destructive of your future happiness."

"The Chief of Badenoch," answered Isabel, "will, doubtless, reflect ere he does that which would surely bring down upon him the vengeance of those who will not suffer my wrongs to pass unavenged."

"You rely too much upon that which will be of little use to you," answered Lord Morton. "It may be months before your father discovers the place of your captivity, and in that fearful interval, what ills—what scenes of guilt may you not be involved in. I tremble at the bare thought, and, though unwillingly, feel myself compelled to inform you that since my arrival here, I have discovered the darkest stratagems already formed against you. You are yourself become the object of designs, hostile not only to the purity of virtue, but to your future fame, your honour and peace."

"I am but too well aware that I am in the power of a monster," answered Lady Isabel, "but surely the Chief of Badenoch, cruel and resolute as he is, will not dare to injure one who is powerless in his hands."

"Your sex and rank will not secure you here," answered the other. "The Chief of Badenoch knows how absolute he is here, nor will he be awed by any sense of justice or forbearance from the accomplishment of his dark purposes. Think then of the consequences which will ensue if you continue unmindful of my advice. This terrible fortress, ofttimes the scene of midnight acts and crimes, abhorrent to the light, is ill calculated to afford the shelter your age and sex demand, and even to continue in it a day longer, is to endanger your future repose, if not to destroy its serenity for ever."

" I can see, my lord," exclaimed Isabel, " that it is your present purpose to terrify me in quitting the castle under your care and protection."

" Nay," he replied, " reflect, Isabel, I entreat you, how perilous a moment's hesitation may render your situation, and what will be the opinions of the world in after times, when people will say,—' The Princess Isabel voluntarily surrendered herself to the bondage of Badenoch's Chief, and regardless of her rank, and in open defiance to the feelings of the injured wife of the chieftain, she usurped her place, trampled on her lawful rights, and gave a sanction to his guilty views towards herself; while at the same time she lived contented and well pleased, the companion of his crimes, and thus for ever severing him from the exemplary and unfortunate Lady Badenoch.' "

" Lady Badenoch !" cried Isabel, with a burst of horror, for at first the astonishment created by the words of Lord Morton, had deprived her of the power to express the strong indignation she had felt. " Is it possible then that Lady Badenoch yet survives the cruelties of a harsh and tyrannous husband ?"

" It is indeed true," answered Lord Morton, well pleased at the effect of his words ; " and as report assures me, she is a resident in this very castle, as a captive. Say, then, obdurate girl, how the world will judge of you should it still be your determination to remain in this place after an opportunity has been offered you to escape ?"

The Princess Isabel felt the full force of these words ; she knew to what mortifying suspicion her present situation would subject her, and she was at the same time too fully convinced that her departure from the castle was utterly impossible unless she received assistance. But she was too well assured that Morton's promises were not to be depended upon, and even now, though strongly urged by the danger of her situation, she had yet fortitude enough to resist this only chance, because it appeared that in seeking to avoid one danger, she was only precipitating herself into another. She paused some little time to consider upon these things, and then regarding Morton with a scrutinising look, exclaimed—

" Virtue, my lord, ever refutes its calumniators, since its trials alone can establish its superiority, and render its possessor superior to those who know not how to value it. I may be unfortunate, and even here have to experience all the evils you have described, but innocence has resources which villany cannot undermine, and I must again add, that after the declaration I have already made rejecting your lordship's proposals, your unwished for presence cannot either change my former determination, or be allowed to prolong its continuance. I am myself," she added, with unceasing vehemence ; " the sole guardian of my own fame, and need not a monitor, such as Lord Morton, since my reliance is placed on Heaven, which can alike confound the presumptuous machinations of guilt, and render impotent the sharpest darts of malevolence, or the envenomed slanders of disappointed calumny."

" Nay, Lady Isabel," he cried ; " deign but to hear me."

" I will hear no more," she replied, " and therefore do I command you to quit my presence !"

The resolution of her manner and animated indignation that accompanied these words, could no longer be misinterpreted, and the crafty nobleman found that in Isabel he had to contend with an opponent, gifted by nature and talents with a strength and superiority of reasoning far beyond what he had expected to meet with. The meek, timid, pliant nature he had hoped to have found in Isabel, was changed for a decision he had not anticipated ; and for awhile the libertine remained silent and confounded by her firmness.

At length, however, driven to despair, by the hopelessness of the views he had formed, he changed his manner, and with more humility thus proceeded :—

"That I have, and do still adore you, Lady Isabel, with a passion firm and unconquerable, my former and present conduct declares. I *cannot* live without you ! nay, start not, for know I *will* not depart till either assured of a milder sentence, or a promise to quit this hateful spot with me. Had you condescended to have trusted me, you would have learnt the sincerity of my truth and devotion to your every wish, and found me obedient to whatever decree you might have pronounced. But to leave you now, and depart with the conviction that I have resigned you to the power of such a villain as Badenoch would be a reproach to which I can never submit. Nor can I doubt your future forgiveness, when you come to reflect that in thus withdrawing you from dangers which I tremble to think of, you will at length condescend to yield to the honourable protection our union will shortly secure you."

Terrified at his latter words, Isabel rose from her seat and would have quitted the apartment, but Morton's daringly avowed purposes prevented her design, and she again exclaimed with mingled feelings of terror and indignation :—

"Be assured, my lord, those unmanly threats will but serve to increase my aversion towards you. You will do well also to reflect that you are no longer empowered to persecute me with your insolent addresses as you were by the haughty monarch to whom you basely sold your allegiance !"

Unawed and unabashed, Lord Morton seized both hands of the Princess, and in spite of all her struggles, forced her to accompany him towards the door.

"This moment is propitious to my designs," he exclaimed ; "for the bustle and confusion that precedes the departure of Badenoch, will favour our flight, and love must plead for the violence I am thus compelled to adopt. Forgive me, lady, that I thus urge you to quit with me a place more ruinous and destructive to your honour that you at present imagine. Nay, it is in vain you oppose my firm purposes, for I have sworn you shall be mine, and no earthly power shall frustrate my will."

"My lord ! my lord !" cried the terrified girl ; "you cannot, dare not mean such an outrage as this ! Unhand me instantly, or dread the consequences which will surely follow if you persist in thus violently in dragging me from hence. The Chief of Badenoch has not yet departed from the castle, and even his protection will I demand against the unmanly force you seek to exercise against a helpless female."

"*His* protection," answered Morton, "can only be purchased by the surrender of your peace, your liberty and fame. Such must be the return he will demand and enforce, whilst the present alternative will secure you both safety and honourable love. Therefore allay thy fears, sweet Isabel ; let us but reach the unfrequented avenue that leads to the vaulted pass undiscovered, and we shall soon be beyond the outward battlements. All is there prepared for our escape, and the power of the dreadful Chief of Badenoch is no longer to be apprehended."

"Villain ! thy baseness and treachery shall be rewarded as they merit !" exclaimed an angry voice in accents of thunder, and ere Morton could drag the princess from the room, the Chief of Badenock, attended by three of his retainers, rushed into the room, and with a furious aim, buried his sword into the bosom of the libertine, Morton. Alarmed by the suddenness with which this had occurred, Isabel fainted, but on recovering a few minutes afterwards she heard the fierce chief thus address himself to her—

"Girl ! you would have deceived me, but at present you have no cause to dread my power, since I shall take time to consider the punishment you best deserve. But for you, my Lord Morton, my vengeance shall find an instant and exemplary doom. Bear him to the rack, slaves, and let him, in lengthened torments, be taught the dreadful punishment that awaits my nod to rid myself of a hated foe!"

"Nay, I can yet defend myself," exclaimed Morton, drawing his sword; "and thus I dare thee to mortal combat."

"Ah! sayest thou so!" cried the chief furiously. "But thou hast only hastened thy doom, for this blow shall for ever silence the presumption that has urged thee to challenge me to single combat."

This threat was no sooner uttered than fulfilled, for Lord Morton fell beneath a mortal thrust, whilst his scoffing, triumphant adversary stood over him, brandishing his wreaking sword, and then pointing its blade towards the heart of his fallen foe, he stood prepared to complete the deed he had thus commenced.

All this time Isabel stood transfixed with horror, yet, though faint and almost powerless with terror at the tragical scene she had thus witnessed, she opposed the fatal purpose of the conqueror, and earnestly implored the life of him who had so recently been her persecutor.

"Hold, Chief of Badenoch!" she cried; "and destroy not the fallen and defenceless man, who has thus felt the vengeance he could not resist."

"I am not obdurate, lady," answered Badenoch; "and therefore, at thy entreaty, will spare his forfeit life on one condition. Swear to be mine, and he is safe."

"Thy purpose is defeated, fell destroyer!" exclaimed the gasping and almost expiring Lord Morton; "for death has already seized upon thy victim, and the Lady Isabel will therefore be spared all further care on my account. Most injured lady," he continued, "forgive and pray for me, for the end of my days have come, and——"

Lord Morton could utter no more, for convulsions seized upon his quivering frame, and sinking back he instantly expired. The princess stood transfixed with horror as she gazed upon the tragic scene before her, and the Chief of Badenoch, as he seized her resistless hand and led her towards the chamber, found her cold and fainting. The peril of her situation, however, soon roused her from the stupifying lethargy into which she was fast sinking, and heaving an agonised sigh, her recollection again returned to all the horrible realities she had witnessed. The Chief of Badenoch watched her returning animation with looks of evident satisfaction, and then addressing himself to his retainers, he said in a tone of undisguised triumph:—

"Thus perish all my foes, and thus may I ever trample upon those who dare oppose themselves against my sovereign will! And now hear me, slaves, take hence the body of this presumptuous lord, and see it instantly thrown over the northern battlements, that the sea may for ever hide from me the hated form of one whom I have detested for the love he has dared express towards this lady."

The Princess Isabel shuddered with increasing horror as she heard the stern commands of the infuriated chief, and a trembling seized upon her heart as she reflected upon the dangers she had to apprehend from one so fierce and merciless.

"Nay, my lord, not to the deep!" she cried, scarcely knowing what she uttered; "do not, I implore you, let them commit his yet warm body to the roaring waves. Pause awhile I beseech you, and let not the madness of triumph lower you even with the roaring monsters of the forests!"

The Chief of Badenoch was, however, resolute, and on a signal being given, the retainers lifted up the body of Lord Morton, and conveyed it in silence from his presence.

CHAPTER XXXIX.

" Nay, if the gentle spirit of moving words
Can no way change you to a milder form,
I'll woe you, like a soldier, at arm's end,
And love you 'gainst the nature of love, force you "
TWO GENTLEMEN OF VERONA.

FAINT and exhausted, the Princess Isabel had sunk upon a chair, whilst the Chief of Badenoch, with passionate haste, closed the door, and approaching her with looks of fearful import, addressed her in stern and portentous words.

"It matters not, lady," he exclaimed, "whether it was through accident or design that Lord Morton gained admission to your chamber, since he has received the just punishment of his presumption, and you are now at liberty to confirm my avowed declarations as there is no longer a rival to oppose me. Every scruple is therefore now at an end, and you are now at liberty to make choice between your chance of certain happiness if shared with me, and the equal certain misery that must ensue should you obstinately persist in rejecting my love. Speak then, Lady Isabel, and deign to confirm the hopes that I cannot bring myself to relinquish."

Roused to the danger of her situation, and terrified by this openly avowed declaration of his purpose, Isabel continued for awhile silent, every faculty rendered torpid by alarm and indignation. Thus compelled, however, to assert the native independance of her mind, she at length, with assumed composure, replied to the insulting declaration.

"The Chief of Badenoch," she exclaimed; "is as much the object of my detestation as was he who has but just now paid the penalty of his life in my presence. Cease, therefore, my lord, from a vain pursuit, nor dare again to insult my ears with language such as you have just uttered. And think not that though, at present, most unhappily your captive, the Princess Isabel can be awed into a submission to a usurped authority, to which she has firmness enough never to stoop. I know your crimes, my lord, and shuddering at them as I do, no earthly power shall ever force me to become the bride of one whom my soul abhors. Unfortunately I am your prisoner, but shall only continue so till my father discovers the place of my retreat, when he will not fail to take full and ample vengeance against the monster who has thus dared to make a captive of his daughter."

"Beware, lady, how you urge me to desperation!" exclaimed the Chief of Badenoch; "and do not rashly tempt me to an act that will end in thy speedy ruin, and make thee hereafter curse the folly that provoked it."

"You have heard me, my lord," she replied, "and no circumstance will ever change my resolution."

"Nay," exclaimed Badenoch, "these haughty tones at once inflame my passions, and give rise to thoughts that are dangerous to thyself. Think well how useless is opposition to one whom kings themselves have stooped to, but never could subdue. The sovereignty of Badenoch is a bulwark so impregnable as to defy all earthly means to conquer it. In its frowning towers I reign sole lord,—my word is the fiat of life or death, and my nod sufficient to secure the destruction of my enemies. The late transaction should, methinks, teach thee, girl, the necessity of submission, for thou hast seen how my foes perish beneath my wrath."

"You threaten me, my lord!" cried Isabel, indignantly.

"Nay, you judge me too harshly," he replied; "for love prompts me in the course I have adopted, and it rests us only with yourself to secure that happiness which it is in my power to bestow. But I can be wrathful, as thou hast thyself witnessed, and therefore I would have thee beware, lest, through slighting my proffered love thou should hereafter have bitter cause to repent the madness that has urged thee to oppose my will. These are no feeble threats, no boyish starts of uncertain passion, as thou wilt ere long learn according to the decision thou may'st think proper to come to. Remember the chambers of Glenroy Castle, and let the midnight deeds thou saw'st there recal the fatal effects that spring from my boundless hate. Death was then decreed thee, but thy beauty came to thy aid, and thou may'st still be happy upon the conditions I have proposed. Banish, then, those looks of scorn from thy brow, and as thou regardest thy future peace, promise that on my return to the castle thou wilt become mine. Do this, girl, or, ere many minutes have elapsed, thou shalt bitterly repent the obstinacy that will have ensured thy destruction."

Isabel could not mistake the fearful import of his words :—his fierce glances, directed towards her, conjured up the most frightful images of approaching violence, for he remained unawed by the indignation that flashed from her eyes, nor did he seem to dread the probability of that vengeance which would pursue him were he to effect the purpose at which he has thus hinted. The security of his present place of retreat would, it was true, afford him shelter for a time, yet she knew him to be crafty and suspicious, and his own personal danger, however distant it might be, would perhaps restrain him for awhile, and thus an opportunity would be afforded her friends to make an effort for her safety. She, therefore, determined to maintain an appearance of firmness, and, regarding him with a steadfast look, exclaimed,—

"Your demands, Chief of Badenoch, will not terrify me into submission, since, like the threat that accompanies them, they are insufficient against one who will perish ere she yields. Your baseness, therefore, will but recoil upon yourself, and thus *you*, instead of myself, must hereafter repent the attempt at violence with which you have been base enough to threaten an unprotected female."

"Proud girl," cried the chief fiercely, "mark my words, and tremble! Three days yet are allowed thee for reflection, at the expiration of which time look for my return, and prepare thyself for the celebration of our nuptials. Be warned, therefore, and urge me not to desperation, for I am resolute in my purpose, and will not be thwarted by any danger that my conduct may produce. At present thou owest thy safety to my forbearance ; but if, at my return, I find thee obstinate and resolved to brave my power, expect all the terrors of my vengeance, and the fearful consequences of the rage thine own conduct will have given rise to. Be wise, girl, and provoke me not to extremities, for there are horrors in this castle thou little dreamest of, but which thou must surely endure should all my hopes be blighted through the antipathy thou hast formed against me."

"Monster!" exclaimed the princess, "thou would'st, coward like, terrify me from the fixed purpose of my soul."

"I would but warn you, Isabel," he replied. "For awhile I leave you to reflect on the consequences that must follow the course you are at present pursuing. Think well on the alternative : in three days thou art mine, with honour and advantage to thy fame, or lost for ever to the world, thyself, and every endearing tie of relative connexion that can cheer thy life with happiness."

Badenoch's glances were terrific as he pronounced these words. He loosened his hold of the unhappy princess who now stood in speechless amazement; but, as her persecutor was turning with a scowl of resentment towards the door, to quit the chamber, she thus earnestly and solemnly addressed him,—

"Oh, my lord! for the last time let me implore you to have pity upon one who never injured you by word or action. My love thou canst never have, for it is already bestowed upon another, but thou may'st yet command my gratitude by granting me that liberty of which I have been unjustly deprived."

"It is in vain you supplicate," answered the Chief of Badenoch; "for at the end of three days you shall be mine, or —"

"The contract is forbidden, lady," exclaimed a female voice at this moment, from the further end of the chamber. "Behold, still living, the wronged, discarded wife of Badenoch, once the object of his fondest love; but now, alas! degraded, despised, and cast off for ever!"

"Hence from my presence!" exclaimed the chief furiously, as his face assumed an ashy paleness, with all the outward symptoms of dread and discovered guilt. "Hence, I say, again, for thou knowest my power, and shall, ere long, receive the punishment thy presumption has brought down!"

"I will not hence at thy bidding, haughty chief," answered the sorrowing Lady Badenoch, as she approached nearer towards our heroine. "Princess Isabel," she continued, addressing herself to our heroine, "I bid thee beware, for the Chief of Badenoch is the husband, still beloved and idolized, of Emmeline! Shun, then, a doubly guilty connexion, and thus save all of us from the woes which must else be ours."

As she spoke thus, Lady Badenoch threw herself in an attitude of supplication at the feet of the Princess Isabel. She was still surpassingly beautiful, though wan and melancholy. Her veil had dropped half way down her shoulders, and the sorrow which marked her countenance went instantly to the heart of our heroine, whose blood recoiled as she thus gazed upon one whose sorrows she so deeply deplored. Aghast, shocked, and burning with indignation, she started as from a lethargy, and, taking a hand of the prostrate lady, exclaimed, in accents of mingled doubt and wonder,—

"To you only do I look for an explanation of mysteries that I in vain seek to penetrate. Merciful heavens! what new horrors encompass me? Oh, fate, dark and terrific!—whither, oh! whither hast thou betrayed my unconscious footsteps?"

"Hence!—begone!—and instantly quit my presence!" cried Badenoch furiously, as, seizing the form of his unhappy wife, he roughly raised her from the floor. "Begone, woman!—leave me, I say, lest, in my uncontrolled rage, I strike thee dead at my feet, even where thou dost now stand!"

"Thou may'st threaten me with death," answered Lady Badenoch, as she again approached our heroine; "but never will I quit this place till I am assured that thy evil designs have been frustrated." Then, addressing herself to Isabel, she continued:—"To thee, lady, do I now appeal for pity and redress. Oh, spare me!—save me from the hate of this man, and thus rescue yourself from the dark guilt of perjury!"

Again Badenoch strode fiercely towards his sorrowing wife. His ashy look of demoniac rage was now bent threateningly upon her, and his words, half stifled with bursting fury, were scarcely articulate as he madly exclaimed,—

"Woman!—thou art lost for ever, nor can any power on earth save thee from my vengeance. I go to prepare the speedy punishment thou hast provoked: I depart, but 'tis to summon my ministers of torture, and too soon wilt thou feel the wrath which thus far thou hast affected to despise!"

With a frown of deadly, withering hatred, the Chief of Badenoch once more regarded the unhappy object of his long persecution, and, then turning from her, as if with disgust, he rushed frantically from the apartment.

"Oh, mercy!—mercy!—and shield me with thy aid from his threatening vengeance!" cried the despairing Lady Badenoch, as she clung frantically round the knees of our heroine, who, scarcely knowing what she uttered, exclaimed,—

"Alas! unhappy woman! Art thou indeed the wife of the tyrannous lord of this castle?"

"I am," answered the other; "Heaven's eye witnessed the performance of the sacred rites, the holy marriage that made me his indissolubly."

A frown of severe anger clouded the countenance of the Princess Isabel as she heard these words, and, regarding the supplicant with a look of mingled scorn and detestation, she exclaimed,—

"Wretch!—begone from my presence! Shame of thy sex, and stain of womanhood, profaner of Heaven's own laws, darest thou sue to me for pity? Dost thou not know and tremble to behold me? Are these features so much changed that no traces now remain to harrow up thy soul's conscious guilt? Oh, Heaven!—was it for this the virtuous, exalted Princess Matilda died? Impious scoffer, hence! and torture my sight no more, for thy presence recals the fatal memory of woes irreproachable that were inflicted by thee on the injured innocent. Hence to thy hidden temple of adulterous secrecy and hateful vice, and presume no more to outrage with thy presence the purity of one who scorns thy vices!"

The Princess Isabel stood severe in conscious rectitude as she thus sternly addressed the abashed, but discovered Emmeline, who, with an internal struggle of conscious self-upbraiding and offended pride, quitted her hold on Isabel, and with alternate flushed, yet timid looks of astonishment and resentment, she said, reproachfully,—

"Am I the abhorred wretch your withering words declare me? Is it a crime to love, and be unfortunate? Oh, lady, think how anguished is the bosom which, while it doats, is scorned for one who tramples thus cruelly on its torn, distracted affection, and with unfeeling, exulting scorn, refuses pity, and rejects her miseries. Say, who art thou? My memory yet retains a faint recollection of features once distantly familiar to its acquaintance. Thy words, too, bitter as they are, awake surmises, but not guilty fears, such as thy speech presages. I tell thee, girl, I know thee not."

"Nor would I satisfy thee upon the point," answered Isabel, "but that my name, when pronounced, may harrow up thy soul, and overwhelm thee with confusion. Hast thou no sense of shame for deeds polluted with every black stain that can deform the loveliness of virtue, and under its richest treasures most baneful?—Oh, when thus baseness like thine can glory in its impious disregard of sanctity and virtue, and avow unblushingly its frailties and dishonour, well may lawless man with unlicenced insolence dare violate the ear of female chastity with words of shame."

"Speak, speak, I charge thee!" cried Emmeline, "and reveal quickly the dreadful import of thy words. I am not yet sunk so low but I can still vindicate my fame and make its calumniators blush when thus they presume to tax its integrity. Say, therefore, who thou art, and why I should tremble at thus finding myself in thy presence?"

"I am the avenger of a wronged sire's dishonour," answered the Princess Isabel,—"the accuser of a guilty wife, speaking from the tomb of my hapless, sacrificed mother, and demanding of her faithless Emmeline, the just account she must hereafter make confession of before the throne of Heaven. I speak to her who, scorning all ties of honour, virtue, or sacred faith, plighted to her husband, Lord Mackenzie, dared burst the barrier of every earthly, every divine law, and in open defiance of every human bond, thus presumest to offend my eyes with thy presence. Quit the sight of the daughter of the Princess Matilda, and tell thy guilty paramour that Isabel will yet avoid his snares, and elude the menaces he has basely uttered against her. Begone, I say, and be it thy torture to learn that the Lord Mackenzie will shortly arrive at this castle, to confound thine iniquity, and overwhelm in ruin the monster whom thou hast made the partner of thine adulterous love!"

"Merciful Heaven!" groaned the unhappy Emmeline, "what dark,—what dreadful tale, half revealed, hast thou been telling me?—Oh, girl, suspend your judgment upon me for awhile. Upon my knee in humble supplication I implore thee answer, and save me if thou canst from the horror, the fearful surmises, that rush tumultuously on my bewildered brain. I have indeed wronged thee, thou injured child of the lost Matilda, for such I now know thou art, but ah! no otherwise than by neglect. Mackenzie long has slept in the tomb,—how then have I wronged him? And though, while living my heart ever respected his virtues, yet have I done no violence to his memory, since the Chief of Badenoch was the first,—only object of my love; and when released by Makenzie's death, I became indissolubly his to whom I was plighted long before my union with the deceased Lord Mackenzie."

"The *deceased* Lord Mackenzie!" exclaimed Isabel; "but this is only a vain subterfuge to conceal thy guilt. My father lives—lives to avenge his own wrongs, and those that I have endured from the libertine Chief of Badenoch."

"It cannot,—cannot be," cried Emmeline, in accents of the most profound grief. "He is dead, and thou wouldst but inflict tortures upon me by those reproaches which I do not deserve. Yet, oh, Heaven! what mean these dreadful tremblings that run in icy chillness through my veins? Distraction, horror, and despair, have seized my senses, and whirl me into madness! Oh, girl, say what thou wilt to inflict tortures upon me, but do not, I implore you, say that Mackenzie lives! Surely, I am not,—cannot be so lost a wretch as to have forsaken one whom I would have perished to save!"

"Thou art lost, indeed," answered the Princess Isabel, "for if thou hast ever indeed doubted, let the appalling truth now avenge all the sufferings thy faithless perjury has inflicted on his heart. These eyes have oft witnessed, and these lips laboured to appease his distracted ravings for thy loss. I have heard him day by day lament his Emmeline, unworthy as she was, scorning all comfort, and bereft of every hope, yet frantically calling upon her to view his anguish, and behold his death,—a death which her cruelty and falsehood alone could have rendered premature. A maniac, and lost to himself and all that was dear to his existence, it had been happiness to a soul like my wronged father's to have quitted a life that Emmeline's ingratitude and baseness had made so hateful. But know, he yet survives thy fatal inconstancy, and shortly will appear to thine and the detested Badenoch's utter confusion and dismay."

"Alas!" groaned Emmeline, "if this be true, what greater misery could have befallen me? Oh, memory, cease thy gnawing pangs of vain repentance and remorse, for sufficient are thy upbraidings and the self-inflicted tortures I endure. Mackenzie lives!—the just, the noble, wronged Mackenzie, still constant and attached to his too guilty wife. Alas! Isabel, I am so lost a wretch, that death at this moment would be the only blessing I can dare hope for. Abject, grovelling in the dust, penitent, and thus sunk lowly at thy feet, as at those of my injured husband, humbly I implore you to pronounce my doom, and bid me die at once."

Scarcely had she pronounced these words, when a sudden noise startled her, and in an instant the Chief of Badenoch and four of his grim-looking retainers strode rapidly into the room.

"Obey my commands," exclaimed the chief, pointing towards the kneeling form of Emmeline. "You know my instructions,—let her be instantly borne to the dungeon!"

"I yield submissively to your will," answered Emmeline, in a meek, subdued tone. "By thee 'tis fit my punishment should be inflicted, for thou hast been the cause of all my errors, and better is it that death should come through thee than from aught else."

"'Tis well I find thee so resigned," he answered, coldly, "for thy doom is fixed, and no power on earth shall save thee."

"Remorseless betrayer!" cried Emmeline, "dost thou triumph in thy cruelties? But I will not shrink from my doom; with transport I go to meet my fate, nor will I deign ask thee to spare me the infliction of a single pang. And you, oh, Isabel, believe me contrite, and disdain not to pray for my no longer guilty spirit, for vengeance will shortly be accomplished, and the wrongs of Mackenzie be appeased by death. Virtue, like thine, Isabel, is Heaven's own peculiar care, nor will yon impious man dare shake its faith and purity. Oh, had the hapless Emmeline been firm as thou art, this hour of retribution, disgrace, and shame, had been spared her."

"Away with her, slaves!" exclaimed Badenoch, fiercely; "bear her hence without delay, and see that all my orders respecting her are punctually carried into execution."

"Aye," cried Emmeline, undeterred by the peril of her situation; "take me to my doom, for no earthly tortures can equal those which are now rankling in my heart. And remember, Badenoch, these feelings must be shortly thine, for thou art lost in guilt, and terrible will be the punishment that awaits thee in another world.   Repent, if thou canst, and heap not yet further crimes upon thine already overcharged conscience, by daring to injure her whom an adverse fate hath thrown in thy power.   Be warned, Heaven's eye is on thee, its angry justice has struck thy victim with its avenging bolt, which shall soon fall with tenfold retributive wrath upon thyself.   I bow with submission to the awful doom, and am thankful that those few moments of sincere repentance have been vouchsafed to me.   But the false delusion of my latter life has passed away, and though the voice of an accusing angel has thus awakened me to a sense of my past guilt, yet let me here avow that I sincerely repent, and that the weakness of my heart has been conquered."

"Woman!" exclaimed the Chief of Badenoch, "dost thou not tremble at the doom which awaits thee?"

"I am meeting fate with resignation," she replied, "and triumph in the thought that Badenoch's hands have deprived me of a life which no longer possesses a single charm for me.   'Tis just that thou art become the instrument that inflicts this retribution on my past misdeeds, and my last prayer is that I may find forgiveness where thou, monster that thou art, will not dare to supplicate for it."

She paused for a few moments, and then directing her gaze towards the princess, earnestly continued :—

"Farewell, Isabel, and pity, if thou canst, one whose errors were not premeditated.   Would to Heaven that my lips might bless thee, ere they are closed for ever; but it may not be that one so excellent as thyself should receive from such a lost wretch as Emmeline, the benediction she would fain have bestowed upon thee."

"Drag her instantly away!" exclaimed the Chief of Badenoch.   "Have ye not heard me, slaves, or must I chastise ye with death, for daring thus long to disobey my orders?"

As the men prepared to carry this command into execution, the Princess Isabel, half relenting the severity of her former words, caught the hand of the despairing Emmeline, and with her feeble arm, sought to oppose those who were preparing to obey the commands of their imperious lord.   Again the ruffians seemed to feel some pity struggling in their breasts, and in spite of the fierce looks of their chief, they stood for some few minutes, as if irresolute what to do.   Isabel observed the opportunity she had thus obtained, and fixing upon Emmeline a look of gentle pity, that she had not till now manifested, she exclaimed with some emotion :—

"Stay, unhappy lady, and if I have indeed wronged thee with reproaches too severe, redeem thy fame, if possible, from that ignominy which thy latter words almost assure me thou dost not deserve.   Say, then, didst thou not know that Lord Mackenzie was living when last, with a haste too precipitate, thou didst leave the Castle of Craiglynn's honourable protection?"

"I will have no further parleying," roared the Chief of Badenoch; "tear them instantly asunder, for he who longer pauses to perform his duty, dies upon the instant!"

This threat was sufficient, and Emmeline was then forced from the hold of the princess, who, however, followed her receding form, as the latter, in faint and almost exhausted tones, exclaimed,—

"Heaven is the witness of my truth, as I solemnly swear my heart acquits me of all intentional guilt towards thy father.   Alas! had I not from strong assurance believed the wronged Mackenzie dead, no wilful trespass had now disgraced my name, or stained my actions with the dark hue of crime.   Stand off awhile, barbarians! deny me not the only balm that now can sooth my soul and dissipate the horrors of my fate.   Oh, generous

Isabel! not thine own heart, gentle and innocent as it is, could have been freer from a thought of premeditated evil than was the bosom of the deceived, undone Emmeline. Deign, then, ere I am gone for ever, to grant me thy forgiveness, if, indeed, the prostrate wretch before thee may dare solicit so much mercy from one who has been thus deeply injured."

"I do forgive and pity thee," exclaimed the princess, fervently; "and oh! may Heaven be merciful to thy errors, and turn aside the never-ending miseries and anguish it has inflicted in the bosom of my long-suffering father, who has ever believed thee guilty of faithlessness and inconstancy."

She could utter no more; her sobs now became audible, and she wept as much over the lost Emmeline as over the irreparable woes of her deeply-injured parent. At this moment two of the ruffians forcibly bore the unresisting Emmeline in their arms. Her agonised spirit writhed in tortures as Isabel's undesigned reproach lacerated her heart with an additional pang of retribution, and with a groan of insupportable anguish she fell fainting into the rough grasp of the men, who, with careless indifference, bore her through the vestibule, and down the dark, winding corridor beyond it. Whilst Isabel, forcibly conveyed back by the gloomy tyrant, Badenoch, was now become so exhausted and worn with the dreadful transactions of the night, as to be unable any longer to support herself.

The Chief of Badenoch placed her in a chair, where for some little time she lay passive and silent, for every feeling of her heart was immersed in horror and distraction at the agonising scene in which she had taken so conspicuous a part. Awhile the chief stood grimly viewing the pale and shuddering girl, who hung down her head in speechless dismay at thus finding herself left alone with the man whose violence she had so much reason to fear, and from whom she could expect neither mercy nor compassion in her present situation. Without a protector she was in the hands of a ruthless enemy, and there was not one within the sound of her voice from whom she could hope for succour, even should she demand it. The chief still continued to regard her with fiend-like triumph, and when at length she began slowly to recover, he said, in a tone that carried agony to her soul,—

"I see, girl, the struggling whirlwind that wrings thy heart, and can read in each look the gathering tempest of the hate thou hast formed against me. Thine eye, too, at intervals lightens with indignant rage, which is suppressed only because thou knowest how futile it would be to bandy words with one who can hear them unmoved."

"Monster!" cried Isabel, "dost thou dare taunt one whom treachery has unhappily thrown in thy power?"

"Aye, girl," he replied, "and I now boldly avow all my guilt, and dare still glory in each gnawing pang it has inflicted on those my soul abhors, for I shall yet live to taste the vengeance of my bitterest hatred."

"Inhuman ruffian, forbear!" cried the princess, in accents of thrilling entreaty.

"Nay, Isabel," he replied, "I still can be merciful—still feel pity for thy helpless condition, and yet would spare thee from further suffering. I can render thee happy, girl, and thou shalt own that I am no vain boaster if you will promise this hour to become mine, and ——"

"Thine! detested monster! Never!" cried Isabel, resolutely. "Avaunt, fell homicide! despair of attaining thy fiend-like purpose; for know, though horrors accumulate, and fate itself should stand with uplifted dart to hurl me to the tomb, I would welcome its grim mandates, and meet it with triumph rather than live the wretch thou hast dared to suppose."

"Dost thou not fear my power, girl?" he wrathfully exclaimed.

"I neither fear thy power, nor tremble at the malice which is dictated by thy hate," she replied; "for my soul's unshrinking firmness shall rise superior to your arts, and hurl on thee, traitor, each bolt of anguish thy utmost fury can devise."

"Nay, this is madness," vociferated the Chief of Badenoch, "for here thou art beyond the aid of those who might serve thee, were it in their power, and the words thou hast uttered may but exasperate me to acts of violence."

"Aye, 'tis well to threaten a helpless female," cried Isabel; "but remember thy villany shall not always triumph, and it may be thy fate ere long to receive the punishment of thy many crimes."

"Listen to me with patience," exclaimed the chief, "and it is possible thou wilt see reason to think less harshly of me."

"Begone!" cried our heroine, firmly; "leave me, I say, lest my curses—the curses of injured innocence, and those of my wronged father, should rise to Heaven against 'thee. The savage, inhuman wrongs thy cruel nature has inflicted pursue thee everlastingly, though hitherto thou heedest not the warning that each moment rings in thine ear. Hence! I say again, and with these empty threatenings awe thy slaves, but presume no more to menace one who rises far beyond thy baleful reach, for the unconquerable resolution of my soul shall yet render vain the dark designs with which thou hast sought to encompass me."

"Isabel!" exclaimed the Chief of Badenoch, "reflect, I charge thee, ere it is too late!"

"My mind is firm in its resolves," she replied. "Surrounded by horrors, stratagems, and treasons—beset by violence, and encompassed by dangers unequalled—still will I rise superior to him who thus basely seeks my destruction. Thou mayest boast, monster, of having me in thy power, but baseness such as thine rarely succeeds, and I am not yet without hope that thy villany will meet the punishment it so justly merits."

Aghast, and surprised into inaction by a display of firmness so heroic and undaunted, Badenoch had at the moment no power to oppose the design of the Princess Isabel; and ere his astonishment and confusion had thoroughly subsided, she had secured herself for the present from the outrage he had been forming in his own mind against her, and had fortunately gained the interior of the next apartment ere he was aware of the purpose she had been meditating. It was, however, the last effort of her exhausted strength that enabled her to secure the bolt which fastened the door, ere she fell trembling and powerless to the floor. And now all the horrors of the late harrowing scene crowded upon her mind, with a weight oppressive and nearly overwhelming, and in a paroxysm of despair she murmured to herself,—

"Oh, why, just Heaven!—why was not the draught of Badenoch deadly and fatal, as his own evil deeds? Why did I ever awake from its lethargic stupor to such excess of wretchedness as that which I am now compelled to endure? Better, far better, had it been to have slept for ever in the silence of the grave than thus to live, recalled to sufferings that are too great for endurance. My father—dear, wronged father! couldst thou know the miseries that now encompass thy Isabel's safety, thou wouldst forget for a time thine own constant unhappiness, and fly to save her from the snares of villany."

Recovering partially from the distraction of her thoughts, Isabel then offered up a prayer to Heaven for the safety of Angus Glenalvon; nor was the young and unfortunate Edwin forgotten in her entreaties for mercy and protection. But her heart seemed to reject even a hope of their escape from the fell rage of their fiend-like foe; and with a shuddering presentiment of their fate, she wept over their almost certain destruction, since it was but too probable they had already perished, to satiate the vengeance of him who had sworn to plunge them into the same abyss of ruin which he had secured for their unfortunate parents.

Raising herself from the prostrate position in which she had fallen, she gazed with a distracted eye round her gloomy, prison-like chamber, to see if any chance of escape might be presented to her view. All, however, seemed as blank and hopeless as her own sad destiny, and, as her thoughts once more recurred to the unfortunate Sons of Glenalvon, she ejaculated with terror,—

"Alas! they perhaps are already disposed of by their ruthless enemy, and even now, whilst my memory clings to them they lie rotting in the tomb to which the tyrant of Badenoch has sent them."

"They live, but are already doomed," cried a deep-toned, sullen voice in her ear. "Angus and Edwin Glenalvon have been thus long preserved from death, but their doom has been pronounced, and ere long they will cease to exist."

"Ah!" she cried despondingly : "are they indeed fated to perish?"

"They are," answered the same harsh voice; "but a word from the Princess Isabel may yet recal them from the dreadful doom that hurries them to an early and bloody grave!"

As Isabel again made an effort to raise herself from the floor she beheld an outstretched arm directed to assist her. The blood froze in her veins with the horrible sensation this sight created in her mind, and scarcely had she strength to support herself against the overpowering sensations of terror with which she had been seized. With an effort, however, she at length raised her eyes towards the form of the intruder, but with equal dread and horror beheld in the expected Chief of Badenoch the no less repulsive figure of the false and treacherous Rupert.

His muscular limbs and dark though livid features bore the marks of internal secret guilt, the momentary contemplation of which aroused in an instant all the terrors of Isabel's soul to action. She now with shuddering fear remembered that this was the wretch whose daring insolence and offered violence had so nearly proved fatal when in the forlorn and desolate chambers of Glenalvon, and while her heart experienced a yet stranger and more perfect sentiment of love and gratitude for that heroic bravery, whose timely aid had rescued her from impending destruction, she shuddered with disgust and horror to think that the violence might now be repeated at a time when no friendly aid was near to rescue her from the villain who stood thus reckless and indifferent before her. She, however, endeavoured to conceal her emotions of terror, lest the ruffian should observe his advantage and basely seek to take advantage of it.

Rupert, or more properly Fergus, for by the latter he is perhaps better known to the reader, soon roused himself from his temporary inaction, and assisting to raise the Princess Isabel from the ground, he said, with a half-concealed sneer :—

"Will the once illustrious, but now fallen Isabel, vouchsafe attention to the suit of Rupert, or must he again remind her that she is now sunk to the level of the man she formerly so much despised, and that he alone can rescue her from the great peril that on every side surrounds her whilst she remains a prisoner within this castle ?"

"I need little reminding of my sad destiny," answered the princess, with what calmness she could assume ; "for, whichever way I turn some new event occurs to assure me that the period of my evil destiny has not yet arrived."

"Trust to me," he exclaimed, "and I will soon convince you that better days are at hand."

"Trust to *you!*" cried the princess, with disgust that she found it impossible to conceal.

"Aye," he replied, "and why not? The Chief of Badenoch's hate, more absolute than his love, cannot go further than mine. Believe me, too, that whilst Rupert, bound for ever in the fetters of eternal gratitude as well as love, will live but to adore and obey the will of the fair object of his passions. Say then, lady—and pause, I entreat you, on the answer you give—say that you will condescend to give me freedom and life, and even Angus, the hated son of Glenalvon, shall accompany our flight, and thus escape the certain fate to which he has been doomed by the vengeance of Badenoch's chief."

Isabel, struggling with an effort that agitated her whole frame as she sought to obtain one last gleam of expiring fortitude, gazed upon the presumptuous vassal with a look of writhing scorn, and waving him off with her hand, she exclaimed in a tone of absolute command:—

"Quit my presence, sirrah! and henceforth presume no more to address me on a subject such as this, lest I bring upon thee that chastisement which thine insolence demands. Here I know I am thy master's captive, but my voice shall yet be raised against thee, and should the Chief of Badenoch learn the presumption of his vassal, he will not fail to pass upon thee that doom which thou hast long ere this deserved."

"Proud girl!" replied the defeated miscreant, bending on the Princess Isabel a terrible look of disappointed rage,—"'tis thou shall tremble and repent this scorn and boasted contempt of the power of him thou hast despised! I go to fulfil my threats—to wreak on the minion of thy choice the vengeance thou hast roused to action; and when the boy, Angus Glenalvon, shall have felt the full power of my rage, then shall these unavailing demonstrations of courage and resistance, yield to force, and give me at once the full possession of her who would thus dismiss me with scorn and ignominy."

"In Heaven's name, what meanest thou?" demanded Isabel, in an agony of terror.

"I mean," replied the ruffian, "that thy favourite, Angus, is in my power. I am his gaoler in this castle, and his life or death equally depend upon my dictum. But thou hast resisted my entreaties with scorn, and since thou hast refused to become mine, it shall be my next care to take those steps that will prevent thy ever becoming the wife of a hated rival. Remember, Lady Isabel, his death will be at your door, for nothing now shall save him from my vengeance."

"Merciful Heaven!" cried Isabel, in accents of the deepest horror; "thou wilt murder him then in revenge for the denial I have given to thy presumptuous addresses?"

"Thou mayst call them presumptuous," answered Rupert, "but I have yet to learn the distinction that exists between myself and her, whose empty title is all she at present possesses in the world. But it is not upon that subject I would now speak. I have freely confessed my passion, Lady Isabel, and as you have thought proper to reject me with scorn, it shall now be my task to destroy him, who it seems you can alone regard with favour or affection."

"Yet stay!" cried Isabel, as she saw the ruffian preparing to quit the chamber on this dreadful errand; "stay, I conjure you, and hear my prayers for one whose life is far dearer to me than my own. Stay, Rupert, and——"

"It is too late, now," he gruffly replied. "A short time since I might have listened to you, but you have pronounced his doom, and from this time forward, you may regard yourself as the murderer of Angus Glenalvon, my hated rival!"

Rupert vanished suddenly from the room as he spoke, and the Princess Isabel sinking powerless upon her knees, exclaimed in a voice rendered frantic with agony :—

"Oh Heaven! upon thee I call in this moment of insupportable terror. Snatch me, I implore thee, from this scene of guilt and woe, or close up mine eyes for ever in the deep sleep of eternity!"

And with a deep groan of anguish that bespoke a heart struggling with its own heavy woes, she sunk back upon the floor, and was for some time happily unconscious of the fresh troubles that had thus arisen in her path.

Rupert had entered through the little chamber that was usually occupied by the attendant, Marianne. This apartment had a double entrance, and one of its doors opened directly on the sleeping chamber of the hapless princess, and through which the ruffian had gained admission. Marianne, who had all this while concealed herself within one of the dark recesses of the larger room, watched the departure of Rupert, and then hurrying towards the unfortunate Isabel, was proceeding to her relief, but had sufficient forethought first to secure the private entrance, by which means the suffering princess, for the night, escaped the threatened infliction of Rupert's return.

For some time, the care and attention bestowed by Marianne upon her unconscious mistress was unavailing, for she remained in a state of utter insensibility, and was thus, for awhile spared the agony which awaited her upon recovery. The first care of the faithful attendant was to

No. 30

raise her beloved mistress upon a couch, where, however, she remained for some hours without manifesting any signs of returning animation.

At length, her heavy sighs, and the half incoherent sentences that she uttered, gave token that the semblance of death was passing away, and by the time that morning had pretty well advanced, the Princess Isabel respired more freely, though she was still feverish, and her mind seemed to wander upon subjects that dwelt deeply upon her mind. It was in vain that Marianne sought by every means in his power to assuage the anguish which thus tore the bosom of her mistress, for Isabel could not but remember the dreadful interview between the Chief of Badenoch and herself, and the peril with which she was threatened, should she persevere in her determination to reject the presumptuous offer that he had made her.

Nor could she drive from her mind the subsequent visit of Rupert, whose vows of vengeance still clung to her memory with startling vividness. Already she believed that Angus Glenalvon had perished by the hands of the assassin, and dwelling upon the last words of Rupert, she in accents of despair, accused herself of having accelerated the death of her lover.

Marianne's affectionate attentions could alone have preserved the princess from a long and dangerous illness, and even as it was, she continued for two days in a paroxysm of frenzy, and happily unconscious of her forlorn condition.

CHAPTER XL.

" Didst thou view him right,
Thou'dst see him black with murders,
Treason, sacrilege, and crimes that strike
My soul with horror but to name them.'
                                        ADDISON.

IT is now necessary, for the better understanding our narrative, that we should pause for a brief time, to advert to some previous eventful circumstances, which will serve to show the various influences that were at work against those who were enduring the oppression and injustice which have been described in the foregoing pages.

The treacherous vassal, Rupert, or Fergus, the husband of Magdalen, were both one and the same person, the former title having been assumed when in the service of the too trusting Lord Mackenzie, whom the Chief of Badenoch had long deceived and misled; and had ultimately placed Rupert in the suite of his basely-wronged cousin, rather as a vigilant spy over his actions, and the occurrences that transpired at the Castle of Craiglynn, than as an attached and faithful domestic. Mackenzie's generous unsuspecting nature never once doubted the sincerity of professions made in apparent friendship, but hollow and deceitful as the breast that framed them; and Badenoch, too deeply versed in treachery and subtle artifice, had sufficient address not only to defeat every suspicion of his real designs, but even to impose on Mackenzie a belief that, though he fought not in the service of Scotland and her king, he never would oppose her noble struggles to redeem her tarnished honour, and rescue the independence of the crown from the grasp of the English usurper.

The dreaded towers of Badenoch had first been betrayed by the artifices of the chief from the King of Scotland to the Monarch of England, and had finally been the secret gift of Edward to the former; but as the situation of the rock was little known to Lord Mankenzie, and as he was certainly unacquainted that Badenoch was in possession of such a place, the chief was well able to screen all his dreadful acts of guilt from every possible chance of discovery.

At the Castle of Craiglynn, where Badenoch had been generously received into habits of strict friendship, he was known only as a knight of Scotland, and a descendant of the ancient house of Glenroy ; but under the title of the Chief of Badenoch he had often been the terror of his country, but had never been suspected, though the deeds of blood and rapine he was thus enabled to commit in disguise were of a nature too horrible to escape detection, had they been less secretly practised.

Of passions fierce, wild, and ungovernable, and swayed by the thirst of ambition, and disdain of the rights of justice or the claims of mercy, he had, under the licensed cruelty of the times, conceived and executed every species of enormity and violence, without either remorse or pity for the savage wrongs his injustice thus inflicted. Ambition was the ruling passion of his mind, nor did he even respect the authority of King Edward himself, from whom he derived his consequence but as the instrumental means of his exaltation and advancement.

The dreadful murder of the unfortunate Glenalvon, had indeed been the result more of hatred than the leading trait of Badenoch's mind ; whilst the fierce flame of sensual love that had burnt in his bosom for the too fascinating Helen, had, if possible, hardened the original cruelty of his mind, and made him reckless of every worldly fear, and every future apprehension ; and to destroy Glenalvon, and force his distracted widow to his arms, were the only gratifications that could satiate the deadly rancour of his vengeance.

It was the disappointment of promised possession which had so balefully kept alive the revenge he had so long brooded over for the loss of Helen, but the latter, by a self-inflicted death, escaped the triumph he had meditated, and which Glenalvon had died to accomplish. Magdalen had, as we have seen, snatched the helpless orphans from inevitable destruction, but Badenoch, even when informed of their supposed death, and believing that the woman's pretended tale had really been true, and that the sons of Glenalvon had fallen, as she narrated, over the alpine bridge that crossed the cataract, on her escape from the Watch Tower, yet still his restless malice was unappeased ; Helen, her husband, and their children, were all swept, as he supposed, away, yet still one relative survived, whom his rage and hatred sought to immolate, but whom a greatness of rank and station rendered secure for awhile from the effects of his deadly malice ; for Lord Mackenzie, the brother of the hapless Helen, was at once an object of terror and abhorrence in his path.

Should any knowledge reach him respecting the horrible fate of his sister and her family, all Badenoch's villany would stand exposed to public odium ; and he for whom he had ever outwardly expressed esteem and lasting friendship would thus become the avenger of the murdered Glenalvon, and at once unfold the long black list of enormities he had practised with so much success.

The beauty of Emmeline had created in his breast a false flame, and he had, with all the dissembling courtesy for which he was conspicuous, gained favour in her sight, even prior to the time when Lord Mackenzie had first declared his passion for her. It was after the death of the Princess Matilda, and Mackenzie's second marriage, with Emmeline, that, like a fiend of darkness, Badenoch again revived the first warm affections of the newly-wedded bride, and thus rendered her life a warfare of anguish, and hopeless struggle, between her love for a forbidden object, and her principles of rectitude and honour to subdue an unfortunate predilection. It is certain she was not a wilful criminal, and that she had been deceived by Badenoch into a belief of her husband's death.

Rupert, the comrade of this base chief, had early displayed passions and propensities the most ferocious; and it was known that some dark misdeeds of suspected murder had banished him from his family. His father was a vassal of the Chief of Badenoch, but the old man had, it was reported, fallen a victim to his son's ungoverned passions. His wife, Magdalen, too, was made an unconscious sharer in his crimes, and had been compelled by him to quit the castle, where suspicion had rendered his longer stay dangerous, for she had discovered this act of atrocity, and it was certain, that had he not forced her so suddenly away, she would have become his accuser. The towers of Badenoch received the villain, but even there the good Magdalen was not to be awed by her ferocious husband, and when first assured by the chief of safety, she with firmness openly avowed her detestation for Rupert, and to Badenoch revealed his foul and horrible crimes. She, however, knew not then that the chieftain's spirit was kindred to her husband's, and that he secretly exulted in the knowledge he had obtained, marking him from that instant as a fit associate in whatever evil deeds he might have to perpetrate.

From this period Rupert rose to high preferment, and hardened as he was in every species of vice, he soon plunged into its wildest excesses, and became the willing tool of his employer. His hand had lighted the first firebrand that destroyed a great portion of the Castle of Glenalvon, for plunder was the promised reward of his assistance; and without his aid the secret entrance to the castle had not been discovered.

Magdalen had been preserved from the effects of her husband's vindictive wrath by the artful policy of the Chief of Badenoch, who had defended her from his fury in order that he might thus possess evidence of Rupert's former guilt, should it at any time be necessary for his purposes. Hence it was that Magdalen was safe for a length of time from the malice of her husband, and the equally destructive hatred of Badenoch, since the latter had an interest in her existence, as her testimony would certainly be required, should he ever find it necessary to get rid of his retainer.

Several years had elapsed since the opening of this narrative, and during which time the chief usually resorted to this castle whenever he was threatened with more than usual danger. During these sojourns Rupert often pondered on the mystery of the undiscovered wealth of Glenalvon, to the ruins of which castle he occasionally ventured, and roaming through its ruined chambers, in vain sought to find the treasure he longed to possess. Oftentimes did he approach the scene of murder, expecting there to discover, unknown to all, the hidden mine of riches. Vainly, however, did he search, for Ronald's fidelity had preserved the records and riches of his master's house, and they were thus fortunately saved from the hands of the spoiler.

Hardened as he was, and reckless of every duty, Rupert had no sooner beheld the Princess Isabel than he resolved to possess himself of her by force. He had been present at her first arrival from the convent, and the subsequent misfortunes that had occurred to her, had added to the chance of making her his. Accordingly he contrived for awhile to follow the ruined fortunes of Lord Mackenzie, in order that, should an opportunity occur, he might take advantage of it and obtain the much coveted prize.

The Chief of Badenoch had also seen and admired the Princess Isabel. On the night the Castle of Craiglynn had been so treacherously betrayed to King Edward, he accompanied the sovereign, and gazing upon her with wonder and delight, he traced in each feature her strong resemblance to the long deceased Helen of Glenalvon—a resemblance doomed to be fatal to her—for from that moment he vowed she should become his, and without delay demanded her the king as the reward of the services he had performed. To this the monarch with little difficulty assented, telling him that his chance to win the princess should be equal to that of Lord Morton's, to whom, as the reader is already aware, he had previously made a similar promise.

At this period Rupert had not the most distant suspicion that his chieftain had seen Isabel, and it is certain his own diabolical scheme would have been successfully accomplished but for the sudden appearance of Angus in the ruined Castle of Glenalvon on the night of his arrival,—an incident that occasioned more dismay to the heart of the ruffian than would have been caused by the spectre of the murdered lord, whose airy form seemed continually to haunt him. On the first sight of Angus he shrank back aghast, and for a moment really believed the grave had sent back its long buried dead; but when he more closely observed the lineaments of Edwin, he at once perceived that the youths were the rescued sons of Glenalvon.

At midnight he visited their chamber, and throwing aside the covering from the faces of the sleeping brothers, convinced himself that all his former suspicions were correct. Thrice he pointed a dagger to their hearts, but the murdered form of Glenalvon seemed to rise before him ; and unable to endure the tortures of a guilty mind, he rushed from the chamber without accomplishing the crime he had intended to commit.

On the second night, however, his resolution was more fixed, for scarcely had he received permission to retire than, hurrying to the Watch Tower, he demanded instant admittance. The ill-fated Magdalen, deceived into a belief that her foster children were again come to seek her protection, hastened to obey the summons, and admitted—not the loved objects of her constant cares —but the incensed Rupert, whose baleful frown foretold her doom and banished every hope of mercy.

" Wretch !" he exclaimed, sternly, " thy last hour is come ! The sons of Glenalvon still survive ; but thus I punish the disobedient rebel that has dared to preserve them in defiance of a husband's commands."

Magdalen saw her danger, and prompted by fear, she fled hastily from the spot, followed closely by the unrelenting Rupert, who, as he overtook the hapless victim of his fury, inflicted a deep wound in her body, and exclaimed, as she sank bleeding at his feet :—

" Down, down for ever! and with thee perish the only evidence of my crimes ! With thy death I am secure, and now can I bid defiance to those who would vainly seek to hurl upon me the ruin I so long have dreaded."

The faithful Magdalen breathed forth a piteous groan, and Rupert, incapable of remorse, waited not an instant to deliberate, but seizing the nearly lifeless body in his gigantic grasp, he hurried with it to the ramparts, and hurled his unfortunate victim into the waters that roared beneath. Then rushing from the scene of his last iniquity, he regained, at day-break, the northern chambers of Glenalvon ; and ripe for yet blacker deeds of outrage, waited the absence of Lord Mackenzie, to practice on the princess his dark designs, which were to compel her, either by terror or force, to quit the place, and from thence convey her for security to the fortress of Badenoch.

Defeated, however, by a being whom he hated as the living avenger of a murdered father ; he hesitated no more to glut his vengeance and destroy the object of his fears, and on the third night entered the chamber where he supposed both his victims reposed. But his dismay was great, when on approaching the bed, he found that Edwin alone occupied it, and struck with conscious guilt, he gazed round the room expecting that Angus was somewhere concealed to watch his movements. The light of his lamp, as he held it over the unconscious youth, revealed the features and exact resembance of his deceased [parents, and Rupert no longer hesitated to execute his deadly purpose; but suddenly the voice of Edwin, piteously crying as he slept, startled the murderer from his design, and the dagger remained suspended in his uplifted grasp. In another moment the boy awoke, and as he beheld the perilous situation in which he was placed, he uttered a cry of horror, and called loudly upon his brother to assist him. But, alas! his Angus was then far away, and ere he could repeat the cry of alarm, Rupert exclaimed in hollow and fiend-like accents,—

"Boy, dare not call for help, for all hope of aid is vain! Thou art in my power, and no human arm can rescue thee from thy doom!"

"Alas! must I then die!" cried Edwin, in a voice of terror. "Hast thou the heart to kill one who never injured thee? Yet too surely do I read my doom in those grim ghastly looks; those frowns that freeze my blood, tell me I must indeed perish."

"Peace, boy," muttered the ruffian, "and tell me instantly where has thy brother concealed himself, and for what purpose has he departed from hence?"

Edwin cast round the room a despairing glance, but his brother was nowhere to be seen; nor could his utmost struggles release him from the powerful grasp of the ruffian, who, with a horrible oath, demanded what had become of his brother. Edwin, however, was too much terrified to reply, when the other, with a violent blow of the fist, struck him insensible upon the floor, and was about to finish the deed with his dagger, when an awful voice echoed through the chamber, and dropping the upraised weapon, the villain stood for a few moments transfixed with horror. But his remorse lasted not long, for danger threatened him on every side, and raising in his arms the form of the insensible boy, he hurried with rapid strides from the chamber.

But still the ghastly visage of the phantom seemed to pursue him, and it was not till he had gained the outside of the ruins that his courage began to revive. Here he briefly paused, irresolute whether to despatch his victim or still preserve him for future vengeance. At that moment his eye encountered the lofty battlements of an old ruined tower, and at the very instant a light streamed through one of its upper casements. This circumstance occasioned him some alarm, and he felt uncertain how to act, since were he to proceed in that direction, he might meet with foes too numerous for his single arm to encounter. Thus impelled by his own guilty fears, he hastened to Badenoch, and having secured his youthful prisoner in a deep dungeon, he hastened to the presence of the chief, to whom he related the discovery he had made. Nothing could exceed the fury with which the imperious Badenoch heard these words, and suspecting that Rupert must have been concerned in preserving the children thus long, he instantly summoned a party of his retainers to his presence, and commanded them to bear the ruffian to the rack, in order that he might be compelled to make a full confession of the share he had taken in the transaction. But Rupert was not to be intimidated, and drawing his sword in his own defence, he exclaimed in a tone of fierce determination—

"Hold, my lord, and ponder what you do ere it be too late! Hitherto I have been faithful to my trust, but this violence may tempt me to say that which will hasten your own downfall."

"You may retire," said the chieftain, addressing himself to the men whose presence he had called for, and on being again left alone with his vassal, he demanded what had become of Magdalen.

"She has perished by my hand," answered Rupert; "and thus has atoned for the rashness that prompted her to save those whom you had doomed to death. Angus is now in the ruin of Glenalvon and may speedily be got rid of, and as for the younger one, he is now in one of your own dungeons, awaiting that death from which he sees no chance of escape."

The displeasure of the Chief of Badenoch vanished as he listened to these words, and after remaining for some time in deep thought, he exclaimed in a tone of more than usual kindness :—

"Thou hast done well, good Rupert, and now, to complete thy services, return to the Castle of Glenalvon, and destroy him whom thou knowest I have most to fear. Be faithful in this transaction, and not only shall gold reward thee, but future honours and advancements shall declare the gratitude of thy master. Away ! do as I have said, and when all is accomplished, return to claim the promised reward of all thy labours in my behalf."

To conquer Glenroy Castle had long been a favourite project with the Chief of Badenoch, and as an opportunity seemed now to offer itself, he prepared to carry his plans into effect by means of stratagem. Lord Mackenzie was the next heir of Glenroy, and after him the Princess Isabel must in right succeed, and it was to defeat those claims that Badenoch summoned nearly the whole of his fierce and lawless band, and on a night when all the inhabitants were buried in sleep, they were, with Rupert at their head, admitted by the hand of Badenoch himself, who had found ready access as a supposed friend. The inhabitants were then made captives, and the fortress taken possession of in the name of Edward, King of England.

Thus Lord Glenroy woke on the morrow a captive in his own towers, and from that moment hope, content, and health were alike strangers to the aged chieftain ; all his faithful servants were debarred from their customary attendance upon him, whilst he himself sunk down the victim of melancholy and despair. The good old warrior, however, still lingered and anxiously dwelt upon the anticipation of Lord Mackenzie's speedy arrival, an event that he trusted would serve to release him from the power of one who had thus basely betrayed him. It is probable he might have been spared to a longer period had not the sudden arrival of the messenger to announce the approach of the Princess Isabel hastened his doom ; for could his death be accomplished before she entered the Castle of Glenroy, the crime might be concealed from her knowledge, and Badenoch avowing himself as the legal heir, would receive her with courtesy, and declare the passion her beauty had inspired in his heart.

But Isabel's resolution in peremptorily demanding to be conducted to the presence of the Lord of Glenroy, excited Badenoch's fears, and to prevent discovery, he had entered the chamber where she reposed, hoping a warning so mysteriously delivered, would deter her from approaching the chamber of the earl ; and it is certain, had she arrived but a few minutes sooner, the Chief of Badenoch would have been awed for a time from the execution of his murderous purpose. At first death was the thought that occurred to him as the only secure means of concealing the horrid secret she had then discovered, and for this purpose he had drawn forth his dagger, when Rupert, who instantly recognised the princess, prevented her discovering his features, by closing the visor of his helmet.

Removed so mysteriously from Glenroy during the long trance in which her senses were bound, Isabel became the victim of a fate which no earthly means could rescue her from. It is certain that Badenoch, when first encountered by Angus, mistook him for the long deceased Lord of Glenalvon, and conscience, awakened with all its tortures, presented to the wild fancy of Badenoch the ideal horrors of past black deeds. Rupert, more hardened at the moment, because assured of the identity of Angus, instantly recognised the armour of his father, and Badenoch, convinced by this explanation, soon recovered from his shock, and by his commands, the youth was almost instantly disarmed and taken prisoner. There were, however, reasons why he should not at present be put to death, and he was therefore thrown into a dungeon till his fate could be more safely decided upon.

The Castle of Badenoch, though impregnable, and not to be subdued by arms, might be reduced by famine; for its excavated base, supported by a slight neck of rock, whose foundation was buried beneath the sands of the sea, could screen the boats of an enemy, and thus prevent the fortress from receiving any stores for the support of the troops. Thus there was a probability of the fortress being obliged to capitulate in the event of a siege, and that such would be the case there was every reason to believe, as one of the companions of Angus had escaped, and it was therefore natural to suppose that he would carry the news to the camp of Robert Bruce, and then obtain immediate assistance in behalf of the young captive.

CHAPTER XLI.

"Hail, Innocence! celestial maid;
  What joys thy blushing charms reveal;
  Sweet as the arbour's cooling shade
  And milder than the verdant gale."

                                        OGILVIE.

WE must now return to Angus, who, buried in a living tomb, alike despaired, when he thought on the fate of a lost brother, and trembled for that of his beloved Isabel, from her he felt assured he was for ever separated. On the day when his imprisonment commenced he had in vain begged to be informed of his own and Edwin's fate; but his guard maintained a sullen silence to his earnest entreaties, and having chained his captive to the wall he left him to his forlorn meditations.

The day was spent by the youth in listless wretchedness, and each footfall that echoed along the gloomy vaults, served but to arouse more and more the melancholy thoughts that rapidly succeeded each other in his brain. The sides of the dungeon were composed of hard rock, high above which was an iron grating which crossed a narrow cavity that admitted a small portion of air and light. This place, however, was far beyond his reach, and giving way to his despair he was about to throw himself upon a heap of straw in one corner of the cell, when the door opened and a female, young and beautiful, advanced towards him. This was Rosalind, the daughter of the stern Chief of Badenoch; but her countenance betokened nought but kindliness and compassion, and advancing with timid footsteps towards the captive, she said :—

"I visited you, Sir Knight, fearing you might be faint and ill;" and taking from an elderly female, who accompanied her, a basket of provisions which she placed before him, she continued. "I trust you will not reject my offered service, since I am come in compassion to your helplessness, and would gladly do all in my power to lighten the sufferings you are doomed to endure. My father, I grieve to say, is your enemy, yet do not on that account hate the guiltless Rosalind, for she knows your sufferings and will lose no opportunity to alleviate them."

Angus, with some surprise, received the offered kindness of Rosalind, who would then have departed had he not with earnest entreaty detained her while he questioned if there were not other prisoners of note in the fortress. For now he had a faint recollection of having heard the cry of a female voice proceed from the covered litter which was borne by Badenoch's men, and which he felt convinced pronounced the name of the princess. Rosalind, however, was unable to satisfy these questions, for as her apartments were situated far from any other portion of the castle, she was a total stranger to the events that had recently occurred. After a pause, however she said :—

"Should I discover your relatives I will exert my utmost influence to mitigate the rigour of their sufferings. But permit me now to depart, for my visit here is a secret one, and were my father to hear of it, I know not how far his anger might carry him. Farewell then, Sir Knight; at this hour tomorrow my attendant or myself will, if possible, return again."

Rosalind and her female companion then left the dungeon, but had scarcely reached the winding passage that led to it, when a heavy footstep was distinctly heard echoing through the dreary vaults. In an instant she extinguished her lamp, and concealing herself behind a pillar waited till the intruder should have passed. As the person hurried by she discovered in him the figure of the sentinel who she had seen on former occasions, and, as she observed him enter the cell which she had just left, she whispered to her attendant :—

"Alas! dear nurse, my heart trembles with apprehension, and I fear that he who is in captivity yonder, is doomed to instant death."

"I am afraid so, too, my lady," answered old Katherine, "for those who once offend the Chief of Badenoch are seldom permitted to escape the vengeance he prepares for all his foes."

"As his child," sighed Rosalind, "I seldom oppose his will; but this young stranger has interested me, and I will make an effort to save him from this cruel destiny."

"Ah, lady!" cried the faithful attendant, "let me implore you to be cautious, for should this feeling of yours be caused by love, you know not the misery you may be preparing for yourself."

"Love!" cried Rosalind; "no, dear nurse, I know not such influence. Pity I can, indeed, feel for the unfortunate, and gladly would I risk my life for the preservation of this noble youth."

"Yet I tremble for your safety, my child," cried the old woman. "But No. 31

come, Rosalind ; let us now return, and we will hereafter consult on the best means for putting your benevolent designs in practice."

But the maiden still lingered on the spot, nor could the nurse withdraw her with all the persuasion she could urge. After a short lapse of time the man returned, and Rosalind, stepping from her hiding place, earnestly besought him to reveal any fresh danger that threatened the unfortunate captive.

"Retire, lady," exclaimed the man, with surprise ; "for should it be known that I have suffered any one to visit the prisoner, the rack will be my punishment. Hark ! the guard approaches ; fly instantly, or I am lost."

"First tell me," cried Rosalind, "what is to be the captive's doom ?"

"Seek to know it in the secret vaulted hall," answered the man as he extinguished the torch, and hurrying down a different avenue, he disappeared, while from an opposite direction a ray of light displayed several armed men descending the rocky pass. Rosalind trembled with terror ; to follow the sentinel who had so hastily retreated, was now impracticable without discovering herself, and ere she could fully determine what course to adopt, the men approached the cell in which Angus was confined and instantly disappeared. It was a moment of dreadful anxiety, and Rosalind was revolving in her own mind whether to advance or retreat, when the men again emerged from the dungeon, and she could see that Angus was amongst them, but they passed by so rapidly that she had not time to resolve upon what course to adopt ; fearful, however, of losing sight of them, she dismissed the attendant in spite of her entreaties to remain, and then following the glare of the torches she glided down a deep descent, and found herself within a spacious vault, from the ceiling of which was suspended a lamp, whose feeble rays only served to increase the horrors of the place. It, however, enabled her to see that at one end was placed a chair on which her father was seated, with the apparent purpose of passing judgment upon his unfortunate captive, whilst, on each side of him stood the lawless ministers of his vengeance, darkly frowning and ready to obey the stern dictates of their imperious master.

Rosalind shuddered as she thus secretly gazed upon the horrible scene ; she had long known there were dungeons beneath the fortress, but never till now was she aware of their extent, or the evil deeds that were perpetrated in them. Whilst she was thus gazing in terror, the iron doors were thrown open, and Angus with a firm step advanced between the double file by which he was guarded. Thus far his courage seemed unsubdued, and taking his place in front of the chair, he awaited with composure the proceedings that were to commence against him. At length Badenoch suddenly broke off a whispered conversation in which he was engaged with one of his people, and addressing himself sternly to the prisoner, he said :—

"Proud boy ! dost thou not now feel that thy destiny is in my hands ? Kneel at my feet for mercy ; confess the vile imposture of thy birth ; acknowledge Edward for thy king, and I may yet spare thee."

"Chief of Badenoch," answered Angus, resolutely, "I treat thy threats with scorn, and call upon thee to kneel at *my* feet to ask mercy for the foul murder of my parents ; or, if thy heart is still hardened, give me a sword, and let us in single combat decide the justice of the cause we both maintain."

"Am I to be thus braved in my own stronghold !" exclaimed the incensed chief, and then motioning for Fergus to stand forth, he continued. "Thou knowest my commands ; teach yon audacious boy the duty of his station, or behold his instant death."

"You have heard our chieftain's commands," said Fergus to the youth. "and knowing them it is now my duty to see that you obey his sovereign will."

"Hah!" exclaimed Angus, indignantly, "dost thou dare thus to address the son of Glenalvon?"

"Boy!" cried the ruffian, "it is in vain longer to persist in this imposture. I am thy father, yet dost thou insolently claim descent from one who, being in his grave, cannot refute the falsehood that has prompted thee to make this assertion. Again, I say, I am thy father, and Magdalen the mother who brought thee forth."

"Badenoch," exclaimed the youth, without deigning to cast a look upon the ruffian, who had last addressed him, "this lie is of thine own invention. But I am not to be subdued by thy shallow artifices. Prepare thy racks, thy tortures, but, ere I perish, learn from my lips that the wrongs I endure will be terribly avenged. Ronald, the faithful vassal of my father, survived the wound thou didst inflict upon him, and his voice, in the presence of witnesses, declared me the son of Glenalvon, and that thou wert his murderer."

"That word has doomed thee," exclaimed Badenoch; "hadst thou accepted my offered mercy thou mightest have lived as the offspring of my vassal, Fergus. But I denounce thee as a traitor to King Edward, and thus the world shall learn that you were sentenced, not from private malice, but on public grounds. Guards, fulfil your office; Fergus, do thou perform the rest, and at my signal let the audacious rebel perish for his treason."

At these words he was seized and dragged towards an arched recess, before which hung a black curtain, which being drawn aside, discovered a cavity, in which a figure clothed in complete black armour, stood like the grim majesty of death.

Rosalind could endure her terrors no longer; she would have shrieked, but the icy chillness that froze her blood refused her utterance. Gasping and faint she clung to the pillar near which she stood, and at that moment all power and strength seemed to forsake her.

Angus was led to the recess and delivered to the figure in black armour, whilst on each side guards were ranged to prevent the possibility of escape. Beyond lay a number of dead bodies; but, oh! what agonies writhed within the bosom of Angus, when at his feet he beheld the pale form of a youth, and gazing down upon it he recognized the features of his beloved Edwin. This sight deprived him of all power of utterance, and falling upon his knees, beside the motionless form of his brother, he at length murmured forth the name of his Edwin. Whilst he was thus absorbed in grief, Fergus stepped forth with a drawn sword in his hand, and raising it he waited but the signal of his chief, when Rosalind, darting from her place of concealment, fell prostrate at the feet of her stern, obdurate father.

"Forbear!" she wildly exclaimed; "slay not the innocent, lest thy daughter, who has been a witness of this night's evil deeds, should hereafter become the accusing testimony that brings thee to an ignominious doom."

"Girl!" roared the infuriated chieftain, "this prying curiosity may henceforth cost thee dear."

"I care not," she replied, "so that my voice saves the innocent from an unmerited doom. Spare, oh, spare this youth, and I will yield up my own life in exchange."

Badenoch trembled with rage, and clenching his mailed fist, he aimed at her a terrific blow which, fortunately for the maiden, missed its intended object.

" Begone from me!" he exclaimed, furiously, " ere my malediction falls upon thee like a withering blight! Take her from my presence, and let her, in solitary imprisonment, repent the rashness that has this night prompted her to become a spy upon my actions. Convey her hence, and see that my orders are obeyed."

Rosalind was instantly seized, and hurried from the place; but, ere the proceedings against Angus had gone further, a loud knocking sounded through the vaulted dungeons, and a voice was heard earnestly demanding entrance. Upon this the door was thrown open, and a retainer, rushing in, exclaimed,—

" Messengers from the English, noble chief, demand your immediate presence at an assembly they are now holding." Then, after a pause, he added,—"There is treason in the castle, I fear, for the sentinel who guarded the western tower is missing from his post!"

Thus circumstanced, Badenoch was for awhile compelled to forego his meditated revenge; and, rising from his seat, he gave orders that Angus should be conveyed back to his dungeon, and a strict watch be set over him. At this command a cloth was thrown over the prisoner's head, and in this state he was hurried from the vault towards the dungeon from whence he had been brought. The chief and Fergus were thus left together, the former of whom, glancing fiercely at the minion, said,—

" Hadst thou struck home upon my signal, all had, ere this, been safe, and Angus, like his brother, had been venomless."

" My lord," answered Fergus, humbly, " be the task mine to finish that which has been left undone. Speak your wish, and doubt not my ready obedience."

" I would be freed from this boy that eats away my peace," exclaimed the Chief of Badenoch, " yet would myself avoid all participation in his death. The younger one is for ever silent: that deed was thine. Be it thine also to remove the other. Hence!—see it done, and the reward of thy service shall be beyond thy hopes."

" Be assured, my lord, it shall be done," answered Fergus, " I know thy wish, and he dies!"

" I rely upon thy word," answered Badenoch, " and now attend me to the chamber of the princess. Be my wishes there accomplished, and thou will find me grateful. Remember —"

" Remember!" repeated a hollow voice that sounded startlingly through the vaults.

" Hark!" exclaimed Badenoch, with trembling alarm; " whence that foreboding cry? Is it not the voice of a murdered victim?"

" A murdered victim!" repeated the same dread voice.

Fergus smiled contemptuously, and his affrighted chieftain shrank back, pale and trembling, and then, in a tone of half-suppressed disdain, he muttered forth,—

" Can a mere echo thus unman one who I thought feared no mortal enemy?"

" This is no mortal enemy," answered the chief.

" I will at least unravel the mystery," exclaimed Fergus; " and, should it prove to be an imposition practised upon us, I will so punish the intruder that he shall never again attempt to pry into our secrets."

As he said this, he seized a lighted torch, and rapidly paced through the dungeon in search of the object which had thus startled them; but, though he examined every part with the greatest care, he could discover nothing which could explain the circumstance he was anxious to clear up. At length, returning to Badenoch, he whispered,—

" Let us quit this place, my lord, without further delay, lest some insidious foe should be concealed here for your destruction. There is some lurking treachery, I feel assured; and, if I may prevail upon you to return to your own chamber, I will take instant steps for punishing those who have thus plotted against you."

Badenoch followed without making any reply; but, in imagination, he still heard sounds that appalled and convulsed his soul. This spot, indeed, had so often been the scene of lawless outrage and violence, that now, when left almost alone in it, the recollection of his cruelties rushed on his memory, and so completely had he become the victim of his terrors, that his limbs almost refused to support him from the place.

Shortly after this the Chief of Badenoch left the castle to obey the summons of the English leaders, and Fergus, rejoicing in the departure of his lord, resolved to carry out certain projects of his own, which he had hitherto been unable to accomplish. He had long sought for the means to release himself from the galling yoke, and from the power of a man whom he at once feared and detested. Thus far he had contrived to disguise the real feelings of his own heart, but how much longer he might be able to do so was uncertain; and, as indications now began to appear of his chieftain's downfall, he determined to save himself, if possible, and, with that end in view, cared not if he assisted in the ruin of Badenoch, so that he could but attain his own ambitious views.

It may be conceived that the unexpected departure of the chief from his castle was a circumstance most favourable to the dark plottings of the treacherous retainer; and, as an opportunity was thus offered, he determined not to let it pass by without making an effort which he believed would raise himself to the highest pinnacle of his hopes. He now revolved in his mind whether it might not be possible to obtain an interview with the English viceroy, and gain his favour by denouncing the man whom he had ever professed to serve. Such a course, he knew, would be attended with the greatest advantage to himself, for Badenoch was by no means a favourite with the English; and, could his ruin be effected, certain honours and promotion would be heaped upon the person who might give the requisite information.

And there were other thoughts which occupied the mind of the treacherous Fergus;—schemes, in fact, that involved the unhappy Princess Isabel in their deep-laid snares, and he resolved to terrify her into becoming his bride, or, in the event of entreaty and artifice failing, to compel her compliance by other and more violent means. With these determinations he doubted not that, ere long, the full accomplishment of his ambitious projects would be brought about.

CHAPTER XLII.

' Poisoned—ill fare!—dead, forsook, cast off!"
KING JOHN.

UPON being led from the cavern, Angus was re-conducted to his former dismal prison, whose solitude was better suited to the purpose of his destruction than even the spot from whence he had been withdrawn. Left once more to the lacerating tortures of his despairing misery, the frantic agonies of his soul defied alike the sympathies of reason, hope, and religion. The pale, ghastly form of Edwin pursued him through the horrors of his dreary confinement; and death, however severe, had been less terrible than a life thus burdened and oppressed.

It was night, and all around the dungeon of the wretched captive was darksome, silent, and terrific. The sea, sometimes rolling its whirling billows against the lowermost bases of his prison, seemed to rock its foundations, whilst at times the hoarse screams of the sea-birds were heard dismally as they flapped their wings under the rude cavity through which air was admitted to the dungeon. At such a moment as this he was startled by a slight noise, and, raising his eyes, he beheld a stream of light faintly flash through the grating of the door, and starting from the ground upon which he had thrown himself, the portal slowly turned upon its hinges, and gave admittance to two figures, dimly discernible as they slowly and cautiously advanced. The foremost, who held the lamp, whispered to his companion, who remained to guard the door, and then advancing towards Angus, threw aside his cloak and discovered a countenance too young and open to portend the doom which the captive had anticipated. He was attired in the Scottish costume, and the golden locks, that fell in parting ringlets over his fair brow, gave a softness to his features which the warlike garb could not divest them of. Angus was at a loss to conceive what could be the object of this visit, but the stranger advancing, offered his hand, and, with an air of encouraging frankness, said :—

"Be not alarmed at this visit, Sir Knight, for in me you behold a friend who has witnessed with admiration the firmness and constancy with which you have sustained yourself. I mourn the fate that has brought you within these walls, and am here either to share your doom or procure your immediate rescue."

"Generous youth," exclaimed Angus, who had listened to these words with wonder, "fortune and fate have spent their utmost malice, and can do but little more against me. I know the relentless hate of him who now holds me captive, and am prepared to meet the doom he threatens to crush me with."

"Nay, it would be weakness to despair whilst hope remains," answered the other. "Will Angus Glenalvon disdain to receive the aid that is offered him, or is the world so valueless and void that there is no remaining motive why he should yet seek to preserve himself from the dreadful fate he anticipates?"

"Thou knowest not all my griefs," exclaimed Angus, "for 'tis a brother's fate, and not my own, that most heavily oppresses my soul."

"But remaining here will not restore him thou mournest," said the youth. "A few moments' delay will render thee guilty of an act of self-destruction; for thy death has been resolved on, and nothing but instant flight can save thee."

"He speaks truly," exclaimed the man who had accompanied the last speaker in his visit, "and it is now my duty to remind you that your own death cannot serve the unfortunate Edwin. We have risked our lives in thus attempting to save yours, and but a few short moments remain ere the choice that offers thee life or death will be allowed. Decide, then, Angus Glenalvon, for longer we dare not tarry."

Full of doubt and astonishment, Angus fixed his eyes steadfastly upon his unknown visiters. The younger of the two bore a countenance marked with the stamp of sincerity and truth; that of his companion was darker and of more rugged aspect, but seemingly characteristic of good intentions. He had been our hero's principal gaoler during his imprisonment, and the captive had certainly experienced some little kindness from him that seemed to invite his confidence in his present offers of service. Still, however, amazed as he was at an occurrence so unlooked-for, he remained for some few moments in anxious deliberation. Yet the milder expression visible in the countenance of the younger person banished his suspicions of treachery, and, addressing the latter, he demanded how his deliverance was to be effected.

"My father," answered the youth, "keeps the keys of the lower portals, which, by a stratagem, I have possessed myself of. One of the gates leads by a private pass directly under the eastern tower, and on reaching the place of destination further means have been taken to secure your escape. Death to us all would be inevitable were our attempt to release you to be discovered, and therefore do I again implore you to hasten from hence ere means are taken to frustrate our design."

"And, should I owe my deliverance to you," exclaimed Angus, "what recompense can you hope from one who is bankrupt alike in fortune and happiness?"

"My only recompense," answered Donald, for such the youth declared his name to be, "shall be the gratification of having done my duty to a fellow creature. Or should any greater reward be bestowed upon me," he continued timidly, "let it be your esteem and love. From this moment I devote myself to your service, and happy shall I be for permission to follow you henceforth as your page."

"We waste time, Sir Knight," again interposed the guard, "for the chance that now offers for escape will be for ever lost unless you instantly prepare to accompany us from the place of your captivity."

"I will no longer delay to accept the opportunity which has thus been offered me," exclaimed Angus; and then addressing himself to the youth, he continued, "to you, Donald, I will, if Heaven permits it, owe my deliverance, and since it's your wish you shall follow my fortunes till better days dawn upon your career."

The guard then advanced, and presenting him with a sword, said,—

"Ere we leave this place, Sir Knight, it will be necessary to disguise yourself, in case we should meet any one in our way from hence. This cloak will serve to conceal you, and should danger threaten, I shall be present to lend my assistance against the foe, should our retreat be interrupted."

"But through what means," demanded Angus, "have I then found a friend in one who I believed to be an enemy?"

"At present, Sir Knight, you must forbear to question me upon that subject," answered the man, "for this is not a moment when I can enter into an explanation of the motives that have led to this change. Suffice it at present to know that I was once in the service of your father, and that at his death I was unwillingly compelled to enter the service of the Chief of Badenoch, from whose trammels I am at length resolved to free myself, in order to transfer my allegiance to the heir of my own loved master."

The seeming honesty depictured in the looks of the man bespoke sincerity and invited confidence, and Angus was too generous to suspect deceit in one who had thus proffered his aid. It was not long, however, ere the treachery of the villain was made manifest, for the figure of a man was seen stealing through the gloom in which the dungeon was involved, and in an instant Fergus sprang forward, and would have plunged a dagger into the heart of Angus, had not the voice of Donald aroused him to a consciousness of his danger. The warning was brief, but it was sufficient to enable the young soldier to protect himself with the weapon which had just before been given to him, and stepping back a pace or two, he called upon the guard to render him his assistance. To his surprise, however, he discovered that the fellow had retreated from the dungeon, and finding himself thus left to his own resources, he prepared to protect himself vigorously against the attack of his implacable enemy. By this time Fergus had also drawn his sword, and a combat ensued, which was carried on with such vigour and determination on both sides, that it would have been impossible for a spectator to have foreseen on which side victory would declare itself. At length, however, the blows of Fergus became more deadly and frequent, for he had received several deep wounds, and, goaded by revenge, he, with tremendous force, raised high his ponderous sword, which he now grasped in both his hands, determined by one tremendous stroke to cleave asunder the skull of his more youthful antagonist. At this moment, however, Donald sprung forward and averted the blow, whilst Angus, stooping suddenly on one side, awaited the opportunity, and grappling his antagonist with one hand he passed his sword through the body of his foe, too, with many a muttered curse, fell upon the ground, never to rise from again with life. This done, Angus, who was also wounded, reeled and would have fallen to the floor, had not Donald supported his tottering frame, and with difficulty supported him to a ledge of the rock, where he sunk down exhausted from fatigue and loss of blood. At this period, a hoarse exulting laugh burst from the lips of Fergus, and regarding his fallen adversary with a look of triumph, he exclaimed,—

"Boy, thou diest; and my revenge, even in death, is more glorious than the imperfect victory thou hast gained, for thy soul shall bear mine company to the darksome regions of the grave. A fatal drug, administered in thy food, now rages through thy veins, and what my sword has left unaccomplished, the poison will, ere long, complete."

Fergus would have continued in this strain of fiendish malice, but he was now seized with the convulsive tortures of death, and after writhing beneath the agonies with which he had been seized, he sank back upon the ground, and yielded up his guilty spirit amidst the most fearful curses and imprecations.

Angus also felt that he was fast sinking, yet he repined not at the treachery which had thus been practised upon him, for death had no terrors greater than the pain he had endured in the loss of all those whom he had loved in the world. Still Donald supported, and would have encouraged him with a hope of recovery, but he smiled feebly at these efforts, and grasping fervently the hand of his generous friend, exclaimed :—

'"I am exhausted, boy, and feel the heavy langour of approaching dissolution creep through my failing limbs. Yet I repine not at my fate, for better is it to perish thus, than to linger out a miserable existence as the captive of a cruel and unrelenting foe."

"Alas ! Sir Knight," cried Donald, "and is it indeed true that you have swallowed the fatal potion you miscreant spoke of ?"

"It is," answered Angus, in yet feebler accents ; "and if you would indeed serve me, mark well the last wishes that my lips will be permitted to utter. Seek out the Princess Isabel, who is somewhere confined within this castle, and say that my last thoughts were fixed upon her, and that Heaven to which I am hurrying. Say that in death I bequeathed her my latest blessing, and that my last prayers were breathed forth in supplication for her future happiness. Entreat her sometimes to remember Angus, and say that in the cheering hope that she will do as I did, contented and resigned to a destiny which I had but too long anticipated."

He now appeared to grow quite exhausted, and sinking back, remained for some moments without motion. The solemn silence that ensued was awful and impressive, and Donald sorrowing deeply for what had occurred, hung mournfully over the form which thus laid outstretched before him. His fixed eye was bent in speechless agony upon the pale visage of the prostrate Angus, and the convulsive sighs that escaped him, told the grief with which the melancholy event had inspired his heart.

The lamp, as it cast its dim light around, displayed at no great distance off the grim and bleeding form of the assassin Fergus, and served to render yet more terrible the dismal scene amidst which this fearful tragedy had taken place. The horrid clang of the recent combat was now buried in the most profound and death-like stillness, and the silence and solemnity that reigned, rendered even more impressive the thoughts indulged in by the sorrowing survivor.

CHAPTER XLIII.

" In some breasts passion lies concealed and silent,
Like war's swart powder in a castle vault,
Until occasion, like the linstock, lights it ;
Then comes at once the lightning and the thunder,
And distant echoes tell thee all is rent asunder."
ANON.

THE many dreary hours of confinement which the Princess Isabel endured,. passed heavily away, for she had been left in all the terrors of uncertainty, and not only her own destiny, but that of Angus was wrapped in the most impenetrable uncertainty. At length, as she was one evening sitting in the solitary chamber that had been assigned her, the shrill blasts of a bugle awoke her from the chilling anguish of despair, and once more brought back her mind to the perils with which she was environed. Wondering what this could portend, she dismissed her attendant to ascertain what had occurred, and during the absence of Marianne, she gave way to the suspense and doubt which were thus conjured up in her mind. She remembered, however, that this was the night on which Badenoch had declared he should return and claim her final decision, and in the full belief that he would now present, himself before her, she gave way to the alarm which it was impossible to subdue.

"Merciful Heaven !" she ejaculated, " is there no hope,—no way left of escaping a doom so terrible as this?"

At this moment she heard sounds afar off, as if persons were hurrying along the corridor, and believing that all her worst fears were about to be realized, she uttered a deep groan of anguish, and sunk, nearly fainting, upon the floor. Presently, however, she was recovered by the care of her attendant, Marianne ; and having ascertained that no one else was in the chamber, she, in wild accents, implored that none might be permitted to enter the room till she had **recovered herself** sufficiently to endure an interview that she so much dreaded.

"Nay, my lady," answered Marianne ; "your terrors have been needlessly excited, for at present you will be spared the visit that you seem so much to dread."

"Is not my dreaded persecutor returned ?" asked Isabel, anxiously.

"I believe not, my lady," answered the attendant ; "and, besides, I have learnt that all the castle is in an uproar, and the people are too much employed in looking after their safety to think of anything else. The sentinel, my lady, had quitted his post when I reached the place, and that was quite enough to convince me that something extraordinary had occurred. The sound of the trumpet, it seems, has spread alarm and dismay through the castle."

"But know you the cause of this alarm ?" cried the princess.

"Why, my lady," answered Marianne, "I ventured as far as I could, and overheard some of the conversation that was going on among the people below, from which it seems they have been pursued almost to the rock itself by a part of the army of King Robert Bruce, who has been able to gain a very important victory of his enemies."

This confused account had in it a dawning of hope that served in some degree to relieve the terrors of the princess, and she was now able to make more minute inquiries.

"Did you hear," she asked, "whether the king was with the party that pursued Badenoch's vassals ?"

"I did not hear them say quite so much as that," replied Marianne, "but they mentioned the name of Randolf ; and if your highness would like to hear anything more of what is going forward, I'll run and listen to what they are talking about, and bring back whatever intelligence I can gather."

Without waiting for a reply, Marianne hurried away from the chamber, and scarcely had she disappeared, when another door was suddenly thrown open, and the Chief of Badenoch presented himself before the terrified princess. The settled character of his deep and hardened villany was now more apparent than ever. His lowering eye expressed at once all the dark emotions that stirred his guilty soul, and approaching the princess, he said :—

"At length, Isabel, the period has arrived which is to terminate my doubts and give you the liberty for which you sigh. I am come to lead you from a wearisome restraint, the conditions of which are, that you accompany me to the altar, and there pronounce those vows which will make you mine for ever."

Isabel withdrew the hand which he had seized within his own, and collecting all the fortitude she possessed, she said, firmly :—

"Must I again remind the Chief of Badenoch that his suit is unavailing, and that even were I disposed to encourage his addresses, I am not so far mistress of myself as to give an answer upon such a subject as this ?"

"And must I also remind you," demanded Badenoch, "that you are now my prisoner, and far removed from those who may once have claimed control over your actions ? Remember, also, how deeply it concerns your peace to accede to my wishes, rather than, by an obstinate resistance, to call down the anger and revenge of him who thus humbly entreats your love."

"I know the worst," answered Isabel, "and am prepared to endure even death itself, rather than submit to the commands of a tyrant. Shall the daughter of the wronged Mackenzie become the bride of him who, with wanton barbarity and lawless guilt, could burst the sacred bonds of love and virtue asunder ?—who, in open defiance of every tie, divine or human, could basely rob a husband of his wife's affections, and then exult in the injury which his own baseness had achieved ?"

"Girl," exclaimed the Chief of Badenoch, "have you reflected upon the consequences that will follow this obstinacy?"

"I have not forgotten that I am in your power," she replied; "but the thought of my own suffering shall not force me into compliance with the hateful terms you have proposed. I may be wretched even beyond my worst anticipations, but no force on earth shall ever compel me to accept the offers of him whom I have so much reason to loathe and execrate."

"This obstinacy," exclaimed Badenoch, "might at any other moment have proved fatal to you; I, however, would abstain from intimidation, and even though thus scornfully rejected, I will still try the gentle powers of persuasion."

"And have you then forgotten Emmeline?" demanded the princess.— "Does she not still live to execrate the hour when she bestowed her hand upon such a monster as yourself?"

"Emmeline no longer possesses my love," he replied; "but I have determined to make such a provision as shall render happy the remainder of her days. Grant but my wish, Isabel, and I will acknowledge Robert Bruce for my sovereign, and, by taking part in his cause, restore him to the throne from which he has been driven. Your father shall have ample recompense afforded him, and then——"

"My father will accept no favour from thee," interrupted the princess indignantly. "He has known thee for a traitor to thy lawful king, and never will his hand be held out to grasp that which has drawn forth the sword of rebellion."

"Nay, girl," the chieftain went on, "it is in vain thus to give utterance to words that may serve to excite that wrath which I would fain subdue. Consent to the proposition I have made, and from that moment thou wilt create peace and harmony between me and all those whom thou callest thy friends."

"Hold, chief," cried Isabel, "and profane my ears no more with words such as those thou hast uttered, for sooner than link my fate with him who was the destroyer of my father's happiness, I will cast myself from the battlements, and thus rid myself of a life which has now become a weary and oppressive burthen."

"Rash girl," exclaimed the Chief of Badenoch, "my vigilance shall prevent the deed thou hast thus hinted at. Reject my offer again, and I will take means to force thee to live until it shall be my pleasure to pronounce the awful judgment that gives thee to the tomb."

"Prepared as I am for all thy deadly malice can conceive against me," answered Isabel, "I can treat thy threats with the scorn they justly merit. But let me remind thee, proud chief, that the time will come when the violence now offered me shall be terribly avenged. I am at present in thy power, but fate is already working against thee, and ere long the Monarch of Scotland will regain his rights, and thou mayest then well tremble, for such punishment awaits thee as thy heinous crimes justly merit."

"Thy prophecy, vain girl, will never be realized," exclaimed Badenoch, "for King Edward's power in Scotland is unshaken, and Bruce is compelled to be a wanderer and an outcast, I am safe from the evils thou hast spoken of. Once more, therefore, I command thee to submit, or my fury will become excited, and thou wilt then endure all the horrors of my vengeance."

"I have already said that I fear it not," repeated Isabel, unmoved by the vehemence with which these words had been uttered.

"Imprudent girl," he exclaimed, "thou hast sealed thine own destiny and that of others whose fate depended solely upon thine own conduct. Remember thou art not my only captive, and a word will be sufficient to crush with one blow all who have dared to raise themselves up against me. What ho!" he cried, stamping furiously upon the floor, and as two murderous-looking ruffians stepped into the chamber he continued,—"thou hast already received my orders ; seize yonder girl and convey her to the subterraneous dungeon beneath the eastern rampart and there leave her till I have considered the doom that will best serve the vengeance it is my intention to take."

"I am well prepared for this violence," exclaimed Isabel, with the same unmoved firmness as before ; "and whether your doom consigns me to instant death or endless imprisonment, I am equally indifferent, for my trust is in Heaven, and in that reliance I can firmly suffer more than it is in the power of the monster Badenoch to inflict upon me."

"And art thou so blind to the interest of thy father and other friends that thou canst consign them to a fate which firmer nerves than thine would tremble at ?"

"Thou hast heard me," she replied calmly, "and, therefore, all further threats would be in vain. Death is my desire, and gladly will I hail the moment which is to end my earthly cares."

"Isabel, thou hast rightly anticipated," exclaimed Badenoch ; "for, great as my love once was, thou shalt find that my hatred can be more intense. Yet a word may still save thee, and, therefore, do I call upon thee to pause ere thou decidest, lest when the hour of repentance shall arrive thou findest thyself bereft of power to change a destiny too terrible for the mind to dwell upon. Speak then, proud girl, and bid me avert the deadly evils which soon must fall upon and crush thee."

"Lead me to my doom," she answered, "for my resolution has been formed, and no threats shall ever force me to retract it. Come then, ye ministers of murder, execute your fell purpose,—strike your poniards to my heart, and with my last breath I will defy the power of him who, coward like, would thus execute his vengeance against a lone and unprotected woman !"

"Let her be instantly dragged to the dungeon I have spoken of," exclaimed Badenoch furiously ; "leave her there in darkness and solitude, and when next I visit her she shall either accept my terms or perish in her obstinacy. Hence, I say, and do my bidding faithfully, or your own lives shall answer for it !"

"Thou shalt find I can be firm in my resolution," she replied, "for death has no terrors equal to those I feel when gazing upon the monster whose crimes have rendered him hateful to all the world. Farewell, proud chief, and be upon thy guard, for the hour of thy destiny is near at hand."

The ruffians now dragged her away, and Badenoch, smarting under the words he had heard, paced up and down the chamber in a state of mind bordering on madness. At last, however, a sudden thought seemed to strike him, and then, hurriedly leaving the room, he in low and muttered words vowed the destruction of his victim.

CHAPTER XLIV.

" 'Tis better to be lowly born,
And strange with humble livers in content,
Than to be perked up in a glistering grief,
And wear a golden sorrow."   SHAKSPERE.

THE ruffians conveyed the hapless princess through innumerable dark winding passages and steep descents ; and when she at length revived to sense and recollection, the first sounds that struck upon her ear were those of the clank of chains dismally rattling near her. Opening her eyes, she beheld the abhorred form of Badenoch approaching from the door, and seizing her hand, he, with a countenance blackened by every baleful passion, led her towards an object which lay stretched in the middle of the dungeon. Isabel involuntarily gazed down on the form to which her attention was directed, and as she recognized the pale and ghastly features of her father, a wild scream of agony escaped her lips, that echoed through the many dungeons with which they were surrounded.

But, alas! Mackenzie knew not his once-beloved Isabel, for his reason had fled, and the scene that ensued was such as harrowed up every feeling in the breast of the hapless princess. This, indeed, was an affliction far more severe than any she was prepared for; her own wrongs she had resigned herself to endure with patience, but a father's sufferings she could not behold without the deepest emotion, and despair now struck upon her heart like an ice-bolt.

"Said I not truly," exclaimed the fiend-like Chief of Badenoch, "when I declared that my vengeance, when aroused, would be terrible? Ill-fated Mackenzie, thy daughter has drawn thee into the same vortex which will destroy herself."

But Isabel heard not these words, for she had sunk at the feet of the poor maniac, little less distracted than himself. Death was depicted in every wild look that shot from his hollow eye, and it was in vain that she sought to console herself with a belief that he recognized her. At length, however, he gazed wildly upon her countenance, but it was only for an instant, and then, tearing himself from her embrace, and dashing her from him with passionate fury, he threw her to the ground, and snatching up a dagger which was lying at his feet, he would have plunged it into her heart, under the idea that it was the faithless Emmeline who thus presented herself before him. But the Chief of Badenoch stepped forward to her rescue, and having disarmed the maniac, he addressed his hapless victim in his usual tones of coolness:—

"Will the Princess Isabel now be mine," he said, "or leave her father to the fate that has been pronounced against him?"

"Leave me, fell homicide!" she indignantly replied—"leave me, I say, for thy presence does but add to the torture that already afflicts me."

"Listen to your doom, girl," exclaimed Badenoch, "and then decide upon the course it will be best to pursue. Swear to become my wife, or never more behold your father. These moments are the last I will grant between the completion of your misery by Mackenzie's death or his restoration, and your own liberty. Choose, then, the destiny that is now offered you, for I will no longer be trifled with by one who is in my power. Become the wife of Badenoch, and your father shall exchange this dungeon's gloom for a more cheerful residence beneath the roof of Glenroy Castle;—dare to refuse me, and his fate is sealed for ever!"

"Glenroy is the tomb of the murdered!" cried Isabel, with a shudder; "these eyes have seen the innocent slain by thy hand, and my lips shall one day denounce thee for thy crimes."

"These words will but madden me to fury," exclaimed the chief: "yet once more do I ask if thou wilt be mine. Bethink you, lady, of the helplessness of your present situation, for Angus is in the power of Badenoch's lord, and —"

"He will murder him!" interrupted our heroine frantically.

"Thy words may prove prophetic," answered the other gloomily. "But Mackenzie shall be my first victim; and for the last time I ask thee, girl, if thou wilt be mine."

As he said this he drew his sword, and held it threateningly over the unfortunate Mackenzie, when Isabel, rushing between the chief and his victim, exclaimed in despairing accents,—

"Spare, oh spare my father!—Badenoch, I am powerless to resist your might ;—you have tortured my soul to madness,—my feelings to desperation and the bitterest anguish! Now you behold me at your feet, and the only boon I ask is that you will plunge your sword into my bosom, and thus end my griefs for ever."

She could utter no more, for a death-like faintness overpowered her, and sinking at the feet of her ruthless persecutor, she became for a time unconscious of the misery to which a cruel fate had consigned her. Finding her in this helpless situation, the Chief of Badenoch raised her in his arms, and bore her from the dungeon, whilst the hapless Mackenzie, as his vacant eye pursued her receding form, uttered a sigh of anguish, in the melancholy belief that she who had been taken from his presence was the faithless Emmeline, whose former conduct had doomed him to a life of wretchedness and despair.

In gaining possession of the person of Lord Mackenzie, the chief had attained an object which he had long sought in vain, for his power was now secure and unquestioned, not only to destroy the man whom he hated and feared, but to seize upon his vast inheritance, which could be easily done by compelling Isabel to become his wife ; and in order the better to accomplish all his designs, he now spread a report that Mackenzie had fallen in the last battle between the Scots and English, a rumour that was at once believed by Robert Bruce and the friends of his cause, since no intelligence could be gathered of the missing nobleman, and it was well known that he would not have deserted the monarch he acknowledged, whilst a spark remained of that life which he had voluntarily sworn should be devoted to the cause of the dethroned King of Scotland.

When the Princess Isabel once more revived, the wild distraction of the late scene had left her exhausted and broken in spirits. For some time she lay upon a couch in the apartment to which Badenoch had conveyed her, but at length advancing footsteps startled her, and as she sprung upon her feet the chief entered, followed by Oswald, the treacherous ruffian who had betrayed Angus, and who it now seemed, was to be entrusted with the duty of watching over her. Isabel shrunk back in terror as she observed them enter, but the chief approached, and having taken from the hand of his attendant a small box of ebony, he presented it to his shrinking victim, and as a flash of triumph shot from his eye, exclaimed—

"Take this, Isabel, for 'tis thine, and full dearly hast thou purchased it. Nay, reject it not, proud girl, for 'tis a gift of costly value, and well worthy thine acceptance. Wherefore hesitate to receive it ?"

Isabel had recoiled back from the gift which was thus offered, for she felt a painful conviction that some dreadful sight was about to blast her eyes, and Badenoch perceiving her repugnance to accept it from his hands, opened the lid of the box, and then continued, in a tone that betrayed the recklessness and savage ferocity that actuated his revenge—

"Behold, girl!" he exclaimed, hoarsely; "that for which the love of Badenoch is despised; 'tis the heart of Angus Glenalvon, and to whose keeping can it be so well entrusted as thine own ?"

For an instant her eyes fell upon the bleeding human heart, on which was placed a label stained with gore, but upon which the name of Angus could be clearly decyphered. With a groan of horror she sank upon the ground, whilst the insatiate monster, without one touch of pity or humanity, gazed upon her with a look of fiendlike triumph. Finding, however, that she was no longer conscious of his presence, he motioned for his attendant to follow, and turning from the room, left the helpless object of his vengeance to awaken in the dreadful consciousness of the sanguinary revenge he had taken.

Leaving her, however, for the present, it will be necessary to observe, that on the night when Badenoch had betrayed the princess from the Castle of Glenroy, he had heard, with unutterable rage, her apostrophe to the name of Angus, when she supposed herself to be upon the eve of death. This served but to increase his vindictive hatred towards the youth whom he had already so deeply injured, and from that moment he resolved upon his death whenever it might be necessary to the furthersome of his own base views.

Badenoch, on the preceding evening, had with difficulty reached his castle undiscovered by the forces of Robert Bruce, who had, by one bold exploit, gloriously regained the principal fortresses that guarded the western isles, and which gave him an advantage that promised future triumph to his arms.

Lord Randolf, impatient for the return of his young friend Agnus, had learnt to his dismay, of his having fallen into the hands of an unknown chieftain, but who he at once conjectured to be Badenoch. Anxious for the safety of Glenalvon, he laboured incessantly to discover the place of his captivity, and at length traced Badenoch to the assembly at Perth, from whence the forces of Bruce had recently driven the rebellious nobles there convened, and following the track of his retreat, Randolf chased him to the fortress of Badenoch, hoping to effect the rescue of his friend, whom he there conjectured to be imprisoned. It was this occurrence which filled the garrison with so much alarm, but having once more secured himself within this stronghold, Badenoch made preparations for its defence, and so certain did he feel of his safety, that he at once began to devise fresh schemes by which he might complete his projects against Isabel, and rid himself of Fergus whose rivalry he so much dreaded.

His first thought was to command the presence of Fergus, who the reader is already aware, had paid the penalty of his crimes by death, and from Oswald the chief learnt a false statement of the occurrence which had deprived him of the assistance of a reckless ally. He, however, secretly exulted in being thus rid of one whose fidelity he had began to suspect; but his joy was yet further increased upon being informed that Angus Glenalvon had also perished. He then commanded Oswald to take the heart from the corpse, and following him to the dungeon, he there beheld the bodies as they lay stretched in death before him. Badenoch cast a slight glance of ruthless malice around, and then sternly addressing Oswald, said :—

" Thou hast told me, fellow, that both these fell by your hand, but your quivering lips assure me that the tale is forged to win my favour with. Be that as it may, however, you now behold me resolute in my purpose, and thou shalt either perish for thy falsehood, or complete the design that brought us here. Place before me the heart of Angus Glenalvon, and I will not only pardon thy deceit, but bestow upon thee such a reward as shall amply recompense thee for the service."

As he pronounced these words he hurried from the dungeon, and being shortly afterwards joined by Oswald, who declared that his purpose had been completed, he bestowed upon him a purse of gold, and to secure his fidelity, placed him in the situation that had been left vacant by the death of Fergus.

His daughter Rosalind, early devoted by a harsh, unrelenting father, to a conventual life, had already experienced the full force of his implacable resentment. Her generous, but ineffectual attempt to preserve the life of Angus, had hastened her own melancholy fate, and without heeding her entreaties, she had been hurried from the castle and conveyed to a distant convent, where her future days were to be passed in seclusion. Badenoch never saw, or designed to think of her after the night when she had aroused his anger against herself.

It is true she had long known the destiny to which she was to be consigned —a destiny now hastened in its conclusion by the decided part she had taken in favour of one whom her father hated. Inflexible and fiercely-determined when once offended, Badenoch took ample vengeance on his guiltless child, and resolving never to behold her again, he had given her in strict charge to the care of a sufficient guard, to be instantly delivered to the superior of the convent, with peremptory injunctions that she should, on the day of her entrance within its portal, commence her profession, and dispensing as far as possible, take without delay the solemn vow of initiation.

The man who was intrusted with this tyrannic mandate had performed his harsh errand in strict conformity with the designs of his imperious master, and witnessed the hapless Rosalind's sorrowful renunciation of a world which she did not bid adieu to without regret. At his return, Badenoch having been assured that the errand was accomplished to its fullest extent, soon lost all remembrance of his injured daughter, and from that moment exulted in the certainty that he had thus secured one whose abhorrence of crime might one day or other have prompted to denounce him of the crimes he had committed. Thus did he add another victim to his cruel tyranny, and he became more than ever resolved to carry out his infamous purposes even though it might be at the expense of more blood.

CHAPTER XLV.

" Oh, ye immortal powers
That guard the just! watch round his couch
And soften his repose;—banish his sorrows
And becalm his soul;—remember all his virtues.
And show mankind that goodness is your care."

ADDISON.

THE chamber now occupied by the unhappy Princess Isabel was a small vaulted room that overhung the dreadful summit of the precipice upon which the fortress was situated; its blackened walls, lined with heavily-carved wainscot, were gloomily lighted by a single window through which the feeble rays of the setting sun were dimly admitted. Isabel had almost unconsciously thrown herself upon a seat fixed in the deep recess, and was watching with a vacant look the sunbeams as they danced upon the waves, and which, under other circumstances, would have called forth her admiration. A solemn stupor had succeeded the agonizing horror of her former feelings, and she was sitting nearly in a state of unconsciousness, when suddenly she was aroused by a light strain of melancholy music that floated by and seemed to have been produced by unearthly agency. This served to recall her to recollection, and then again remembering the last fearful interview she had had with the Chief of Badenoch, a frenzy appeared to seize upon her brain, and as she rose to flee from the apartment, a dizziness overpowered her, and she fell fainting and insensible on the ground.

Oswald shortly afterwards entered the room, and hastened to raise her, and, having once more restored her to consciousness, he delivered a hasty message from his chief, and then retired, leaving her once more to the agonizing reflections that oppressed her weary soul. Hers was indeed a melancholy situation, and she shuddered convulsively as she pondered on the long train of sufferings she had already endured, and those that were yet to come.

From these harassing reflections she was at length aroused by the deep tolling of a bell, that announced the eleventh hour, and for the first time she glanced round her forlorn prison, and discovered that it was not the one she had been accustomed to inhabit. This revived afresh the recollection of re-

cent occurrences, and she remembered that Badenoch had commanded his
ruffians to convey her to the dungeon on the east side of the castle, where she
had subsequently found her father, a captive in the power of his insatiate
enemy. To release him was, therefore, the first object of her care, and,
snatching up a lamp, she found that the door was open, through which she
passed into a spacious corridor, and then continuing her way, she resolved
to make, at least, this one desperate effort to restore her frenzied parent to
liberty.

Impelled by filial love and duty, the princess, with eager haste, proceeded
onwards ; but amidst the numerous intricate openings that branched out in
various directions, she found herself at a loss which road to pursue. She,
therefore, abandoned herself to the guidance of chance, and thus prompted to
adventure, pursued her progress exactly as fate directed her footsteps. One
arm sustained the long veil she wore, whilst her lamp, as it trembled in her
hand, threatened almost every moment to expire.

The winds now howled dismally, seeming to shake the castle even to its
very foundation, whilst at times the loud, tremendous roar of the sea, agitated
by the tempest of the night, mingled in the wild, unearthly chorus, and carried
dread to the heart of the sad and nearly broken-hearted wanderer. At last, a
sudden gust of wind rushing through the vaulted passage, extinguished her
lamp, and almost at the same instant she discovered before her the dark outlines of two human figures, at no great distance in advance. Presently the
glare of a torch borne by one of them, enabled her to see the intruders more
distinctly, and shrinking behind a buttress, she could hear the conversation
that was passing between them.

" Did you see nothing move swiftly yonder ?" demanded one of the men, in
tones of alarm.

" Where?" asked the other, pausing abruptly in his speed.

No. 33

" Yonder, in the deep shade of the cavern," was the reply. " Something in black flitted across the path, and vanished almost as soon as my eye caught sight of it."

" I saw nothing," muttered his comrade, " so rouse you, and be a man, or we shall miss the object that should employ us to-night."

" I am no more a coward than you are, Oswald," exclaimed the other, " but, to confess the truth, I like not this dismal place, so let us make haste and quit it. They say it is the haunt of spirits, and no wonder at it, for these old frightful towers have witnessed many a foul deed, and, between ourselves, comrade, I have no great fancy for the job our lord has thought proper to give us."

" Why, how now, Robert," exclaimed Oswald, " hast thou no more courage in thee than a woman? remember the reward we are to have for this business, and either follow me to the eastern wing, or leave me to finish the deed by myself."

" The eastern wing!" cried Isabel, with sickening faintness, " alas! 'tis then my father they are about to murder!"

By this time the ruffians had nearly reached the extremity of the gallery, and suddenly passing through a low gothic portal they were almost instantly hidden from her sight. This aroused her, and hurrying after them, she soon found herself traversing another passage, through whose distant space the reflection of the torch was still discernable.

For a considerable distance she continued to follow the receding footsteps of the ruffians through many a dreary corridor, damp with unwholesome vapour and blackened with age and desolation. At length the men reached the top of a flight of spiral steps which they precipitately descended, and Isabel attempted to follow them, but a faintness overpowered her, and for a few moments she was obliged to pause. Reflection, however, still urged her to proceed, and passing down the steps she once more beheld the men as they passed on more slowly than they had done before, and crossing a sort of court-yard, they approached the low gothic porch of a building that appeared at one time to have been devoted to religious worship. This they stealthily entered, followed at some little distance by Isabel, who found herself within the castle chapel, the gloom of which served to increase the terrors with which her soul was already inspired, and the storm which just then burst forth with redoubled violence, seemed to warn the murderers from the guilty purpose which had thus brought them out at the solemn hour of midnight.

Quickening her pace, the princess now hurried after them, but suddenly she lost all traces of them, though the glare of their torches flashing upwards still continued to afford some clue to guide her in the pursuit, and after some time she found herself in a more remote part of the fabric. Pausing here for a moment, she became convinced that she had pursued a different path to that which had been taken by the men; but presently she observed, by the light they bore, that they had turned on one side, and proceeding in that direction, she soon found herself in what appeared at one time to have formed the burying place belonging to the chapel. Frantic with terror, she still continued to move onwards, when suddenly she stumbled forward, and would have been precipitated into a new-made grave had she not caught a pillar and thus saved herself from almost certain death.

At that period she observed the two men approaching from an opposite direction, and stepping back for concealment, she heard Oswald say,—

" This spot will suit our purpose well; for the sea, our former burying place, might chance to give forth its secrets, and thus involve our chief in danger."

"And do you think his crime may not be discovered, even though we bury the victim in this secluded spot?" demanded Robert, gloomily.

"What is that to us?" asked the other. "For my own part, I am but like yourself, an agent in this business, and so let the guilt and punishment fall on him that conceived and commanded us to do the deed. A good and valiant soldier ever obeys the will of his leader, without troubling himself about the motive or cause for which he is to act. If, however, your conscience is troubled with any qualms of cowardice, depart and leave me here alone to the performance of this adventure."

"Oswald," exclaimed the other, angrily, "I have seen good reason to believe that you are not all you would make the world think. This villany has come too suddenly upon you to be real; for I can remember the time when you would have shrunk from the mention of such a crime as this, and yet you are now willing to take the whole crime upon your own shoulders."

"And what is it to thee if I have seen reason to change my opinion upon these subjects?" exclaimed Oswald. "Let it suffice that I see my own advantage in it, and if thy abject spirit be not frightened with the sight of my sword, draw forth thine now, and shew that thou hast not yet lost all thy manhood."

"What means this frenzy?" asked Robert.

"Draw and defend thyself," exclaimed the other, "for thy courage has began to fail, and there is but too much reason to believe that thou wilt henceforth seek to betray me. Draw, I say, for this tomb shall soon receive one or both of us."

"Nay, this is madness," replied Robert; "for though I may not like the deed we are engaged on, it follows not that I should draw my sword against one who has hitherto been my friend. It may be that I spoke words in haste just now, but, trust me, no insult was intended, nor will I raise my weapon against a man to whom I bear no malice. And now, having thus explained myself, I am willing to proceed onwards, and complete the task which has brought us forth at this dark and midnight hour."

"I will have none of thy aid," exclaimed Oswald; "for, suspecting thy fidelity, I will myself perform the deed which fills your coward soul with terror. Alone will I execute the mandates of our chief, and alone will claim the gold with which he has promised to reward the service. Dare to follow me, Robert, and I will slay thee without remorse, for thou hast provoked me, and thou shalt find I am no feeble foe, but one equal to the chastisement of cowards who fear to obey their master's commands, because a little blood must be shed. Hence to thy lord, and tell him the deed is done;—tell him, also, of thy dastard fears, and rebel disobedience to his orders, and when thou hast done that, bid him recompense thee as thou deservest."

For an instant Robert paused irresolutely; his livid features quivered with ill-suppressed rage, yet the threat still rang in his ears, and he dared not follow his comrade. His eye, however, pursued him with a deadly and rancourous malice, and in hoarse, yet scarcely articulate tones, he exclaimed, resentfully,—

"Insolent minion, these words shall cost thee dear, for though I have now quailed beneath thy vain bravado, yet be assured the time is not far distant when I will revenge myself for what thou hast now dared to utter."

Speaking thus, the ruffian slowly departed, and Isabel, who had partially recovered herself, became convinced of the necessity of immediately quitting the spot. To follow Robert, would, perhaps, lead her in safety to the place from whence she had started; but, in pursuing the more remorseless Oswald, it was beyond all doubt she would certainly be conducted to the dungeon in which her father had been left to languish, and where it was but too probable he would meet the dreadful fate to which he had been doomed. She, therefore, no longer hesitated as to which course she should adopt, and though her bosom had become the seat of tumult and increasing terror for the safety of a beloved parent, she felt at this moment an almost supernatural courage that permitted her not to sink under the horrors which on every side thickly surrounded her. Having thus resolved, she pursued the track Oswald had taken, and was fortunately guided by the faint gleams of the torch which he had taken to aid his own footsteps.

Passing beneath the arch through which the ruffian Oswald had disappeared, the Princess Isabel suddenly found herself in a long and dismal cloister, the walls on either side of which were lined with ancient memorials of the dead. Escutcheons, tombs, and mouldering monuments displayed here and there the frightful chapless heads and other fragments of human skeletons horrible and ghastly to view. The light borne by Oswald but faintly rendered these dreadful objects visible, and with noiseless tread she moved after him, anxious only to behold how all this was to terminate. Nor was she left much longer in doubt, for presently Oswald paused to open a low iron door, which, with some difficulty, he succeeded in doing, and then, descending a few steps, disappeared from her view.

Isabel's terror had by this time rendered her almost powerless; but the hollow echo of a faint moan once more roused her courage, and, tottering forward, she descended the steps, and in one instant after found herself in a low square vault, whose blackened walls added to the gloom which was but dimly illumined by a small lamp, high suspended from the roof. Within a recess opposite was to be discerned a rude couch, on which a human figure lay stretched and motionless, apparently in the last stage of human suffering. Towards this object the form of Oswald was seen stealthily advancing; and, as with noiseless footstep he reached the pallet of the wretched being, he held aloft the torch he carried with him, and then, starting back with surprise, exclaimed, in muttered accents,—

"What! not yet dead? Miserable victim of ambition and remorseless cruelty, canst thou so long endure these wrongs, and still cling to thy miserable existence?"

The captive either slept, or was unconscious of the presence of a stranger, for Oswald received no answer; and, after a fearful pause, he murmured to himself :—" I was in hopes to have found thee dead ; but, since thou still livest, the dreadful task of ending thy wretched life must be mine !"

Isabel's wild shriek at this moment rung loud and piercingly through the vaulted space ; and, rushing forward, she, in piteous accents, implored the ruffian to forbear his dreadful purpose. Oswald was startled as these sounds met his ear, and he stood aghast, as if some messenger from the other world had been sent to arrest his murderous intent. He, however, quickly perceived Isabel ; and, believing that it was an apparition that he beheld, his courage failed him, and, making towards the door, he precipitately fled, leaving the princess fixed and motionless with horror. At length, however, a feeble voice was heard, and, rousing herself from inaction, she sprang towards the couch, and in a few hurried words explained to the unfortunate captive that she was now in the dungeon.

" Dost thou say, my Isabel is here ?" faintly murmured the prisoner. " Blessed spirit, art thou sent from Heaven to whisper consolation in the ear of the dying Emmeline, and to assure her that she is forgiven ?"

" Emmeline !" cried the princess, with surprise, and looking more stedfastly on the form before her, she recognised the wan features of her whose name she had just pronounced. She, however, started back, and was about to quit the cell in order to continue her pursuit after her father, when the same faint voice once more broke upon her ear.

"Stay,—in mercy stay!" cried Emmeline, "and do not leave me thus to perish without one friend to soothe my dying moments."

But Isabel was deaf to these entreaties, for she thought only of her father's safety, and hurried from the cell ere the words of the dying woman were finished. Too much time had, however, been lost to admit the possibility of overtaking Oswald, not the faintest trace of whose torch flashed through the murky darkness of the place, and without the aid of a light it would be in vain to continue her search. No other alternative, therefore, remained but to return to the dismal spot she had quitted, and slowly retracing her steps she once more entered the dungeon from whence she had so hastily departed.

Sickening with the disappointment, Isabel was unable any longer to support herself, and she was sinking upon the couch of the hapless Emmeline, when the latter, uttering a heavy groan, again revived from the fainting fit into which she had fallen, and perceiving who was present, she exclaimed :—

"Isabel, do my dim eyes again behold thee as they have in happier days? Yet no; 'tis some spirit sent to watch beside my couch and assure me that all my faults have been forgiven."

"What shall Isabel do for thee?" asked the princess in accents of compassion. "Teach me how to alleviate thy sufferings, and restore thee to thyself. Or say, shall I not fly to bring that aid which thou so much needest?"

"All is in vain," gasped forth the wretched captive, "for my sand of life has nearly run, and a brief time will serve to set my soul free from its bondage."

"Speak not thus sadly," cried Isabel, tenderly, "for now do I feel assured thou art not the guilty creature I once believed. Thy words when last we parted, bade me hope thy trespass was involuntary, and that I might yet pardon thy desertion of my unfortunate father."

A sudden spasm at this moment agitated the whole frame of Emmeline; thrice she essayed to speak, but could not give utterance to her labouring heart; a dying pang shot through her every nerve, and the princess became more terrified as she observed these convulsions continue, and knew not how to alleviate them. The excessive agonies, however, which she beheld filled her mind with sudden dark suspicions, and she felt almost convinced that the horrible pangs she witnessed must proceed from having swallowed a poison mixed with her food, and it seemed equally certain that the open grave she had seen was prepared to receive the ill-fated wife of the Chief of Badenoch. But from these reflections she was presently awakened by the voice of the sufferer, who in accents of despair called faintly for food, declaring that for the last three days none had been brought for her sustenance.

At that moment a distant gleaming light, streaming from the upper avenue, was seen faintly in the distance, and Isabel, forgetful of her own situation, screamed loudly for assistance. But even the faint hopes which thus inspired her, were doomed speedily to vanish, for she recognised the grim form of Badenoch, who, having left his attendants on the outside, strode with a foreboding frown into the dungeon. For an instant, Isabel shrunk back aghast from his presence, but remembering the necessity for immediate aid, she again advanced, and throwing herself upon her knees at the feet of the tyrant, earnestly implored him to procure food for the dying victim of his cruelty and injustice. He, however, regarded her with a look indifference, and turning away his head, exclaimed :—

"Thou pleadest in vain, Isabel, for to no prayers of thine will I listen till thou hast first consented to become mine. Swear to obey me, and not only Emmeline, but thy father also shall be saved from the fate to which they have been doomed.   Speak, then, girl, for 'tis thy voice alone that can give life to those who are now languishing in my power."

"Inhuman monster!" cried Isabel, "and dost thou think with such an example before my eyes I can consent to become the bride of a relentless murderer ?"

"Remember Glenroy," he exclaimed, "and tremble to again provoke my anger.   The terms I have proposed are not difficult, and thou wilt do well to grant them ere it is too late to save those for whom thou pleadest."

"Alas! thou hast at length subdued me," cried Isabel ; "my spirit can endure no more; grant, oh, grant the favour I have asked, and I will be yours.   But think not this act of lawless outrage will escape punishment, for the time will ere long arrive when Heaven's severest inflictions will fall upon him who has thus persecuted helpless innocence."

"Psha! I fear not the inflictions you speak of," exclaimed Badenoch ; "and from the world's censure I have nothing to fear, since you must sign this instrument by which an acknowledgment is made that you voluntarily bestow your hand upon me.   That done, our union shall immediately take place, and the release of your friends will follow without delay."

"Once more," cried Isabel, earnestly, "I implore thee to have mercy upon me, and do not thus force a compliance from one who never can voluntarily be thine."

"'Tis in vain you plead," he exclaimed, "for my resolutions are immoveable, and never will I rest satisfied till the hand of the Princess Isabel is made securely mine."

"Alas!" she sighed, "I but too well understand the ambition that has urged thee on, for had my fortune been less princely, and my birth less exalted, thine acts of violence had never been perpetrated.   Take then my envied dignities ; take all, and banish me and my wronged father to some remote country, far from my native Scotland, where never more our names may inspire thy heart with fear.   Do this, and most solemnly do I promise never to utter a word that may serve to publish the cruel injustice I have endured."

"And can the high-born Princess Isabel stoop to such dissimulation as this?" demanded Badenoch, scornfully, "or does she in truth imagine me so weak as to trust my future hopes,—nay, even life and fame upon a promise extorted in a moment of danger ?   Here thou art absolutely beneath my control, and shall either yield to my demands, or, by a refusal, pronounce thy father's doom."

"Ah!" cried the frantic princess, "is there no other alternative left to save *his* life ?"

"Thou shalt see that presently," answered the chief, ferociously, and then having given a signal for the approach of his minions, he added,— "Bring forth your captive, slaves, and remember, whatever commands I give, must be promptly and willingly obeyed.   Away, then, and see that you speedily place before me the old man whose existence depends upon the submission of yonder trembling girl."

The men, whose ferocious aspect had alarmed the Princess Isabel, immediately quitted the dungeon, and in a brief period returned, dragging with them Lord Mackenzie, who they cast down with some violence at the feet of their imperious master.   Badenoch eyed our heroine with an inquiring look, and having satisfied himself that her terrors had been excited to the highest pitch, he said :—

"Isabel, thou seest thy father, perhaps for the last time ; speak then, for his destiny is in thy hands, and a single word from thee will force me to become his executioner !"

CHAPTER XLVI.

"Not to me,
Oh ! not to me, stern death ! art thou a foe ;
Thou art the welcome messenger which brings
A passport to a blest and long repose."

MRS. ROBINSON.

THE last effort of Isabel's firmness was now entirely overcome, and she felt that fate itself could not have a pang in store more agonizing than the one she now endured. Her resistance was at an end, and the horrors of such a spectacle had nearly overpowered her, when the voice of Badenoch was again heard muttering :—

" Will the Princess Isabel now sign the instrument I hold in my hand, or by a refusal condemn her father to death ?"

For a moment the hapless girl looked around her in wild uncertainty, but at length her recollection dawned, and rendered desperate by the peril in which her father was placed, she took the parchment from the ruthless villain, and signed it, without reflecting further upon the consequences it would bring upon herself.

" It is done !" exclaimed Badenoch, joyfully, as he snatched it from her ; " my design is at length accomplished, and the Princess Isabel is at length the reward of my deeply-laid stratagem."

" 'Tis indeed done !" groaned our heroine, in accents of despair, and then as she once more perceived the form of her father, she added :— " Yet I have saved the life of him who gave me existence, and let that thought repay me for any sufferings I might have to undergo."

With these words she sprung towards her father, who was supported by one of the ruffians, and with a cry of mingled tenderness and grief, sank fainting in his arms.

And now were Badenoch's projects all but accomplished, for he well knew the real condition of Lord Mackenzie, who was fast drawing towards that eternity, between him and which but a very few minutes interposed. The wild paroxysms of the last fatal night had worn nature to her utmost limits ; for hours after the sudden appearance of Isabel in his dungeon, he had raved of Emmeline in all the frantic desperation of madness, and at length, with a heavy groan, he fell to the earth in that state of lethargy which is the sure fore-runner of death. Unconscious, however, as she was of his danger, Isabel, on recovering herself, could not restrain the feelings of her heart, and in accents of grateful joy, she exclaimed :—

" Heaven be praised that I am thus once more permitted to hold a beloved father to my heart, and that from this moment we shall be no more separated through the ruthless tyranny of our cruel oppressor."

Mackenzie, however, knew his fate, and sighed to think that its near approach must give fresh sorrow to his hapless child. For himself he experienced no wish to linger on, for death was to him the long-desired bourne of every earthly hope, and, but for the pang of parting, he rejoiced that at length the period of his miseries had arrived. Yet much he wished to learn the fate of others who were dear to him, and, clasping the hand of his child, he said,—

" Dearest Isabel, tell me by what strange means thou hast discovered and thus pursued me hither ? This scene of lawless oppression and cruelty suits not thy gentle nature to encounter ; and though, to see thee ere I die, and take of thee a last farewell, is a joy beyond what I had dared to hope, yet am I not without fears that thou hast been betrayed hither as

I have. But, Isabel, thy care is all in vain, for the hand of death presses heavily upon me, and a brief space will remove me from a world in which I have endured so much misery and despair.''

"Merciful Heavens!" cried Isabel; "am I, then, doomed to endure yet further horrors than those I have already gone through? Is it not enough that I have promised to become thy slave, obdurate chief?—but I must now behold my father, dying through the foul means thou hast used to rid thyself of one whose just rights have been surrendered up!''

At that instant a deep groan sounded fearfully through the dismal vault: its tone seemed familiar to the ear of Mackenzie, and he cast around him a wild and inquiring look, as if anxious to convince himself whether some new horror was not about to burst upon him. The princess stood aghast, for the recollection of Emmeline's presence now crossed her mind; and, ere she could sufficiently recover herself to prepare her father for this unexpected interview, he slowly raised himself, and, in trembling accents, murmured,—

"Was this last pang required to fit me for that departure which is so near at hand? Alas! Emmeline, how art thou changed!—how have thy broken vows recoiled upon thyself, when not even thy love towards the remorseless destroyer could avert the heavy hand of fate with which his tyranny has oppressed thee.''

"My father," cried Isabel, imploringly, "be merciful to her whose sufferings have been far greater than you imagine. Alas! you know not the horrors she has endured, nor with what steadfast meek submission she has atoned her errors. They were involuntary, and, trust me, for I have seen its bitter proof, she erred not wilfully, nor knowingly. She has fallen beneath a villain's snares, and is now deeply penitent for the wrongs you have endured.''

"Indeed, indeed I am," cried Emmeline, struggling forward, and throwing herself upon her knees before Mackenzie; "and here, prostrate at your feet, I implore you to withdraw the heavy curses you have heaped upon me. Pardon, my lord, is all I ask, and when that is granted I care not how soon death comes to release me from the deep afflictions I have endured.''

"Thou art, indeed, dying," murmured Lord Mackenzie, as he gazed earnestly in her face, "and if my forgiveness may serve to remove any portion of the weight that oppresses thee, it is already bestowed. The scene of trial to us both is hastening to a period, and in the hour of death I will pardon the errors of my once loved, but erring wife. Yet thou, too, hast been much wronged, for I know the falsehoods with which thou wert betrayed, and the sad tale of thy early affliction lives recorded in my memory. Take, then, my entire forgiveness, for the hand of death, I see, has struck thee low, nor shall I linger long behind thee.''

"I am no longer accursed, then!" cried Emmeline, in a delirium of joy, "and all my frailties are from this moment blotted from thy remembrance. This is, indeed, a happiness that I had not dared to hope for; but, since it has been vouchsafed to me, I thank Heaven and thee for the blessing, and will now die content.''

"And all these sorrows," exclaimed Mackenzie, "have been brought upon us by the monster who now stands by and triumphs at the ruin and destruction in which he has involved us!''

"He is, as thou sayest, the cause of all," returned Emmeline, "and yet in our last hours we will not reproach him for the misery he has brought upon us. Let him reflect deeply upon the crimes he has committed, and, unless his heart be adamant, he will feel such tortures as will prove ample atonement for the sin which has urged him to take this course. Thy forgiveness, my lord, has rendered me happy; and, though but few more moments

remain to me in this world, I can hail the approach of death with joy, and take my departure from hence with u a murmur."

Emmeline could utter no more, for the moment of their separation had arrived ; and, grasping the hand of her husband, she pressed it to her lips, and then, sinking back, expired in the arms of the princess. Mackenzie turned sickening from the sight, and Isabel, as she clung round the nearly lifeless frame of her father, cast her eyes upon him with looks so piteous and agonizing as entirely subdued his every effort of resignation or fortitude.

"Alas ! my child," he exclaimed, " I have no consolation to bestow, for the final blow is struck, and, to deceive thee with a hope of living, would be in vain. Spare me, then, in these, my last moments, the dreadful aggravation of witnessing thy severe distress. Retire, my love, and leave me to my fate,—let me conclude, undisturbed, the short remainder of my weary pilgrimage, and harrow not these final minutes with the tortures of such a parting."

" I cannot, will not depart," cried Isabel, endeavouring as much as possible to conceal her emotion. "Oh! do not drive me from the last sad indulgence Heaven has left me ; but struggle yet a little to prolong existence, be it but to save thy daughter from despair and madness ! Oh! think how she has loved thee, and remember that if she now loses thee, all that has power to make life valuable is for ever torn from her, and the grave only remains as a refuge in which she may find rest."

" Nay, forbear this grief, if thou lovest me," exclaimed Mackenzie, with increasing languor. "I do not bid thee cease to regret awhile my loss, but to learn the duty of submission, which can alone restore thee to serenity and peace."

At this period the Chief of Badenoch advanced from the distant part of the dungeon in which he had placed himself, and, taking the hand of Isabel in his own, he ferociously exclaimed,—

No. 34

"Remember your promise, Isabel, and here, in the presence of your father, once more declare your readiness to become my bride. Nay, it is in vain you would shrink from me, girl, for I am resolute, as you well know, and, having received your solemn pledge, I would have you render it even more sacred by repeating it in the presence of this dying man. Swear to become mine this night, or, short as his time is in this world, I will plunge my dagger in his heart, and thus throw upon yourself the crime of his murder!"

Mackenzie's eye was raised for an instant on Isabel, and then rested on the hardened villain who had thus oppressed them.

"Thinkest thou," he said, sternly, "thy deeds will for ever escape the retribution of Heaven's avenging wrath? I do not curse thee now; for, with me, the power to judge or to punish guilt is ended. Hence from the sight of those thou hast so deeply wronged, and learn, proud chief, that even this helpless woman may yet find a protection from the violence with which you seek to make her yours. Begone! villain that you are, and no more blast my eyes with a sight so loathsome and abhorrent!"

Abashed and dismayed, Badenoch turned away, but the effort made by Mackenzie proved too much for him, and sinking back upon the ground, it became evident that he had but a few more moments to live. Rousing himself, however, to what little energy remained, he said,—

"Let not the breath of calumny canker the future frame of Emmeline; but for thy father's sake, my Isabel, shield her memory from detraction, and let not the world learn that she was once faithless. Bury us, my daughter, in one grave, and let the same earth mingle ours together. Promise me this, and all my soul holds sacred here will then be accomplished. Promise me too, that when the power of retribution shall be thine, thou wilt redress all those fearful wrongs that have been heaped on us and those we hold most dear. Pledge thyself to this, and my wearied spirit will depart in peace."

Isabel needed not to hesitate, for, alas! the power to fulfil these injunctions she felt assured never would be hers. For some few moments she struggled with the agonies of her grief, but could not give utterance to the words that almost choked her. In a voice that grew more and more faint, the dying man repeated his injunctions, and not till then was his heart-broken child able to give the promise he demanded.

"Thou hast given ease to my heart," he then exclaimed; "for I know thou wilt respect the dying wishes of thy father. They will become a duty to thee, and the thought that thou art fulfilling my last request will urge thee to leave nothing untried till all has been accomplished according to my desire. The noble Angus, too, were *he* but your protector, would hazard even life itself ere you became the bride of him who has involved thee in this misery. It would have glad my soul to go hence in the certainty of having bequeathed you to each other, but Heaven seems to have willed it otherwise, and it is our duty to submit with resignation to the decree."

He paused from exhaustion, and the increased difficulty with which he breathed, showed the nearer and more rapid strides that death was making. At length, however, he seemed to collect together what little strength remained to him, and pressing the hand of Isabel, said,—

"Adieu, my child, and forget not the last injunctions with which I have charged you. Think that in Heaven I shall behold their fulfilment with rejoicing, and let that recollection urge you in the task I have imposed. Obey me, and the last blessing of a dying father shall be your eternal reward."

These were the last words he could utter, but his eyes remained fixed in solemn sadness upon the form of his beloved child, and as at length they closed in death, a smile of tenderness played upon his features, proving that even to the last his thoughts were fixed upon her from whom he was thus separating.

No tear relieved the overcharged heart of the sorrowing girl, but at length a half-stifled groan escaped her lips, and then falling upon the lifeless body of her father, she remained for some little time in a state of utter insensibility. The lamp now but duskily gleamed over the dismal scene as it shone upon the features of the silent dead, than whose pale features Isabel's were scarcely less wan. The thunders of the night, too, burst forth in terrific peals, and thus added to the horrors which such a scene was calculated to inspire. The Chief of Badenoch strove to shake off the fear which these events had occasioned, but all his efforts proved unavailing, and at length he retired from the dungeon, leaving Isabel, still fainting as she was, in the dreary solitude to which his own cruelty and tyranny had consigned her.

On the day succeeding, the castle became the seat of tumult, for scarcely the dawn appeared, than it was discovered that the rock was surrounded by innumerable armed vessels, manned and equipped for all the purposes of a siege. The sentinels that paraded the ramparts were the first to give the alarm, which passing quickly through the garrison, soon reached the ear of the chieftain himself. Equally astonished and alarmed, Badenoch hastened to the highest Watch Tower, and as he cast his glance around, he saw but too plainly that in this instance the enemy had come in power and might enough to render vain all hopes of resistance. At this moment an arrow, conveying a scroll, fell at his feet, and hastily picking it up, he discovered that it was a summons from Robert Bruce, commanding him instantly to surrender the castle to those who had come determined and prepared to wrest it from his hands; the document then went on as follows :—

" If the usurper, Badenoch, can plead ought in extenuation of his crimes, let him come boldly forward and claim our royal clemency, for, notwithstanding the rebellion he has been guilty of, we hereby promise him grace and pardon upon condition that he surrenders himself, his lands, and this strong fortress, into our hands, and that he foregoes for ever his alliance with the usurping English powers. But should he dare demur, or rashly presume to oppose our demands, we will seize upon his lands and territories, as forfeit to the state against which he has rebelled ; and his person we not only banish for ever from this our kingdom, but do hereby command all our loyal subjects, wherever he may secrete himself, that straightway he be seized upon and imprisoned until our further will be made known. Further than this, we also command him upon his peril, that without delay, he instantly deliver and restore to our guardianship, the person of the Princess Isabel, together with all such other prisoners as have been unjustly detained in his fortress.

(Signed) " ROBERT BRUCE."

As the Chief of Badenoch perused this, rage, mingled with hate and fear, struggled for supremacy in his breast. Aghast, and for a time thrown off his usual guard, he deeply mused upon the peremptory mandate, and felt that the strength of his own resources for resistance were insufficient when compared to the will of a sovereign, who had lately been fortunate in war, and who he knew was idolized by the country in general. He reflected that though he might in his fortress defy a greater power than that which had been brought against him, yet it was only here that he could be defended from future vengeance. The rock was his last and only resource, for it was invulnerable, and he knew also that it contained stores and ammunition which would enable him to hold out for a long time to come. Still, to resist Robert Bruce, and by boldly opposing, make him eternally a foe, would be to defeat his long-cherished hopes and crush them for ever.

The pardon offered in the event of his submission was lenity beyond his utmost expectation ; yet he felt assured that he had silenced every living evidence against him, and as his thoughts once more recurred to Isabel, he resolved to make her his bride without delay, and thus shield himself under the protection, he believed it would be in her power to bestow. Yet to this thought succeeded another that startled him, and with fresh alarm he again perused the summons, for from whom, or from what unknown cause could have proceeded the discovery of his retreat and the captivity of the Princess Isabel. The manner in which she had been spirited away from the Castle of Glenroy, was, he well knew, of so dark and mysterious a nature, as to prevent every chance of discovery, and yet it now appeared the secret of her detention was no longer unrevealed.

Numerous were the suggestions that now crowded on his mind, to evade, if possible, the demands of the king; and at one moment he determined boldly to deny the princess, and by an act of violence, put the final period to his enormities in her death or compel her to acknowledge him her chosen lord and husband. This seemed to be the only alternative left him, and was, indeed, the long-laboured object of his ambition. Still, however, neither these dark objects, nor the absolute power he possessed to complete them, could silence the inward alarms he felt, and it was now that his guilt began to prey upon his spirit in continual purturbation and doubtful suspicion. His soul, teeming with rage, malice, and despite, could ill-brook the change his fortunes sustained, and at one moment he felt desperately inclined to hurl down ruin on the Scottish king and his followers, but from projects so fatal to his future interests, his cooler judgment withheld him.

There was then no course but to soothe the resentment of Robert Bruce, and by previously compelling the princess to become his bride, thus at once secure himself from the dangers and obloquy of that public investigation of his crimes, which he trembled should be brought to light. Cursing the necessity which thus compelled him to court the sovereign against whom he had so long waged rebellion, he sullenly and unwillingly prepared for the only alternative left him. A herald was therefore despatched from the rock to deliver the answer he had, after much deliberation, prepared; in which it was stated that the Princess Isabel had come to the fortress as a voluntary visitant, and had never been detained, but should be speedily restored, though as the wife of the Chief of Badenoch.

The astonishment and doubt with which this reply filled the king and his warriors, suspended for a time their operations, and in the meantime Badenoch was not inactive. The climax of his fate now approached, and it was certain that either by one bold stretch of lawless guilt, he must defeat the opposing danger that encompassed him, or by yielding to his doom, fall ignominiously and for ever. The latter choice his haughty spirit disdained, for he was deeply steeped in villany, and his passion and reason had too long submitted to his evil propensities to divert their channel. He no longer deigned even a semblance of pity for Isabel's condition, and, as we have lately seen, he, with menace and threats of violence, forced from her a promise to become his wife.

Throughout the remainder of the day, Badenoch had been too much employed in matters of the deepest import to visit the unfortunate princess. He, however, despatched Robert and five or six others of his retainers to the dungeon, with orders to bury the bodies of Emmeline and Lord Mackenzie, and when that was done, to convey the princess to the chamber which she had formerly occupied. It was with no little difficulty, however, that they could prevail upon Isabel to part from all she loved dearest upon earth, but at length she silently assented, and as the bell tolled the hour of ten the sad procession commenced, the princess following with haggard mien and slow trembling footsteps, till she found herself beside the open grave which she had seen on the preceding night.

Isabel here uttered no frantic exclamations, but her eyes were bent in subdued anguish upon the body of her father, which they lowered into the tomb beside the unfortunate Emmeline. The grim beings who had borne the corpses retreated, whilst the others, with their torches, grouped themselves at the foot of the tomb. At the head stood a monk who pronounced the solemn ritual of the dead, and having finished the ceremony retired, followed by all present, except Isabel and her attendant, Marianne. Robert and another retainer of the chief, at some little distance, awaited the departure of the princess to close up the sepulchre.

Isabel had fallen beside the grave, where she remained for some little time in earnest and solemn prayer. At length, however, sobs broke from her lips as she thought of the misery she had endured, and that which was still in store for her, and dreading the violence of the Chief of Badenoch, she gradually sank upon the earth, and her soul became steeped in temporary oblivion.

CHAPTER XLVII.

" To Heaven I swear,—
To Heaven and all the powers that judge mankind,
Never to mix my plighted hands with thine."
ADDISON.

IN a state of unconsciousness, Isabel was borne from the dreary spot, and when again her senses became restored, her eyes encountered the dark visage of Badenoch, who stood impatiently awaiting her revival, and then holding forth the fatal paper she had signed the preceding night, he bade her prepare for their nuptials. It was in vain she implored to be allowed some little time, for the priest was instantly summoned, and the paper having been placed in his hands by the chief, he read aloud as follows :—

" By this free deed of gift I place the guardianship of my person in the hands of the Chief of Badenoch, to whom, in solemn contract, I thus willingly resign myself, and empower him to claim me for his bride, giving him my firm assurance to ratify the marriage whenever he may think proper to claim the fulfilment of this pledge. (Signed) "ISABEL."

Having concluded this, the monk, without a single comment or a pitying glance on the hapless victim, returned the scroll into the hands of him from whom he had received it, and beginning the marriage ceremony, paused not until he had brought it to a conclusion. The princess, constrained to submit to the mockery, and too weak to offer opposition, attempted none, but scarcely had the rites been brought to a conclusion, when the door of the chamber was forced open and two figures made their appearance, in one of whom she beheld, with wonder and amazement, the well-known features of Angus Glenalvon, whose supposed murder she had so deeply mourned. Badenoch also started with terror at this unexpected apparition, and he would have fled with conscious guilt from the room, but Angus rushing furiously towards him, was in the act of plunging his sword into the body of his hated foe, when Donald, with a cry of horror, sprang between them and earnestly besought mercy for the guilty chief. The helmet of the youth fell to the ground as he rushed forward, and instantly the features of Rosalind were revealed to the wondering spectators. Still, however, Angus was firmly bent upon the destruction of the Chief of Badenoch, and he was again preparing himself for a second attempt, when Lord Randolf, followed by several armed men, hurried towards the scene of action.

"Angus Glenalvon," he exclaimed, "this impetuosity, if persisted in, will ruin all, for our king has declared that he will himself be the judge of Badenoch's guilt, and should the traitor perish by your sword, the anger of Robert Bruce will be turned against yourself. Forbear then, and leave the justice of your revenge to him who will not fail to hurl punishment upon the evil doer."

The youth acquiesced to this advice, and sheathing his sword, he hastened to the assistance of Isabel, and raising her from the ground on which she had fallen at the moment of his appearance, endeavoured to restore her once more to animation. During this period, Lord Randolf, addressing himself to Badenoch, said :—

"It is now my duty, proud chief, to tell you that your power in this fortress is at an end; the castle now acknowledges King Robert for its master, before whom I here cite you to appear and answer to the charges about to be preferred against you."

"I submit, my lord," answered Badenoch, "and having done as you will, yield to me the Princess Isabel, who is now my wife."

"If she consents to such a demand, it shall be granted," returned Lord Randolf; "but if otherwise, our duty commands us to guard her in safety till your claim has been inquired into by the king."

But as no answer was returned to this, either by Isabel or the Chief of Badenoch, the whole party immediately quitted the chamber and proceeded to the hall of state, where, upon a throne, sat the royal Bruce, by whose side was placed a chair for the accommodation of the princess who had scarcely recovered from the shock which recent events had occasioned her. Sadness and resignation marked every feature, yet her eyes beamed with joy on Angus whenever he addressed her, and already she half forgot the dreadful trials it had been her sad destiny to undergo.

On the left of the throne stood, clad in armour, the Earls of Murray and Douglas, the inseparate companions of their heroic king; whilst around the hall sat the nobles and warrior knights, and in the back ground were arranged the warriors who had accompanied the king in this expedition. Then the herald having proclaimed silence, led Badenoch forward, and read aloud the several charges of which he stood arraigned. These consisted of many foul acts of atrocity and bloodshed, among the foremost of which, were the murders of the Earl of Glenalvon, his countess and youngest son, together with that of Glenroy; with the imprisonment and violence offered to the persons of Lord Mackenzie, and the Princess Isabel, his daughter. The herald then demanded of the prisoner if he had anything to advance in his defence that could refute them.

"It is needless to urge any," replied Badenoch, "and I shall therefore content myself by demanding who are my accusers?"

At this moment Angus stood forward, and looking sternly upon the captive chief, he exclaimed,—

"In me you behold the heir of Glenalvon, and here, before the majesty of Scotland, do I impeach thee of foul practices against the lives of both my parents, my brother, and myself. Praying for justice, I then humbly bend my knee before the king, and beg permission to support my charge in single combat against the usurper of my rights."

"These accusations are false," exclaimed Badenoch, fiercely; "and knowing my own innocence, I here declare my readiness to accept the challenge that has been given."

The murmur that ran through the court at this bold denial created universal surprise. Every eye was now bent on the king, and amidst the silence that ensued, the herald called upon the Princess Isabel to stand forth and give her testimony against the prisoner.

"It is forbidden; *her* evidence cannot here avail," cried Badenoch, "nor will I plead against the accusations of *my wife*, whose testimony it is endeavoured thus to extort."

As he spoke he handed up the paper which Isabel had been compelled to sign, and the king having perused it, demanded of her whether she acknowledged the writing.

"I do, my liege," she tremblingly replied.

"And knew you the nature of the contents ?"

"Only in part," answered Isabel, "and I signed it to save the threatened life of my father."

"Then thus do I destroy the claim he has basely advanced ;" exclaimed the king, tearing up the paper and scattering the fragments upon the floor. "The consent was extorted by force, and from this moment thou art free from the bonds with which he sought to enthral thee."

The defeated Badenoch trembled with passion, but ere he could utter the maledictions of his boundless hatred, the princess left her seat; and, accompanied by one of the pages, retired to her own chamber. Angus then handed a paper to the herald which was read aloud, in which the whole transaction of the Earl of Glenalvon's murder was minutely related by Ronald, the old and faithful domestic whose signature was appended to it. To this the guilty chief listened with impatience, and at its conclusion he demanded with a sneer whether Ronald was living to confirm his testimony.

"He no longer lives," replied the king, "for I myself was present when he died, and heard the narrative which we have just now listened to. With his dying breath he declared your enormities, and should further testimony be required, we have one present whose testimony will confound thee."

At this juncture, Stephen, a former retainer of the chief's, stood forward, and in a few words confirmed all the charges that had been brought against his master. This done, he announced that there were yet other witnesses at hand, and the door being thrown open two persons were seen advancing, one of whom was Edwin Glenalvon, and the other Magdalen, the generous foster mother who had brought up the sons of Glenalvon, in spite of all the danger with which they had been threatened. To convey an idea of the rapture that filled the bosom of both the youths at this unexpected meeting would be impossible, but when at length their joyful expressions began to subside, Magdalen was desired to approach the throne, and in obedience to the king's command, she related all the occurrences of the last few years, but with which the reader is already acquainted down to the period when her life was sought by her relentless husband, and from which point we will continue in her own words :—

"The dagger of Fergus," she went on to say, "had entered my side, but fortunately the wound was not so deep as to prove mortal. My body sunk not to the bottom of the water into which it had been precipitated, but floating on the surface was drifted to the opposite bank, where I was discovered by Stephen, who bore me to this castle, and in one of the dungeons afforded me the secrecy and safety I so much required. There I continued to remain, and the chief source of consolation I derived, was in the cheering intelligence that both the sons of Glenalvon were still in existence. By the kindness of Stephen, I was often permitted to wander through the dungeons, and thus frequently become a secret witness of the cruelties inflicted upon those who were unfortunate enough to fall beneath the displeasure of the stern Chief of Badenoch. It was on one of these occasions that I heard a project planned for poisoning both the brothers, unless Angus would consent to resign his birthright and disavow all claims to the earldom of Glenalvon, by acknowledging himself to be the son of Fergus and myself.

"Frantic with dread, I sought the prison of Edwin, which I had by accident discovered, when the terrific chief himself had entered it to murder the youthful inmate. My unexpected appearance, however, awed him, for he believed me to be an unearthly visitant ; and for that time the life of Edwin was saved. But I had heard enough to assure me that the brothers were to be destroyed by poison administered in their food ; and having related my alarm to Stephen, we examined the viands, and discovered that my fears were but too well founded. In this difficulty, we destroyed the food which had been prepared for Edwin, and having infused into his drink a powerful sleeping powder, it was placed in the dungeon of the youthful captive, and drunk without suspicion or distrust. The effects were such as I had anticipated, for Edwin shortly fell into a profound slumber, and a little before midnight, Stephen came to inform me, that if I wished to behold Angus, I must secrete myself in the subterranean hall of judgment, where some terrible scene of crime was about to be enacted."

It is needless here to recipitulate the mock trial which succeeded, but to the narrative of which the auditory listened with the most breathless attention. Nor did she fail to describe the agony of Angus when he beheld, as he supposed, the dead body of his unfortunate brother, and having dwelt sufficiently long upon this subject, she thus proceeded :—

"When the hall was again cleared, and Badenoch had retired with the guilty confidant of his crimes, I left my hiding place, and hastening towards the spot where Edwin lay, to all appearances lifeless, I raised him in my arms, and bearing him to my own dungeon once more recalled him to animation. Relying on Stephen's solemn promises, and thus anxiously employed in the service of the younger brother, my apprehensions for the elder were somewhat diverted, and it was not till long after midnight that, with a feeling of transport only to be equalled by that I now experience, I learnt from Stephen that Angus was far beyond the reach of Badenoch's power, guarded by his sovereign's protection, and with every prospect of regaining his long-lost rights."

Here Magdalen's narrative concluded, and it is now only necessary to observe in this place that it was through Stephen's means that Rosalind had been prevented becoming the inmate of a convent, and in order to account for the reappearance of Angus, it is only necessary to observe that the wound he had received in his conflict with the ruffian was not mortal, and that in consequence of the darkness of the night, the heart of Fergus had, by a mistake, been taken instead of his own.

After Magdalen had concluded her narrative, the king highly extolled her faithful services in behalf of the orphan sons of Glenalvon, and having promised that she should be liberally rewarded for the generous sacrifices she had made in their cause, he addressed himself sternly to the Chief of Badenoch, and demanded whether he would offer any reason against the judgment of death about to be pronounced.

" Gracious sovereign," exclaimed Angus respectfully ; " to me alone should belong the punishment of my parent's murder. Let me, then, stand forth the champion of their wrongs, and with Heaven's aid I will yet avenge their death."

" It cannot be," answered the king, " for I now doom him to an instant and ignominious death, as a traitor to his king, his country, and his God."

A shriek of agony at this moment echoed through the hall, and soon was seen a female form wildly rushing through the crowd, and sinking at the feet of Bruce, she exclaimed :—

" Mercy, sire, mercy ! and spare my father the dreadful fate to which you have just doomed him. Angus, plead for me, for surely you cannot be ungrateful, nor forget that Rosalind, in a moment of danger, once preserved your life."

" Rosalind did indeed preserve thy life," cried Magdalen ; " I was a secret witness of the deed, and my heart blessed her for the act, since, in saving the stranger Angus, she obeyed the instinctive voice of nature, and saved a *brother* when every other hope of preservation was denied him."

" A brother !" exclaimed Angus and Edwin in amazement. ..

" Aye, it is even as I have said," replied Magdalen ; " in Rosalind you behold the daughter whom your parents so long mourned as lost."

" I must—I do believe you," cried Angus, and clasping the trembling girl in his arms, he fondly welcomed her under her new title of relationship, and Magdalen proceeded to explain the mystery in the following words :—

" It is now, about eighteen years ago, sire, that the infant and her attendant Katherine, were suddenly taken from the Castle of Glenalvon and never more heard of. Every search proved fruitless, and not till long after the murder of my lord and lady did I learn her fate. It was then that I discovered from my husband that the little Rosalind had been stolen by him at the command of his master, and conveyed to this fortress, where it had been determined that she should perish, but that the former wife of the Chief of Badenoch, pitying the forlorn state of the innocent child, had adopted the infant, and at her death left her under the care of Katherine, who was faithful to her charge, and never revealed the secret to anybody but myself. The evidence of her veracity is to be found in some papers that were entrusted to my keeping, and the perusal of them will convince all persons of the truth of the story I have related."

Shortly after this the court broke up, and Badenoch having been conveyed to one of the dungeons of the castle, shortly afterwards slew himself with a pionard, which he always had concealed about his person in the event of such a moment of jeopardy as the present arriving. Rosalind, when informed of her long supposed father's death, felt shocked and wept bitterly, for she forgot the cruelties she had endured from him, and dwelt only on the thought that till now she had ever been accustomed to regard him as a parent.

On the succeeding morning the king departed, accompanied by the Princess Isabel and the Sons of Glenalvon, and having conveyed our heroine to the

No. 35

convent of St. Columba, the remains of Lord Mackenzie and Lady Emmeline were removed there from the fortress and honoured with a magnificent funeral. This done, Bruce, accompanied by Angus and the chief of his nobility, went to join the army which had been collected together to oppose the invading hosts of the English monarch, and from that period victory was his constant attendant till the foe was finally driven from the country by the great and decided Battle of Bannockburn.

Magdalen, Rosalind, and Edwin, for the first two months of the princess's retirement continued her companions at St. Columba, and at the expiration of that time, they prepared to visit Glenalvon. During this interval Isabel had secretly employed agents, who had, even in this short space of time, wonderfully changed the face of the ruined castle, so that the greater part of it was once more made habitable. The secret repository which contained the riches of the house of Glenalvon had also been opened, and its immense treasure was found entire, together with every record necessary to the re-establishment of heirs to their lawful inheritance.

Many months passed away, during which the Princess Isabel gradually regained that peaceful tranquillity of mind so long despaired of. The horrors she had endured by imperceptible degrees faded on her memory, and the blissful quietude of her days had restored her mind to its former happiness. With filial sorrow she ever dwelt on her father's misfortunes, and cherished his remembrance, but when at length her grief yielded to the conviction of reason, she no longer continued to repine, but resigned herself to a destiny over which she had no power to control.

Angus, during this long interval, though constantly engaged in the duties of his warlike profession, often found leisure to visit St. Columba, amidst whose deep embowered solitudes he had drawn from his Isabel a confirming assurance that he was still dear to her affections.

It is now, however, necessary that we should retrace our way for some little distance, in order that we may explain a portion of our narrative that would otherwise be obscure.

The paper given by the hand of the dying Lady Emmeline to the Princess Isabel, contained a sad memorial of her unhappy story ; it was worded in strong expressions of mental suffering, and our heroine, as she wept over its contents, fully exonerated the treacherously-betrayed and ill-fated Emmeline from all premeditation of an intentional lapse from virtue, or the innocence and dignity of her sex.

The paper alluded to was of considerable length, but its contents may be thus compressed, as it is somewhat material to our story, and involves some points that it is highly necessary should be elucidated :—

Badenoch and Emmeline had from infancy shared with Lord Mackenzie in the affections of the countess, the mother of the latter. Emmeline was an orphan, ward of the earl, and distantly related to him, whilst Badenoch was more nearly connected to the family of the countess, being nephew to herself and her brother, the powerful and almost princely Earl of Glenroy.

The character and dark propensities of Badenoch need no further delineation in this place ; by his deep artifice he had early entwined himself into the affections of the artless and unsuspecting Emmeline, long before Mackenzie's impassioned love had declared itself for that unfortunate lady. In fact, from her earliest remembrance, Emmeline grew up in the habit of loving the Chief of Badenoch, beyond every other being upon earth, and when afterwards commanded by the haughty Earl of Inverness, the father of Lord Mackenzie, to reject the addresses of his son, she had, as may be supposed, obeyed the injunctions placed upon her.

It was the fierce passions and ruthless ambition of Badenoch, which had early sundered the intimacy between himself and Lady Emmeline, but nothing could ever subdue the growing hopes she had formed, and the fixed attachment of her young and unsuspecting heart,—and when the death of the Princess Matilda subjected her to the addresses of Lord Mackenzie, who had thus been left a widower, Emmeline had not courage or resolution to declare her want of love for him, or that her heart's affections were irrevocably bestowed upon another object.

The weakness and humility of her timid mind shrunk from the task of giving pain to a being whom she had long been convinced regarded her with an ardent passion that she could not return ; she knew also that even as the husband of the Princess Matilda, he had regarded her with a breathless affection, and when at length Mackenzie enthusiastically declared his passion, and demanded her hand, Emmeline, though she mourned over the fatal promise she had made the princess on her death-bed, had not courage to recant its solemn obligation, or avow the sacrifice its fulfillment must impose upon her inclination. This irresolution was an evil, the consequences of which she thought not of at the moment, but at length the period arrived when she had bitterly to deplore the want of nerve, which was productive of much bitter grief. Nor did Mackenzie know the all-absorbing passion with which she regarded his haughty rival, and thus were brought about that series of miseries that have already been detailed to the reader in the course of the foregoing pages.

At the period above-mentioned, too, Badenoch had been three years absent, during which interval he had totally neglected Emmeline. It is certain he guessed the secret attachment to him, but other objects just then occupied all his attention, and he affected to take no notice of a circumstance that he might hereafter use for his own base purposes. With many painfully hidden struggles, therefore, the Lady Emmeline had at length yielded a reluctant consent to the importunities of the still youthful and ardent Lord Mackenzie. Her mind, though not strong in its intellectual capacities, was naturally good and susceptible of great and lasting gratitude, and, therefore, was too generous to refuse to bestow happiness on others, though unfortunately doomed to know none herself ; and that compliance to his wishes, which Mackenzie had vainly believed originated in the kind returns of mutual affection, was but the offering of gratitude and esteem for one who had been so faithfully devoted in his love. But he was blinded in his love for her, and the joy which the acceptances of his offer inspired, prevented him from seeing the fatal precipice which yawned at his feet, threatening him with certain destruction.

It was at this juncture when the Chief of Badenoch had fatally resolved to destroy for ever the peace and happiness of the unsuspecting Mackenzie, that he remembered and felt an interest in the discovered attachment of Emmeline ; and with demoniac malice, he resolved to make it his instrument of ruin to his generous and too confiding cousin. His artifices were numerous, and at length, unfortunately, but too successful, for not only did the artless Emmeline, through the false representations he made, become really convinced of the death of her husband, but even the attached household of his victim were equally convinced by the artifice he made use of to carry out his nefarious designs ; for the Chief of Badenoch it was who had, by repeated messengers, given rise to the general belief that the death of Lord Mackenzie had happened during the time when he was engaged in the noble struggle that was taking place to rid his country of the foe that had dared to invade it.

At length the crisis of Emmeline's fate was decided. On the night succeeding the day in which the hypocritical Chief of Badenoch had sent to her his false intelligence of the death of Mackenzie, he himself was treacherously, and with much secrecy, admitted to the presence of the sorrowing Emmeline ; and his basely-contrived forgery, too artfully contrived for credulous unsuspecting faith such as hers, prevailed, and with a readiness that he had scarcely anticipated, she listened to the news he pretended to be the bearer of, and gave full credit to the artfully-contrived tale he had prepared for the purpose of carrying out his intentions.

Badenoch, with all the hypocrisy he was capable of, pretended to lament deeply the fate of a friend who he declared he loved with the utmost sincerity; and so well did he play his part, that Emmeline suspected not the falsehood he had thus carefully covered. She, in truth, began to regard him as almost the only friend that now remained to her in the world, and yielding to the belief of his honest intentions, she made him the confidant of all her griefs, and implored that he would watch over her interests against those who she unfortunately believed were most opposed to her happiness. This was arriving exactly at the point Badenoch had been aiming at, and repeating his assurance of friendship, he bade her to be of good heart, since he was resolved to perish in her cause rather than suffer any arm to befall her. And Emmeline implicitly believed him, for he took care that his language should be smooth and hypocritical, and thus did she lay the foundation of that misery which was afterwards to be her lot.

Having thus far succeeded in his base designs, the Chief of Badenoch delivered to her a paper couched in the hand-writing of her husband, together with a ring, the former gift of Emmeline to her lord soon after their marriage. The contents of the forged letter were as follows :—

"Before this reaches the hand of Emmeline, her faithful Mackenzie will have been numbered with the dead. Receive this pledge of my love and my remorse, for the sorrows and disappointment my fatal passion has occasioned you; but in my death your wrongs and sufferings shall be atoned, and the faithful affection of Badenoch repay your too generous sacrifice to the lost peace of Mackenzie. This will at least be some consolation to me, and I can die happy in the certainty that joy and peace remain to you.

"Fly instantly from the place where you have so long sojourned; trust not any of its treacherous vassals, for they have betrayed me and my rights to ruin, and ere long the English forces will invade my territories, and make yourself the prisoner of their lawless violence. This I have learnt accidentally through a spy, and believe me, Emmeline, I tremble lest my warning to you should come too late. The dread of dangers to which I too well know your innocence and beauty will be exposed, harrows my last moments, and makes death tenfold more hideous.

"Therefore, my loved Emmeline, if the solemn wishes and commands of a dying husband are sacred to your obedience, lose not a moment, but fly *instantly* and *secretly*, and in the honourable protection of the Chief of Badenoch, shield your unprotected purity from the dangers with which it is threatened by those who are preparing to seize upon the castle and all who may be found within it. You have, I know, loved Badenoch, and must ratify the contract of your plighted faith. To him, who I have ever found my best and most faithful friend, I bequeath my wife, my Emmeline, and may ye both be as happy as I hope shortly to be.   "MACKENZIE."

Badenoch's testimony confirmed the tenour of this infamous forgery, and the dissembling villain was believed by the too credulous victim of his artifices. Emmeline's mind, indeed, was ever too unsuspicious for the destiny it was her misfortune to be placed in; guiltless herself of deceit, she never for a moment doubted the veracity of Badenoch's words; not, however, because she loved him as she had formerly done, but because her heart's conviction was satisfied that a man placed in his exalted situation would never stoop to commit an act that was base or dishonourable. He was thus secure even from a passing doubt, and we have already seen with what perseverance and duplicity he could pursue his designs to a termination.

This will serve to prove how deeply the hypocrite had acted his part, and how completely he had deceived all the world as well as the more inexperienced Emmeline ; and it will be seen that he did it with an outside semblance of those virtues which he had never known but by name, and only assumed the appearance of, for the most diabolical of purposes.

The hand-writing of Lord Mackenzie had been exactly imitated, and the ring which Badenoch had surreptitiously obtained from his lordship, was a fatal evidence that confirmed his death beyond the possibility of Lady Emmeline to doubt, for when her husband took leave of her at their last separation, he had solemnly vowed never to part with this token which had been given to him by herself, but with life, which, if he should be sensible was terminating, he would then restore it, as the undoubted testimony of his death, to her who had given it to him. There then was an evidence that she could not controvert, and bursting into an agony of tears, she placed the token in her bosom, resolving to keep it as a sad memorial of him who had been thus suddenly taken from her.

Badenoch had been present when the above-mentioned solemn contract was made, and treasuring its remembrance in his mischief-working brain, he thus darkly made it the grand instrument of all his nefarious plot, and the ruin of her for whom he was professing so much love and veneration. The hapless Emmeline, indeed, while she tenderly and sincerely wept over the supposed death of her husband, could not but feel a strong repugnance to the commands which had been laid upon her to quit the castle secretly with the Chief of Badenoch. At length, however, duty and affection prompted her to follow the instructions that had been given in the letter, and after some hesitation, she expressed her willingness to take her departure whenever it might be necessary.

This was the great end for which Badenoch had been aiming, and it was with no little difficulty that he could conceal the demoniac joy which filled his heart when he found that his base efforts had not been made in vain. It was still, however, necessary that he should urge motives for immediate flight, and successfully playing on the credulity and weak timidity of her mind with false accounts of her personal danger, both from the inhabitants of the castle and the fierce hordes, who he assured her would be sent to plunder it, he, at length, in an evil hour, prevailed upon her to quit the fortress, and then, without loss of time, conducted her to one of his own castles, where it would be almost impossible to trace her.

He was now, by this one rash step of hers, not only the master of her person, but her only dependance, for Lady Emmeline had no living relatives to take any interest in her sad fate, and she was thus rendered helpless and powerless in the hands of the villain who had so successfully plotted for her destruction. Nor did her misfortunes end here, for she was taught by Badenoch to believe that all the possessions and wealth of her late husband had been wholly confiscated to the English government, from whose despotic power there was for her no appeal towards obtaining a restoration of the lands and property, the loss of which rendered her an abject and penniless beggar. This was a situation that she had not anticipated, and yielding to the melancholy occasioned by the utter ruin that had fallen upon her, she gave way to the grief which she found it impossible any longer to control.

The Chief of Badenoch beheld her drooping spirits with a feeling of fiend-like joy that it would be impossible to describe, for mischief and deeds of darkness were ever prominent in his mind, and having once resolved upon accomplishing the destruction of his hapless victim, he would suffer no remorse of conscience to interfere in her behalf. He, however, affected a show of kindness whenever he was in her presence, and even condescended to remonstrate against the grief which the death of her late husband had occasioned.

And so completely was Emmeline blinded by the artifices he practised to secure a successful termination of his views, that she discerned not the villany which lurked within his heart, nor had she the least suspicion that he had in any way deceived her. Thus she became an easy prey to the arts of the destroyer,—yielding her full credence to the heartless monster who was imperceptibly leading her to destruction, and believing that in him she had found one friend who would shield her from the perils with which her present destitute condition threatened her. But she knew not the heart of the man she thus relied on, or her subsequent fate might have been a far happier one.

At length, after the lapse of a twelvemonth given to the memory of her husband, Lord Mackenzie, Emmeline, without one really wrong intent or thought of evil, consented to ratify the wishes of the Chief of Badenoch, by bestowing upon him her hand at the altar, and thus she unsuspectingly plunged herself into a vortex of ruin, from which it was never afterward possible to extricate herself. Never was a villanous deception carried on with more success than the present, for he imposed upon her with the profanation and mockery of the marriage rites, and she was not awakened from this delusive trance till the discovery of the Princess Isabel had fatally aroused her to a sense of the misery and degradation into which she had fallen, and it has been already seen with what agony of remorse and despair she was seized when the full measure of her griefs became known.

After the marriage, Badenoch lost no time in possessing himself of the property which he had represented as having been confiscated to the English crown, and then, the better to conceal his own base treachery, he immured her in a miserable dungeon, from which he intended she should never be liberated. Emmeline's heart sank under the heavy misfortunes that now fell upon her, and with a mind naturally weak, she soon became a prey to the idiotcy that was so greatly aggravated by the subsequent cruel treatment she received. But this moved not the obdurate heart of the morose Chief of Badenoch, who hourly expected to see her numbered among the many other victims of his baseness and cruelty, and often did he plot means for destroying her, which he was only prevented carrying into execution, lest by so doing, he should hasten his own fate. From the time of her being first immured within the dungeon he rarely went to visit her, for his heart, stern as it was, quailed as he beheld the unfortunate object of his duplicity, and he could not endure a sight that reminded him of the treachery by which he had secured her downfall.

It may here be necessary to remark that the Princess Isabel was never aware that her father had so base a relative as the Chief of Badenoch; for, from the death of her mother, the Princess Matilda, she had been removed while yet an infant, to the protection of an aged female relative, and had but very seldom returned to the castle of her nativity, till she wholly quitted the Convent of St. Columba, to watch over the health of that parent whose mutual suffering had been caused by the supposed falsehood of his second wife, the Lady Emmeline.

Gladly turning from the foregoing melancholy details, we now approach that bright period of history, when the King of Scotland, at the renowned battle of Bannockburn, freed his country from the aggressors who had so long harassed it with their usurpation, and carried fire and sword from one extremity of the kingdom to the other. The event was indeed a stirring one, and the historians, whether they be Scottish or English, unite in giving honour and glory to the brave band of men who, rousing themselves with all the fire of patriotism, within a few short hours succeeded in restoring the faded honour of their native land, and driving forth the invaders who had oppressed them.

At the Battle of Bannockburn, the gallant heroic Bruce, gathered wreaths of immortal honour for his country, and with thirty thousand ill-disciplined and half-armed men, subdued an army of a hundred thousand, composing the flower and excellence of the English nation. Heroically great were the almost superhuman deeds of the conqueror on that proud and triumphant day.

Hand in hand with victory, the invincible royal champion of his country's honour, and his three inseperable companions, Randolf, Douglas, and Glenalvon, became the terror and wonder of their enemies, and the idols of their friends; and while on the night preceding the battle, the English forces, confident in their superior numbers, gave way to the most riotous voluptuousness and licentious debaucheries, Bruce with solemn sacrifice had purified his army, and offered to the God of battles and of divine justice, the homage and incense of the heart's pure libation.

It was night when the monarch of Scotland, calm in intrepidity, and strong in the confidence and hope inspired by the justice of his cause, and his faith and reliance on Providence, was seen passing from rank to rank, cheering and encouraging his men, and filling their minds with his own unconquerable resolution, to die in the field rather than become again the slaves and hostages of a foreign yoke that was no longer to be endured. He taught them to rely on Heaven for succour in a righteous cause, and reminding them of the consequences that would follow a defeat, earnestly besought them to strike boldly for victory, and added an assurance that their efforts would not be made in vain. Everywhere he was received with enthusiasm by his faithful soldiers; his presence was regarded as a certain foreboding of victory, and the few who had previously wavered, became fixed in their resolution never to yield, whilst life remained to enable them to strike a blow in the behalf of their long oppressed country.

And whilst the army of the gallant Bruce was thus engaged in making preparation for the next day's strife, that of the enemy was indulging in the most shameless excesses, and frequently might be heard in loud and boastful scoffs to sneer and deride the foe whom, in fancy they had already vanquished, and felt so sure of defeating, that they neglected every means of securing that which their numbers warranted them in anticipating. But the chief thing that produced the result of the next day's battle, was the want of a wise and efficient leader to guide and direct the energies of the army, so as to secure the other advantages which the English possessed. King Edward the Second, it is true, was among them, but he was a sad substitute for his more brave and energetic father, and when the moment for action arrived, he was incapable of performing the onerous duties he had in an evil hour taken upon himself.

At length the decisive morning of battle dawned—the King of Scotland, confident of the result, and completely armed from top to toe in bright steel armour and vestments of tyrian and crimson dye, came forth from his tent. Upon his now awful front, sat stern resolution, and that invincible courage which could alone serve to fix the destinies of that important day. Every heart in his small but gallant army offered him its homage and love, and every soldier to a man, was eager and panting to approve himself worthy of so renowned a leader. Upon his crested helm he wore a gem of inestimable quality and value, and which, in the battle's greatest fury, rendered him the more conspicuous both to his own soldiers and those to whom he was opposed. His exhortation to his army was brief and comprehensive.

"Not for your king," he cried, "but for your country's freedom and independence, you are this day to bravely fight and conquer. Remember, my countrymen, the deep injustice, the heavy wrongs which we have all endured from those who now stand against us as an enemy. Our wives and children look up to us for that peace of which we have been but to long deprived; —they also have felt the power of the oppressor, and shall we, who boast of the name of men, stand idly by, and see those we love trampled in the dust, and spurned by the feet of a proud and usurping host? But I speak to those who have suffered wrongs, and are panting to resent them ; the foe stands before us exulting in the power of their numbers ; but Heaven is for us, my friends, and with your aid we will this day drive the hated intruders from our soil. On then, my gallant comrades, and die or conquer !"

That they *did* conquer is well known, and therefore, it is not required that we should enter into a full description of the great events which marked the celebrated battle of Bannockburn. Fame has shadowed it with immortal trophies, and the dignity of history given to after ages a lasting reward that never can be forgotten.

Robert Bruce was himself the first of the Scottish heroes that bravely rushed singly into the field of battle, and the first man that fell beneath his more than mortal prowess was Sir Henry Bohun, an English knight, whose bravery had before been tried in many a hard-fought field. This event acted like an electric shock, and the ardour of the Scottish army was in an instant roused into a flame of courage and fierce intrepidity that it was impossible to subdue.

The example of their gallant king created in the breasts of his followers an invincible boldness and amelioration to great achievements, which, while it prompted them to deeds of desperate exploits, gained them a rank and celebrity in their country's history that renders them famous down even to the age in which we live. Through the exertions of Bruce, their ranks kept entire and compact ; his eye was ever watchful to detect where the least weakness manifested itself in any part of his army, and when he saw any signs of giving way to the force of the enemy, he was instantly on the spot, and inspiring his men to maintain their firmness, and by opposing a bold front, prevent the further advance of their English assailants. In this way, he preserved his troops in the same order that they had commenced the battle, and to this circumstance, in a great measure, may be attributed the decisive victory that followed.

The English, in fact, were completely overthrown and routed by the hardy valour of the Scots ; their king narrowly escaped with life, and was pursued by the triumphant conquerors into the very heart of his kingdom. Immense was the treasure and spoil that day acquired to Scotland by the defeat of her former aggressors, who had come adorned with all the riches and gay sumptuous splendours of an oriental victor. In fact, they seemed rather coming to a certain triumph than to an encounter with a hardy, brave, and warlike nation, fighting to re-establish its ancient liberties, and the independence of which they had been unjustly deprived.

The English, it must be admitted, were not deficient on that day in their accustomed bravery and valour ; but their leaders were of weak capacity, and they had vainly imagined that their treble superiority over the small forces of the enemy must of itself frighten the latter, and make them give way without even striking a single blow. But they reckoned not on the courage and patriotism of a hardy race of men, who had been deprived of their liberties, and were determined on restoring them. Former victories had, in fact, been of easy achievement, for the Scots at first believed their enemies to be invincible, and it was not without some difficulty that they could be prevailed upon to take up arms to prevent the further encroachment of the foe.

At length, however, the valour of Robert Bruce inspired the people of Scotland with a feeling of courage, and roused them to action. He proved to them that intrepidity and resolution were alone required to obtain the freedom of their country, and having pointed out to them the shame and degradation they were enduring, succeeded in collecting together the army with which he had now come into the field. The result did not disappoint his expectation, and we have seen how successfully their valour was exerted.

Against such a leader as Bruce there was in the English army no equal opponent, and their vanity and arrogance in solely relying on the amazing magnitude of their army over that of the enemy, had thrown away the certainty
of victory from the folly of thinking it won before the battle had in reality
commenced. The event was such as the hardy valour on one side, and the
supine inactivity and sudden panic it created in the other, might have been
expected. The supremacy of the throne of Scotland from that day regained
entirely its ancient prerogative and independence, and the power of its enemies
was humbled. Never, indeed, was it more complete, for the invaders were
compelled to evacuate the country they had overrun, and the triumph of the
day terminated in a peace that gave security and liberty to the nation that had
so bravely fought for it.

Bruce's illustrious queen, the Princess Mary, his sister, with the Lady
Buchan, were exchanged for English prisoners of note taken at the battle of
Bannockburn, together with all the Scottish captives who had so long groaned
under English bondage. The gallant patriots who had fought and bled with
Bruce for the freedom of their country, from this eventful day found their
valorous deeds and constancy amply rewarded. Scotland once more exercised
her rights, and formidably checked the encroaching greatness of her intestine
as well as foreign enemies ; and Bruce, the great founder of her happiness
and future grandeur, lived idolized by his people—adored by his family and
friends—feared by his enemies—and admired as a hero and conqueror by
every power in Europe.

Very many months had passed since the decease of Lord Mackenzie, during
which long interval of succeeding unbroken serenity the Princess Isabel had
gradually regained that peaceful serenity of mind so long despaired of. The
horrors of the Castle of Badenoch, and the cruelties she had endured from its

No. 36

ruthless chief, by degrees imperceptibly faded from her memory, and the blissful quietude of her even days had restored her mind to her happy equilibrium to which she had for years past been a stranger. She had now, too, friends about her who were anxiously solicitous to restore that cheerfulness which at one period seemed to have fled for ever, and Isabel was too grateful for the kind attentions bestowed upon her not to make every effort on her own part to prove that she merited the goodness which had been exercised in her behalf.

Still, however, there were periods when, left to herself, she could not refrain from giving way to the grief that remembrance would occasionally bring to her mind. With filial sorrow she would at such times dwell on the misfortunes that had been endured by her hapless parent. But when at length her grief yielded to the conviction of reason, which told her that his death was the only balm that could assuage sorrow so deep as his, she no longer continued to repine at the afflicting event, but resigned herself to the mournful bereavement, though she ever continued to lament the sad destiny which had pursued him even to the very brink of the grave, to which he had been hurried by the persecution of a ruthless enemy.

It was after the final battle of Bannockburn, that the princess, with mingled sensations of joy and tender regrets, prepared for her departure from the convent in which she had found so secure a refuge. Bruce himself, mindful of his promise, had with Angus, hastened there to conduct her to the home from which she had been so long exiled. Her heart was now satisfied, and all her late alarms for the safety and life of Angus, ended in once more beholding him returned from the battle's dangers, and unharmed, amidst the perils through which he had passed.

The king led the youthful hero towards the princess. He had learned from Randolf the story of their lives, and though the modesty of Angus forbade his lips to avow the passion that filled his heart, the king had observed quite enough in his manners to read the full confirmation of the intelligence he had previously received.

"Receive, my Isabel, a monarch's proudest gift," cried the king, with benign regard, as he placed the hand of the princess in that of Angus Glenalvon. "The heroic defender of his country is deserving no less a reward than it is now my happiness to bestow upon him. Accept him, Isabel, and by that act prove your ready obedience to the request of a guardian and a sovereign."

"When I prove unworthy of such a reward," exclaimed Angus, fervently; "may the sharpest tortures of fate punish my ingratitude, and may the bounty of Heaven and my king for ever forsake me. But may I—dare I hope my Isabel will bless my future days by fulfilling the one joyful anticipation that has ever sustained me through all the trials and vicissitudes it has been my lot to endure?"

The princess was endued with too much candour to hide the genuine emotions of her soul, and with full conviction of her lover's worth, yet with a sigh of painful recollection, she timidly replied :—

"My loved father with his dying breath, bequeathed me to Angus Glenalvon, even when he knew not that my heart confirmed his wishes. I promised to obey his injunctions, and need I add that nothing more remained to increase my happiness than to know that our union would give satisfaction to my king and guardian."

With these words she sank into the arms of Angus, and the monarch, with a tear of gladness that spoke the feelings of his almost paternal joy, exclaimed, as he raised his hands in benediction over them :—

"Sacred and happy may this contract be which I thus solemnly confirm ; and may Heaven sanctify your union, my children, with years of increasing happiness, and honours. May its choicest blessings attend and guard you both from the severe misfortunes of your hapless parents!"

"Ah!" sighed Isabel, "would that my father had lived to witness this moment of his daughter's happiness!" But the cloud which overshadowed her countenance was quickly dispelled, and the voice of gratitude and love had power to charm away each rising remembrance of past happiness to present joyfulness and peace.

Led between her royal guardian and Angus, the princess took a lasting but affectionate farewell of St. Columba's convent, and was soon conveyed over to the opposite shores of Craiglynn, where, with shouts of joy and acclamations she was welcomed by the numerous tenantry, and conducted to the ancient castle of her forefathers. Here a numerous assemblage of nobles awaited to receive and congratulate her, and amidst assembled multitudes, she, in a few days after her arrival, resigned herself to the arms of Angus Glenalvon, and found in his society that happiness and domestic peace which had been so long denied her through the unjust persecution she had endured.

On the day of their marriage the princess presented to her husband the rich portions of the earldoms of Glenroy and Mackenzie, together with a royal warrant obtained from the king, empowering Angus to assume the princely titles of both these domains.

Magdalen was also nobly rewarded, such being the thoughtful care of Bruce, who with gratitude remembered the constancy of her virtues, and the heroism with which she had watched over the the offspring of Glenalvon. It was not, however, without some difficulty that she could be prevailed upon to accept the bounty of her sovereign; and, even when she at length yielded, it was only on condition that she might be permitted to reside amongst those in whose behalf she had displayed so much regard and constant affection.

The title and estates of Glenalvon were, by Angus, bestowed upon his brother, Edwin, who thenceforth became its earl, whilst the future fortunes of Rosalind were liberally provided for by the Princess Isabel, who would suffer no diminution from the revenue of Glenalvon and its young possessor; but had, from her own unbounded wealth, made her dowry equal with the most illustrious females of Scotland.

As we have already observed, the marriage of Angus and Isabel was solemnized with regal pomp and courtly favour, for they were honoured and regarded by all parties, and there were few persons who absented themselves on the day that witnessed the solemnization of their nuptials. From the King of Scotland himself Angus received the hand of the princess; and, after the happy ceremony of the marriage, a banquet followed, the gorgeous magnificence of which exceeded anything that had ever before been witnessed within the ancient walls of the Castle of Craiglynn.

Beneath a gold and purple canopy of state, adorned with the victorious trophies of Bannockburn, sat the royal and illustrious Bruce. On either side of him were placed his daughter, the Princess Margaret, and his niece, the Princess Isabel. Next to the latter was the beauteous Rosalind, and on the opposite side the Lady Mary Bruce, the king's sister, accompanied by her friend the Countess of Buchan, and almost all the high-born dames of Scotland present to be witnesses and partakers in the joyful triumph of that auspicious event.

Angus, with the Earls of Randolf and Douglas, and many others among the invincible defenders of their country, jousted in the court-yard of the castle in honour of their ladie loves, and largely added to the triumphs of their king, and the joyous event which had thus assembled them together.

The bards and minstrels, who had been brought together by the rumours of this high festival, attuned their harps, and exalted the song of victory to the immortalizing honour of the deeds of the king and his assembled heroes. The festival, it is said, lasted some days, and few events disseminated more joy than did the union of Angus and the beauteous Princess Isabel.

Thus closes our narrative, and, should the tale happily inculcate the lessons of virtue, and persevering patience under evil, the end of our labours will have been attained, and the time devoted to the perusal of these pages be not altogether unprofitably employed.

THE END.